B. J. Daniels is a *New York Times* and *USA TODAY* bestselling author. She wrote her first book after a career as an award-winning newspaper journalist and author of thirty-seven published short stories. She lives in Montana with her husband, Parker, and three springer spaniels. When not writing, she quilts, boats and plays tennis. Contact her at bjdaniels.com, on Facebook or on Twitter, @bjdanielsauthor

Nichole Severn writes explosive romantic suspense with strong heroines, heroes who dare challenge them and a hell of a lot of guns. She resides with her very supportive and patient husband, as well as her demon spawn, in Utah. When she's not writing, she's constantly injuring herself running, rock climbing, practicing yoga and snowboarding. She loves hearing from readers through her website, www.nicholesevern.com, and on Twitter, @nicholesevern

Also by B. J. Daniels

Steel Resolve
Iron Will
Hard Rustler
Rogue Gunslinger
Rugged Defender
Cowboy's Redemption
Dark Horse
Dead Ringer
Rough Rider
Restless Hearts

Also by Nichole Severn

Rules in Blackmail
Rules in Rescue
Rules in Deceit
Rules in Defiance

Discover more at millsandboon.co.uk

AMBUSH BEFORE SUNRISE

B. J. DANIELS

MIDNIGHT ABDUCTION

NICHOLE SEVERN

MILLS & BOON

First Published in Great Britain 2020
by Mills & Boon, an imprint of HarperCollins*Publishers*
1 London Bridge Street, London, SE1 9GF

Ambush before Sunrise © 2020 Barbara Heinlein
Midnight Abduction © 2020 Harlequin Books S.A.

Special thanks and acknowledgement are given to Nichole Severn for her contribution to the *Tactical Crime Division* series.

ISBN: 978-0-263-28033-3

0620

MIX
Paper from
responsible sources
FSC™ C007454

Printed and bound in Spain
by CPI, Barcelona

AMBUSH BEFORE SUNRISE

B. J. DANIELS

This book is for anyone who's fallen for the wrong person—and gotten lucky and found the right one. It's never too late for love.

Chapter One

JoRay "Jinx" McCallahan stormed into the sheriff's office, mad, frustrated and just plain beside herself.

Sheriff Harvey Bessler looked up from his desk in surprise, saw her and groaned good-naturedly. "Let me guess. T.D.?"

"What am I supposed to do about him? I'm already divorcing him. I've got a restraining order against him—like that does a lick of good. I've run him off with a shotgun. But short of shooting him, he just keeps coming back."

"All you have to do is call when he breaks the restraining order on him and we'll pick him up."

"And he'll be back on the street within hours even madder and more determined to drive me crazy."

Harvey nodded sympathetically. "Unfortunately, we don't have anything else we can hold him on. Unless he is caught in the act doing something illegal…" The sheriff motioned her into a chair before he leaned back in his own to eye her over the top of his cheater glasses. "How are you doing other than that?"

She scoffed as she took a seat. She'd been coming to this office since she was a child. Her father and Harvey had been best friends up until Ray McCallahan's recent death. Because of that, Harvey was like a second father to her. She'd been fortunate to have such good men in her life.

Until T. D. Sharp.

The sheriff got to his feet and came around his desk to call out to the receptionist. "Mabel, get this girl a cola from the machine. Get me one, too." He turned back to Jinx. "Remember when you were little and you'd come in here with your papa to visit? I'd always get you a cola. It always made you feel better."

Just the mention of her father made her eyes burn with tears. She missed him so much and she knew Harvey did, as well. "That was back when the worst thing that happened to me was falling off my bike and skinning my knees."

He laughed. "True enough. Not that you let a little thing like a skinned knee stop you. You've always been strong, Jinx."

She didn't feel strong as she heard Mabel come to the door with two bottles from the old-timey machine in the break room. Harvey took them and gently closed the door.

"I'm afraid this is the best I can do right now," he said as he handed over her cola. "What's T.D. done now?"

She took the drink, feeling embarrassed for the way she'd barged in here. T.D. wasn't Harvey's problem; he was hers. She took a sip from the bottle Mabel had opened for her. It was ice-cold. For a moment she felt like a kid again as the sheriff went around behind his desk and lowered his weight into his chair with a creak and groan.

"Other than bad-mouthing me all over town? He's got it where I can't find anyone to work out at the ranch and I've got cattle that if I don't get them to summer pasture…" Her voice broke. She took another sip.

"I don't doubt T.D. did everything you're saying," Harvey said quietly. "He been out to your place again?"

She waved that off, knowing if Harvey picked him up it would only make T.D. worse, if that were possible. She hadn't come here for that. She knew she had just needed to see him because she needed to vent and she knew that he'd listen. "I keep getting offers on the ranch even though it isn't for sale. T.D. is determined to take half of whatever I could get for the place, even though we were married such a short time. He actually thinks he deserves half the ranch."

Harvey shook his large gray head. "I'm sure you had your reasons for marrying him."

Jinx laughed. "You know that you and Dad tried to warn me but I was in...*love*." She practically spat the word out. "How could I have been so blind?"

"It happens, especially when it comes to love. T.D. can be quite charming, I've heard."

"Not for long." She took another long drink of her cola. "What does that leave me?" she asked, her voice sounding small and scared even to her. "I'm going to have to sell the ranch to get rid of him. My only other option is to—"

"You're not going to shoot him."

She smiled. "You sure about that?"

Harvey sighed. "I know things have been rough since Ray died. Maybe you should think about getting away for a while. Maybe take a trip somewhere. Give T.D. time to cool down."

She narrowed her eyes at him. "Or maybe I should sell the cattle and take a loss and forget about driving them up into the mountains to summer range." But that would be admitting defeat and she wasn't good at that. When backed against a wall, her tendency was to come out fighting, not give up.

He said nothing for a moment. "What did your father want you to do?" he asked quietly.

Jinx felt the shock move through her and realized of course her father had told his best friend what he wanted her to do once he was gone. "I'm going to have to sell the ranch, aren't I?"

"Sweetie, I know it's not what you want. Are you that determined to keep ranching?"

"It's all I know, but it's more than that. That place has been my home since I was born. I don't want to give it up just because of T.D."

"That's the real thorn in your side, isn't it? T.D. has you against the ropes. But I can't believe you're not that set on ranching it alone. Then again, you're so much like your father," Harvey said, smiling across the desk at her. "Stubborn as the day is long and just as proud. But if you're keeping the ranch to show T.D. or people in this town…"

"It isn't right that T.D. should force me into this or worse, take half."

"I agree. You hired yourself a good lawyer, right?"

She nodded. "He says T.D. can ask for half of what the ranch is worth on paper. No way can I come up with that kind of money. I don't have a choice. In the meantime, T.D. has it where I can't even find any wranglers to work for me."

His expression softened. "I'm worried about you. If T.D. breaks the restraining order again, you call me. I can pick him up, maybe even keep him overnight."

She shook her head, finished her cola and stood. "Thanks."

"I didn't do anything."

Jinx smiled at the older man. "You listened and the cola tasted just like it did when I was a kid. I do feel better. Thanks."

The sheriff rose, as well. As she started to take the

empty bottle back to the break room, he said, "I'll take that." She handed it to him, their gazes meeting.

"I'm going to go have a talk with T.D.," he said and rushed on before she could say it would be a waste of time. "He's a cocky son of a bitch and I would love nothing better than to throw him behind bars—that's just between you and me. Maybe we'll get lucky and he'll take a swing at me."

She laughed. "Good luck with that. In the meantime, somehow I'm going to get my cattle to summer range. I'm not going to let T.D. stop me even if it means taking the cattle up there by myself. Don't worry, I've advertised out of state. Maybe I'll get lucky. After that…" She shook her head. She had no idea.

Her hope was that T.D. would give up. Or his girlfriend would keep him busy and away from her. Her father used to believe time healed most things. But with a man like T. D. Sharp? She had her doubts.

"Jinx?" She turned at the door to look back at the sheriff. "Just be careful, okay?"

T. D. SHARP THREW his legs over the side of the bed and hung his head. A cool breeze dried the sweat on his naked body as he sat for a moment fighting his mounting regrets and frustration. At the feel of a warm hand on his bare back, he fought the urge to shake it off.

"Come on, baby," Patty Conroe purred. "You don't have to leave. You just got here."

He reached for his underwear and jeans, anxious to escape. Coming here tonight had been a mistake. After his run-in with the sheriff earlier, he'd thought what he needed was a kind word and a soft, willing body. But it hadn't worked tonight. His body had performed but his mind had been miles away—out on the Flying J Bar MC Ranch.

"I need to go out to the ranch and talk to my wife," he said as he stood to pull on his jeans, foolishly voicing the thought that had been rattling around in his head. The sheriff thought he could threaten him? That old fool didn't know who he was dealing with. If T.D. needed to go talk to Jinx, he damned sure would. She could take her restraining order and stuff it up her—

"She isn't your *wife*," Patty snapped. "She's your *ex*."

"Not yet." He heard her sit up behind him. "We don't sign the papers until the property settlement is finished and it sure ain't finished. Which means she's still my wife. And I can damn well go see her if I want to."

"What about the restraining order? You go near her and she's going to call the sheriff."

"Let her. She already went whining to him, but there isn't a thing he can do to me. Anyway, I'm not afraid of Harvey Bessler."

"He's the law, T.D. You better watch yourself or he'll trump something up and lock you behind bars. Have you forgotten that he was her father's best friend? He would love nothing better than to put you in one of his cells."

He scoffed, more than aware how tight Ray McCallahan had been with the sheriff. But Ray was dead and gone and if Harvey kept harassing him, he'd get the old fart fired. "Let him try."

"You think he won't arrest you? Well, I'm not getting you out of jail this time. You hear me? *Let Jinx go.* She sure didn't have any trouble letting *you* go."

Her words were like a gut punch. He wanted to slap her mouth. "Watch it," he warned. He wouldn't put up with her saying anything bad about Jinx, whether the woman was his almost-ex-wife or not.

He looked around for his boots, knowing that if he didn't get out of this apartment and soon, they were going to fight. He was already fighting with Jinx. He didn't need another woman on his case.

"Why do you need to talk to her *tonight*? Anyway, shouldn't your lawyer be handling this?"

He didn't answer, knowing better. He wished he hadn't brought the subject up about his soon-to-be ex to start with. But she'd been on his mind. Nothing new there. Jinx had caught his eye and he'd fallen for the woman. Fallen hard. When she'd told him it was over and sent him packing, he'd been in shock. The woman needed him. How was she going to run that ranch without him?

But somehow she'd managed in the months since he'd been booted out. He'd put the word out that no one he knew had better go to work for her if they knew what was good for them. He chuckled to himself since he'd heard she was having trouble hiring wranglers to take her cattle up to summer range.

That would teach her to kick him to the curb. He'd thought for sure that after a week or two she'd realize the mistake she'd made and beg him to come back. So he'd made a few mistakes. Like hooking up with Patty.

But Patty wasn't even the reason that Jinx had thrown him out. She'd said she didn't care about his girlfriend, his drinking, his not working the ranch like he should have. She said she was just over him and wanted him gone.

Maybe as his friends said, the only reason he wanted her back was because of his bruised and battered ego. But he knew in his heart that wasn't all of it. He still wanted Jinx. She was the sexiest woman he knew. He was crazy about her.

If she hadn't made him feel like he was a hired hand,

he wouldn't have needed Patty. But from the day they married, he'd been too aware that it was her ranch. Not that she didn't always tell him that it was their ranch and that was why she wanted him more involved. But he knew better.

Once she threw him out, though, he threw her words back at her. *Our ranch, huh? Well, then I want half of it.* Not that it was even about the ranch and the property settlement anymore. He couldn't stand that he'd let a woman like her get away. Just the thought of another man touching her drove him insane.

He told himself he could change. He could be the man she needed. She had to give him another chance. He figured if the two of them could just talk—or even better, hit the sack together—they could work this out. Once he got her in bed, she'd listen to reason.

"You're bound and determined to go out there, aren't you?" Patty said behind him, sounding close to tears. She was wasting her time. Her tears no longer moved him. For months she'd been trying to get him to divorce Jinx and marry her. The woman was delusional.

"Maybe I should drive out to that ranch myself," she said, sniffing dramatically. He heard the threat, the anger, the spite, dripping with jealousy. "I'd like to tell her what I think of her."

T.D. refused to take the bait as he found his boots and began to tug them on. Now, if he could just find his shirt…

"I think it would do her good to know that you've been sneaking over to my place the whole time you've been married to her. Her lawyer might want to hear about it, too."

The words swung at him like a baseball bat to the back of his head. He spun around, going for her throat before he could call back his fury. The woman was threatening to ruin *everything*. Before she could move he was on her. He saw the shock and fear in her eyes as his large hands clamped around her scrawny neck. She opened her mouth, gasping like a fish tossed up on the bank, but no sound came out.

He'd known about the bad blood between Jinx and Patty. Apparently, they'd gone to school together. Jinx had dated Patty's brother in high school. When the fool had gotten drunk and driven off the switchbacks on the highway west of Jackson Hole, Patty was convinced that he'd done it on purpose because of his breakup with Jinx.

T.D. had known how jealous Patty was of Jinx. He'd always suspected that was the reason she'd come after him, determined to get him into her bed not long after his marriage to Jinx. As if it took a lot of effort on her part. Patty was a nice-enough-looking woman with willing ways.

But tonight she seemed to have forgotten her place in the scheme of things. Leaning closer, he tightened his hold on her throat and, pressing his lips to her ear, whispered, "You listen to me. You won't go near that ranch. You won't go near Jinx. You ever say a word to her and I'll…" He felt her go limp and let go of her, dropping her back on the pillows.

For a moment he thought he'd killed her, but then she came to, gasping, eyes wild, hands going to her red and bruising throat. He watched her wheeze for breath as she scooted across the bed out of his reach.

Good, he thought. She needed to know exactly what she was dealing with if she ever betrayed him. She'd been getting a little too cocky for her own good lately. All that talk about the two of them getting married as soon as his divorce went through. Like he would tie a noose around his neck again, especially with a woman like her.

He found his shirt and pulled it on. As he walked out, he didn't look back. Let her wonder if he would ever return. Women like Patty Conroe were a dime a dozen. Women like JoRay "Jinx" McCallahan were another story.

Regret flooded him as he climbed behind the wheel of his pickup. He'd blown it with Jinx. Talk about cocky. Once he had that ring on her finger, he thought he could just coast with her. He'd been dead wrong.

Letting out a snort, he still couldn't believe that she was going to divorce him, though. But then again when Jinx threatened to do something, look out, because the woman was going to do it, come hell or high water.

As he started the engine, he reached over and pulled a can of beer from the near-empty six-pack he'd left on the seat. He told himself that he'd get Jinx back because he couldn't live without her. He knew that now, he thought as he opened the beer and took a long pull on it.

Admittedly, he shouldn't have cheated on her. He should have helped out around the ranch more. He should have done a lot of things differently. With a second chance, he would.

Not that it was all his fault. Jinx wasn't an easy woman. She was too damned independent. Truth was, she didn't need him and that stuck in his craw.

But now with her daddy in his grave, Jinx was all alone except for Max, that old cook of hers—and all those cattle that needed to be taken up to summer range in the high country.

Maybe she would realize that she couldn't live without him, either. He'd heard that she was so desperate she had even advertised for wranglers out of state.

T.D. smiled to himself. Thanks to him, she was high and dry right now. No one around here was going to work for her. He knew most of the wranglers for hire because of all the years he'd gone from ranch to ranch as one. Unless they wanted to get on his wrong side—a bad place to be—they'd stay clear of Jinx and her ranch. And they had.

What better time to have a talk with her, he thought feeling good. He'd make sure it was just the two of them, restraining order or not. He'd charmed her into marrying him. Surely, he could charm his way back into her life—and her bed.

JINX MCCALLAHAN SLOWED her pickup as she spotted two trucks and horse trailers sitting in her ranch yard. She didn't recognize either of them. After parking, she climbed out and took in the group waiting for her.

She shoved back her Western hat as she considered what looked like a straggly bunch of wranglers standing in the glow of her yard light. She told herself that beggars couldn't be choosers since she had several hundred head of Herefords to get into the high country and time was running out.

Normally, she had no trouble hiring on help this time of year. She was no fool. Her inability to find local help was T.D.'s doing. He'd put the word out, forcing her to look for help much farther from home, but hadn't heard anything. Unfortunately, word traveled fast among ranching communities about her "problems" with her soon-to-be ex-husband. She couldn't blame anyone for not wanting to get into the middle of it, especially if they knew anything about T. D. Sharp.

But after stopping at the sheriff's office, she'd run some errands, bought herself some dinner and made up her mind. She wasn't going to let T.D. put her out of business even if she had to take the herd to summer range all by herself—just as she'd told the sheriff. Maybe she wouldn't have to if any of these wranglers were decent hands, she thought now.

She stepped to the first cowboy who'd climbed out of the trucks and stood waiting for her. As he removed his hat, she looked into the bluest eyes she'd ever seen and felt a start. Was it the scar on his chin or something about his eyes? What was it about him that made her think she knew this man? Or had at least run across him sometime before? Surely, she would have remembered if she had stumbled across such a handsome cowboy.

Stress and lack of sleep, she told herself. Her mind was playing tricks on her. Or her body was. Because she felt strangely close to him as if they'd once shared something almost...intimate? She knew that was crazy. There'd never been that many men in her life.

Jinx shook her head. Her father's illness, his death, T.D.... All of it had taken a toll on her, she knew. She couldn't trust her mind or her body or her instincts. And if she and this man had met, wouldn't he have said something?

"What's your name?" she asked him.

"Angus Cardwell Savage, ma'am."

"Cardwell?" Her eyes narrowed. "Any relation to the Cardwell Ranch in Montana?"

"Dana Cardwell Savage is my mother."

She considered the tall, lanky, good-looking cowboy for a moment, telling herself that she had to be wrong about having met him before and stepped to the next one. "And you're..."

He quickly removed his hat. "Brick Cardwell Savage, ma'am."

She felt a start as she did a double take, looking from Angus to Brick and back. "You're twins?"

"Identical," Brick said with a chuckle. "Except I'm more charming."

Jinx ignored that. A charming cowboy was the last thing she needed. She'd married one and look how that had turned out.

She considered the two for a moment. Angus had a small scar on his chin in the shape of a crescent moon. Other than that, she couldn't tell the brothers apart. She moved on to the next wrangler.

As the cowhand removed the weathered straw hat, a long blond braid tumbled out. "Ella Cardwell," the wrangler said, lifting her chin in obvious defiance.

Jinx shook her head. "I said I needed men. Not—"

"I can do anything these two can do," Ella said, aiming her elbow at the two cowboys next to her who were also from Cardwell Ranch. "Usually better," the cowgirl added, lifting her gaze until Jinx was staring into emerald green eyes that flashed with fire.

She shot a glance at the two Cardwell men, expecting them to object. Neither did. Turning back to the young woman, she said, "Ella Cardwell, huh?"

"My mother's Stacy Cardwell. Dana's my aunt."

"What are you doing riding with these two?" Jinx asked, indicating Ella's cousins.

"I like wrangling. I'm more at home on the back of a horse than anywhere on this earth." She shrugged. "My cousins watch out for me and I watch out for them."

Jinx studied the young woman whom she estimated to be in her late twenties, early thirties—about her own age and that of her cousins. They were all young when what she needed was seasoned help. Unfortunately, there was none to be had right now because of her almost-ex-husband. It was why she couldn't afford to be picky and yet...

"Why aren't you all working on your family ranch?" she asked, concerned about their ages and lack of experience. Also their possible safety, given what was going on.

"I will someday, but in the meantime, we wanted to see more of the country and experience life before we settled down," Angus said.

Brick chuckled. "Just sowing some wild oats, ma'am."

That was what she was afraid of. "There won't be any of that on this cattle drive. We have to get my herd up into the mountains for the summer and I'm already running late. If you're looking for fun, you've come to the wrong place."

"We're good hands and we aren't afraid of hard work, ma'am," Angus said, giving his brother's boot next to him a kick. "Don't mind my brother. He likes to joke, ma'am."

She'd had more than enough of this ma'am stuff. "Call me Jinx," she said as she moved to the next two wranglers who'd answered her help-wanted ad.

"Royce Richards," said the fourth cowboy. At least he was older. "Cash and me here used to wrangle for—"

"Huck Chambers," Jinx said, nodding as she eyed the men more closely. She'd seen them around Jackson Hole. Cash looked to be in his early forties, much like Royce. He removed his hat and said, "Cash Andrews." While Royce was tall and wiry-thin with a narrow, pinched face and deep-set dark eyes, Cash was larger with a broad face as plain as a prairie. But when her eyes met his pale brown ones she felt something unsettling behind them.

She tried to remember what she'd heard about the men and why they were no longer with Huck. She thought about calling Huck, but told herself if they didn't work out, she'd pay them off and send them packing. She only needed them for a few days, a week at most, depending on the weather and how long it would take them to move the cattle.

Looking the lot of them over, she reminded herself that she was desperate, but was she *this* desperate? She hesitated. She could use all of them, but hiring a young woman wrangler? That seemed like a recipe for disaster on a cattle drive. She thought of the spirit she'd seen in the young woman's eyes, a spirit that reminded her of herself.

"All right," she said with a sigh, hoping she wasn't making a mistake—not just with the Cardwell bunch but with Royce and maybe especially Cash. What was that she'd seen in his gaze? Just a flicker of something she couldn't put her finger on. A lot of cowboys didn't like taking orders from a woman. She hoped that was all she'd seen.

"See your way to the bunkhouse. We ride out at first light in the morning. I notice that you brought your own stock," she said, glancing at the two pickups parked in her yard and the horse trailers behind them. "You can bed them down for the night in the barn or that corral. Cook will rustle up something for you to eat. I wouldn't suggest going into Jackson Hole tonight." *Or any other night*, she thought. But since they would ride into the mountains early tomorrow, they'd have little chance to get into trouble.

At least that was what she told herself as she headed inside the ranch house to talk to Max about feeding them. She found him in the kitchen finishing up washing some pots and pans, his back to her. The cook was short and stocky as a fat thumb with a personality as surprising as what he often cooked. He'd been with Jinx's family for years. She didn't know what she would do without him. Or vice versa if she sold the ranch.

But as she studied the man from behind, she realized Max was getting old. He wouldn't be able to handle a cattle drive much longer. For him, her selling the ranch might be a relief. He could retire since she knew her father had left him well-off.

The moment he turned around and she saw Max's face, she knew he'd seen her wranglers. "They might not be as bad as they look," she said defensively.

"Didn't say a word."

"You didn't have to." She leaned on the counter. "Can you rustle up something for them to eat?"

He nodded and began digging in the refrigerator. He came out with a chunk of roast beef. She watched him slice it and said, "They're young, I'll admit."

"Unless my eyes are going, that one looked distinctly female."

She sighed. "I like her."

Max laughed, shaking his head. "Bet she reminds you of yourself."

"Is that so bad?" He said nothing, letting that be his answer. "You hear anything about Royce Richards and Cash Andrews?" she asked, changing the subject. "They used to work for Huck Chambers."

He looked up from the beef he was slicing. "If you have any misgivings, send them on down the road."

"I can't. I have to take a chance with them. I need the help and at least they're older and probably more experienced." She looked toward the window and wondered what her father would have done. In the twilight, the pine trees were etched black against the graying sky. Beyond that, the dark outline of the mountains beckoned.

She told herself that she had to follow her instincts. First, she would get the herd up to the high country to graze for the summer. It would buy her time. Then she would decide what to do. She couldn't think about the future right now.

But of course that was all that was on her mind. "Once this cattle drive is over..." She didn't finish because she didn't know what she would do. Just the thought of ever leaving this ranch brought her to tears.

"I'll run sandwiches over to the bunkhouse," Max said. "You should get some sleep. You worry too much. You have five wranglers. With a little luck—"

"My luck's been running pretty thin lately." If the wranglers had heard what was going on at her ranch, they wouldn't have wanted anything to do with the Flying J Bar MC and she'd really be out of luck.

"I have a feeling your luck is about to change for the better," Max said as he picked up the plate of sandwiches and started for the door. "You're due. You want one of these sandwiches? I don't remember you eating much for dinner earlier."

She shook her head. "I'm not hungry, but thanks. Max," she called, stopping him at the door. "You didn't have anything to do with those three showing up from Cardwell Ranch, right? You didn't call Dana Savage, did you?"

He didn't turn as he said, "Go behind your back? I know better than to do something like that. I'm no fool." With that he left.

Jinx sighed, still suspicious. Her mother had been friends with Dana and it would be just like Max to try to help any way he could. She let it go, telling herself not to look a gift horse in the mouth. She had five wranglers, and tomorrow they would head up into the high country. Maybe Max was right and her luck was changing.

Still, she stood for a long time in the kitchen, remembering how things had been when both of her parents were alive. This house had been filled with laughter. But it had been a long time ago, she thought as she heard Max leave the bunkhouse and head out to his cabin. Her father's recent illness and death had left a pall over the ranch even before she'd finally had it with T.D.

You need a change. Don't stay here and try to run this ranch by yourself. I don't want that for you. Her father's words still haunted her. Did he really think it would be that easy just to sell this place, something he and his father had built with their blood, sweat and tears?

She shook her head and was about to head up to bed when she heard the roar of a vehicle engine. Through the kitchen window, she spotted headlights headed her way— and coming fast. "T.D." She said his name like a curse.

Chapter Two

After they took care of their horses, Angus could tell that something was bothering his cousin and wasn't surprised when Ella pulled the two of them aside.

"Maybe we should have told her the truth about why we're here," she said, keeping her voice down. The other two wranglers were still inside the bunkhouse.

"I thought the plan wasn't to say anything unless she didn't hire us," Brick reminded her. "She hired us, so what's the problem?"

"It doesn't feel right keeping the truth from her," Ella said more to Angus than Brick. She knew how Brick felt. He'd found them a job up by the Canadian border where one of his old girlfriends lived on the ranch. The last thing he'd wanted to do was come to Wyoming instead. Especially knowing the circumstances.

"We don't want to stomp on the woman's pride," Angus said. He knew firsthand where that could get a person. "Jinx needs three good wranglers and that's what we're doing here. Once it's done you can go anywhere you want to go."

Brick sighed as they reached their pickup and unloaded their gear before continuing on to the bunkhouse. Angus found himself looking out into the growing darkness. He'd felt it the moment they'd driven into the ranch yard. He wondered if the others had, as well, but wasn't about to ask. Trouble had a feel to it that hung in the air. An anticipation. A dread. A sense of growing danger. It was thick as the scent of pines on this ranch.

He understood why his brother hadn't wanted to come—and not just because of that cowgirl up by the Canadian border. "Don't see any reason to buy trouble," Brick had argued. "I know this woman's mother was a good friend of our mother's, but *Wyoming*?" Brick had never seen any reason to leave Montana. Angus felt much the same way.

But Jinx McCallahan was in trouble and their mother had asked them to help her—but to keep in mind that she was a strong, independent woman who wouldn't take well to charity. She just needed some wranglers to get her cattle up to summer range, Dana had said.

While Brick had been dragging his feet, none of them was apt to turn down Dana Cardwell Savage. But what his brother and cousin didn't know was that he would have come even if their mother hadn't asked them. The moment he heard that JoRay "Jinx" McCallahan needed wranglers, he'd been on board.

"Once she can get her cattle up to summer range, things should get better for her," their mother had said. News among ranch families traveled like wildfire, but Angus had the feeling Dana had heard from someone close to Jinx. "The trouble is her ex-husband. He's got all the local ranchers riled up. She can't get anyone to work for her other than Max, the ranch cook, and while he's like family, he's getting up in age."

Angus had talked Brick into it. All it had taken was the promise that when the cattle were in their summer grazing area, they'd hightail it back to Montana.

Ella hadn't needed any talking into it. "The woman

just buried her father? She's running the family ranch single-handedly and now the ex-husband is keeping her from getting her cattle to summer pasture? Of course we'll go help."

Dana hadn't been so sure that her niece should go, but Ella wasn't having any of that. She'd been riding with her cousins since college. She wasn't sitting this one out. So the three of them had packed up and headed for a small community south of Jackson Hole, Wyoming.

Angus had been looking forward to seeing Jinx again. He remembered her red hair and her temper and was intrigued to find out what had happened to that girl. *That girl*, he'd seen tonight, had grown into a beautiful woman. Her hair wasn't quite as red, but her brown eyes still reminded him of warm honey. And those freckles... He smiled to himself. She didn't try to hide them, any more than she tried to hide the fact that she was a woman you didn't want to mess with.

For a moment earlier he'd thought that she had remembered him. But why would she? They'd just been kids, thrown together for a few hours because of their mothers.

He'd seen her looking at the scar on his chin. If anything could have jogged her memory, the scar should have, he thought as they entered the bunkhouse.

"It's more than Jinx needing wranglers to get her cattle up to summer range," Ella said quietly beside him.

He nodded, having felt it since they'd reached the ranch. Jinx had more trouble than a lack of hired help.

Back in the bunkhouse, he'd just tossed his bedroll onto the top bunk when he heard a revved engine growing louder as a vehicle approached the ranch.

"Stay here," he said to Ella, signaling to his brother to stay with her.

He picked up his weapon from the bed, strapped it

on and stepped out of the bunkhouse into the darkness to see the glow of headlights headed straight for them.

JINX PICKED UP the shotgun by the front door on her way out to the porch. The moment she'd heard the engine, she'd known it was T.D. and that he was going to be a problem. By now he would have had a snoot full of beer and have worked himself up. She didn't need to see her ex-husband's pickup come to a dust-boiling stop just short of the house to know that he was in one of his moods.

The driver's-side door was flung open almost before he'd killed the engine. *Drunk again*, she thought with a silent curse. Tucker David "T.D." Sharp stumbled out of the pickup, looking nothing like the handsome, charming cowboy who'd lassoed her heart and sweet-talked her all the way to the altar.

"You get out here, JoRay!" he yelled as he stumbled toward the house. "We need to talk."

"I'm right here," she said as she stepped from the dark shadows of the porch. She saw his eyes widen in surprise—first seeing her waiting for him and then when he spotted the shotgun in her hands. "You need to leave, T.D. I've already called the sheriff."

He smirked at that. "Even if you did call him, it will take Harvey at least twenty minutes to get out here."

"That's what the loaded shotgun is for," she said calmly, even though her heart was racing. Just seeing him in this state set her on alert. She knew firsthand what he was capable of when he got like this. He'd torn up the kitchen, breaking dishes and some of her mother's collectibles during one of his tantrums.

"Come on, JoRay. I just want to talk to you," he whined as he took another step closer. "Remember what it was like? You and me? You *loved* me. I *still* love you."

He took another step. "I deserve another chance. I swear I can change."

"That's close enough." She raised the shotgun, pointing the business end of the barrel at the center of his chest.

He stopped, clearly not sure she wouldn't use it on him. She saw his expression change. "You had no business kicking me off this ranch," he said, his tone going from wheedling to angry in a heartbeat. He spat on the ground. "I got me a lawyer. Half this ranch is mine and I intend to take what's mine. This ranch and you, if I want it. You're still my wife. I can take it all." He started toward her when a voice out of the darkness stopped him.

"Not tonight you aren't."

A wrangler stepped from the shadows into the ranch-yard light by the bunkhouse. She saw the faint gleam of the scar on his chin. She also saw that Angus was armed. He hadn't pulled his gun, but it was in sight and T.D. saw it, too.

"Who the hell are you?" her almost-ex-husband demanded.

"The lady asked you to leave," Angus said, his voice low, but forceful.

T.D. scoffed. "You going to make me?"

"If it comes to that, yes." The cowhand still hadn't moved, hadn't touched the gun at his hip, but there was something like steel in his tone.

She could see T.D. making up his mind. He'd come out here looking for a fight even if he hadn't realized it. But with T.D., like most bullies, he preferred better odds.

He swore and shot Jinx a lethal look. "This isn't over. You might have hired yourself some…cowboys," he said as some of the other wranglers came out of the bunkhouse and watched from a distance, "but when they're gone…"

She heard the promised threat, saw it in his gaze. He'd be back for more than the ranch.

Jinx felt a shudder. How could she have not seen the mean side of this man before she stupidly married him? Because he'd kept it well hidden. Drunk, he was even worse, filled with an unexplained rage. She'd felt the brunt of that anger. He'd never hit her. He wasn't that stupid. But he'd beat her down with his angry words every time he drank until she'd had enough and sent him packing at gunpoint.

Her father, Ray, had been in the hospital then. Once he died, T.D. got it into his head that he deserved a second chance. When that didn't work, he'd decided the ranch should be his. And so should Jinx. He'd refused to sign the divorce papers until she settled up with him.

The problem with the man was that he never took no for an answer. Egged on by his friends he drank with and some of the other ranchers he'd grown up with who'd tried to buy her out the moment her father had died, T.D. felt both the ranch and she were his legal right.

Legally, he might have some right to the ranch, unfortunately, because they were still husband and wife technically. She hadn't had the sense to get a prenuptial agreement signed before they'd married. She'd been in love and stupid. But no matter how much of a fight T.D. put up, she was divorcing him. And while he might get his hands on half the proceeds from the ranch, he would never get his hands on her again if she could help it.

T.D. started toward his truck, stopped and tilted his head as if listening. With a smirk, he turned back to say, "If you called the sheriff, he's sure taking his time getting here." His gaze locked with hers for a moment. "Liar, liar, pants on fire, all Miss High-and-Mighty. You didn't even call the sheriff."

"If I'd called the sheriff," she said quietly, "he would have stopped me from shooting you, if you'd taken another step in my direction."

The words seemed to hit T.D. like a strong wind. He wavered, his gaze locking with hers. "So why'd you bother with a restraining order, then?" he snapped, thinking he was smarter than she was.

"Because it will look better in court after I kill you. 'I tried to keep him away, but he just wouldn't listen.'"

"Best keep it loaded and beside your bed, then," he said, smirking at her. "Because I'll be back."

She didn't doubt that. He would come back when it was just her and Max alone on the ranch. "And I'll kill you before I let you touch me again."

Her words inflamed him—just as she knew they would. But he wasn't the only one with a temper. She'd put up with all she was going to from this man. She didn't want him to doubt that she would pull the trigger on both barrels when he came back.

T.D. slammed his fist down on the hood of his pickup as he stumbled to the driver's-side door and jerked it open. He shot her a hateful look before climbing behind the wheel. The engine revved. He threw the truck in Reverse and tore off down the road, throwing dirt and gravel.

Jinx let out the breath she'd been holding. Moments before, she'd half expected T.D. to turn and charge her like a raging bull, forcing her to shoot him or pay the price for even a moment's hesitation. She figured the only reason he hadn't was because of Angus.

As she turned to thank him, she saw that the spot where he'd been standing was empty. Like the others, he must have gone back inside the bunkhouse. Apparently, he hadn't wanted or needed thanks. But now he'd put himself in the line of fire. T.D. wouldn't forget.

ANGUS STEPPED AROUND the side of the bunkhouse, listening to the sound of T.D.'s pickup engine fading in the distance. He hoped the man had enough sense not to come back, but he wouldn't bet on that.

He thought of the way that Jinx had handled the situation and he smiled. Angus had come down here believing that it was to save not just Jinx's cattle—but the woman herself.

After seeing her with that shotgun tonight, staring down her husband, Angus realized Jinx McCallahan could take care of herself. It didn't surprise him. He thought of the girl he'd met just that once. She'd made an impression on him all those years ago. She'd done it again tonight.

Her almost-ex-husband thought he could bully her. Well, T. D. Sharp had picked the wrong woman to try to intimidate. Angus could have told him that just based on knowing her a few hours years before. You didn't want to mess with that redhead, he thought, smiling to himself.

So as he stood in the dark, pretty sure T.D. wasn't headed back this way—at least not yet, he reevaluated what he was doing here. Helping Jinx get her cattle to summer range, but after that…he wasn't so sure.

Angus thought of the woman standing on the porch with the loaded double-barrel shotgun trained on her not-soon-enough-ex-husband. He realized he wasn't here to rescue her. She could rescue herself. But maybe, with some luck, he could keep her from killing T.D. and going to jail.

PATTY STOOD IN front of the bathroom mirror inspecting her throat. It was still red in spots and bruised in others.

She could make out T.D.'s fingerprints where he'd choked her. She touched the spot tenderly and cursed Jinx. Just the mention of her name sent T.D. in a tailspin. Until he was done with that woman, he wasn't himself. She had to remember that.

Stepping out of the bathroom, she thought she heard a vehicle. T.D. would come back. He'd be all apologetic and loving. He'd done it before another time when he'd gotten rough with her. And like tonight, it had been over Jinx McCallahan.

Oh, how she hated that woman, she thought, fisting her hands, fingernails biting into her palms. She'd give anything to get that woman out of their lives.

And now T.D. had gone out to her ranch to see her as if he could talk her into giving him another chance. The damned fool. It would serve him right if he got himself arrested—or shot. She wouldn't put it past Jinx to shoot him. Maybe then he'd realize that she didn't give two hoots about him.

Tears burned her eyes. What was wrong with the man? He had a woman who loved him unconditionally and still he couldn't stay away from that…ranch woman. He'd left her to go to Jinx. It burned at her insides. What if he didn't come back tonight? What if Jinx gave him a second chance? The thought made her sick to her stomach. Why couldn't she just let T.D. go?

She felt bitterness roiling in her stomach. If only Jinx would sell her ranch and leave town like most people thought she would after her father died. Let her move far away. Then T.D. would come to his senses. As long as Jinx was around, she'd keep him stirred up.

Her phone rang. For a moment she thought it would be T.D. Maybe he'd gone down to the bar and had started feeling guilty about their fight and was now calling to apologize. Or maybe invite her down to the bar to have a drink with him. Wouldn't it be something to be able to go out in public together? That would show Jinx.

She checked her cell phone, instantly disappointed. It was only Wyatt, T.D.'s friend, probably calling to ask if she knew where the man was. "Hey," she said, picking up. Maybe T.D. had asked him to call her.

"Are you all right? I saw T.D.'s truck down at the bar. Figured you'd be alone. You two have a fight?"

Patty's heart dropped. If T.D. was at the bar, then maybe he *wasn't* planning to come back tonight.

"You okay?" Wyatt asked.

She felt touched by his concern. The shy cowboy was so sweet. Too bad she couldn't fall for him instead of T.D. "Wyatt, you have to stop worrying about me." He'd found her sobbing her eyes out the last time she and T.D. had had a bad fight. He'd run a clean washcloth under the cold-water faucet in the bathroom, wrung it out and handed it to her. He'd asked if he could get her anything to eat, something to drink.

He was so thoughtful. She wished T.D. was more like him. And while she appreciated the fact that Wyatt cared, at the same time, it felt a little creepy. Sometimes she wondered if he watched her apartment just waiting for T.D. to leave in one of his moods.

"I could come over," Wyatt said now.

She touched her throat. It still hurt. Wyatt would notice the bruises and the dark spots that looked like fingertips. "I don't think that's a good idea. You know how T.D. is. He wouldn't like it." Who was she kidding? T.D. wouldn't care.

"Was he alone at the bar?" she asked.

"I don't know. I didn't go inside. Patty, what do you see in him?"

It was a question she'd asked herself many times over the year she'd been seeing T.D. He'd never made it a secret that he loved his wife and yet, she'd been convinced that one day he would leave Jinx and marry her. Instead, Jinx had thrown him out and now T.D. was determined to get the woman back.

"I'm in love with him," she said simply. "You know that."

"I know. It's just that…he doesn't treat you right, Patty. You need a man who values you for who you are. You have so much to offer a man. A man who deserves it."

She couldn't argue that. Like tonight, she didn't need Wyatt to tell her that it was mean of T.D. to come by only to leave right after they'd had sex. She knew he was using her and it broke her heart, but what could she do? The alternative was to not see him at all.

"You have to know how I feel about you. What can I do to show you? Just name it, Patty," Wyatt pleaded. "I would do anything for you."

She walked back into the bathroom and stared at her reflection in the mirror for a moment. Wyatt was right. She deserved better. "There *is* something you could do. Where are you now?"

"Just down the street." His voice sounded hopeful and she knew he'd meant it about doing anything for her. With a little persuasion, she thought she could get Wyatt to do the one thing she might ask.

"Come on up. But make it quick. T.D. will be coming back soon."

AFTER LEAVING THE RANCH, T.D. had considered going back to Patty's. But he wasn't up for another fight. Nor was he up for apologizing. Patty just didn't get it. He wanted Jinx, as much as he hated her right now. His wife thought she had the upper hand at the moment. Maybe she did. Maybe that was why he was so angry.

He'd driven straight to the bar, telling himself that maybe he would sneak back out to the ranch later tonight and surprise Jinx. A need stirred in him like none he'd ever felt, and he kept reminding himself that she was still his wife. She'd better not be seeing anyone else. Just the thought of that cowboy who'd come out with his six-shooter strapped on his hip...

He ordered a beer even though he could tell Marty hadn't wanted to serve him at all. But Marty also didn't want any trouble, as if he could sense that T.D. was just spoiling for a fight. It had been a long time since he'd broken up a bar.

"One beer, T.D., and then you head on home," the bartender told him.

"Home? And where exactly would that be, Marty?" he asked angrily as he picked up the cold beer the man had set in front of him. He took a long drink. It did little to cool down his fury. Jinx had no right to treat him this way. She'd made him the laughingstock of town. He couldn't let her get away with it. Half that ranch was his and damned if she wasn't going to give it to him. If she thought they were finished, then she didn't know him very well.

He smiled to himself and took another gulp of beer. From what he'd seen out at her place, she was planning to take that herd of hers into the mountains tomorrow. It would take her a few days of good weather and good luck to get them up to the high country.

T.D. had made that trip with her last year. He knew the route she took and where she camped each night. As he finished his beer, he realized that he hadn't believed she would get anyone to help her take her cattle up to summer range. Now that she had, she'd forced his hand. He could no longer just threaten to follow her up into the mountains. He had to do it. He had to show her. And he knew just how to do it.

WYATT FELT SHAKEN to his core as he left Patty's apartment. His hands actually shook as he started his truck. On one hand, he couldn't believe his good luck. On the other... He left, driving aimlessly through town, his mind whirling.

He'd had a crush on Patty since grade school. Not that she'd ever noticed him except on those few occasions when he'd stopped into the café where she waitressed. She was nice enough then, smiling and chatting him up. He wasn't stupid. He knew she was like that with everyone because she hoped for a good tip.

Over the years, he'd watched her go through a couple of bad marriages and twice as many equally bad relationships. But nothing had cooled his ardor for her. He'd always known he was what she needed. He'd only hoped that one day she would realize it.

Now he had finally told her how he felt and to his surprise, she'd made him an offer. The offer was less than what he'd hoped for and yet more than he'd expected. He felt as if full of helium. This must be what people meant when they said they were floating on cloud nine.

Of course, there was a catch, he thought, feeling himself come back to earth with a thud.

"Word is that Jinx is driving her cattle up to summer range tomorrow," she'd said once they were seated on the couch in her living room. She'd sat so close to him that her perfume had filled his nostrils making him feel weak. He couldn't help but notice that she'd forgotten to button the two top buttons on her blouse, making it gap open. Sitting this close he could see the swell of her full breasts above her lacy black bra.

He'd also seen the red marks on her neck, a couple of them deep bruises, but he'd known better than to say anything. He'd figured it was why she'd invited him up so he waited for her to bring up the subject.

"Wyatt, you're his best friend," she'd said, leaning to-ward him. "You know T.D. is planning something. Once Jinx gets those cattle to the high country, T.D. will lose his leverage—or at least what he sees as leverage."

He'd nodded, surprised that Patty knew this about T.D. and yet still wanted the man. "He's threatened to follow her up into the mountains," he'd admitted. "But I think it's just talk."

She'd scoffed at that. "He'll get himself all worked up tonight after a few beers and then he'll want you and Travis to go with him since he doesn't have the guts to do it alone, and the two of you don't have the guts to turn him down."

He'd winced, knowing it was true and that she was right. He'd agree to go once T.D. started pressuring him. You just didn't say no to him, and Wyatt hadn't since they were kids growing up. T.D. had gotten him into so much trouble over the years. But like she said, the man was his best friend.

What she'd said next had floored him. "I want you to make sure that Jinx McCallahan never comes out of those mountains."

At first he'd thought he'd misunderstood her. "I don't know what you mean."

And then Patty had leaned toward him, her full breasts brushing his arm as she kissed him. "Do this for me and I promise you won't regret it." She kissed him harder, giv-ing him a little of her tongue. He'd about lost it right there.

But when he'd reached for her, she'd pushed him away. "Not until you do me this favor." Then she'd taken his hand and put it on her warm breast. He'd felt her nipple harden under his palm. And just as quickly, she'd pulled it away. "Now you should go. You wouldn't want T.D. to catch you here."

He'd stumbled out of her apartment to his rig and started driving aimlessly. She wasn't serious about any of it, he told himself. Not the offer. Not the favor she'd made him promise to think about as he was leaving. The woman didn't realize what she was asking. Or what she was offering.

"If you and T.D. get up in those mountains trying to sabotage Jinx and her cattle drive, anything could happen," Patty had insisted as she'd walked him to the door. "Accidents happen. No one even knows who did what."

There was no mistaking what she'd asked him to do for her. Kill Jinx. As if the woman was Patty's only problem. It astounded him that she didn't know T.D. at all. Even if Jinx wasn't in the picture, T.D. wasn't going to marry her. He'd string her along until he found someone else he thought he deserved more. Then he would break her heart all over again. But this time Wyatt would be there to pick up the pieces. Unless he let Patty down now.

He saw T.D.'s pickup parked in front of the bar and their friend Travis getting out of his rig to go inside. He pulled in, honked his horn and Travis stopped to wait for him.

That he'd even given a second thought to Patty's favor was insane. He couldn't kill anyone, especially his best friend's wife, he told himself as he climbed out of his truck in the glow of the neon bar sign. Why would Patty think he was capable of such a thing?

Because she knew how much he wanted her.

Patty was the only woman in town who saw him as anything but a shy, awkward cowboy who lived with his mother when he wasn't working on some ranch or another. She was offering him something he'd only dreamed of for years. He could still taste her on his lips as he and Travis pushed into the bar.

Chapter Three

As T.D. finished his beer, he tried to understand where he'd gone wrong. Too bad his father wasn't still around. His old man would have told him how worthless he was, happily listing every mistake he'd ever made, and the list was long.

He'd thought marrying Jinx would change him. Even his father would have been surprised that a woman like Jinx would have given two cents about him, let alone married him. But now she was divorcing him, proving that his father was right. He didn't deserve Jinx. He really was worthless.

But Patty aside, he wanted to argue that he'd been a pretty good husband. Just not the one Jinx wanted. He ground his teeth at the thought. What the devil had she wanted anyway? A man she could boss around? Or one who would take over the ranch and run it the way he saw fit? He could run that ranch with one hand tied behind him—if she'd give him another chance. So he'd made a few mistakes when she'd let him run it. He wouldn't make those mistakes again.

He fumed at the thought of the way Jinx had treated him at the end. He'd looked into her beautiful face and he'd seen the disgust he'd grown up with. He wasn't good enough for her, never had been, her look said. He saw that look every night when he closed his eyes to try to sleep.

The only thing that kept him sane was drinking. If he drank enough, sometimes he'd pass out and didn't have to see that look.

"Another beer," he said, banging his empty bottle hard on the bar and getting a side-eye from the bartender.

"You've had enough," Marty said as he came down, a bar rag in his hand. He picked up the empty bottle. "I told you I was only serving you one. Why don't you call it a night, T.D.?"

"What don't you—" The rest was cut off as his two friends came in on a rush of spring air. He could see how this was going to go if he stayed. He was in one of his tear-this-place-apart moods.

"Let's get out of here," he said to his friends, sliding off his stool before they could join him. "If they don't want our business here, we'll take it somewhere else. Anyway, there's free beer at Patty's. She's a little mad at me, but I still have my key." He picked up his change, leaving no tip for Marty as he pocketed the few coins. Marty acted as if he didn't care. He seemed glad to see him go.

"Why don't we go to my place?" Travis suggested. "I've got beer and there's no one there to give us any trouble."

T.D. laughed. "Good idea. I need to let Patty wonder where I am for a few days anyway."

Outside, the cold spring night air took his breath away for a moment. Warm, summerlike weather was a good two months away in this part of Wyoming. He started toward his pickup when he spotted the sheriff standing across the street leaning on his cruiser. He swore under his breath. The SOB was just waiting for him to get behind the wheel. Harvey had been laying for him, hoping to catch him at something so he could throw his butt behind bars.

T.D. laughed. "Let's walk. It's a nice night," he said to his friends.

"Are you kidding?" Travis squawked. "It's freezing out."

"Man up," T.D. said as he gave Travis a playful shove and then the three of them were making their way down the street, leaving their vehicles parked in front of the bar. It wasn't as if they hadn't done that before on those nights when they were too drunk to drive home.

"You're awfully quiet," T.D. said, throwing his arm around Wyatt's shoulder. "I'd suspect you had woman trouble if I didn't know you better." He laughed at his own joke as Wyatt shrugged off his arm.

"I might surprise you someday," Wyatt said.

"Right," T.D. said with a chuckle. "But in all seriousness we need to talk about tomorrow. I hope you're both ready to ride up in the mountains. We've got to catch up with Jinx and do a little damage."

"What kind of damage?" Travis asked, sounding worried.

"You know," T.D. said, feeling the alcohol he'd consumed. Sometimes it made him feel invincible. He was going to show everyone, especially Jinx. "Get ready for some...high jinks."

WYATT HAD BEEN hopeful that Patty was wrong and T.D. would give up on trying to stop Jinx's cattle drive. He should have known better. T.D. was at loose ends after the breakup. One day he was determined to get her back; the next he just wanted half the ranch so he could get on with his life.

Going up into the mountains after Jinx and her herd, though, was just plain crazy. Nothing good could come of that. Someone could get killed. Wasn't that what Patty was hoping? The reminder sent a chill through him. That he would even consider her request... Was he so desperate for anything that Patty offered that he'd even consider it?

Once they reached Travis's trailer, they consumed more beer and listened to T.D.'s account of what had happened earlier tonight, first at Patty's, then out at the ranch with Jinx. Wyatt watched as T.D. worked himself up for tomorrow. Just as Patty had said, the cowboy was talking about chasing after the herd and Jinx as they headed for the high country and doing anything he could to ruin her life.

"It's time I showed Jinx what was what," T.D. blustered, fueled by the booze and the anger he had going.

"Come on, T.D., what's the point in going all the way up there after her?" Travis argued. "Sounds like it could get us all killed or thrown into jail and for what? Just to mess with your ex-wife?"

T.D. swore. "She's not my ex yet. I need to show her that I mean business. And up in the mountains, the sheriff won't be watching me like a hawk. That old fart is out to get me because of her."

Wyatt had to ask, "You got a plan?" He still held out hope that all this was just the booze talking. Maybe by morning, T.D. would be so hungover he'd have changed his mind. The thought both relieved him and upset him. He hated to think how it would disappoint Patty. Wyatt couldn't stand the thought of her thinking less of him.

T.D. grinned. "You know how dangerous a cattle drive can be. Accidents happen. And let's face it. Jinx is due for some bad luck the way I see it. She can't just toss me

out without a dime. Before I'm through with her, she'll
be begging me to take half the ranch. Maybe more. If
something were to happen to her... Well, we're still legally married. That entire ranch could be mine...if my
wife should meet with one of those accidents."

"I don't like the sound of this."

"Damn it, Travis," T.D. snapped. "Stop your whining.
You don't want to come with us? Fine. Stay here and work
at your old man's hardware store. Or you could tell him
that you have a cattle drive to go to and won't be back
for a few days."

"You're going to get me fired, T.D."

"Quit. Once I get the ranch, I can offer you a good-
paying job and you won't have to put up with your old
man ever again. How does that sound? You, too, Wyatt."

Wyatt couldn't imagine anything worse than working for T.D. "Sounds great," he said, which seemed to be
what the cowboy needed to hear right now.

"Sure," Travis said, sounding about as enthused by
the idea as he was.

He had to hand it to Travis for trying to talk sense
into T.D. But ultimately, Wyatt knew that Travis would
come along with them. T.D. would beat him down. Just
as he would Wyatt if he'd raised objections. So he hadn't
bothered, because as T.D.'s best friend, it was a foregone
conclusion that he was going along.

"Then we should get some sleep," Travis said, climbing to his feet.

"Mind if I stay here, Trav?" T.D. asked as he finished
his beer and stood.

"Take the guest room down the hall."

T.D. laughed. "Guest room. That broom closet of a
room? You're really living large, Trav."

"I'm going home," Wyatt told the two as he got to his feet.

"I'll pick you up first thing in the morning," T.D. said. "Be ready." It wouldn't be the first time T.D. had sat outside Wyatt's mother's house, honking his horn and yelling for him to get moving.

And just as quickly, T.D. changed his mind. "Wait, first we should have one more beer to celebrate," he said, pulling Wyatt to him as Travis went to the refrigerator for the beers. "A toast to us!" he said, putting his arm around each of their shoulders. They clinked beer cans together, T.D. sloshing his own beer on the floor.

"We're going to need to pick up a few things in the morning before we head out. I promise you, this is going to be fun," T.D. said. "Something all three of us will remember when we're old men. Isn't that right, Wyatt?" He pulled him closer.

Wyatt hoped the cowboy didn't smell Patty's perfume on him. He could still smell it on his shirt, still remember the feel of her lips and the sweet touch of her tongue in his mouth. He swallowed, afraid he couldn't do what she asked. More afraid he could.

ANGUS HADN'T SLEPT WELL. Seeing Jinx now grown-up and so beautiful and self-assured, he'd felt a sense of pride. *I knew her when*, he'd thought. But that wasn't all that stole his sleep.

Last night he'd seen how strong and capable Jinx was when facing down her soon-to-be ex-husband. He worried that if he hadn't been here, T. D. Sharp would have called her bluff and gotten killed. Unfortunately, that would have been something Jinx would have had to live with the rest of her life.

Now Angus had found himself lying awake, listening for the sound of a pickup on the road into the ranch. The one thing he'd learned about T.D. last night was that he wasn't through with Jinx and that made him dangerous—just as dangerous as the situation he, Brick and Ella had ridden into.

He must have drifted off, though, because the clang of the breakfast bell brought him up with a start. By then, Ella and Brick had been already dressed and headed for the chow hall. Angus had quickly followed. The other two wranglers had straggled into the ranch kitchen a little later.

"I'd like you to ride point with me," Jinx told him at breakfast.

"Happy to," Angus said. He and the ranch woman would be riding at the head of the line of cattle. He'd felt her studying him as if trying to understand why he seemed familiar, he figured. Maybe he'd tell her once they were alone on the cattle drive. Not that she would probably be happy to hear their first meeting story, he thought, touching his scar.

Jinx turned to Ella and Brick. "I thought the two of you could work the flank and swing positions farther back." She considered Royce and Cash. "You'll be the drag men bringing up the rear, picking up stragglers and keeping the line moving."

"Whatever you say, trail boss," Cash had said with a smirk.

Jinx seemed to ignore him. "We'll see how that works out. Max will be bringing up the rear in the chuckwagon."

At daybreak Angus and the rest of the wranglers saddled up and began to move the large herd of cattle toward the mountains. They left the valley floor for the foothills dotted with tall pines. Angus felt a sense of relief to be riding away from the ranch.

The days ahead would be filled with long hours on horseback, herding cattle up into the towering mountains of western Wyoming. He loved cattle drives and always had. It was a peaceful existence. *At least for the moment*, he thought as he looked back down the road. Soon they would start the climb up into the mountains.

He found himself looking over his shoulder, wondering how long it would be before he spotted riders coming after them. How long it would be before he saw T. D. Sharp again. By then, they would be far from civilization. They would be on their own since Jinx had said their cell phones wouldn't work until they reached the top of the mountain—and even that was sketchy.

They moved cattle all morning and now trailed them along a creek through the pines. Cattle tended not to trail in a group, but string out in a long line. There were natural leaders who would take their places in front, while all the rest trailed behind. A head of a thousand could stretch out a mile or two so the wranglers worked in pairs on each side of the line.

The day had broken clear and sunny, reminding Angus how much he loved this work. He breathed in the spring air, rich with sweet pine, the scent of bright green spring grasses. It mixed with the scent of dust and cattle on the warm breeze. He lived for this and couldn't imagine any other life, he thought as he turned his face up to the sun. He knew his mother hoped that one day he would return and help run Cardwell Ranch in the Gallatin Canyon near Big Sky, Montana.

Lately, the ranch had been calling him. He could feel his time of being a saddle tramp was almost over. He just wasn't sure his brother Brick realized it. Or how his cousin Ella would take the news. Knowing her, she had already sensed his growing need to return home.

He'd grown up on Cardwell Ranch, fished the blue ribbon trout stream of the Gallatin, skied Lone Peak and ridden through the mountains on horseback from the time he could sit a saddle. But as he took in this part of Wyoming, he thought nothing could be more beautiful than its towering snowcapped peaks.

His gaze shifted to the woman who rode opposite him. He could see her through the tall pines. Like him, she, too, was smiling. "Beautiful, isn't it?" she called to him as if sensing him watching her.

"Sure is." Jinx in her element was more beautiful than the country around her. Her long, copper-colored hair was tied off low on the back of her neck. Her straw cowboy hat was pushed back and her freckled face turned up to the morning sun making her brown eyes sparkle. He couldn't help staring.

At a sound behind him, he turned as his brother rode up, all smiles. "You have a nice herd here," Brick called to Jinx. "Excuse me for saying it, but you look real pretty this morning." With that he spurred his horse before he turned back to his flank position.

Angus rolled his eyes at him and rode off to pick up one of the cows that had wandered off, before falling back into line. He saw that Jinx had dropped back to say something to Brick and shook his head. His brother. If there was a pretty woman around, Brick was going to try to charm her.

But Angus suspected his brother was wasting his time. Jinx had already fallen for one cowboy whom she was now trying to get rid of. He didn't think she was in the market for another.

ELLA SAW THE exchange and chuckled to herself. Her cousins were so competitive that her aunt Dana said they had probably arm wrestled in the womb. Ella wouldn't have been surprised. She'd grown up with the two of them always trying to outdo each other as boys and now as men—especially for the attention of women.

She wasn't worried this time, though. Jinx, she suspected, could see through anything the two did to impress her. She just hoped they all knew it was only for fun. Maybe she needed to remind Angus of that, though. She'd seen the way he had looked at Jinx earlier this morning. It surprised her and worried her a little.

Right now both Jinx and Angus were vulnerable. Jinx, because of her father's death and her upcoming divorce. Angus, because he'd finally gotten over his heartbreak from the last woman he'd fallen for and he now exhibited signs of a growing restlessness. She suspected he would be returning to Cardwell Ranch soon to stay.

Ella turned in her saddle to look back, making sure they hadn't lost any cattle. In the distance she could see the chuckwagon bouncing up the trail behind a team of two horses with Max at the reins. Closer, Royce and Cash were riding next to each other, appearing deep in conversation. As if sensing her watching them, they separated to move some of the slower cattle up into the line.

She didn't like the vibes she picked up from the two men and planned to sleep with her sidearm handy. She'd been a little surprised that Jinx had taken them on. But the ranch woman was desperate or Ella and her cousins wouldn't be here.

"First cattle drive with a woman wrangler," Royce said as he rode up next to her. But when he saw Jinx riding in their direction, he pretended to turn back to look for cattle.

"Doing all right?" Jinx asked her as she brought her horse alongside Ella's.

"Just fine."

Jinx rode astride her for a few minutes. "You let me know if anyone bothers you."

Ella laughed. "I can handle myself."

"I don't doubt that. But there's two of them and I don't trust either of them, do you?"

"No. Don't worry. I've been keeping an eye on them. I'm not sure why, but I don't expect them to stay with us long."

"Funny you should say that. They both hit me up for an advance on their wages before we left this morning," Jinx said. "I turned them down, but I suspect I'll be paying them off before we ever reach summer range."

If that was the worst they could expect, Ella thought. They rode along for a few minutes, the herd of cattle a rust-colored mass of slow movement. "I heard about your father," Ella said without looking at the woman. "I'm sorry."

She felt Jinx's surprised gaze on her for a long moment before the woman said, "I wondered how much you all knew about my...situation." Ella said nothing. "I suppose it's no secret that my mother and Dana Cardwell Savage were friends." Ella knew that the two women had met at cattlewomen conferences and stayed in touch until Jinx's mother's death. "I suspect that's why the three of you showed up on my ranch."

Ella kept silent, riding along through the spring morning, glad, though, that Jinx knew. She didn't like keeping anything from the woman. She liked Jinx.

"I guess what I'm saying is that I appreciate you being here, but it could get...dangerous."

Ella looked over at her and smiled. "Then I'm glad we're here to help."

The ranch woman chuckled at that. "We'll see how you feel when the shooting starts—so to speak."

She met the woman's gaze. "We know what we're up against. We didn't come into this blind."

"I just hope you don't regret it." With that, Jinx rode off.

STILL HALF-DRUNK and sound asleep in Travis's spare bedroom, T.D. came awake with a start at the sound of someone banging hard on the door.

"Tucker David Sharp, we know you're in there," a deep male voice called from outside.

He froze, wondering how they'd found him. He considered going out the only window large enough that he could fit through. Then he swore under his breath, realizing that going out the window wasn't going to help. He needed to try to settle this and hope for the best.

"Give me a minute," he called as he rolled over to look at his cell phone. He couldn't believe he'd slept so late. He swung his legs over the side of the bed and put his throbbing head in his hands. The cattle drive. Jinx would have been up before first light. Who knew how far she'd managed to get by now. Cussing his hangover along with his bad luck, he wondered when his fortune would change. Trouble just seemed to dog him.

"Goin' to bust down the door if you don't open it," said the voice on the other side.

"What's going on?" Travis asked from the spare room doorway. "You know this guy?"

Pushing past Travis, he said over his shoulder, "Don't worry. I'll take care of it." In the living room, T.D. took a deep breath, let it out and stumbled to the door.

The man standing outside was big and beefy with a bulldog face and dark eyes as hard and cold as a gravestone.

"Shawn, come in," T.D. said as the man pushed his way in sans an invitation. He closed the door and turned to face him, a little surprised that Shawn had come alone. Little did he doubt that there were more men, probably waiting in the car in case T.D. caused any trouble. "Look, I know I owe you money."

The man laughed, setting his jowls in motion. He stopped abruptly to narrow those death-like eyes on him. "You *owed* money. Now it is past due. Perhaps you didn't read the fine print when you took out the loan."

"This is a small town so I assume you know what's happened to me." He waited for Shawn to say something. When he didn't, T.D. continued even though he knew his words were falling on deaf ears. "My wife is divorcing me. I have a lawyer who says I can get half of her ranch. You know the spread, so you know how much money we're talking about here. So it shouldn't be that long before I'll have what I owe."

Shawn smiled at that. "Don't forget interest and the late fee that is added every day you don't pay. But here's the problem. My boss doesn't want to wait."

T.D. remembered his father's expressions when bill collectors came around. *They can't eat you.* But they darned sure could mess you up. *Can't get blood out of a turnip.* Another of his father's expressions. But Shawn wasn't your normal bill collector. It was T.D.'s blood that was going to run free if he didn't come up with a plan and quickly.

And it wasn't as if he'd taken out a loan at the bank. He'd gambled on being able to pay what he owed, just as he'd gambled away any money he could get his hands on. "Five thousand. I can get you that by the end of the week."

Shawn raised a brow. "You don't have two nickels to rub together. Where will you get five grand?"

"Leave that to me. One week. Five thousand to hold your boss until I can pay him everything I owe him."

"With interest and late fees."

"Right," T.D. said, thinking how large a chunk that was going to take out of his half of the ranch. But when he considered the alternative, what choice did he have? Jinx had no idea just how deep his gambling debts had gotten. Not that she was going to bail him out again. She'd made that clear before she'd thrown him out.

His future looked bleak. Unless he got the entire ranch. Like he'd told his friends, anything could happen on a cattle drive.

Chapter Four

The day passed in a blur for Angus as they worked the cattle up through the pines and began the long climb to the high mountain range. Saddle sore after eating the dust the cattle kicked up, they had stopped midday for a quick lunch and to let the cattle drink from the stream. Then it was back in the saddle. Jinx had said she wanted to make it up to the old corrals the first day so they pushed ahead and reached the spot by the time the light began to fade.

Angus climbed off his horse now to close the gate to the corral that held the horses. The herd lowed from a large vibrant green meadow, the cattle glowing in the last of the day's light.

He felt the hours in a saddle. But it was a nice tired feeling of accomplishment. Also, he was thankful that they'd gotten the herd this far without any trouble. He'd actually been a little surprised. But then again, T. D. Sharp might be the kind of man who made threats when he was drinking, then didn't follow through on them.

At least he hoped that was the case. He'd seen Jinx watching the trail behind them. She expected her ex to make trouble. But they'd been moving at a pretty good pace all day. He figured T.D. would wake up with a hangover this morning and not be anxious to jump on a horse and head for the hills.

But Angus didn't doubt that the man wasn't through making trouble for her. He just didn't know how or when the cowboy would strike, only that he would if he could get some friends together to buoy his confidence. Angus had met men like him before.

All day he'd kept an eye on Jinx—as well as Royce and Cash. He'd seen Jinx's expression when she'd hired the two. She'd hesitated more with Royce and Cash than she had with Ella. That told him a lot. She didn't trust them and neither did he.

After unsaddling his horse, he left it in the fenced enclosure and headed for the chuckwagon, following the smell of something good cooking. He could see flames rising from a large campfire not far from the wagon where Max was dishing up dinner. There was steak, potatoes and beans with fresh homemade sourdough bread to soak up every bite.

Angus took his plate over to the fire, pulled up a log and sat down next to Ella and Brick.

"Good grub," Brick said as he cleaned his plate and went back for more.

Royce and Cash were still taking care of their horses. Angus didn't see Jinx. Max was busy in his wagon kitchen slopping more beans and potatoes on Brick's plate along with another steak.

"How are you doing?" Angus asked Ella quietly. He knew she never complained and that she could hold her own. He also trusted her instincts. She had a sixth sense about some things, especially people. But sometimes he worried about her. She would get quiet and he'd know that something was bothering her. Like now.

"I'm doing better than your brother," she joked. "He is getting nowhere with Jinx."

He smiled and shook his head, letting her deflect

his question for the moment. "You know Brick. He'll keep trying."

"She likes you, though," Ella said, glancing over at him. "She isn't sure she can trust you, though. I've seen her watching you and frowning."

Angus chuckled, knowing trust wasn't the problem. But he said, "I would imagine she won't be trusting any man for some time to come. However, I asked how you were doing."

Ella smiled, but it didn't quite reach her eyes. "I'm fine."

"Well, if you want to talk about it..." He let that hang, seeing that whatever seemed to be bothering her, she wasn't ready to share it.

Over by the chuckwagon, Brick had struck up a conversation with Jinx as she came to get her plate. Ella shook her head as she and Angus watched him. "She sees right through him and yet he still thinks he can charm his way into her good graces. You, however, haven't tried to charm her."

"Nor am I going to try." Jinx wasn't like the other women he and Brick met. He wasn't interested in making it a competition. The other women had recognized it as a game and had enjoyed the attention. But none of the other women were Jinx.

He ate and watched the flames rising into the wide-open sky overhead. It wouldn't be full dark for another hour or so, but by then, he figured most everyone would be out for the night except for those assigned to stand watch over the herd.

"I'm worried about Royce and Cash," he said. "You let me know if they give you any trouble."

Ella chuckled. "You sound like Jinx. But like I told her, I can take care of myself."

"I'll still be watching them both," he said and followed her gaze to where the two men had finally finished putting their horses and tack away by the old corral. Rising, he took his cousin's empty plate and his own and started toward the chuckwagon.

Brick was headed back to the campfire and stopped him. "We made good time today, don't you think?" his brother said. "Another couple of days and we'll be in the high country." Brick looked toward the towering peaks, dark against the fading light. "This job isn't going to last that long. I was thinking we could still go north for the summer and work that ranch up by the border."

Angus laughed and shook his head. "You know you aren't serious about that woman up there."

Brick cut his eyes to him. "Who says I have to be serious?" Jinx had been talking to Max at the chuckwagon, but now made her way toward them and the campfire. Brick had seen her, too.

Angus grabbed his arm to detain him for a moment. "I'd tell you that you're wasting your time but that would only make you more determined," he said with a sigh. "Emotionally, Jinx is no place good right now. The last thing she needs is a wolf like you tracking her. In case you care, I'm not interested in her so let's not make this a contest."

Brick grinned at him. "Nice speech, my brother. But I've seen the way you look at her."

"I'm worried about her and what T. D. Sharp is going to do next. You should be, too, since the man is dangerous."

"You're just *worried* about her." His brother laughed. "I turn on the charm and get nowhere while you just quietly worry. I've also seen the way she watches you. Come on, we've been doing this since grade school." He glanced toward Jinx, who'd stopped to turn back to say something to Max. "But you should know. I could be serious about a woman like Jinx."

Angus shook his head and muttered, "I knew I was wasting my breath. You aren't serious about this woman or even the one up on the Canadian border and we both know it. Leave Jinx alone." With that he turned and walked over to the wagon where Max was watching Brick get a log for Jinx by the fire. What made him angry wasn't even his brother, but the surge of jealousy he'd felt.

"She forgot her bread," Max said, more to himself than Angus.

"I can take it to her."

Max studied him for a moment before handing him the plate with the bread on it. As he handed over his dishes and walked back to the campfire, he thought about how protective Max was of Jinx. The woman seemed to bring that out in all of them. He reminded himself that this was just a job, even though he knew it wasn't. They were here because Jinx needed their help and not just with her cattle, he feared. But his cousin and brother were right about one thing. He was determined to protect Jinx, for old times' sake, he told himself. It was more than a job for him.

"Happy with the progress we made today?" he asked Jinx as he handed her the plate of bread Max had sent for her.

Jinx took a piece and he set the plate down on a spare log and sat across the fire from her. Brick had taken a log between the women.

"We're on schedule but last I heard there's supposed to be thunderstorms tomorrow," she said. "We won't be able to get any cell phone service until we get to the top of the mountain, so there is no checking to see if the storm has been upgraded or not." She sighed. "Spring in the mountains. I'm hoping we can beat the bad weather to the next large meadow where we have another corral at least for the horses."

She took a bite of her meal. Angus suspected she didn't even taste it. A lot was riding on getting the cattle to summer range. But he knew it was also a distraction from what had been happening down in the valley with her ex.

"That's why I want to leave at daybreak. To get as far as we can before the bad weather hits us," Jinx was saying. "If you could let the others know?"

"I'd be happy to," Angus said. He could tell that she was exhausted from more than the cattle drive. He wished there was something he could say to make things better for her, but unlike his brother, he thought Jinx probably needed silence over sweet words.

"I'll go tell Cash and Royce," he said and rose.

"Tell them chow's on, too," Max called as Angus headed over to where the men were standing and talking next to the corral holding the horses. He felt every mile in the saddle as he stretched his long legs. Walking through the tall green grass, he found himself looking forward to turning in early. They'd gotten through the first day without any trouble. No disgruntled almost-ex-husband. But a thunderstorm could change all that. Lightning was the major cause of stampedes on cattle drives.

Even if T. D. Sharp didn't show his face, they were in for a rough day tomorrow.

JINX WATCHED ANGUS GO. She still hadn't figured out why he seemed so familiar. Nor had he said anything. She sighed and rose to take her dishes back to Max.

"I can take those for you," Brick said, shooting to his feet.

She smiled but shook her head. "Stay here by the fire with Ella." She was glad when he sat back down. She needed to be alone. Brick was sweet and a good wrangler. He amused her with his blatant attempts to charm her, but he was wasting his time. While he resembled his brother, they didn't seem to be anything alike. Angus was a mystery to her.

The more she was around him, the more she felt a strange sense that they'd been here before. She couldn't shake the feeling that she knew this man, as in another life. It was crazy. Sometimes she'd find herself studying his face as if a memory was so close she could almost touch it.

"He's handsome, isn't he?" Max asked, startling her. She hadn't realized that she'd reached the chuckwagon. Her mind had been miles away.

"Pardon?" she asked, turning to face him as she conjured up her most innocent face.

Max laughed. "You were staring at Angus Savage—and not for the first time, I might add."

"I don't know what you're talking about. I was…thinking."

"*Thinking*? I can just imagine." He turned back to his cooking.

She didn't want to know what he'd imagined. Nor did she want to continue this conversation. Still, she asked, "Have you ever run across someone you felt as if you knew in another life?"

He chuckled. "That your story?"

"I'm serious."

Max turned to look at her. "I can see that. I suppose it's possible the two of you met before. Your mother and his were good friends." The cook frowned. "I think she took you with her up to Cardwell Ranch once years ago." So that could have been it, she thought. "You don't remember?"

She shook her head and yet as he said it, she had an image come to mind of mountains shooting up from a green river bottom and a large red barn set against a wall of rock and pine trees. A memory teased at her. "How old would I have been?"

"Eight or nine," he said as he turned back to his cleaning up. "You didn't stay long, just overnight, I think. That's probably why you don't remember."

But she did remember a little. Now it really nagged at her. It wasn't just that she'd seen him before. She couldn't shake the feeling that something had happened during that visit; she was sure of it.

She turned to look at Angus again. He'd rejoined his brother and cousin on a log by the fire. His face shone in the campfire light. Max was right about one thing; the cowboy was handsome as sin. Had he remembered her? He would have been a little older than she was by a couple of years at least.

"Why don't you just ask him?" Max said with a laugh. "Otherwise, it's going to drive you crazy."

He was right about that, as well, but what if Angus didn't remember her? She'd feel foolish. Then again, what if he did? What if he was just waiting for her to say something?

"While you're making up your mind, why don't you hand me your dishes?" Max said with a shake of his head as he took them from her.

Leaving camp, she checked the cattle, glad that Brick and Royce had volunteered to take the first shift. She didn't expect trouble. Not tonight. T.D. was angry and vengeful, but he never planned ahead. He knew she was taking the herd up into the high country for summer grazing today. Maybe he would even wait until she returned to continue threatening her, rather than try to catch them. His laziness might pay off for her.

But unfortunately, she also knew that her being up here in the mountains put her at a disadvantage. T.D. wasn't stupid. He would realize how vulnerable she was up here. Anything could happen in the mountains on a cattle drive. People got injured. Others died. And T.D. was desperate to get his hands on her ranch. He would come after her.

In the distance she heard a coyote howl. Another answered, then another. She was more worried about wolves and bears, than coyotes. But she could only protect her herd so much. It was the nature of the business.

The camp was quiet as she walked back toward the fire. From out of the dark shadows, she spotted a lone figure still illuminated in the flames. Ella gave her a nod as she pulled up the log next to her again. The heat of the blaze felt good this high in the mountains since it was only early June.

Jinx could feel the long day in the saddle in her muscles. She yearned for sleep, but it had been hard to come by for some time now. It wasn't just T.D. who haunted her dreams. She didn't want to think about any of that. Instead, she was curious about this young woman and her lifestyle.

"If you don't mind me asking, why this life?" she asked after a few moments.

Ella smiled. "Probably same as you. I was born into it. When you're raised on a ranch, you do what you know." She shrugged. "I like what I do."

"But you aren't working your home ranch."

She shook her head almost wistfully. "It would have been too easy just to stay there. But I wasn't ready to settle down. I wanted to experience other places, other people. It's tougher as a woman to find that kind of freedom. That's why traveling with my cousins works. They give me space. I give them space."

Jinx looked toward where Angus had spread out his bedroll in the fallen dried pine needles beneath a stand of pines some distance away. "They seem nice enough," she joked.

Ella chuckled. "They'll grow on you."

"That's what I'm afraid of," Jinx said.

"Brick can be a little much."

The ranch woman shook her head. "He doesn't bother me. Has he ever been serious about a woman?"

"Not to my knowledge," Ella said. "A sure sign of fear of intimacy, huh?"

She waited a beat before she asked, "And Angus?"

"Oh, he's been in love. Got kicked in the teeth not all that long ago, so he's gun-shy."

"Aren't we all?" Jinx considered the young woman. "What about you?"

"If you're asking if I've ever met someone who made me want to settle down..." Ella shook her head. "By my age my mother had been married a few times. I'm hoping I'm a whole lot pickier than she was."

"Sorry. I didn't mean to pry. I thought everyone met someone, got married, lived happily-ever-after. That's what my parents did. They were high school sweethearts. That was the kind of marriage I'd wanted. The kind I'd just assumed I would have."

"Everyone makes mistakes when it comes to love. I'm sure I will, too."

Jinx eyed the woman, thinking how much she liked

her. If they didn't live in different states, miles from each other, they could be good friends. She was going to be sorry to see Ella go when the job was over. "You seem like a woman with her head squarely set on her shoulders."

Ella laughed. "Maybe. At least when it comes to some things. I've seen my cousins make fools out of themselves over love. I swear I'm not going to do it, but then again no man has ever swept me off my feet. I've seen what love has done to some of my seemingly normal friends, as well."

Jinx knew the woman was trying to make her feel better. Just talking to her did. She stared into the flames, letting them lull her for a while before she pushed to her feet. She had no idea what tomorrow would bring other than thunderstorms, but she needed to at least try to sleep.

"You'll put the fire out?" Ella nodded. "Sleep well. We leave again at daybreak." With that, she turned and left.

The weight of the job ahead and the day in the saddle pressed on her. Taking her bedroll Jinx found herself a spot some distance from the others. Spreading it out, she lay down and stared up at the night sky through the pine boughs. She'd never seen so many stars—even back at the ranch—as she did up here. Breathing in the last scent of the campfire and the pines, she closed her eyes. She found herself smiling, glad she'd hired on the Savage brothers and their cousin Ella.

Exhausted, she fell asleep, only to be awakened to what sounded like gunfire and yelling.

Chapter Five

Angus woke to what he soon recognized as the banging of pots and pans, followed by cussing. He sat up abruptly, afraid T.D. had found their camp already. He turned in the direction of the racket. Through dawn's thin haze he saw Max standing next to the chuckwagon, his shoulders hunched in anger, a large dented pan in one hand and a huge spoon in the other. He was beating the bottom of the pot and staring off into the trees. What the—

Rolling out of his sleeping bag, Angus pulled on his boots and strapped on his gun, then headed for Max. "What happened?"

"The son of a bee broke into the wagon, made a mess and took most of our food," Max said, toning down his cussing as Jinx quickly joined them.

"Who broke into the chuckwagon?" she asked, sounding as confused by what she'd awakened to as he'd been.

Max huffed. "Dang black bear. Made a hell of a mess. I heard someone moving around in the wagon." Max slept under the wagon, but was clearly a heavy sleeper. "I looked in half-asleep and there are these red eyes staring out at me. 'Bout scared me out of my wits."

Angus chuckled and relaxed. He'd been afraid it was T.D. or someone in camp who'd gotten into their food.

"I thought you kept the food up so the bears couldn't get into it?"

"Had it locked up, but these bears... Smart as whips. Figured out how to get into the container, I guess. I should have hoisted it up in a tree, but I thought for sure it was safe in the metal box."

"How bad is it?" Jinx asked.

"You mean other than the mess?" Max rubbed his grizzled jaw for a moment. "Bear got all the meat. I'd say that was enough, wouldn't you? We have at least two more days up here before we head back. It can't be done on empty stomachs."

"Can we make do with what the bear didn't get?" she asked quietly as if not wanting the whole camp to know about this.

Angus figured it was too late for that given the racket Max had made. He could tell that the older man was still shaken by coming face-to-face with the bear. As he looked over his shoulder, he saw Brick and Ella were headed this way.

Max stared at the ground for a moment. Angus could tell that the bear had startled the cook. Max had scared it away by banging the spoon on the bottom of the pan— which now looked like the surface of the moon.

"We still have flour and sugar, salt and lard." Max raised his head. "I hope you like biscuits."

"I *love* biscuits," Angus said. "Also, I can get a couple of blue grouse and my cousin Ella is one hell of a fisherwoman." He turned and caught Ella's eye. She nodded and turned back to her gear. If he knew her, she'd have some fish from the creek for Max to fry in minutes. "We'll be fine," he said, turning back to Jinx and Max. "It's only a few days."

"Three to get back out of the mountains." Jinx smiled

at him and mouthed "Thank you," before turning her attention to Max again. "We'll make do."

Max nodded sullenly. Clearly, he hated being outwitted by a bear. Not to mention the rude awakening he'd had. Jinx was also visibly upset about the loss of the food, but she appeared to be holding it in as if afraid that letting it out would only make things worse.

"Get some breakfast going," Jinx said. "I'll get the others up. If they aren't already." As she started to walk away, she touched Angus's arm. "Can I speak to you for a moment?"

He followed her away from the chuckwagon and Max for a short distance before she stopped and turned to him. "A *bear.*" She shook her head as if relieved it hadn't been T.D. "Sure gave Max a scare." She let out a huff of a laugh. "I had expected trouble but I figured it would come from T.D. and his buddies." She sobered. "I know him. He won't be far behind, though. Still, my first thought was that maybe Cash or Royce was behind it. Maybe T.D. didn't put them up to hiring on with me. Maybe I'm just overly suspicious now."

Angus nodded. "You're not."

"I should send them packing right now." She met his gaze. "Problem is, we could use them. Especially with thunderstorms coming today. We only have two more days before we reach the high country if nothing slows us down."

"If you're asking my advice, I'd keep them where we can see them until then."

Jinx sighed and smiled. "I was and you're right. Fine, but I'll be watching them."

"You won't be alone," he said and walked back to where Max was still swearing as he stood looking at the mess in the wagon. "Let me help with breakfast."

The older man turned to stare pointedly at him. "You ever cooked on the trail?"

"I have," Angus said. "You want me to make the biscuits or the fire?"

Max's face broke into a grin. "We got trouble enough without you making the biscuits, son. See to the fire." He climbed back into the wagon, mumbling to himself.

"I make some damned fine biscuits, I'll have you know," Angus called after the cook. Inside the wagon, Max huffed, but he was no longer cussing.

Angus smiled as he set about making the fire. Brick joined him. Ella had gone down to the stream. She always carried fishing line and had a knack for catching things. Angus figured it was her infinite patience. Brick went to help Max clean up the mess the bear had made.

When he had the fire going, he looked up and caught Jinx watching him.

AFTER A BREAKFAST of fried trout and biscuits, they rounded up the cattle and traveled higher into the mountains. Ella had proven her skill at catching pan-size trout. This morning he and Brick cleaned them before turning them over to Max, who dusted them with flour and dropped them in sizzling lard.

"Good breakfast," Jinx had said as she finished hers and thanked Ella for the fish before her gaze shifted to Royce and Cash. "I'd like the two of you to ride pickup again today. Keep an eye out for stragglers. If the thunderstorm is bad, I'll need you to help keep the herd from spooking."

Both men nodded. Angus had noticed that Royce and Cash had eaten plenty of fish and biscuits. There was nothing wrong with their appetites. What did surprise him was that they hadn't asked about the ruckus this morning, keeping to themselves as usual. He found that strange. Also suspicious. He wondered if there was a reason the bear had been able to get into their supplies so easily. The men made him nervous, just like they did Jinx and Ella.

But after breakfast and the excitement of having a bear in camp, they'd gotten a fairly early start, riding out as they had the day before. The sun rose and moved lazily across the canopy of sky above the treetops.

As the morning and early afternoon slipped away, the sun began its descent into a horizon filled with gunmetal-gray storm clouds.

Just as Jinx had predicted, a thunderstorm was headed their way. Angus could hear the low rumble in the distance. He rode over to join her. "How far to the next corrals?"

She shook her head as she glanced at the storm moving toward them. "We can't make it in time. There's a large meadow a half mile from here. I don't think we have a choice but to try to hold them there."

As Angus rode point again on his side of the herd, he saw Jinx riding back to give the others the news. He could feel the electricity in the air. It made the hair quill on the back of his neck. He could smell the scent of rain.

Behind him, he felt the lightning strikes growing closer along with the thunder and rain as he found the meadow and circled back to help with the herd. He knew what could happen if even a few of the cattle spooked and took off. He'd seen a herd stampede in a thunderstorm and knew that was Jinx's greatest fear.

Or maybe her greatest fear was what T.D. might do if he'd decided to follow them into the mountains. If T.D. took advantage of the thunderstorm to hit just then, Angus doubted they could keep the herd from stampeding.

PATTY HAD BEEN so sure that T.D. would have come by her apartment last night—if he wasn't in jail. She needed to know what had happened so she dressed in her uniform for work, but left early so she could stop by T.D.'s favorite bar.

Sliding onto a stool down the bar from several regulars having their morning coffee, she asked Marty if he'd seen T.D. last night. She and Marty had gone to school together. He was older and had married young. He had three kids and another on the way with his wife of many years.

She'd always liked him. Always thought how different her life would have been if she'd married someone like him and now had a home and kids.

Marty poured her a fountain cola and set it down on a napkin in front of her before he answered. "He was here. I let him have one beer and then asked him to leave. From the marks on your neck, I probably don't have to tell you that he was in one of his moods."

Self-consciously, she touched her neck. She'd thought she'd covered the worst of it with makeup. "Did he say where he was going when he left?"

"Yeah, he wrote down his entire itinerary for me." He shook his head. "He left with his minions, Wyatt and Travis."

Well, at least he hadn't been thrown in jail after going out to Jinx's ranch. Maybe she hadn't called the law on him. Or maybe he'd changed his mind and hadn't gone. Maybe he'd just come here to the bar.

She took a sip of her cola. "So you don't know where they went after they left? T.D. didn't say what his plans were?" She had to get to work soon, but first she had to know if T.D. had mentioned going after Jinx.

Marty seemed to study her for a moment. "They

stopped in this morning for…supplies for a trip. They were all in T.D.'s truck with a horse trailer and three horses in the back. I would imagine you know as well as I do where they're headed." Marty leaned toward her on the bar, his gaze locking with hers. "Why do you waste your time on him?"

She chuckled and looked away, embarrassed. "I need something to do while I'm waiting for you to ask me out."

"I'm married, but I know that's like bear bait for you." Marty shook his head. "Patty, I'm serious. You're better than T.D., better than any of the men I've seen you… date. Come on, Patty, wise up. There are some good men out there. Try one of them for a change."

She put down her glass of cola a little too hard, splashing some out onto the bar. "We all can't be like you, Marty," she snapped. "In a dead-end job, with a mortgage on your double-wide and a bunch of kids."

He sighed. "Sorry, you're right. It's none of my business and what do I know anyway, right? But I'm happy, Patty. Are you?" He turned to go down the bar.

"I'm sorry. Marty? *Marty!*" But he kept walking. What made it worse was that she knew he was right. She thought her problem was Jinx. Or that her problem was T.D. She knew it was her and always had been. She was like her mother. She always went for the lowest denomination when it came to men. But that didn't mean she loved T.D. any less.

As she finished her cola and left Marty a tip, she felt her chest tighten as she thought about what she'd asked Wyatt to do. Too late to change anything, she told herself. Wyatt probably couldn't do it anyway.

For a moment, though, she felt the enormity of what she might have put into motion. She'd known Wyatt'd had a crush on her for years. She'd seen it in those puppy dog eyes of his and the way he shuffled his boots, dropping his gaze to them when he was around her, as if half-afraid to meet her eyes.

Until last night. It did amaze her how easy it had been to seduce him. All it had taken was one kiss and he'd been ready to do anything for her. He hadn't said he'd do it, though. He might chicken out. But at least she'd put the notion into his head and had given him a taste—so to speak—of the payoff if he did it.

Now, though, she felt nervous and worried. She told herself that what was done was done. Too late for second thoughts since there was nothing she could do about it. And if something did happen up there in the mountains and Jinx didn't return... Well, T.D. would be free of Jinx—and he'd have the ranch. And he'd have Patty to thank for it.

Sheriff Harvey Bessler pushed through the door as she was leaving. "Patty," he said. "I'm hoping I heard wrong." She had no desire to talk to him. Also, she was running late for work. But he was blocking the door.

"Sorry?" She made a point of looking at her phone to show him that she was on her way to work—that was if he didn't notice the waitress uniform she was wearing.

"I heard T.D. and his buddies have gone up into the mountains. But you wouldn't know anything about that, right?"

She shook her head. "Did you ask his wife?"

Harvey gave her a sad smile. "I hope he's smart enough not to go after Jinx and make trouble."

Patty glanced again at her phone. "I wouldn't know, Sheriff, but if you don't move I'll be late for work. I'd hate to tell Cora that I was late because of you. Who knows what she'd put in your food the next time you come into the café."

He sighed and stepped aside. "You have a good day, Patty."

"I'm going to try, Sheriff." As she stepped out of the bar, she saw the dark clouds moving swiftly across the valley. She glanced toward the mountains where by now T.D. would be. The air smelled of rain and the wind had picked up, swirling dust up from the gutter to whirl around her. She shielded her eyes, Marty's words still stinging her.

As the first drops began to splash down, she made a run for the café wondering where T.D., Wyatt and Travis were right now. She knew it was too early, but she couldn't help wondering if maybe Wyatt might already have Jinx in his sights.

Chapter Six

Lightning splintered the sky in a blinding flash. Thunder followed on its heels, a boom that seemed to shake the earth under their feet.

Angus pulled on his slicker to ride the perimeter of the herd. He could feel the wind at the front of the storm kicking up. The pine trees swayed, creaking and moaning as dust devils whirled around him.

Clouds moved in, taking the light with them as the sky blackened. It was like someone had thrown a cloak over them, snuffing out the light, going from day to night. In a lightning strike, he saw the woods illuminated for a moment in sharp relief before going dark again.

When the rain came, it slashed down horizontally in hard, huge drops that pelted him and cascaded off the brim of his Stetson. Through the downpour, he could barely see Jinx on the other side of the herd, running point. He watched as the cattle began to shift restlessly. It wouldn't take much for them to panic. All it would take was for a few of them to take off at a run and spook the others and soon they would all be stampeding.

The wind tore at the trees, ripping off pieces of the boughs and sending them airborne. The rain fell in sheets, obliterating everything. A bolt of lightning zigzagged down in a blinding path in front of him. His horse reared and he had to fight to stay in the saddle as thunder exploded directly overhead in a boom that set some of the cattle at the edge of the storm running.

The herd was already jumpy. It wouldn't take much to set off more of the cattle. Too many of them running would be impossible for the two of them to turn by themselves. They would be caught in the stampede.

Angus spurred his horse as he went after them, hoping to cut them off and turn them back before the others began to move. He rode blind, the rain painful as it pelted him. The wind lay over the grass in front of him, moving like ocean waves in an angry sea.

He turned the handful of spooked cattle, steering them back toward the herd. As he did, he spotted Jinx through the rain. She and her horse appeared almost ghostlike in a lightning flash. She'd ridden out and had turned the others. The rain was so loud that when it suddenly stopped, he felt as if he'd gone deaf.

He looked over at Jinx. She sat on her horse, glancing around as surprised as he was. Just as quickly, it began to hail. Ice pellets the size of quarters fell in a wall of white that blotted out everything. He ducked his head to it, the noise as deafening as the thunder and rain had been. The hail pummeled him and the side of the mountain, quickly covering the ground and the backs of the cattle.

He rode his horse under a high, large pine tree to wait out the hailstorm. As he did, he could hear the lightning and thunder moving off over the mountains. It wasn't until the hail began to let up, that he saw Jinx again. She sat astride her horse under a pine tree only yards away. He saw the relief on her face.

More than relief. She smiled with the kind of joy that comes with knowing you made it through something challenging. He returned her smile as he took off his hat and shook off the melting hailstones. The herd stood, backs coated white, the storm over. Angus settled his Stetson back on his head and felt himself relax a little as droplets of moisture fell from the sodden pines as the storm moved on as quickly as it had appeared.

WYATT WATCHED THE storm pass from under a large pine tree low on the mountain. Next to him, Travis Frank wrung out his hat. "This has to be one of your worst ideas ever, T.D."

"Quit complaining," Wyatt said as he looked around the sodden camp. "It isn't like that was your first thunderstorm—or your last if you're lucky." Travis grumbled under his breath as T.D. emerged from the tree he'd been under, stretched and walked over to them.

"One hell of a storm," the cowboy said, laughing. He'd clearly used the time trapped under the tree while waiting for the hail to stop to take a nip or two from one of the bottles of whiskey he'd brought along.

"You realize that he's going to get us killed or thrown in jail," Travis said under his breath to Wyatt.

"Ready to ride?" T.D. asked jovially. The man had never made it a secret that he loved storms. T.D. loved loud and boisterous, disorder and confusion. He loved chaotic frenzy—and often caused it. It was no wonder the cowboy would enjoy a storm like the one that had just moved through, Wyatt thought as he and Travis left the shelter of the tree.

"What now?" Wyatt asked, clearly not enjoying this. Like him, Travis had noticed that T.D. had been hitting the bottle. His face was flushed, his eyes bright. Sober, T.D. was trying. Drunk, he was hell on wheels.

"Now we catch up to the herd and let the fun begin," T.D. said, grinning. He looked excited, anxious to do

whatever he could to cause trouble. Wyatt knew that
Jinx would be expecting nothing less. He wondered if
T.D. realized that or if he thought he was really going to
surprise her when he showed up.

Wyatt hated to think what mayhem T.D. was planning.
More than likely the man was playing it by ear, which
was even more frightening. He hated to think how drunk
T.D. might be by the time they reached Jinx and the herd.

He went to the large pine where he'd tied his horse,
swung up into the damp saddle and looked to the towering pine-covered mountain ahead of them. How long
before they caught up to the herd? Like T.D., he was anxious. He'd brought his hunting rifle with the scope. Patty's favor rode with him, like a secret tucked in his jacket
pocket. A secret that warmed him all through the storm
and chilled him the closer they got to catching up to Jinx.

AFTER THE STORM PASSED, the sun had shone bright. They
moved the cattle farther up the trail, making better time
than Angus had expected. With the storm over, there
was a more relaxed feeling in camp that evening when
they finally stopped. They'd reached some more of the
old corrals along the trail to summer range.

He'd gone out and killed two blue grouse. Though out
of season, he didn't think anyone was going to turn him
in after Max fried up the birds until they were crisp on
the outside and juicy in the middle. Max had made gravy
out of what was left of the cracklings in the huge cast-
iron skillet and served it with a large batch of homemade
biscuits. Nothing went to waste.

"We're sure as the devil eating better than I expected,"
Cash said and stuffed half a biscuit into his mouth. "You
know what I mean," he said as he swallowed the mouthful. "After the bear got into our grub."

Angus saw Jinx and Max share a look. He had a pretty good idea what it was about. Max had been so sure that he secured the box with the metal meat cooler in it. When Angus had a chance, he'd gotten a good look at the box. He knew that bears were much smarter than most people thought.

He'd once had a cooler stolen off his cabin porch at the ranch by a grizzly bear. That bear did everything possible to get into that old rounded-edge metal cooler, much like the one in the chuckwagon. When Angus had found it, the grizzly had scratched and clawed and even rolled the cooler down a hillside, but still hadn't been able to get inside it.

There was only one way the black bear had gotten into the one in the chuckwagon. Someone had propped it open like a calling card for any bear in the area. Max was lucky he hadn't awakened to the noise to find a grizzly staring out of the wagon at him.

"Excellent meal," Brick said and everyone around the campfire agreed. This high in the mountains, the temperature began to drop even though it was early June.

After everyone had finished, Royce pulled out a well-used pack of cards and challenged anyone who wanted to play with a poker game. Angus passed, but Brick and Cash said they were in. Ella announced that she would watch and make sure no one cheated.

Jinx got up and walked with Angus to the chuckwagon where Max was seated, watching all of them after cleaning up the dishes. As they approached, the older man rose from where he'd been lounging and announced he was calling it a night.

"I'm sleeping in the woods tonight," Max said. "No more sleeping under the chuckwagon." With that he took his sleeping bag and disappeared into the darkness beyond the campfire.

"Max isn't wild about bears," Jinx whispered with a laugh.

"Hope he doesn't run across one then out in the woods." They both chuckled as she and Angus sat on a log with their backs to the chuckwagon.

"With his luck, Max will run across one on its way to the chuckwagon," she said.

They grew quiet as the campfire popped and the card game grew louder. "I think that's the second time I've heard Royce speak," Jinx said. "You think he deals off the bottom of the deck?"

"I think you can count on it," Angus said with a laugh.

"Your brother—"

"Can take care of himself. Anyway, Ella is looking after him." He smiled to himself, thinking about the three of them working their way across the west from ranch to ranch, camp to camp. It wasn't Brick's first card game. Nor the first one that Ella had watched to make sure he wasn't cheated.

"I'm going to miss this," he said, surprising Jinx—and himself—that he'd spoken his thoughts out loud.

"Are you quitting wrangling?" she asked, turning to him. Her brown eyes had darkened with concern.

"I'll never quit ranching. My parents are counting on me coming back and pretty much taking over running Cardwell Ranch. It's what I was born to do." He smiled and shook his head. "I'm looking forward to it. But I will miss this. Who knows what Brick is going to do. He wants nothing to do with running the ranch."

"You two look so much alike and yet you're so different." He could feel her gaze on him. "What about Ella? What are her plans?"

Angus glanced toward the campfire. Ella's pretty face was lit by the golden firelight. "I don't know. She's welcome to help with the ranch. She's family. But you know how that goes. She could meet some man in a three-piece suit and follow him to the big city."

Jinx laughed. "Can't see that happening, but like you said, you never know. The big city definitely isn't for me. Then again, I have no idea what my future holds."

At the poker game, sparks rose up from the campfire to burn out in the velvet starlit sky overhead. Angus stretched out his long legs, content after a good day in the saddle and a good meal. It didn't hurt that he was sitting here with a beautiful woman, one who intrigued him and always had.

Jinx seemed as relaxed as he felt. He told himself not to get any ideas. The woman needed him. He was a hired man. Once the cattle were at summer pasture, his job would be over.

Still, as he breathed in the night scents that floated around him, he was aware of Jinx next to him in a way he hadn't been aware of a woman in a very long time. The night air felt heavy and seemed too busy with that feeling that anything could happen. He wondered if Jinx felt it or if it was all his imagination.

The thought made him smile. Whatever it was he felt right now, he knew that this was where he belonged at this moment in time. Fate had brought him here. Brought him to this woman whom he'd never forgotten.

"You almost look as if you're enjoying this," Jinx said as she also stretched out her legs to get more comfortable.

He chuckled. He loved nothing better than being in the mountains, listening to the lowing of the cattle and feeling tired after a day in the saddle. But there was also something about Jinx that drew him to her and it was more than a chance meeting all those years ago. It was also more than his being protective.

"I guess it shows, how much I enjoy this," he said, looking over at her. Her brown eyes shone in the ambient firelight; her hair seemed to catch fire, reminding him of how red it was when she was but a girl.

"It does show," she said. "This life gets into your blood. It would be hard to give up."

"I don't plan to. What about you?"

She seemed to be watching the flames of the nearby campfire, the light playing on her face. "After my mother died, my father lost interest in the ranch," Jinx said. "He lost interest in life and went downhill fast. I buried him earlier this spring. I've been running the ranch alone since then. T.D. was supposed to help take up the slack." She looked away. "But I realized right away that all he wanted to do was sell the ranch and live off the profits."

"I'm sorry," Angus said as he focused his gaze on where Brick tossed another log on the fire. A shower of sparks rose up in a flurry of bright red to disappear into the sky overhead.

"This ranch has been in my family for only two generations," she said. "Around here that doesn't mean anything. Most of these people are at least fifth generation ranchers."

"That doesn't mean you aren't wedded to the life and the land. It's hard to let go of something you love. Or someone," he added, remembering what his brother had said.

She smiled over at him. "I let go of T.D. months ago. Unfortunately, getting rid of him isn't as easy as I'd hoped. I filed for divorce but he's contested it, determined to force me to sell and settle with him." Jinx shook her head. "We've only been together less than two years and yet that's enough, according to my lawyer, that T.D. can force me into a settlement. I can't believe what a fool I was."

Angus chuckled. "We've all been there, trust me." Only the crackle of the fire and the occasional burst of laughter or curse broke the stillness around them. He wasn't surprised that in a few minutes, Jinx changed the subject.

"I can't believe my good luck, getting three good hands from Cardwell Ranch," she said, lightening the mood. "Your cousin Ella is just as good as she says she is."

He smiled. "Yep, she can ride circles around me and Brick."

Jinx glanced over at him, the firelight dancing in her eyes. "The two of you let her."

Angus grinned. "Maybe a little, but don't underestimate my cousin. She's special, that one."

"I love how close you three are. Do you have other siblings?"

"An older sister, Mary, and older brother, Hank. And lots more cousins."

"I always wanted a large family."

He studied her in the firelight. "Maybe you'll have one of your own someday." She looked skeptical. "Just because you climbed onto a rank horse once, doesn't mean you quit riding."

She laughed at his analogy. "Rank horse covers T.D. well. I know there are good horses out there as well as men. I'll be much more discerning next time. If there is a next time."

"There will be," he said and met her gaze. He held it, wishing he could take away the hurt he saw in those eyes.

"Your father is a marshal, right?" He nodded. "Your family must miss you."

He smiled, thinking of his mother. "If my mother had her way, we'd all live in the main house and would park our boots under her dining room table every night for dinner."

Jinx nodded. "I've heard about Dana Cardwell Savage. Our mothers were friends, both involved in the cattle-women's organizations, but I'm sure you already know that. What about Ella's parents?"

"Just her mom, Stacy. She's always taken care of all of us and helped Mom running the house rather than the ranch. She lives on the ranch in one of the cabins up on the side of the mountain." He could feel Jinx's curious gaze on him.

"I'm sure your mother can't wait to have your boots back under her table."

"There's no hurry," he said, chuckling at the truth in her words. "My family, especially my mother and uncle Jordan, have everything under control. My sister takes care of the books for the ranch. They don't need me yet."

"But when they do?"

"I reckon I'll head on home."

Jinx stared up at the swaying pines overhead for a moment. "When my father got sick, I promised myself that I would keep the ranch or die trying."

"Is that what he wanted you to do?"

She seemed surprised by the question. "No, actually, on his deathbed, he made me promise two things. Get rid of T.D. and then the ranch. He thought it would be too much for me and that I would kill myself trying to hang on to it. I guess it's no wonder so many ranchers are selling out to those large companies that move cattle with helicopters and are owned by even larger corporations."

"Ranching isn't an easy way to make a living, that's for sure," Angus agreed. "So your father gave you good advice."

She chuckled. "You mean by kicking T.D. out?" She shook her head, looking rueful. "I'd kicked him out of my bed a long time before that. I should have kicked him off the ranch sooner. But I think I just hated to admit what a mistake I'd made."

"What about selling the ranch?"

Jinx stared again at the campfire for so long, he didn't think she was going to reply. "That's the hard part. I'm not sure I can do it." She let out a bitter bark of a laugh. "But I'm not sure I can keep it, either. T.D. is forcing my hand. I think I'm going to have to sell it just to settle up with him."

"I'm sorry it's come to that."

"My own fault. And maybe my father was right and it's for the best. Just doesn't feel that way right now. Admittedly, T.D.'s got me digging in my heels just out of orneriness." She sighed and seemed glad to see the poker game break up. Angus noted that neither Cash nor Royce looked happy as they headed off to bed. Brick, however, was grinning and joking with Ella, which told him that she'd kept the game honest. That was his cousin. Now his brother had the two men's money in his pocket and had probably made enemies in the process.

"It's going to be another early morning tomorrow," Jinx said but didn't move. "I heard that a male grizzly was seen in this area recently. I thought I'd put Royce and Brick on first watch. Brick's already volunteered."

Angus just bet he had. "I can relieve Brick."

She nodded. "I'll let them know." Like him, she must have hated to leave this quiet spot. There was an intimacy to it. When she looked over at him, their gazes locked for a few long moments.

Jinx pulled her gaze away first and rose to her feet. "I best get some shut-eye," she said. "It was nice visiting with you."

"You, too. Sleep well," he said as he watched her stop by the campfire to speak with Brick and Ella. Jinx was chuckling to herself as she went to find Royce and Cash before heading to her sleeping bag spread out in the dried pine needles some distance from the fire.

Angus watched her go, telling himself that there was nothing he could do to help Jinx other than to get her cattle to the high country. But even as he thought it, he knew that wouldn't be the end of her problems. And they hadn't gotten the cattle to the high country yet, he reminded himself as he made his way to his own sleeping bag.

All they needed was another long day of moving the herd and then a short one without any more trouble than they'd had and the cattle would be on summer range. Then it would be just a matter of returning to the valley. The job would be over.

As he walked through the darkness of the pines toward where he'd dropped his sleeping bag earlier, he saw Royce ride off with Brick and then part company as they split up to take the first night shift.

He looked around but didn't see Cash. The two worried him, especially after the incident with the bear in the chuckwagon. Since then, though, nothing had happened. So maybe Max had gotten forgetful and left the box holding the meat locker unlocked and cracked open just enough that a bear caught wind of it.

He told himself that in another day and a half they would have completed the job they were hired on to do.

He and Ella and Brick could head back to Montana. They would have accomplished what they'd come here for.

Unless Jinx's almost-ex had other plans for them before then.

ELLA COULDN'T SLEEP. She felt restless, even as tired as she was. For a while, she lay staring up into the darkness. Clouds from the aftermath of the storm hung low over the mountainside, blocking out the stars like a thick, dark cloak.

Finally, she rose and walked away from the camp, feeling as if she couldn't breathe. She wasn't sure what was causing it. Earlier she'd tried to reach her mother. But she couldn't get cell phone coverage.

From as far back as she could remember, she'd "sensed" things. She'd been uneasy when they'd stopped by Cardwell Ranch before heading down here to Wyoming. Her mother had been acting strangely. It wasn't anything she could put her finger on. Just a sense that something was wrong.

That feeling had only gotten stronger. Her instincts told her she should saddle up and go home. But she'd signed on to this job and she would stick it out. Especially after meeting Jinx. She wasn't about to leave the woman shorthanded. In a few days they would be headed home. She just hoped that would be soon enough, as she reached the horse corral.

With the clouds hanging so low over the mountainside, she could only make out dark shapes behind the corral fence. She leaned against the railing, breathing in the cold night air, and tried to still her growing unease. She and her mother had always been close since from the beginning it was just the two of them—and of course the rest of the Cardwell/Savage family. As to her father, she knew little about him, only that he'd never been in the picture.

Not that she hadn't had an amazing childhood growing up on Cardwell Ranch. Her mother had seemed happy there after having split with her family years before over what would be done with the ranch following Mary Cardwell's death. Ella knew only a little about the argument that had caused the siblings to fight over the ranch. Apparently, Dana had refused to sell it, while Ella's mother, Stacy, and her uncle Jordan wanted the cash from the sale.

When their mother's will was finally found, it settled the squabble, but by then the damage had been done. It had taken time for Stacy and Jordan to come back to the ranch. Stacy had come back after she had Ella.

She felt fatigue pull at her and started to push off the corral fence when she heard a sound that made her freeze. Someone was moving through the darkness in her direction. Instantly, she was on alert, aware that whoever was moving toward her was moving cautiously, as if not wanting to be heard.

Whoever it was hadn't seen her. She stayed still as the figure grew larger and larger. She knew it wasn't an animal because an animal would have picked up her scent by now.

The shape grew larger and larger until the man was almost on top of her. She watched him look around in the darkness as if to make sure that no one had seen him. She could tell he was listening because the night was dark; he couldn't see any farther than she could.

Then, as if believing he was alone, he reached for the latch on the corral holding the horses.

"Cash?"

He jumped and then froze for a moment before he

slowly let go of the latch. Turning just as slowly, he squinted into the darkness. He took a few steps in her direction. "Oh, it's you. I didn't see you standing there." He sounded winded as if she'd scared him. Or worse, she'd caught him.

"What's going on?" she asked, even though she had a pretty good idea.

"Nothing," he said as he moved closer. "Just checking on the horses."

"Looked like you were going to open the gate and let all the horses out."

He let out a nervous laugh as he closed the distance between them. "Why would I do that?"

"I was wondering the same thing." He was close now, so close she could see the dark holes of his eyes.

He glanced around and then said quietly, "I thought everyone was asleep."

"I figured you did."

His gaze settled on her. His lips curled into a smirk. "What's a woman like you doing up here on this mountain with a bunch of men anyway?"

"You have a problem with it?"

"Me?" He leaned toward her. "Naw, but some men would think a young, good-looking woman riding with a group of males was just asking for it."

His words sent a chill through her, but she didn't let it show. Except for the fact that she'd eased her hand down to the holstered gun at her hip. "Men like that end up dead. Good thing you're not one of them. Otherwise, I'd advise you to sleep with one eye open."

He cleared his throat as his gaze dropped to her hand resting on the butt of her pistol. "That sounds like a threat."

"Only to men who don't respect women."

Ella heard a soft chuckle from the darkness before Jinx materialized out from behind Cash.

"There a problem here?" the trail boss asked, startling the already nervous Cash.

He spun around. "Not from me," Cash said quickly and took a few steps away from Ella.

When Jinx shifted her gaze to her in question, Ella simply shook her head and said, "I believe Cash was just on his way to bed. He's thinking about sleeping with one eye open."

He shot her a mean look before checking his expression and turning to Jinx. "In case either of you care, I'm a light sleeper." He touched the gun at his hip.

"Sleep well," Jinx said.

As Cash headed toward camp, Ella heard him mumble something about women not knowing their place.

Jinx sighed as she watched him disappear into the darkness before she turned back to Ella. "Now, what was really going on out here?"

"I couldn't sleep. Cash didn't see me out here in the dark. I think he was planning to release the horses. He was starting to open the gate when I spoke up. He said he was just checking his horse."

"But you don't believe him." Jinx nodded. "Best get some sleep."

Chapter Seven

Wide awake now, Jinx saddled up her horse. Royce had offered to take the first watch, along with Brick. So far it had been quiet. Other than the black bear that had gotten into their larder, they hadn't seen any more bears.

But with the grizzlies out of hibernation and hungry, they were a threat to the herd. She'd seen how easily one could take down beef on the hoof. She and the others had to be cautious, especially of the ones with cubs, she thought as she rode out toward the south end of the herd.

But the wild animals weren't the only threat. She thought about what Ella had told her, trusting the woman's instincts along with her own. Cash needed to go. But maybe after being caught, he wouldn't be a problem. Jinx sighed. She needed him just a little longer. If he'd hired on to cause her trouble, then maybe he was already working with T.D. Otherwise, there was a good chance he would turn on her once her almost-ex did show up. It was only a matter of time before that happened. T.D. was too predictable not to follow her up here.

Pushing thoughts of him away, she considered what to do about Cash. As the last of the clouds passed, the night sky was suddenly ablaze with stars and a sliver of moon. Nothing seemed to move in the dark stillness as she rode south along the edge of the herd.

On nights like this, she couldn't help but think of her father. She missed him so much it took her breath away. He'd been everything to her since she was a girl. He'd always been there when she needed him. When her mother had died, he'd comforted her more than she could him. He would have known what to do about Royce and Cash.

Just as he'd known that T.D. was all wrong for her. He'd tried to talk her out of marrying the cowboy, but she'd been in love.

Love. She could laugh now at how starry-eyed she'd been. T.D. had definitely charmed her. He'd made her feel beautiful. Her feelings for the few boyfriends she'd had seemed silly in comparison. T.D. had been her first honest-to-goodness love affair. He took her to fancy restaurants in Jackson Hole, getting her out of her jeans and boots, making her feel like a desirable woman.

That thought made her heart ache. She'd felt like a princess with T.D. Why wouldn't she marry him? He'd said and done all the right things.

"I know you want your father to walk you down the aisle," T.D. had said one night. "I want that for you. That's why I don't think we should put off getting married."

She'd been dragging her feet. There'd been little red flags. T.D.'s credit card not working. Times when he'd forgotten his wallet. She'd been happy to pay. Another time there'd been the man whom T.D. had purposely avoided at the rodeo, saying the man was a poor sport at cards. Later, she would learn about his gambling habits. But back then, there'd been enough that she'd been wary of when it came to marrying T.D. He had talked a good line, but she questioned how much help he would be on the ranch.

But then her father had gotten sick. T.D. had been

right. She'd dreamed of her father walking her down the aisle. They'd decided to get married, rushing into it even as her father was telling her to wait and be sure this was the man for her.

An owl hooted down at her from a tree limb, startling her out of her thoughts. She reined in her horse, realizing that she still hadn't seen Royce. He was supposed to be riding herd tonight along with Brick. She could hear Brick to the north playing his harmonica, but there was no sign of Royce.

A horse whinnied from the darkness. She spurred hers forward, following the sound to find Royce's horse tied to a tree. Quietly, she slid off her mount and approached the man on the ground, gun drawn, only to find him sound asleep under the large pine.

Walking up to him, she kicked the worn sole of his boot. He shot up, fumbling for his gun as he blinked wildly and tried to wake up.

"Sorry," he said, scrambling to his feet. "Mother Nature called. I got off my horse and sat down for a minute. Guess I fell asleep."

"Guess so," she said. "Go on back to camp. I'll take it from here."

Royce picked up his Stetson from the dried pine needles and, head down, untied his horse. He hesitated for a moment as if he wanted to say something more in his defense. But apparently, he changed his mind, swung up on his horse and left.

Jinx watched him go, figuring she knew why Huck Chambers had let the two go. If just being lazy was all she had to worry about, she could live with that a few more days. But she feared there was more when it came to those two, especially after Ella's earlier suspicions about Cash.

ANGUS WOKE SHORTLY before he saw Jinx ride out. He rolled out and headed for his horse, figuring he'd relieve his brother so Brick could get some sleep. It didn't take much to find him at the front of the herd. Angus simply followed the sound of Brick's harmonica. His brother always carried the musical instrument in his hip pocket, seemingly lost without it.

As he approached, his brother kept playing an old Western song that their grandfather Angus had taught him. He and Brick had been named after their grandfathers. Angus Cardwell played in a band with his brother Harlan, while Brick Savage had been a marshal, like their father.

Brick finished the tune, holding the last note until Angus rode up alongside him. "We've got company," his brother said quietly. His first thought was a grizzly. "Three of them. I spotted their fire. It's almost as if they want us to know they're down there."

"T.D.," Angus said. He'd been expecting him before this. Three riders on horses could easily catch a slow-moving herd. The question now was what happened next.

"What do you think his plan is?" Brick asked.

T.D. didn't seem like a man who would have a plan. Instead, he bet the cowboy made decisions on the spur of the moment. It was another reason, Angus knew, that the man was dangerous. He'd learned from his marshal father that one of the most volatile situations involved a domestic dispute. And now he and his brother and cousin were right in the middle of Jinx and T.D.'s.

"I would imagine he plans to surprise us," Angus said.

"You sure we shouldn't go down there and surprise them?"

He shook his head. "Short of shooting them, all we would do is play into T.D.'s hands. He wants to torment

Jinx. Better to ignore them as long as we can. Otherwise, I'm afraid there might be bloodshed."

His brother nodded, but looked disappointed. Brick wasn't one to back down from a fight. He'd gotten his namesake's temper and his other grandfather's musical talent, while Angus had taken more after their father. Hudson Savage was easygoing, solid as granite and just as dependable. He thought before he spoke and it took a lot to rile him.

"Get some sleep," Angus told his twin. "Jinx said we're moving out early again."

He saw his brother glance down the mountain to where the men were camped.

"Let's not say anything to Jinx," Angus said. "Not yet. No reason to worry her when so far, T.D. and his friends haven't done anything."

"Not yet," Brick said as he pocketed his harmonica and rode back toward camp.

T.D. took a drink from the pint of whiskey he'd brought and stared into the flames of the campfire. He felt antsy but he knew that Wyatt was right. They'd had a long day on the trail, pushing hard once they finally hit their saddles at almost midday. They'd caught up to Jinx and the herd before sundown.

Wyatt had insisted that it wouldn't be smart to do anything until they'd rested their horses and come up with a plan. *Wyatt and his plans*, he thought with a silent curse as he raised his gaze from the fire to consider his friends.

"You really hit the bottom of the barrel with these two, didn't you, Junior?" his father had said when he'd begun running with Wyatt and Travis at a young age. "But then I guess it isn't easy to find two dumb enough to tag along with you given where you're headed."

He thought of his father's smirk, his words harder than a backhand and more hurtful. Tucker David Sharp Senior had never given him any credit. The man had been convinced early on that his namesake wasn't going to amount to anything and neither were his friends.

Well, all that was about to change. At least for him. Once he got the ranch…

The more he'd thought about it, the more he wanted the whole thing. Half would force Jinx to sell her precious ranch, which should have been satisfaction enough, he supposed. And it would put a good chunk of change into his pocket—temporarily. Once he paid off his gambling debts, he wouldn't have all that much left. Also, he knew himself well enough to know that money burned a hole in his pocket. He'd gamble, trying to use the money to make more money and probably lose it all.

But if he had the whole ranch, then he could show his father that he'd been wrong about him. Too bad the senior Sharp was in his grave, but he could watch from his special place in hell. *Look at me now, Dad. See how wrong you were?*

He would rename the ranch after himself and make it the best damned ranch in the valley. He took another sip of the whiskey. Or maybe he'd just sell it and live off the money. Maybe he'd have to sell it to pay his gambling debts. If he couldn't borrow against it. He imagined walking into the bank and asking for a loan against his ranch. *His* ranch. He liked the sound of that.

"You might want to go easy on that stuff," Travis said from across the fire as he watched him take another slug from the whiskey bottle. T.D. shot him a dark look. "Just sayin' I agree with Wyatt. We should have a plan so we don't get our fool selves shot. Jinx ain't alone up there."

"Don't you think I know that?" T.D. snapped. He

thought of the cowhand who'd come to his wife's rescue the other night at the ranch. He'd seen the others, as well. A motley bunch if there ever was one. He'd recognized two of them, Royce Richards and Cash Andrews, both worthless as the day was long. Working for Jinx was probably the only job they could get after Huck had booted them off his place.

But dumb and worthless aside, they'd all be armed. And Jinx was no fool. She'd know he'd be coming after her—if she didn't already. He got up to throw another tree limb onto the fire. He couldn't wait until tomorrow. When he got the ranch he was going to buy himself a brand-new pickup, the best money could buy. He'd show them. He'd show them all. T. D. Sharp was somebody.

Chapter Eight

The next morning Jinx pulled Royce aside. "Here's your pay," she said, handing him the money she'd brought along, already anticipating that Royce and Cash wouldn't last more than a day or so. "I think it's best if we part company now rather than later."

"You have to be kidding me. Just because I fell asleep?" Royce said incredulously. "I suppose you've never done that while on watch?"

"No, I haven't, and I've been doing this since I was six."

He shook his head. "I guess we all can't be as perfect as you, Ms. Trail Boss. By the way, how'd you get the nickname Jinx anyway?"

"It was just something my father called me, if you must know."

"Oh, I thought it was because you brought bad luck to everyone around you," Royce said, his eyes narrowing angrily. "Seems all those things T.D.'s been saying about you are true."

She didn't bother to comment as she turned. Over her shoulder, she said, "You're welcome to have breakfast before you pack up and leave."

"No, thanks," he said to her back. "I've had enough.

At least now I understand what your husband had to put up with."

Jinx kept walking. It was hard not to take the bait. Royce had a lot in common with T.D. Both blamed other people for how their lives had turned out. They really seemed to think that if their luck changed, everything would come up roses. They preferred to blame luck rather than their lack of hard work.

As she was headed down the side of the mountain to where the chuckwagon sat, she saw Max and knew, even before she heard him carrying on, that something else had happened.

By the time she reached him, Angus and Brick had joined him. Angus was squatting on the ground in front of one of the wagon's wheels.

"What's wrong?" she asked as she moved closer.

"Someone sabotaged the wagon," Brick told her.

"Don't worry. Angus thinks he can fix it," Max said, disbelief in his tone. "Then again, he thinks he can make eatable biscuits."

She caught Angus's amused grin. "I'm going to have to make my biscuits before this cattle drive is over just to show Max," he said to Jinx.

"If you must," she said, unable not to smile.

"My honor is at stake," he said as they all stood around the wagon wheel in question.

"So you think you can fix the wheel?" she asked.

"A couple of spokes were pried loose," Angus said. "Brick and I can knock them back into place. They should hold enough that we can get the wagon off the mountain. You can get it fixed once we get back to civilization, though."

"Civilization? You do know this is Wyoming, right?" she joked, then sobered. "So this was done purposely?"

Angus nodded. "There's something else you should know." He hesitated as he saw Cash headed their way. "T.D. and his friends have caught up to us."

"You think they did this?" she asked.

He shook his head. "It was someone in camp."

She let out an angry breath. Turning, she saw Royce riding off. Did he do this?

Cash joined them. "What's going on?"

JINX CONSIDERED CASH, wondering if she shouldn't send him down the mountain with his pay, as well. But she figured Royce had done this after her encounter with him last night. "My ex-husband and a couple of his friends have followed us. It could be a problem."

"Looks like it already is a problem," Cash said, eyeing the wheel on the wagon.

"We aren't sure who did that," Angus said as Royce disappeared over a rise.

Cash followed his gaze. "So you paid off Royce?"

"I did," Jinx said, half expecting Cash to quit and go with his buddy. "I'm saying it could get dangerous. I know you didn't sign on for that."

He nodded his head in agreement before shrugging. "I hate to ask what's for breakfast," he said, as if losing interest in the conversation.

"Ella caught more fish and I know there are biscuits," Brick told him.

"That'll do," Cash said and started toward the fire Max had already laid that morning. "It's just another day and a half, right?" he asked over his shoulder.

"Right," she said to his retreating backside before looking at Angus. He shook his head as if to say it was her decision whether or not to keep him on.

The news about T.D. hadn't come as a surprise. She'd

known he couldn't leave well enough alone. It gave her whiplash the way one moment he was begging for her to take him back and the next threatening to sue for half the ranch. More and more, she just wanted it over.

"Should have killed T.D. when I had the chance," Max mumbled under his breath.

"And what would I do without you while you went to prison?" she demanded.

"Starve," he said flatly.

"Exactly." She coaxed a smile out of him as he dished up her breakfast and she went to sit near the campfire. Cash got up without a word to go stand in line for his breakfast. She told herself it was just another full day and night. They would reach summer pasture with the herd by noon tomorrow and then head off the mountain.

Not that it would be over for her, but at least she didn't have to worry about her wranglers and Max up here in the mountains with T.D. and his friends. She felt anxious, though, knowing that he was so nearby. She would double the patrol tonight. Knowing T.D., he just might decide to strike once he was drunk enough.

"You're awfully quiet," Angus said as he sat down next to his cousin after getting his breakfast plate. Everyone else had eaten while Angus and Brick had worked on the wagon wheel. They would be moving out soon.

"It hit me that this is probably the last time that we'll do this together, the three of us," Ella said.

"Why would you say that?" he asked, surprised.

She shot him a don't-con-a-conman look. "Because it's time. I've suspected you've known it for a while." Her gaze left him to find Brick. "I'm worried how your brother is going to take it. But I'm sure he'll fall in love, get married, have a passel of kids and be just fine."

Angus shook his head. He couldn't see it. Brick loved women. Loved the chase. But once he caught one, he was already looking for his next challenge. He studied his cousin for a moment. It would take a very special woman for him to ever settle down.

"What about you?" he asked. Ella looked surprised. "There a cowboy out there for you?"

"A cowboy?" She chuckled. "I'm thinking more like a banker or a stockbroker, someone who wears a three-piece suit to work. What are you smiling about?"

"You. I know you, cuz."

"Maybe I'm tired of cowboys and want something different."

"Maybe a man who drives a car that has to be plugged in."

"Nothing wrong with saving the planet."

Angus scoffed. "Seriously, what would you do with a man who didn't know how to drive a stick shift or back up a trailer or ride a horse?"

"Anything I wanted," she said with a laugh.

He shook his head. "Well, I hope you find him, but it's not going to be on this mountain."

"I know." She met his gaze. "So you're saying it's time we grew up and settled down. I guess this is the last time for the three of us to be wrangling together."

"It makes me sad to think about it," Angus said and took a bite of his breakfast. He didn't have much of an appetite after seeing what someone had done to the chuckwagon wheel. Talking about this wasn't helping. "We've had some good times. I wouldn't take anything for the years we've been on the road."

Ella nodded. "What will you do?"

"Go home. The ranch needs some young blood." He studied her out of the corner of his eye as he ate. "I know your mother wishes you would stay on the ranch. You know there is a place for you in the business."

"I know. I don't know what I'll do. But I'm not worried. It will come to me."

He shook his head. "You amaze me. You have so much faith in how things will work out. Don't you ever worry?"

"Of course I worry. But I do think a lot of it is out of my hands."

"Stacy will be disappointed if you don't stay on the ranch."

Ella smiled. "My mother can handle disappointment. She's had plenty of it in her life. Anyway, she's told me repeatedly that she just wants me to be happy."

He laughed. "My mother told me the same thing."

"You don't think she means it?"

"She does. And she doesn't." He shook his head. "Dana has her heart set on me coming back to the place. Fortunately, I'm a born rancher. It's what I want to do, always have."

"You're thinking of Brick."

Angus nodded. "He doesn't want to ranch. But he doesn't know what he wants."

"I predict that one day he'll meet a woman and everything will be clear to him. But that doesn't mean it will be easy."

"You see that in the campfire flames?" he joked.

"Pretty much." She met his gaze, smiling. "Same thing is going to happen to you. If it hasn't already."

Angus finished his breakfast and rose, laughing. "I trust your instincts, cuz, but a woman isn't always the answer and from what I've seen, love is never easy."

Ella merely nodded. But as he walked away, he heard her say, "We'll see."

THROUGH THE MORNING mist hanging in the pines, T.D. saw Royce coming and picked up his rifle where he'd leaned it against a tree. He ratcheted live ammo into the chamber as the man rode toward him. "That's far enough," he said, raising the weapon.

"Take it easy," Royce said and reined in to lift his hands in surrender.

"What do you want?"

"I just got fired by your wife. What do you think I want? A kind word, a soft bed, a decent meal?" he said sarcastically. "I want to get even with her. Then I want the other stuff along with a stiff drink or two. I heard you were offering a...reward of sorts for anyone who...didn't help your wife." Royce chuckled. "I've done my part."

"By hiring on to help her get her cattle to summer range?" T.D. demanded.

"Maybe I made it more difficult for her. They're probably trying to figure out how to fix one of the wagon wheels right now."

T.D. smiled. "Why don't you swing down out of that saddle and we can talk about it? I do have a little whiskey."

"I just thought you might," Royce said as he dismounted and tied his horse to the closest tree limb.

Resting his rifle against the tree again, T.D. dug in their supplies for another pint of whiskey. "Have a sip and then tell me what's going on in the other camp."

Royce took the bottle, unscrewed the lid and gulped.

T.D. snatched it from him. "I said a sip." He wiped the top off with his hand and took a drink.

"Where are the others?" Royce asked, looking around.

"Doing some surveillance work. How many men does Jinx have?"

The cowboy pulled up a log next to the fire. "Four at

the moment, not counting the old cook and the woman she hired on."

"I thought I saw a cowgirl by the bunkhouse the other night." He laughed. "She's that hard up, is she, that she had to hire a woman?"

"The woman's good. Definitely wouldn't underestimate her," Royce said.

"That's it?"

"Cash Andrews is up there. At least for the moment. She's only got another day and a half and she'll have the cattle to the high country. Cash will do what he can to make it harder for her." Royce smiled. "He was going to let the horses out but that...cowgirl, as you called her, caught him."

T.D. shook his head. "Sometimes it feels as if women will take over the world unless we do something about it."

"I'd take another drink. The trail boss didn't allow liquor."

He laughed, knowing all about Jinx's rules. He'd played hell living by them. He handed the whiskey bottle to the man, ready to grab it back.

But this time Royce took a drink and passed it over to him again. "She's already been having some bad luck," he said, grinning as if he knew this was music to T.D.'s ears. "A black bear got into the food. Seems someone left the metal box with the meat and eggs in it open. This morning the chuckwagon wheel had been worked over. Thought you might like to hear that."

"Poor Jinx." He eyed the cowboy. "If you're not in a hurry to get back down to the valley, maybe you'd like to hire on with me."

"You're offering me a job?"

"I'm going to be running the Flying J Bar MC soon," T.D. boasted. "But this job is more about getting even. The wages aren't good, but the satisfaction is guaranteed."

Chapter Nine

The day passed without any trouble, surprising Angus. When Jinx rode over to him late in the afternoon, he mentioned his surprise to her.

"He'll wait until tonight," she said. "He'll wait until he thinks we are all asleep. It could be a long night since I plan to double the patrol tonight. But tomorrow will be an easy day and then it will be over."

It just wouldn't be over for Jinx. Not that Angus thought they would get by that easily. T.D. had ridden a long way. He wasn't going to let them get away without making trouble for Jinx and the herd.

It was dusk by the time they made camp and Max cooked the grouse Angus and Brick had shot. Cash straggled in, limping.

"Stepped in a hole," he said as he plopped down on a log by the fire. "It's killing me." He turned as Jinx walked up and asked what was going on. "I don't think I can ride watch tonight. I can barely walk. Hurts like hell even in the saddle."

Jinx seemed to study him for a moment. Like him, Angus figured she had been expecting something like this. "You quitting, Cash?"

He shook his head without looking at her. "Just not sure I'll be much help."

She nodded. "I'll settle up with you in the morning. Unless you're thinking of taking off tonight?"

"Mornin' will do," he said, still not looking at her.

All day Angus had seen her watching for T.D. while keeping an eye on Cash. The wrangler had seemed restless. When they'd stopped for lunch, Angus had noticed that Cash barely touched his biscuit sandwich of leftover fried fish from that morning. Normally, the man ate as if he feared it would be his last meal.

"I'll be glad to have Cash gone," Jinx said later as she and Angus rode out to take first watch. "I'm kicking myself for hiring him and Royce."

"You did what you had to do," Angus told her. "Anyway, they haven't caused that much trouble."

"There is still tonight," she said as she looked down the mountainside.

He'd seen the campfire below them. He'd also seen four men standing around it. Royce had joined ranks with T.D. and his friends. *No big surprise there*, he thought. That just left the question of Cash. He made Angus nervous, like he did Jinx.

To make matters worse, the night was dark, the clouds low. A breeze in the pines made the boughs moan woefully. It was the kind of night that you wouldn't see someone sneaking up on you until it was too late. Worse, they'd had to leave Cash in camp alone except for Max. Brick and Ella were on patrol on the other side of the herd.

Angus felt anxious and he knew that was what was really bothering Jinx. Knowing T.D. was out there and not alone… "Cash'll be gone in the morning."

She nodded, but still looked worried as they rode slowly around the northern perimeter of the herd. "What if Royce hooks up with T.D.?"

He hated to tell her. "He already has, I'm pretty sure."

She let out a bark of a laugh. "Cash is bound to join them, as well. They'll outnumber us."

He couldn't argue that. "We'll do what we have to do." He'd been thinking about what they could do if T.D. attacked them. He thought the cowboy would be more sneaky than that. But neither of them knew what the man would do.

"I just don't want to have to kill anyone," she said.

He didn't, either, but what neither of them said but both knew was that they would if they had to.

JINX CONSIDERED RIDING down the mountain and confronting T.D. But they would merely have the same argument. Worse, he'd be with his friends so he'd show off. She couldn't chance making things worse by embarrassing him in front of them. At this point she had no idea how to handle T.D. He'd gone off the rails and she couldn't see this ending any way but badly.

She wondered what he had planned. As if he ever planned anything. Maybe he thought he could intimidate her by simply following her up here. If he'd hoped his presence would rattle her, well, it did. She'd been waiting for the other shoe to drop for some time now. T.D. was nothing if not determined. He wouldn't give up. Now more than ever he had to save face with his buddies and everyone else in the county. Too bad he didn't put that kind of determination into a job.

She thought of T.D.'s father and what little he'd told her about him in a weak moment. The man had sounded horrible, which she knew could explain partially at least why T.D. was the way he was. He saw himself as a victim. Right or wrong, he believed his actions, no matter what they were, were warranted.

Like now, it was clear that he felt he had to do something to make this right when this was the worst thing he could do. But there would be no reasoning with him. The only thing she could control were her own actions. Keep fighting T.D.? Or give in?

Giving in meant putting the ranch up for sale. She couldn't afford to borrow against it, not when she knew that she and Max couldn't run it by themselves.

Before her father died, he'd seen the handwriting on the wall. "I'm getting too old to do this anymore," he'd told her. "Even if T.D. was worth his salt, this place takes more hired hands than we can afford. It's why so many families are selling out. Even the ones with a half dozen sons who could run the place are being sold because younger folk want more out of life than feeding cattle when it is twenty below zero, calving in a blizzard or branding in a dust storm or pouring rain."

"We've done all of that and survived," she'd argued. "I love this life. I'm not ready to give it up."

"It's dying, Jinx. I need you to promise me that when I'm gone, you'll put the place up for sale and move on with your life."

She hadn't been able to do that. "I'll try." That was all she'd said that time and then again later when her father was on his deathbed. He'd known how hard it would be on her to let go of the ranch—especially being forced to by her soon-to-be ex-husband. The property settlement was the only thing holding up her freedom. But if it meant giving up the life she loved, what kind of freedom was that?

She'd already been offered a fair price for her herd—if she got the cattle to summer grazing land. She wouldn't even have to bring them back down in the fall. Also, there were several ranchers around, interested in her place.

A local Realtor had come out not long after Jinx's father's death.

"With what you'd make off the ranch, you could do anything you've ever dreamed of," the woman had said.

"What if running this ranch is what I've dreamed of?" Jinx had asked her.

The woman had nodded and given her a pitying look. "Then I guess your dream has come true." She'd handed Jinx her card. "In case your dream changes," she'd said and left.

WYATT SMELLED DINNER cooking and felt his stomach roil.

"You goin' to have one?" Travis asked. T.D. had put him in charge of the food they would need. "Just a couple of days' worth. Keep it simple," T.D. had said foolishly.

"Hot dogs again?" Wyatt asked.

"Hey, T.D. said to keep it simple. I cut you a stick to cook yours on. What more do you want?"

Real food, he wanted to say. Like his mother cooked every night. He picked up the stick with the sharp end Travis had whittled with his pocketknife and looked around. "Where's T.D.?" Travis shrugged. Digging a hot dog out of the insulated pack, he wondered how long they could survive on hot dogs, cookies and trail mix. Not long since the supply was dwindling fast.

"Maybe he changed his mind." Travis sounded hopeful.

Like him, Wyatt figured Travis was ready to get off this mountain. It was cold at night this time of year and hot during the day. They'd spent hours in the saddle following Jinx and her herd of cattle, only to stop when Jinx did and make camp below the mountain. T.D. had done nothing but drink and complain about his soon-to-be ex-wife. Hopefully, this foolishness would be over soon because they were running out of food and now they had Royce to feed, as well.

Speaking of the devil, the wrangler ambled out of the woods. "I'll take one of those," Royce said of the hot dogs. Travis pointed at the stick he'd made him. "Where's T.D.?"

They both shrugged. Wyatt saw that his hot dog was pretty much black and pulled it out of the fire. Travis tossed him a bun and a plastic squeeze container of mustard.

"You have any ketchup?" Royce asked.

"We're roughin' it," Travis said. "It's mustard or nothing. We didn't know we'd have…company."

Royce laughed at that. "Well, when the fireworks start, you're going to be glad you have my company."

Wyatt shared a look with Travis. What had T.D. told Royce? Fireworks? He didn't like the sound of this.

At the sound of a twig breaking off to their right, they all froze for a moment. Wyatt was going for his gun, thinking the smell of the hot dogs cooking had brought a bear into camp. It wouldn't be the first time.

Fortunately, it was just T.D. He came walking into camp, grinning.

"The fun is about to begin," he announced and looked at Travis. "That one for me?" he said of the hot dog Travis had cooked perfectly.

Travis looked from the hot dog to T.D. and back before he sighed and said, "Why not?"

"Then we'd better pull up camp," T.D. said, taking the hot dog and bun and reaching for the mustard. "We might have to move fast."

Oh, hell, Wyatt thought. What has the cowboy done now?

Chapter Ten

Angus caught a whiff of something on the breeze that froze his blood. *Smoke?* Jinx must have caught the scent, as well. She shot him a look and then the two of them were yelling for the others as they raced toward the smoke rising on the horizon.

Angus hadn't gone far when he saw the flames licking at the grass along the tree line—and in the direction of the herd. He jumped off his horse, pulled off his jacket and began beating the flames back. Next to him, Jinx was doing the same.

As Ella and Brick joined them, they formed a line, pushing the fire back. Had it been fall, they wouldn't have been able to stop the wildfire. But with the new grass mixed in with what was left of the dried fall vegetation, the fire wasn't moving fast.

The four of them worked quickly, beating back the flames. Angus had no doubt who had started the fire. He'd seen firsthand what T. D. Sharp was like that night at the ranch. He'd expected trouble, but not this. The man was a damned fool. Didn't he realize that he could start a forest fire that could spread through the mountains— killing everything, him included?

Every year forest fires burned across this part of the west. They often grew even with the states throwing everything they could at the flames. Most weren't put out until the first snows in the fall. That was Angus's fear now. If this fire spread, it would kill more than Jinx's herd.

At first it appeared that they would never be able to hold the fire off. Then as if granted a miracle, a spring squall came through just before daylight, drenching them and the mountainside with a soaking rain shower. The rain did most of the work, but they still had to finish putting out hot spots.

By then it was midday. But they'd kept the fire away from the herd and they'd put it out. With most of the mountainside wet from the rainstorm that had come through before dawn, T.D. would play hell getting another fire started until everything dried out. By then they would have the cattle in the high country and have returned to the valley.

Angus figured T.D. would lose interest once Jinx was no longer on the mountain. There would be no reason to kill a bunch of cattle, especially when it sounded as if he would get half the ranch in the divorce. So half the cattle would also be his. That was if the man had thought that far ahead.

But first they had to get the herd the rest of the way to summer range. What else did T.D. have planned for them before they all went back down into the valley?

"Here's where it started," Brick called. Jinx walked over to where his brother was pointing at the ground and Angus followed.

He knew what he was going to find even before he reached his twin. Boot tracks in the soft, wet, scorched earth and the charred remains of a bandanna soaked with fuel oil.

"Whoever started the fire had planned this," Jinx said

with disgust as she took a whiff of the bandanna. The cowboys wouldn't have had fuel oil on them. They had to have brought it with them. She shook her head, planting her hands on her hips as she looked out across the pasture to where the herd moved restlessly. If Angus hadn't smelled the fire so quickly... If the flames had gotten away from them...

"What now?" She sounded close to tears but quickly cleared her throat. "What's he going to do next?" She looked at Angus, but it was Brick who spoke.

"What if it wasn't your ex?" Brick said as he looked around. "Anyone seen Cash?" Angus realized he hadn't seen Max, either.

They made their way back to camp. Angus wasn't surprised to see Cash's horse gone. Max was busy finishing making breakfast. "I thought you might all be hungry," he said as he took them in. "Figured I was better here than fighting the fire."

"When did Cash leave?" Jinx asked.

"Soon as he smelled smoke," Max said. "He hightailed it out of here. Said he'd catch up with you at the ranch to get his pay."

Jinx mumbled something under her breath.

"I think we should end this now," Brick said and looked at him. "Let's go pay them a visit."

"No," Jinx said, her gaze on Angus. "We have cattle to move. That's why we rode up here. That's what we're going to do. We've lost some time, but we're going to get these cattle to the high country. But first I'm going to wash some of this soot off. Thank you all for being here." With that she turned on her boot heel and walked away.

"I think we're growing on her," Brick said with a chuckle.

Angus smiled. "That is one determined young woman

and she's right. We take care of the herd. That's our job."
He felt his twin's gaze on him.

"She likes you," his brother said.

"I'm not trying to—"

"That's just it, Angus. You don't have to try." With
that, Brick turned and walked away.

Angus sighed, tired of his brother's need to compete. He doubted it had anything to do with Jinx. Brick
just liked to win. Angus was determined, though, that it
wasn't going to be a problem between them. After this
job was over…well, as Ella said, maybe it was time that
the three of them went their own way.

Smelling of smoke and covered with soot, Angus
headed for the creek. He needed to cool down anyway.
He and Brick weren't that much alike sometimes. He had
wanted to go after T.D., too, which told him that Jinx was
right about ordering them not to. He'd never been impulsive. Now wasn't the time to start.

And what if some of T.D.'s men hit the herd, scattering
it, while he and Brick were off looking for him?

Reaching the creek, he stopped under a large old pine
tree and pulled off his boots. Pulling his gun, he pushed
it down in one of his boots and then took off his belt and
tossed it beside the boots.

He considered stripping down, but realized his clothing could use a wash. Or at least a dip in water. He
stepped to the edge of the stream, picking a dark spot
where the water ran deep and then in a few strides dove
headfirst into the shimmering pool.

He'd known it would be freezing cold. Just as he'd
known it would take his breath away. But knowing was
one thing; feeling it clear to his bones was another.

He shot up out of the water and let out a yell and then
a laugh.

"How's the water?" asked Jinx from the shadow of the large pine.

"Warm," he lied, grinning as he watched her pull off her boots, then her holstered gun, before she did what he had done.

He moved aside to give her plenty of room. She dove in and came up fast, spitting out the icy water as she did. He couldn't help but laugh.

"Cold enough for you?" he asked, still grinning even though he realized he couldn't feel his lower extremities.

"I've felt colder," she said and then laughed as the two of them rushed to the shore, grateful to be out of the snow-fed water.

Angus pulled off his shirt and hung it over a limb to dry in the sun. A warming spring breeze rippled over his bare flesh.

Jinx had sat down on a rock, leaning back to close her eyes. "Maybe your brother is right," she said.

"Brick is seldom right," he joked. "That you even think he might be proves you've lost your mind."

She smiled and opened her eyes to look at him. "If anything happens to you and the others because of me…"

"We knew what we were getting into."

She studied him on the rock where he'd sat down beside the stream. He'd stretched out his long legs in the hopes that his jeans would dry some in the sun without him having to remove them. "Ella told me. Your mother asked you to come help me?"

"It's what neighbors do."

She laughed at that and she freed her hair from the braid she'd had it in. The wet coppery mass of curls fell around her face, dropping down past her breasts. "We're hardly neighbors."

"We're ranchers. Ranchers help other ranchers."

"Maybe where you live."

"Don't blame the other ranchers. They're in a tough spot."

She met his gaze. "Do you always give everyone the benefit of the doubt?"

"Hardly. But I try," he admitted. "Few people want to get in the middle of a family squabble."

"Is that what this is?" she asked, holding his gaze. "But the three of you did."

He chuckled. "By now you must realize that we lack good sense."

She pulled her gaze away to look toward the stream. "I hate that everyone knows my troubles."

"Don't. We all need help sometimes."

She smiled, shaking her head. "You must be wondering what I saw in T.D. What would make me marry someone like him?"

"That's your business."

"Still, you must think me a fool."

He laughed softly, turning his face up to the sun. "If you'd met my last girlfriend… We all have a mistake in our past that we'd like to forget."

"You're an awfully nice man, Angus Savage."

He could feel the sun warming his chest and hear the quiet babble of the stream. But what really warmed him were her words. Sitting here with her, he felt a contentment that he hadn't felt in a long time.

His eyes opened as he sensed her closeness. She stood over him for a moment, before she sat down next to him and turned until she was facing him only inches part. He held his breath as she reached toward him. His heart thundered in his chest as he felt her cool fingertips trace the scar on his chin.

"I'M CURIOUS," JINX SAID, her voice sounding strange even to her. "How did you get that scar?"

She watched Angus swallow, then seem to relax, his blue eyes bright with humor. "Well, it's kind of an amusing story." He smiled. "I got pushed out of a barn loft when I was eleven."

"That's awful."

He sat up straighter until they were eye to eye. "It was my fault. I asked for it."

"You asked to be pushed out of a barn loft?"

"I was teasing her. She warned me that if I didn't stop she would knock me into tomorrow."

"She?" Jinx felt goose bumps break out over her skin and for a moment she could smell the fresh hay in the barn, feel the breeze on her face, remember that cute cowboy who'd taunted her. Her heart began to pound.

His smile broadened. "She was a spitfire, as fiery as her hair back then."

Jinx felt heat rush to her cheeks. "Tell me her name wasn't JoRay McCallahan."

"Sorry, I'm afraid so," he said and laughed. "I wondered if you would remember."

"When I saw you, I thought I'd met you before, but I couldn't think of when that might have been. Then Max told me that my mother took me up to the Cardwell Ranch for a short visit when I was about nine." She groaned. "Your mother must have been horrified by what I did to you." Jinx didn't think she could be more embarrassed.

He shook his head. "My mother said, 'What did you do, Angus?' I confessed that I'd been giving you a hard time and that you'd warned me what would happen if I didn't knock it off."

"Oh, I can imagine what my mother said."

"Actually, both mothers had trouble hiding smiles, once they realized that no one was hurt badly. Your mother told you that you couldn't go around pushing boys just because of something they said or you'd spend the rest of your life fighting them."

"You'd think I'd have learned that lesson."

He grinned. "When your mother said that, you replied, 'Well, if the boys are smart, they won't give me a hard time—especially standing in front of an open window two floors up.'"

She laughed with him. "Oh, that sounds so much like me. I'm so sorry."

"Don't be," he said as he seemed to fondly touch the scar. "It was a good learning experience for me." His blue eyes hardened. "And I never forgot that girl."

"I suppose not." She shook her head in disbelief. "Still, you came down to help me get my herd up to summer range."

"Like I said, it's what neighbors do," he said and grinned again. "Also, I was curious to see the woman that girl had grown into."

She couldn't help the heat that rushed to her cheeks wanting to blame it on the sun beating down on them. "Now you know."

He smiled. "Yes. I wasn't disappointed." He leaned toward her and she knew even before his lips brushed hers, that he was going to kiss her—and she was going to let him.

The kiss started out soft, sweet, delicate, but as her lips parted for him, he looped his hand behind her neck and pulled her down for a proper kiss. She felt the warmth of his bare chest against her still-damp Western shirt. A shiver moved through her as he deepened the kiss. She touched the hair curling at the nape of his neck, wanting to bury her fingers in his dark hair, wanting the kiss to never stop.

At the sound of Max ringing the chow bell, he let her go. She drew back, shaken by the kiss. "We shouldn't have done that."

"I'm not going to apologize for kissing you. I've wanted to since the first time I laid eyes on you. Only back then, I was just a boy who thought the way to get a girl's attention was to give her a hard time."

"I'm still a married woman," she said, hating that she sounded breathless. Had she ever been kissed like that? "And I'm your boss."

He nodded. "If you're saying that I have bad timing, I couldn't agree more." He grinned. "But I'm still not sorry." With that, he touched her cheek, a light caress before he rose, retrieved his shirt from the tree, pulled on his boots and left, saying, "I'll see you back in camp, boss."

JINX WATCHED HIM GO. Her face still felt hot, her cheeks flushed, and her heart was still doing loop-de-loops in her chest. She touched her lips with her fingertips, remembering the feel of his mouth on hers, and couldn't help but smile. Of course the kiss had been wrong. But she was glad that Angus hadn't apologized for it.

As he disappeared into the pines, she couldn't remember ever feeling this good. This free. And if she was being truthful, it hadn't been the first time she'd thought about kissing Angus. He was handsome as the devil. Just the image of his broad chest as he'd come out of the stream, the water rippling over taut, tanned muscles... She shivered, realizing that she wanted more than just a kiss.

That, too, surprised her because for months she hadn't given men, let alone sex, a thought. But that Angus had released this in her, didn't surprise her. She liked him, trusted him, felt close to him. Now that she knew about their earlier connection, she thought with a laugh. But Angus was also the kind of man her father would have approved of. Too bad he hadn't come along before T.D.

Shaking her head, she reminded herself of the mess her life was in right now. She was a woman who'd foolishly married a handsome, smooth-talking man. Now she was living a bad country song, she thought as she rose and pulled on her boots.

The best thing she could do, she told herself, was to keep her distance from Angus. The cattle would be settled into summer range by tomorrow. Once they reached the ranch, he would no longer be in her employ.

But didn't that mean he would be headed home to Montana? He'd told her he was going back to help run Cardwell Ranch. It was just as well, she knew. She certainly wasn't ready for even a man like Angus.

But she felt a shiver as she thought of the way he'd cupped the back of her neck, drawing her down as he deepened the kiss. She found herself smiling again.

She pulled her long hair up into a ponytail and tried not to think about Angus or the kiss or her uncertain future. He would return to Cardwell Ranch. She would sort out the mess she'd made of her life.

Her cheeks still felt hot, though, and she could still taste him on her lips. One look at her and would everyone know when she returned to camp? She realized that she didn't care.

T.D. had failed in his attempt to get the mountain on fire and scatter her herd. She felt ready for whatever else he had up his sleeve, determined to get through this or die trying. Soon she would be free of him. Her step felt lighter as she followed the smell of freshly baked biscuits.

ANGUS HAD WALKED away from Jinx, telling himself to be careful. He thought about the last woman he'd let get this close and how that had turned out. Jinx...well, she was a whole different rodeo in so many ways, including, he reminded himself, that she was married with a crazy not-yet-ex-husband.

He finished buttoning up his shirt. It had dried nicely. As he neared the camp, his brother stepped out of the trees.

"Have a nice swim?" Brick asked, grinning.

"I did." He saw his brother look past him toward the creek. "Don't even think about it."

Brick gave him his best innocent face. "I don't know what you're talking about."

"Jinx. She isn't some prize to be won. She's got serious problems and is in no shape to even think about getting involved with another man."

Brick cocked his head. "Is that what you keep telling yourself?"

Angus sighed. "We're almost done here. Once the cattle are in the high country, there will be nothing keeping us here."

His brother shook his head. "And you'll just be able to leave her knowing that her jackass of a husband isn't through tormenting her?" He didn't give Angus time to answer. "That's what I thought. You don't want a part of this, brother, trust me. How do you even know that she's over him?"

He thought about the kiss still tingling on his lips. Jinx was over T.D., that he was sure of. But that didn't mean that she was ready for another relationship, especially after her last one. "I'll cross that bridge when I come to it, but you definitely won't have to stay. You and Ella can go back home and—"

Brick was shaking his head. "The three of us signed on and the three of us will leave together. You stay here and you'll get yourself killed."

He wanted to argue that his twin didn't know squat, but unfortunately, Brick was right. He would only make things worse if he stayed. But how could he leave knowing the kind of trouble Jinx was in?

"I just hate to see you falling for her," Brick said. "You're dead right that she's not ready for another man. Hell, she hasn't gotten rid of the one she has."

"There's no reason to be talking about this," Angus said as he started past his brother. "Let's just get these cattle safely up to the high country. That's the job we're being paid for. That's enough to worry about since I really doubt that T.D. and his friends are through with us."

His twin caught his arm to stop him. "I'm just worried about you, Angus."

"Maybe it's time you quit worrying about me."

Brick laughed. "We're brothers. Womb mates. I'm going to worry especially when I see you headed down a dangerous path. You just can't stand to see a woman who needs rescuing and not try to rescue her. It's in your DNA. But you almost got killed the last time you got involved in a domestic situation that wasn't any of your business."

He'd gotten between his girlfriend and her former boyfriend, a mistake in so many ways. "This is different."

"Is it? Jinx can divorce T.D., give him what he wants and be done with him. But maybe she's dragging her feet on the property settlement because she is still in love with him. Like you said, she needs time to figure it all out."

"I know that," he said as he stepped past his brother and started again toward camp. He glanced back. It had crossed his mind that Brick might go down to the creek. But to his surprise, his brother now followed him.

"He'll hit us again," Brick said, thankfully changing the subject. "Maybe we *should* try to find him no matter what Jinx says."

"We can't leave the camp unprotected. Jinx is right. With two of us gone, it would be a perfect time for T.D. to strike."

Brick said nothing, but Angus could tell his brother was chewing it over. He just hoped Brick didn't do anything impulsive.

WYATT THOUGHT ABOUT riding out of the mountains and not looking back. T.D. had sent him out to see what damage had been done to Jinx and her herd after the fire. He hated to report that Jinx and her crew had put out the fire with the rainstorm finishing the job. He knew that news was going to put T.D. into a tailspin. He'd thought he was so smart starting the fire.

"Well?" T.D. demanded as he dismounted. "Took you long enough. I thought I was going to have to come look for you."

Wyatt already anticipated the cowboy's reaction to what he had to tell him. "They fought the fire, putting it almost out. Then the rain did the rest. The fire's out."

"What about the herd?" T.D. demanded. "Surely it scattered some of them."

He shook his head. "Sorry."

T.D. swore and stomped around the wet camp. Royce was trying to get a fire going again but everything was soaking wet after the squall that had come through. He and Cash were arguing, Cash saying he was hungry and might ride down to town.

"We should all ride out of here," Travis said, watching them. He looked wet and miserable. "I don't know what we're doing up here anyway."

T.D. turned on him so quickly Travis didn't have a chance to react. The blow sent him sprawling onto the wet ground. "I'm sick of your whining. Nothing is keeping you here and while you're at it, take those two with you."

Royce looked up, seeming surprised that T.D. meant him and Cash. He'd managed to get a small blaze going. He continued building the fire. Cash, Wyatt noted, had gone silent.

"That's all you saw?" T.D. asked as Wyatt hung up his slicker on a tree limb to dry in the sun. "I thought for sure that the fire would spook the herd. Or at least scatter them."

Wyatt shook his head. All the way back, he'd debated telling T.D. what he'd seen through his binoculars near the stream. Maybe it would end this once and for all. Or maybe it would make T.D. even crazier.

He had no idea what T.D. would do if he told him that he'd seen Jinx and one of her wranglers down by the stream swimming together, then talking while sitting in the sun and then kissing.

Wyatt had watched, unable to pull his eyes away. The two had been so close, so intimate. He wouldn't have been surprised if they'd stripped down and made love right there beside the water. The scene had been so passionate, it had made him wonder if the kiss was the first between the two of them.

He saw that Travis had gotten to his feet and was now busying himself hanging his wet clothing on a tree branch, his back to the rest of them. After T.D. had punched him, why hadn't Travis left? Wyatt told himself he would have gone with him, but he knew that was a lie. T.D. would expect him to stay. Even if he wouldn't, Wyatt wasn't finished up here, was he?

After what he'd seen, he'd been telling himself that Jinx deserved what she was going to get. She was cheating on T.D. Not that it was his place to do anything about that, Wyatt told himself. But if he told T.D., he knew the cowboy would go ballistic, riding up to the camp, guns blazing.

He thought of Patty and the promise she'd made him—and the one he'd kind of made her. T.D. was pacing, worked up because his fire had fizzled out and his attempt to hurt Jinx had failed. So far, nothing that anyone had done had stopped the woman. Suddenly, T.D. stopped pacing and looked at him. "We're going to have to stampede the herd."

Travis turned to glance back at him, but then quickly turned away again. Royce threw a handful of dry dead pine needles onto the fire. "Count me in," he said. Cash just looked uncomfortable but nodded.

Wyatt realized that everyone was waiting on him, including T.D. He told himself that now was the time to put an end to this if he was going to. If he rode back to town now, he suspected the others would follow. He knew Travis was just looking for an excuse to bail but wouldn't unless someone else did first.

He could stop this before it was too late.

Before anyone got killed.

Chapter Eleven

"Hey! Watch out!"

Patty felt the plates of food she'd been carrying tilt dangerously as she collided with one of the café customers. "Sorry."

The man was busily looking at his sleeve and then his pants to make sure that none of the café's evening special had spilled on him. Patty heard his wife say from the booth, "It was your fault. You got up right in front of her."

"Are you kidding?" the man demanded. "She wasn't watching where she was going. If you'd been paying attention, you would know that she's been in a daze this whole time. She screwed up the orders at that other table."

"Seems one of us has been watching the waitress with a little too much interest," the wife snapped.

Patty felt the heat of embarrassment on the back of her neck as she delivered the orders to a far table. The man was right. Her mind hadn't been on work for some time now. She put on her plastic smile, tried to say all the right things, but she was only going through the motions and at least one person had noticed.

"Everything all right?" her boss asked when she returned to the kitchen.

She had no idea. "Fine." Her mind was in the mountains with T.D. Had he caught up to his wife? For all she knew, the two of them could have made up. She kept seeing a campfire and the two of them rolling around on a bedroll next to it. The image burned through her stomach like acid.

Not that she believed it. Jinx wouldn't take him back. There was no way the two of them were reconnecting, not with all those others up there on the mountain with them. Not only did Jinx have wranglers working for her apparently, but she also had several hundred head of cattle to tend to. She wasn't rolling around with T.D. on any bedroll.

But not knowing what was happening was driving her crazy. Wouldn't she have heard if T.D. and the others had returned to town? Of course she would have. Which meant they hadn't.

So T.D. was still up there in the mountains. Which meant Wyatt was still up there, as well. For a while, she'd forgotten about that.

She thought of the promise she'd made him—and what she'd asked him to do. She'd seen the way he reacted to her. He would do anything for her—just as he'd said. Just as she'd known he would.

A thought made her heart begin to pound.

By now Jinx could be dead.

Unless Wyatt chickened out.

She went to pick up an order for a table that had just come up and tried to still her nervous anticipation. Wyatt wouldn't let her down.

"DON'T YOU THINK we should call the sheriff on T.D.?" Ella asked as she joined her cousins around the campfire later that evening. Max was busy in the chuckwagon and Jinx was seeing to her horse.

They'd spent the day moving cattle, getting as far as

they could. Tomorrow was their last day. They should reach summer range before noon, Jinx had said. "And tell him what? I'm sure he knows T.D. followed us up here, but there was little he could do. It's a free country and a huge mountain range," Brick said.

"Brick's right. Nor can we prove he started the fire," Angus said. "I'm not even sure the sheriff could arrest him on the restraining order. T.D. hasn't gotten close enough to break it yet. Also, Jinx said we wouldn't be able to get cell phone service until we reached the high country above the tree line and even then, she said it would be sketchy."

She knew they were right and yet she couldn't shake the bad feeling she had. "You know he's not finished."

"He'll hit us tonight. He has to," Brick said. "This time tomorrow we'll be in Jackson Hole. I don't know about the two of you, but I plan to kick up my heels. But first I'm going to treat myself to a big fat juicy beef steak and all the fixings. Maybe find me some sweet-smelling woman who wants to dance."

Ella shook her head. "I wouldn't be counting your chickens just yet."

"She's right," Angus agreed. "I don't think the fire did the kind of damage T.D. was hoping for. Whatever he has planned it will be tonight and I suspect it will be much bigger."

Ella poked the fire with a stick, sending sparks into the air. "I don't get why he's doing this. Just to torment her?"

Angus shrugged. "I'm not sure T.D. has a point. He's angry, probably drunk most of the time and feeling he has to do something to save face."

"It's stupid and dangerous," Brick said. "If that fire had gotten away from us or that rain squall hadn't come through when it did…" He shook his head. "The cowboy's crazy."

At the sound of someone coming out of the darkness, they all turned. "Brick's right. T.D. is crazy, stupid and dangerous," Jinx said. "That's why we aren't going to get much sleep tonight."

"I still think we should pay him a visit," Brick said.

"Don't you think they're expecting that?" Ella asked only to have her cousin shrug.

"Also, there's five of them now," Angus said, having earlier seen them trailing the herd. It didn't surprise him that Cash had joined their ranks. "Riding into their camp would be more dangerous than staying where we are and waiting for them to hit us."

"Except we have several hundred head of cattle," Ella said. "If I were him, I'd try to use them against us."

Jinx looked over at her and nodded. "My thought exactly. He'll try to stampede the herd tonight when he thinks we're all asleep. He'll drive them right at us."

"Unless we stop him," Brick said. "That's why we have to hit him first."

Ella saw that Angus was studying Jinx and smiling as if they'd just shared a secret. "You have a plan?"

"Once it's dark enough where we can't be seen, we booby-trap one side of the perimeter," Angus said and Jinx gave him a knowing smile.

Brick caught the exchange and said, "Bro, why do I get the feeling you told her about what we used to do when we were kids to catch critters?"

"Subject must have come up some time or another," Angus said.

"They have us outnumbered," Jinx said, clearly warming to the plan. "We have to better our odds. I suspect they'll come riding in fast, yelling and shooting to spook the herd. To drive the herd right at us, they'll come in from the north. We just need to be waiting for them, subdue the ones we catch and quell the attack. Any we can get on the ground, should be fairly easy to tie up and gag, right?"

Brick laughed. "I like the way you think. Less blood-shed."

"Hopefully, no blood will be shed." She looked at Angus. "It's going to be another dark night. We weren't going to get any sleep anyway. At least this way we'll be ready for them."

Unless we're wrong and T.D. came at us another way, Ella thought. She wondered how far she'd have to ride to get cell phone coverage should things go as wrong as she feared they would.

"You mind staying here with Max and making sure everything is all right?" Angus asked her as the others rose to go to work.

Ella nodded, knowing exactly what he was telling her to do.

THEY WORKED QUICKLY and quietly, setting up the traps some distance from the herd in the path T.D. would have to take to stampede the cattle into their camp.

Angus checked with Brick to make sure he was ready before he went to the spot where they'd left Jinx. He let out a soft whistle as he approached to let her know it was him coming through the trees and was careful not to trip any of the booby traps.

"You ready?" he asked when he reached her. He could tell she was nervous. They all were. "It's going to be all right."

She smiled. She really did have the most beautiful warm smile. There was a gentleness to her along with strength. He found himself drawn to her in a way he hadn't ever been with another woman. He didn't believe in love at first sight and yet he hadn't forgotten how taken he was with that redheaded girl who'd turned up at Cardwell Ranch, all those years ago.

He touched her cheek, unable to stop himself any more than he could hold back the feelings that swam to the surface when he saw her. He felt connected to her in a way he couldn't explain. He would have said fate had thrown them together not once but twice, years apart, if he believed in it.

Ella would have understood what he was feeling better than he did. She believed in a lot of things he didn't including love at first sight and destiny and true love. But this feeling was so strong that had he believed in true love, he would have been tempted to call it that.

Brick always said that falling in love was like falling off a horse. You had no choice but to get back on. Well, Angus much preferred falling off a horse. To him, falling in love was like jumping off a cliff and not knowing if you would survive. He knew one thing. The landing could be hell.

He'd survived his last breakup, but even as strongly as he felt, he knew he wasn't ready to make another leap. Especially if that leap involved Jinx McCallahan, he told himself. Even if she wasn't married and in the middle of a divorce and didn't have a crazy, dangerous ex who wouldn't let her go. Jinx was a mess. It didn't matter that she'd kicked T.D. out months ago, filed for divorce and didn't want him back under any circumstances, apparently. Her husband wasn't through with her yet. Angus feared she might lose more than her ranch because of T.D.

"Is everything all right?" Jinx asked quietly, no doubt seeing the battle going on inside him.

"Fine," he lied. "How about you?"

"Fine."

He could see that she was as confused as he was. "We're going to get through this," he said, hoping what he was saying was true.

"I hope so," she said as if she knew he didn't just mean tonight.

He was so close, he could see the pain in her face even in the darkness. He knew what it felt like to have a failed relationship. His hadn't even involved getting to the altar. His relationship hadn't lasted that long. But he recalled the pain quite easily. He knew that Jinx wasn't ready for another man any more than he was ready for another woman.

He breathed in the cold mountain air, feeling tired from a long day in the saddle and working hard to get the traps set. It wouldn't be long now. He should get back to his spot.

Yet, he didn't want to leave her. A premonition? He was worried about her and would be until she was free of T.D. In the meantime, he knew she would stay in his thoughts. What was it about her? Those few seconds when she let down her guard and let him see how vulnerable she was? At those moments it took all his strength and good sense not to step to her and take her in his arms, everyone be damned if they didn't like it.

"I should go," he said. Her ex was going to show up at any time. Crazy bitter and probably drunk, nothing good was going to come out of it when T.D. did strike again.

Every time a lock of her coppery hair came loose from her braid and fell over those big brown eyes, he wanted to push it aside. But he knew if he touched her, he'd kiss that mouth again with its bow-shaped full lips.

He realized the trail his thoughts had taken and reined

them in with a groan. His brother was right. Something about this woman had him twisted into a knot. His gaze followed her whenever she was around. He couldn't quit thinking about her.

Worse, if he was being honest with himself, he'd been smitten with Jinx from the moment he'd laid eyes on her when they were nothing but kids. It had only gotten worse when he'd seen her again. He recalled the way she'd come out of her house that night at the ranch, shotgun in hand, facing down her ex with courage and determination. She'd shown a strength that had chipped away a corner of his ice-encased heart.

Since being on the cattle drive, he'd felt his heart melting at just the sight of her. She refused to show weakness even when he knew she had to be as exhausted as he was at the end of the day. More and more he felt drawn to her in a way that made him both scared and exhilarated.

He felt like one of the bears that had come out of a long hibernation. He was hungry again in a way he'd never experienced before. Bad timing be damned. He wanted this woman.

JINX SHIVERED IN the darkness. She was so close to Angus that she could look into his blue eyes. This was it, she thought. They could all die tonight. She yearned for Angus to take her in his arms.

He brushed a lock of her hair back from her face. She felt her eyes widen, but she didn't move. "Why are you looking at me like that?"

"I'm counting your freckles. I've wanted to since I first laid eyes on you," he whispered, so close now that she could hardly breathe.

She smiled to hide how nervous it made her. "I take it you have a lot of time to kill?"

He met her gaze and smiled. "Not as much as I'd like right now," he whispered. "You don't have any idea how beautiful you are."

She chuckled self-consciously and dropped her gaze. "Angus—"

With his warm fingers, he lifted her chin until their eyes locked. "You're beautiful, Jinx, and I haven't been able to take my eyes off you this whole time."

Her pulse jumped as he bent to brush his lips over hers. The heat of her desire rushed through her veins, hot as liquid lava. She'd never felt this kind of need before, knowing only one man could satisfy it.

Angus pulled back to look into her eyes for a moment before he dropped his mouth to hers again. She surrendered to his kiss as he parted her lips and delved deeper. His arms came around her, pulling her against him until she could feel the beat of his heart in sync with her own.

She opened to him, no longer fighting her feelings. Desire flared, his kisses fanning the flames. She lost herself in his kisses, in the strength of his arms drawing her to him, in the low moan she heard escape his lips as she pulled back.

"Jinx," he whispered her name on a ragged breath. "Jinx." Angus said it low, soft, a caress that sent a pleasurable shiver across her skin. Then his fingers touched her face, drawing her closer until she was looking into his eyes, losing herself in them.

His mouth was dropping to hers again. Her lips parted, as if there had been no doubts between them. One arm looped around her waist, pulling her into his solid body. She felt his need as much as her own. Like her, she knew that he feared tonight might be their last.

She surrendered to him, needing this man's strength as well as his gentleness. What surprised her was the fire he set ablaze inside her. T.D. had never ignited such passion. He'd been rough and demanding, believing that was what every woman wanted.

Angus seemed to know what she needed, what she desperately desired, as if he knew instinctively that she hadn't been truly satisfied. Because of that, she felt vulnerable and exposed. Had it been any other man other than Angus...

His breathing was as labored as her own as his hand slipped up under her coat to her warm flesh. She arched against him, wanting and needing more, as she let out a moan of pure pleasure and whispered his name.

They both froze at a sound in the trees lower on the mountain. For a while, she'd completely forgotten T.D., forgotten everything but the feel of this cowboy's arms around her.

Angus groaned quietly and let go of her, drawing back. "When this is over," he said on a hoarse breath. "Jinx, I promise, when this is over..."

She touched her finger to his lips and shook her head. They couldn't make promises. Not tonight. Not under these circumstances.

Angus looked as if he couldn't bear to leave her. She knew the feeling. She gave him a gentle shove.

Nearby, they heard one of the traps being sprung. Then silence.

ANGUS WAS FURIOUS with himself as he rushed back to his spot on the mountain only to find that a deer had tripped one of his traps. The pretty doe bound off into the distance. But it could have just as easily been T.D. or one of his men. He shouldn't have left his traps unattended. He wouldn't again.

He'd let himself get carried away. It wasn't like him

and yet when he'd looked at Jinx… He thought of what he'd seen in her eyes. A need like his own. A fear matching his own. Tonight everything could go wrong and there could be bloodshed.

Forcing that thought away, he told himself it was why they'd both been vulnerable. Just the thought of the two of them on the side of this mountain in the dark and what he'd wanted to happen… He knew it was insane, but he'd felt as if they were the last two people in the world. Neither of them had wanted to stop, but fortunately, when the deer tripped the trap, they had.

What if it had been T.D. instead of a deer? What if he'd seen the two of them? He shook his head at his own impetuousness, let alone his foolishness. He could have gotten both Jinx and himself killed.

Tomorrow they would reach her grazing land with the herd, then… But that was the problem. Then Jinx would be back at her ranch dealing with her problems and there would be no excuse for him to hang around. That was if they lived through tonight, he reminded himself.

He heard a meadowlark whistle close by. "You all right?" Brick whispered as he came out of the darkness of the pines. "I heard one of your traps go off."

"Deer. A little doe." His voice sounded strange even to him.

"You all right?" his brother asked suspiciously.

"Just jumpy. You should get back to your traps."

He nodded but didn't move for a moment. Angus wondered if his twin could tell from his expression even in the darkness what he'd been up to.

"We'll be done tomorrow," Brick said.

"I was just thinking about that," he said, honestly.

"I bet you were."

"I'm looking forward to going home to the ranch."

"Glad to hear that." Brick slapped him on the shoulder. "Be careful."

"You, too." He watched his brother disappear back through the pines and tried to concentrate on staying alive tonight.

Chapter Twelve

As they waited for the cover of darkness, T.D. thought about sneaking into camp, finding his wife and collecting on at least some of what she owed him. She hadn't just kicked him off the ranch. She'd kicked him out of her bed months ago.

He'd been fine with it at the time. He'd had Patty, and Patty was always willing. But she wasn't Jinx. Patty couldn't fill a need in him that had little to do with sex. Jinx had filled that need. He'd been married to her and the ranch. He'd felt he finally belonged somewhere.

What bothered him was that he'd thought Jinx would come begging for him after a few weeks, let alone a few months, without him.

But she hadn't. It seemed impossible that she hadn't seemed to miss his lovemaking as if he hadn't been giving her what she needed. Was that true? If so, it shook the very foundation of what he believed about himself. All he'd ever had was his looks and his way with women. That Jinx might have found him lacking drove him insane with fury.

Patty never complained, he told himself. And yet the fact that Jinx didn't want him back ate at him. When he got the chance again, he'd remind Jinx what she'd been missing.

"Let's get ready to go," he ordered everyone gathered around the fire. He sensed they weren't as into this as he was and that annoyed him.

"Don't you think she's going to be expecting this?" Travis asked without moving.

He didn't bother to answer him. Travis was right about one thing, though. Jinx knew him too well. She'd know he'd come for her tonight, their last night on this mountain. But not even Travis knew what he had planned. In the dark there would be confusion. At least that was his hope. Jinx would anticipate what he had planned. Too bad there was nothing she could do about it, though.

Still, it made him wonder if he was too predictable. Is that why she thought she could live without him? Maybe it was time to prove to her that he could still surprise her. He smiled to himself.

"Here's what I want you all to do," he said and told them their part of the plan, keeping his own to himself. He knew he couldn't depend on Travis or Royce or Cash. But at least he had Wyatt here with him. They'd been buds since grade school. Wyatt would have his back.

Stepping away from the dying coals of the campfire, he pulled his binoculars from where he'd left his saddlebag to look toward her camp. He couldn't see a damned thing, it was so dark tonight. He thought about last night when he'd spotted Jinx and he'd felt his pulse jump like it always did when he caught her unawares.

She'd been standing not far from the light of their campfire. He'd been studying her when he realized that she wasn't alone. His heart had begun to pound wildly. He'd felt weak with shock and fury. She'd stood talking to one of her wranglers—the same one who'd come to her rescue back down at the ranch.

He'd seen the way she was standing, the way she had

her head tilted to look up at the cowboy. She liked him. Maybe more than liked him. He realized that he hadn't even considered what his wife had been doing all these months when she wasn't letting him into her bed. How many other wranglers had there been since she'd kicked him out? Did everyone in the county know what had been going on but him?

His blood had pounded so hard in his head, he'd felt dizzy.

That was when he knew that he could kill her. She'd humiliated him for the last time. When he'd seen her standing with that cowboy, he could have grabbed his rifle and taken a shot right then, but suddenly a cold calm had come over him. As his wife had stepped away from the cowboy, he'd lowered the binoculars. For possibly the first time in his life, he hadn't gone off half-cocked. He was going in prepared this time because now he knew what had to be done.

He would find her while the others kept everyone else busy. He'd find her and finish this.

ELLA PUT OUT the campfire as planned and watched the smoke rise slowly into the darkness. Quiet fell over the mountainside. The plan had been to make everything seem as it had been other nights. As predicted, clouds had rolled in, smothering any starlight tonight.

She listened, knowing it wouldn't be long before this moment of peace was interrupted. Brick, Jinx and Angus had left to be ready. Jinx was closest to camp but Ella couldn't see her. She thought about their traps. They didn't have time to dig holes or pits, but would use the pine tree boughs to make a swinging log that could be released as a rider passed. Another one would have a large rock that swung down from a tree.

"Even if some of them miss, they will be enough of a distraction that we can attack," Brick had said, clearly enjoying this.

"We need to immobilize as many of them as we can before they reach the herd," Jinx had said.

Ella had opted to stay in camp to set up some booby traps of her own just in case the others were wrong about how and where T.D. would strike.

"You're a smart woman," Max said now as he left behind his beloved chuckwagon to take refuge in an outcropping of trees next to a wall of rock some distance from the camp. She'd talked him into it, wanting him out of the line of fire no matter what happened tonight.

"You should have a good view from there," Ella had said as she'd tried to sell him on the idea. "But you'll also be armed so if any of them decide to come this way…"

The older man nodded, clearly seeing what she was up to. "I would love to get that man in my sights."

She gave him a disapproving look. "We're supposed to wound them unless we have no other options."

"I'll be sure to keep that in mind."

Leaving him, she went back to where the campfire had died to nothing but a tiny stream of smoke before climbing into the chuckwagon to get the pots and pans she needed. Her trap wasn't lethal, but it would alert them if T.D. and his men were circling around behind them. Max would be safe as long as he stayed out of sight.

ANGUS FINISHED THE last of the swinging branch booby traps and looked through the trees to where he could barely see Jinx. He knew that like him, she was waiting and listening. Jinx thought that T.D. would come roaring in, all liquored up, shooting and yelling and out of control.

They wouldn't have any trouble hearing them coming, if that was the case. Jinx didn't expect T.D. to approach this rationally. She just assumed he would be drunk, angry and acting out rather than having a plan.

But Angus thought that she might be wrong and that expecting him to act as he usually did could be a mistake. T.D. knew this was his last night to stop them from reaching summer range—or at least cost them another day or so, if he scattered the herd. So Angus stood listening, suspecting T.D. would try to sneak up on them instead.

He couldn't help but worry. Ella had stayed back at camp to take care of things there. She'd looked worried but he knew she would take care of Max and herself.

They were all worried, he thought, as on impulse, he moved quietly through the pines to where Jinx was waiting. He drew her into his arms, unable to fight the bad feeling that had overcome him. She leaned into him as if glad to let him take some of the weight off her—at least for a moment.

At the sound of something moving slowly, cautiously toward them, they separated. Brick came out of the darkness, whispering, "Is it safe?"

Angus wasn't sure if he meant from the booby traps or because he had spotted Jinx in his brother's arms. "We're as ready as we can be."

Brick nodded. "I'm going back up the mountain to my spot." He pulled some strips of leather from his jacket pocket. "If I get one down, I'll make sure he won't be any more trouble until I untie him at daylight." He pulled out the wad of torn dish towels he planned to use as gags. His brother gave him a grin before disappearing back up the mountainside.

Angus just hoped this worked and that no one got hurt or worse, killed. But that would be up to T.D., he thought with a shudder as the darkness seemed to take on a life of its own. "They're coming," he whispered as he heard a horse whinny in the distance.

Chapter Thirteen

As Brick hurried back up the mountainside, Angus returned to his spot. Jinx could tell he hadn't wanted to leave her. The night felt colder not being in his arms. She tried to concentrate on what had to be done, rather than the wrangler.

With luck, this would work. Even if T.D. stampeded the cattle into their camp, the only thing that would be destroyed was Max's beloved chuckwagon. A chuckwagon could be replaced. Max, in the meantime, would be safe away from camp, Ella had assured her.

She knew they were as ready as possible and still she couldn't help being scared. With a man like T. D. Sharp... Had he followed her up here just to torment her? To keep her from getting her herd to summer range? Or was his motive even more treacherous? She remembered the look in his eyes the other night at the ranch and knew at that moment, he'd wished her dead.

Jinx swallowed the lump in her throat, telling herself the man didn't scare her even as she knew it wasn't true. There was something about him, a feeling that he'd stepped over some invisible barrier and now he felt he had nothing to lose. If he ever got her alone again...

She shivered and pushed the thought away. His attack on them tonight would get him sent to jail. At least temporarily. With luck, she could get a loan against the ranch until she had it sold. Dangling that kind of money in front of T.D., she thought she could get him to sign the divorce papers. She wanted this over.

Right now the thought of losing the ranch didn't seem so overpowering. Standing here in the dark, trying to gauge what T.D. would do next, she had a whole different set of priorities. She wanted to live. Angus had made her realize there were more important things than a piece of land or a herd of cattle. There could be a life after T.D., after losing her mother and father, after even losing the ranch.

Not that she was ready for that life. Not that Angus might even be in it. But he'd made her see that her mistake in marrying T.D. wasn't the end of the world. It was only the end of this life. She could put this all behind her without knowing what the future held for her—just that she had one.

If she lived past tonight.

Waiting in the dark, the night getting colder, she regretted her own stubbornness. She should have sold her cattle, taken a loss and put the ranch up for sale. She'd put not just her life in jeopardy. Now Angus, Brick and Ella along with Max were in danger because she was so damned determined to get the herd to summer range.

As much as she hated to admit it, she'd done it not just out of stubbornness. She'd wanted to show T.D. that he wasn't going to run her life, let alone ruin it. Her stubborn pride could get them all killed. She couldn't bear the thought. Angus, Brick and Ella had answered her ad because Dana and Jinx's mother had been close. They should never have had to come all this way. None of them should be on this mountainside right now knowing there was a madman out there in the pines set on vengeance.

Another horse whinnied from deep in the pines above her on the mountain. She heard a branch snap under a horse's hoof. They were moving more slowly than she'd expected. Did they expect a trap?

She pulled the weapon at her hip, hoping she wouldn't have to use it. The plan had been to cause enough confusion to drive them back—if not subdue any who fell into their traps. By cutting down their numbers, it would make T.D. think twice. At least that was the hope. She knew he was basically a coward. He needed his two close friends to bolster his courage—that and alcohol.

Unfortunately, he had them and two more men who would follow his orders if he offered them the right incentives.

The sound of the riders grew closer. She could hear the creak of saddle leather, the brush of tree boughs and whisper of high grass against the horses' legs as their riders kept coming.

Jinx found herself holding her breath. She knew how quickly everything could go south. Behind her, the cattle lowed softly. If she was right, the approaching riders would begin firing their weapons and yelling as they tried to stampede the herd back toward the camp.

And if she was wrong?

ANGUS FELT THE hair rise on the back of his neck as he realized the riders had spread out and at least one would soon be almost on top of him. Even in the pitch blackness of the spring night, he waited for the shapes to materialize out of the dark.

The trick, he knew, was to stay calm until it was time to attack. The booby traps were spring-loaded. All a horse had to do was trip the rope hidden in the tall green grass and all hell would break loose. Jinx could handle this, he told himself. At the same time he was reminded that all of this was about her.

T.D. had ridden all the way up here with his friends to cause her trouble. He wanted to torment her. To make her pay for not taking him back. To hurt her.

And that was what scared Angus the most. If T.D. got his hands on her, how far would the man go?

He couldn't see her through the trees, but he knew she was still there. He hadn't wanted to leave her alone, still didn't.

A swishing sound off to his left on the mountain-side was followed by a cry of pain. He could hear what sounded like a struggle, then silence. He listened hard for the all-clear signal and finally heard his brother whistle a meadowlark's call.

He tried to relax. Brick had one of them down. Four to go.

The riders seemed to be quickening their pace through the pines. One of his log swings snapped in the darkness. He heard an *ooft* sound followed by a loud thump as a body hit the ground. An instant later, a horse ran past him—sans its rider.

Angus sprang into action, moving quickly toward where he'd heard the man fall. As he neared, he heard mewing sounds. Gun drawn, he pounced on the man only to have him cry out in pain.

"My arm," the man cried. "It's broken." His eyes widened as he saw the gun in Angus's hand. "Don't kill me. None of this was my idea." The man began to cry.

Angus saw that there was no way to tie the man's hands, so he took the man's weapon and tied his ankles together along with the wrist of his good arm.

"You have to get me a doctor," the man pleaded. "I don't want to die out here."

He hurriedly put his hand over the man's mouth. "Where's T.D.?" he asked the man quietly and released his grip on the man's mouth long enough to let him answer.

"I don't know. I thought he was with us, but I haven't seen him since we left camp."

He quickly gagged the man, fearing it was too late. The others could have heard him. But none of them had come to his aid. At least not yet.

In the distance he heard another of the booby traps snap off to his left. Brick had another one down, followed by the meadowlark whistle. As another booby trap went off, he waited but heard nothing. That one must have missed. Or maybe the man had wised up and gotten off his horse.

To Angus's count, they had three down. That left two men. Did Brick have T.D.? If not, was he one of the two left? He hoped they'd heard what was going on and had headed back. He listened, hearing nothing but the pounding of his own heart.

That was until he heard an earsplitting racket coming from camp and then dead silence.

THE FIRST SIGNS of daylight cast an eerie dark gray shadow over the mountainside. From her perch in one of the large old pines, Ella saw that a riderless horse had set off her alarm in the camp. She watched the horse head for the corral where their horses whinnied and moved around restlessly.

So where was the rider? She felt anxious, worried about what was happening in the forest beyond the camp. But she wasn't about to leave Max. She'd promised Jinx she would make sure he was safe.

He sat with his back against the rock rim, his shotgun

resting in his lap. She watched from her tree perch. The clouds had parted some. The sky to the east lightened in the area around her, and she wondered how long before dawn. Her eyes felt dry and scratchy from staring into the darkness of the pines.

She listened but heard nothing but the cattle lowing in the meadow higher up the mountain. Closer, she heard the steady beat of her heart as she waited and prayed that the others were all right. And yet as she waited, she feared something had gone wrong. She kept thinking about the horse that had set off her alarm—and its empty saddle. Where was the man who'd been riding it?

JINX TENSED AS she heard the noise coming from camp, but before she could react, she heard a rider bearing down on her. She had her gun ready, hoping she didn't have to use it. A riderless horse burst out of the darkness and ran past her.

She let out the breath she'd been holding and tried to relax. The horse had come from the direction of the camp. She told herself that Ella would take care of whoever had set off the alarm back there—just as she would make sure Max was safe. If she was able.

Listening, Jinx heard nothing. The quiet was more unnerving than the racket had been. She had no idea how many of the men were down. Or if any of them had turned back. All she knew was that unless they had T.D., he was still on this mountain somewhere. Maybe even closer by than she knew. That thought sent a shudder through her. She feared how badly things could go on this mountainside.

The sound of the gunshot made her jump. It had come from higher up on the mountain. *Brick*. Her heart dropped. She knew Angus would go to him. She could hear movement through the pines off to her right. It was still pitch black in the pines, but the sky was lightening in the distance. Soon the sun would rise. Soon she would be able to see who was coming at her.

A closer sound made her freeze. She sensed T.D. even before she heard the swish of his boots through the tall grass behind her, followed by the smell of the alcohol on his breath as she swung around, leading with the pistol in her hand.

T.D. was on her so quickly she didn't have time to even pull the trigger. He covered her mouth with his gloved hand before she could scream as he ripped the pistol from her grip. Tossing the weapon away into the darkness, he put his face against the side of hers and whispered, "Hello, wife. Don't you wish you'd just paid me off when I asked nicely?"

Chapter Fourteen

Angus ran through the pines toward the sound of the gunshot, knowing where it had come from. His brother was in trouble. There hadn't been the meadowlark whistle as hard as he had listened for it. The clouds had moved off, leaving a lighter ceiling overhead as daylight peeked through the pines.

He could make out shapes through the trees. He saw two horses, both tied to a limb. That meant three men down, just as he'd thought. He hadn't heard another trap being sprung. What had happened that there'd been a gunshot?

Because there were still two men out there, he reminded himself as he ran through the pines. He'd known at once that the gun report had come from the spot where Brick had set up his booby traps. As he ran, he prayed for the sound of his brother's meadowlark whistle. But it didn't come to let him know that Brick was all right. Because in his heart, he knew he wasn't.

He didn't even consider that he might be running into a trap. All he could think about was getting to his twin. He'd felt that shot as if the bullet had entered his own body. Because they were identical twins, they'd always shared a special bond. Not that they'd dressed alike or were alike in so many ways. They'd never had a special language that was all theirs. Nor had they ever sensed when the other was in trouble. Until now.

Angus was almost to Brick when he heard the second gunshot. He burst through the pines, shoving aside boughs to find his brother lying on the ground next to two bodies. In that instant, he saw that Cash had been gagged and tied up but had managed to free himself.

At the sight of Angus, the man jumped up, ran to his horse and pulling the reins free, took off down the mountain as if the devil himself was after him. On the ground next to Brick, Royce lay dead from a gunshot wound to the chest. There was a gun dangling from the man's fingertips even though his wrists were bound.

He saw what had happened as clearly as if he'd witnessed the whole thing. Royce had pulled a second gun that Brick hadn't found on him before his brother had tied the cowboy up.

Angus dropped down beside his brother. Brick was trying to say something. There was a dark blood spot on his upper chest that was getting larger and darker. Angus quickly pulled off his coat and pressed it to the wound.

As he did, he heard someone coming through the trees. He didn't go for his gun, knowing he wouldn't have time to pull it. He picked up Brick's gun and turned it as the figure burst through the pines.

Ella. He eased his finger off the trigger as she dropped to the ground beside Brick. "Help is on the way," she said as she took over holding the coat to her cousin's wound. "I was able to get cell service from the top of a pine tree."

Angus felt a surge of relief. Help was on the way. But her next words turned his blood to ice.

"I think T.D. has Jinx," she said. "She's not where she's supposed to be and there are drag marks going down the mountain. His horse set off my alarm. I had a bad feeling so I called for help, then climbed down the tree. I was on my way to check when I heard the second shot."

His heart had dropped to his boots. Brick was shot and T.D. had Jinx?

"I'll take care of Brick," his cousin said. "Go find her. Before it's too late."

As T.D. DRAGGED her through the woods, Jinx tried to fight him. He held her by the throat, his boozy breath next to her ear as he told her what he was going to do to her. When he'd first jumped her, he'd thrown her down, knocking the air out of her.

She fought him, scratching and kicking and biting, only to have him slap her so hard she saw stars. He'd sat on her and quickly bound her wrists and gagged her with her bandanna. He'd thought she would scream for help. She could see that T.D. was just hoping someone would come to her rescue so he could kill them.

With his arm locked around her neck, he dragged her. When she tried to fight him, he cut off her airway until she quit struggling. At first she'd been terrified, knowing at least in part, what he planned to do to her. But the more she fought him, the more furious she got. How dare he think he could treat her this way?

She knew she needed to save her strength for when she had a chance of actually getting away from him, but the mad she had going felt good. And it was so much better than terror right now.

He stopped under a large old pine tree far from the camp. Throwing her down, he climbed on top of her. She glared at him, putting all her disgust into the look.

"It's not rape," he said as if reading her gaze clearly enough. "You're still my wife, which means you are still mine to do whatever I want with." His idea of marriage astounded her. She tried to tell him what she thought of him through her gag but he only laughed, not understanding a word.

"Come on, you like this," he said as if he could still charm her. "I love you. I just want to show you how much, remind you of what you've been missing. You have been missing it, haven't you?" His gaze narrowed for a moment. "Don't you remember what it was like with the two of us? You know you still love me. We can stop this right now. All you have to do is admit it was a mistake when you threw me out. It isn't too late for us."

She knew it was a lie, but she wondered if T.D. did. Maybe he believed everything he said. If she submitted to him, it wouldn't be over. Even now, she could see that he didn't trust her. Didn't trust that he could charm her anymore. She could see the fear in his eyes. Even if she were stupid enough to take him back, his anger and insecurity would make their lives a living hell. He'd always said, when he was drinking, that she thought he wasn't good enough for her. He was the one who believed that until he'd proven to her he was right.

T.D. wasn't good enough for her. He wasn't the kind of man she wanted in her life. Not now. Not ever.

He stared at her in the growing light. Was he having second thoughts about this? Was he wishing like she was that none of this had ever happened?

Slowly, he leaned down to kiss her, but she moved her head from side to side each time he tried and attempted to buck him off. But he was too strong for her. She wouldn't submit to him. She couldn't.

Swearing, he said, "Fine. We don't have much time so let's get right to it." He unzipped her coat and then grabbed her Western shirt and unsnapped it in one quick, hard jerk. "I'll just take what's mine. You want it rough? Well, too bad, because that's the way you're getting it."

She'd told herself that she would kill him if he ever touched her again. He'd bound her wrists behind her with duct tape and had her lying partially on her side. She felt a little give in the duct tape. He'd been in a hurry and he hadn't done a good job.

As he leaned over her, grabbing her chin to hold her head still while he kissed her hard, she moved her hands down her side and pulled her legs up until she could reach her boot with the knife in it.

Drawing the knife from the sheath, she clutched it tightly in her fist. She knew she could do little damage with the knife the way she was bound. But right now just getting him off her would be a start. Leaning back, she got the blade between her wrists and felt it cut through most of the tape. Just a little more.

T.D. took her movements as her getting into what was happening. He deepened the kiss as he groped her through her bra. The tape gave. Her wrists free, she swung the knife.

He must have sensed that her hands were free because he moved just enough that the blade cut into his side—rather than his back. He let out a howl of pain, grabbing her wrist with such force that she dropped the blade before she could stab him again. Still on top of her, T.D. snatched up the knife, his blood staining it.

Her breath caught in her throat as he leaned over her, flashing the blade in her face. She closed her eyes as he wiped the blood off on her cheek. "You stupid bitch," he breathed, sounding as if in pain. She knew it was only a flesh wound. She had succeeded in only making him angrier with her.

But she opened her eyes, defiantly glaring at him. If

he didn't know before, he did now. She would rather die than let him do this to her.

Holding her wrists down above her head with one hand, he laid the cold knife blade against the bare skin of her chest for a moment, before he cut her bra open. She felt the cold night air on her exposed breasts and heard his chuckle when he saw her puckered nipples.

It's the cold, you idiot, she wanted to say, even more contempt in her gaze.

He recognized it because he growled, "I could cut your throat just as easily."

Please do, she thought.

"Maybe I will cut you, once I'm through with you," he said, so close that she wanted to gag on the alcohol fumes. He pocketed the knife and rolled her over, duct-taping her wrists again, this time more roughly.

Flopping her back over, he held her down with his body as he stared at her for a long moment. She felt a chill because the look was clear. This was goodbye. He would never let her leave this mountain alive.

She heard him unzip his jeans before he began fumbling to get hers undone, shifting to one side as he did. Jinx brought her knee up hard and fast and caught him in the groin. As he let out a howl and leaned to one side, she bucked him the rest of the way off and rolled to the side to scramble to her feet.

He reached for her, grabbing a handful of blue jean fabric and dragging her back. She kicked at him, but he pulled himself to his feet and slapped her so hard she tasted blood.

His voice was hoarse with fury and pain as he locked one arm around her throat again, pulled his pistol and held it to her head. "You're a dead woman."

WYATT TRIED TO hold the rifle steady. His finger brushed over the trigger. All he had to do was pull it. Pull it and Jinx would be history. Patty would be grateful.

At the thought of her, his finger hovered on the trigger. If only he could quit shaking—and get his crosshairs on Jinx. Since the moment T.D. had grabbed Jinx, he hadn't had a clear shot.

Just when he had the crosshairs on her, they both moved. He swore. He could feel himself sweating profusely under his coat even though the early morning was freezing cold. The sky around him was lightening. He had a clear view of the two and wasn't sure how much longer he would.

He hadn't heard any of the others for some time now. Not since the sound of that gunshot had broken the silence. Earlier T.D. had spelled out the plan to them. Even as he was talking, Wyatt knew he was lying. T.D. wanted them to quietly sneak up on the herd before they started shooting and hollering and scattering them.

But just before they left camp, T.D. pulled him aside to tell him that he had a different plan for him. "I'm going to sneak into the camp from the other way, find Jinx and finish this. I want you to cover my back."

Wyatt had nodded numbly, thinking that the cowboy's plan worked out perfectly for his own plan. They'd ridden for a way with the others and then cut off through the pines to ride up almost to the camp. It had been T.D.'s idea to let his horse go into camp as a decoy. The man wasn't stupid. He knew Jinx was expecting the attack.

Wyatt had hung back but kept his eye on T.D.

Now he stood some yards away. The rifle was getting heavy. He didn't know how much longer he could wait to take a shot. Worse, he thought he'd heard a helicopter in the distance.

When he'd lowered the rifle, then lifted it again, he'd been shocked to see that Jinx had almost gotten away from T.D. The rifle wavered in his hands. Surely he hadn't missed his chance at a clean shot.

He fought now to get the crosshairs on her. T.D. had his arm around her neck and a pistol to her head. What the hell? Was he only threatening her? He couldn't believe that this situation might solve itself. If T.D. killed Jinx, he wouldn't have to and yet he could take credit when he saw Patty. T.D. would be going to prison...

Wyatt felt a surge of hope that everything might work out for him. But T.D. had to pull that trigger. He watched as Jinx tried to fight him off. Any moment the wranglers working for her would be coming. What was T.D. thinking, taking this risk? *Shoot her!*

Couldn't the man feel time running out? It struck him that T.D. was crazy. He always had been, but lately he'd been getting worse. He was going to get them all thrown in jail—if not killed.

As he watched through the scope, Wyatt realized that T.D. wasn't going to shoot her. If Jinx was going to die, it would be up to Wyatt to finish this and soon. He'd missed a good shot earlier when he'd lowered the rifle for even a moment and was now mentally kicking himself. This could already be over. He could have killed Jinx.

The rifle wavered in his arms, the crosshairs going from Jinx's face to T.D.'s as the two kept moving around. Wyatt thought of how disappointed Patty would be if he didn't do what had to be done. How disappointed he would be in himself because any hope he had of ever being with Patty would be gone.

Not that T.D. stood a chance now of ever getting Jinx

back—and freeing Patty. Hadn't Wyatt been hoping that his friend would return to Jinx and break it off with Patty for good? He could have seen himself comforting the brokenhearted Patty. He'd seen it as a chance to win the woman's heart.

But now it was clear that Jinx was never going back to T.D.—not after this. T.D. had blown any chance he had by following her up here into the mountains. Not that it seemed he stood a chance anyway since now there was a wrangler in the mix. Jinx had moved on—and damned quickly, if he said so himself. Patty thought she had to get rid of Jinx to get T.D. back. Jinx was already long gone.

Through the rifle scope he tried to get a shot at Jinx. T.D. wasn't going to pull the trigger. Instead, his friend seemed to be looking back up the mountain. For a moment Wyatt feared that he'd seen him and almost lowered the rifle. No, T.D. must have heard some of the others coming. Time had run out.

He put the crosshairs on Jinx's red head and assured himself that no one would know who fired the fatal shot. T.D. would be blamed for all of it—not that he wouldn't probably get away with it, just as he had all of their lives. He'd dragged them up on this mountain, gotten him and Travis in trouble, and T.D. would somehow shift the blame.

If T.D. shot Jinx he'd go to prison and Patty would be free. But even as he thought it, Wyatt knew the man didn't have what it took to pull the trigger.

Wyatt settled the crosshairs on Jinx as the sun caught in her red hair. "This is for you, Patty."

As DAWN BROKE over the mountains, Angus followed the drag marks down the mountain at a run, his pistol drawn, his heart racing. He had to find Jinx.

He came to a sliding stop as he saw them—and they saw him. T.D. pulled her out of the darkness of a large pine, using Jinx like a human shield. She was gagged and from what he could see, her hands seemed to be bound behind her. Her coat was open, along with her shirt, her bare breasts covered by her long hair.

T.D. had a gun to her head and was grinning as he locked his free arm around her neck, pulling her back against him. "Drop your gun or I'll kill her right now," he ordered. "I wouldn't try me on this."

Angus could see the fear in Jinx's face, but suspected that it was more for him than for herself. He felt his finger on the trigger, the barrel pointed at T.D.'s head. But it was a shot he knew he couldn't take.

He thought about what to do as he considered his options. They were limited. He could rush the two of them and hope for the best. There was a desperation in T.D.'s expression. He looked nervous, like a trapped animal, and that made him even more dangerous. The man knew that he'd never get out of this, not this time. Brick had been shot. Royce was dead. T.D. would have heard the gunfire.

What Angus feared was that the man would panic and shoot Jinx if he didn't drop his gun. He slowly lowered his pistol to the ground, knowing that there was nothing stopping T.D. from shooting him.

But Angus was ready. If T.D. even started to pull the gun away from Jinx's head, he was ready to launch himself at the man. There was a good chance he would be shot, but if he could save Jinx, it was a chance he had to take.

"I know she's been with you," T.D. said, anger marring his handsome face. "Just the thought of you and her…" Jinx let out a cry as T.D. tightened his hold on her.

Angus started to take a step forward, but T.D. quickly

said, "Don't do it. I'll kill her. You know I will. If I can't have her, then no one can, especially you."

He could tell that Jinx was having trouble breathing. "You don't want to go to prison."

T.D. laughed. "I've been headed there my whole life. The only thing good I ever had was Jinx. And now that's gone." He pressed the pistol barrel harder to her temple, making her wince. "This is all your fault, Jinx. You only have yourself to blame."

The air filled with a sound of a gunshot report.

Chapter Fifteen

Angus started at the sound. He had no idea where the shot had come from—just that it had happened fast. Suddenly Jinx was on the ground and T.D. was standing over her splattered with blood. Angus was instantly moving, grabbing up his gun from the ground as he rushed toward T.D.

Another shot filled the air, biting the bark of a tree next to T.D. as the man turned and ran into the pines. Angus launched himself down the hill to cover Jinx from the gunfire. He still wasn't sure where the shots were coming from or who was firing them. He shielded Jinx, terrified that she was already badly injured by the first gunshot.

"Jinx!" he cried as he hurriedly removed the gag from her mouth. "Jinx?" As the gunfire stopped, he heard someone take off on horseback. Pulling his pocketknife, he cut her wrists free and turned her onto her back to lower her to the soft ground.

Her eyes were open. But like T.D.'s, her face was splattered with blood to the extent that he couldn't tell where she'd been hit.

"Angus," she said, her lips curving into a smile before her eyes closed.

"Jinx, don't leave me. Jinx?" He moved closer. In the

growing light of day, he could see where a bullet had grazed her temple. He checked her pulse. It was strong. She didn't seem to have any other injuries, he realized with relief. He could hear a helicopter approaching. Closer, he heard someone moving through the tall grass and trees toward him.

He spun around, pistol ready, and then relaxed. "Max, Jinx has been hit."

Max stumbled up to them and dropped to his knees next to her. Jinx opened her eyes. "Max." The older man took her hand as her gaze shifted to Angus. "T.D.?"

"He got away," he said.

"No," both Max and Jinx said almost in unison.

"A helicopter will be here in just a minute," Max said. "I'll stay with Jinx. Don't let T.D. get away."

Angus saw the worry in the older man's eyes. Unless T.D. was stopped, Jinx would never be safe. He felt torn. He didn't want to leave her, but he damned sure didn't want T.D. to get away.

"Go," Max urged him. "She'll be all right. I'll stay with her and make sure of that."

Swearing, Angus took off down the mountain, following the blood trail T.D. was leaving as the sun topped the mountain and fingered its way through the pines. T.D. hadn't come at them as they'd both anticipated. Instead, he'd sent his flunkies in while he circled around to come up the back way. He'd never planned to stampede the herd. The man had only been after Jinx, letting the others be the diversion he needed.

The bad feeling Angus had had since they'd taken this job had now settled in his bones. He had to find T.D., if it was the last thing he did. As he looked into the dark shadows of the pines, he knew it could very well be just that.

T.D. RAN, SLUMPED over from the pain. He still couldn't believe that Jinx had stabbed him. But that was the least of his worries. He was bleeding from a gunshot wound to his upper chest and because of that, he was leaving a trail. Worse, he knew someone was behind him coming after him—just as he knew who it would be. Jinx's wrangler.

The thought turned his stomach. Earlier, he'd had a nice drunk going. He'd felt cocky and self-assured. He'd outsmarted his so-smart wife. He'd had her in his clutches.

Now he was running scared. He could just hear his father telling him how he'd really screwed up his life good this time. He was looking at jail. Maybe even prison. Why hadn't he let it go? Why hadn't he let Jinx go? But he knew the answer. She was the best thing that had ever happened to him.

But following her up on this mountain? It had been as stupid as Travis had said. He blamed his pride. Everyone in the county knew that Jinx had kicked him out. What was he supposed to do? He couldn't stand looking like a beaten dog with his tail between his legs. He couldn't just let her get away with that.

Now as he stumbled through the pines feeling sick to his stomach and scared, he didn't want to be that man anymore. He wanted desperately to be different, but he had no idea how to make that happen. He felt as if he'd been forced into his bad behavior his whole life. First, by his father's taunts. Later, by the knowledge that he wasn't any good. He wasn't good enough, especially for Jinx. It was why he drank. The more he drank, the worse things got, but he hadn't been able to stop. He'd never been able to stop himself on any of it. For the life of him, he couldn't just let things alone.

Like now. He kept running instead of doing the smart

thing and surrendering. He could hear a second helicopter coming. Why not just give up? He needed medical attention. He was still bleeding. He wasn't even sure he could get away. Why not make things easier for himself?

Because there was something in his DNA that wouldn't let him. *That and arrogance*, he thought. Then again, a part of him believed he could get away. He knew this mountain. He knew how to get off it to the closest ranch. He knew how to get help from someone who wouldn't call the cops. He could get away and save himself, and knowing that was what kept him going.

What he didn't know was how badly Jinx had been hit. He'd felt her drop to the ground when he'd released her. There'd been blood everywhere. He hadn't known if it was his or hers. Now he knew that at least part of it was his. But he was sure she'd been hit. Who had fired the shot, though? Not the wrangler. Maybe one of his buddies. Or maybe even Max. Max hated him, just as Jinx's father had.

He pushed those thoughts away as he ran, one surfacing that made him stumble and almost fall. What if Jinx was dead?

The thought hit him so hard that he had trouble staying on his feet. He loved her. His heart broke at the thought that she might be gone. He knew he'd said he was going to kill her—and he might have—but it wasn't what he'd wanted. He hadn't pulled the trigger. He wasn't sure he ever would have been able to.

He'd just had to let her know he wouldn't be simply sent away like some orphan child she was tired of having around. He thought of his mother who'd deserted him when he was nine. He remembered standing at the window, snot running from his nose as he cried and pleaded for her not to leave.

His father had found him and practically tore off his arm as he'd jerked him away from the window. "I'll beat you to within an inch of your life if you don't quit crying. She's gone. Accept it. I have. I never want to hear her name spoken in this house again. Now man up. You and me? We're on our own so make the best of it."

The memory still hurt. He had to stop for moment to catch his breath. Each breath was now a labor. What if the bullet had clipped one of his lungs? What if it was filling with blood right now?

T.D. knew he had to keep moving—even if it killed him. He took off again, holding his hand wrapped in his bandanna over his wound, aware that the bandanna was soaked with his blood.

Growing more light-headed, he felt as if he'd been running his whole life. He was a runner like his mother, he thought. She had gotten away. He feared he wouldn't be so lucky.

Chapter Sixteen

Angus stopped to look ahead in the pines. Had he lost T.D.? He glanced down and saw a drop of blood on the dried pine needles. He looked for another and saw it a few yards away. The blood drops were getting farther apart and smaller, which meant the man wasn't bleeding as badly as he'd been earlier. He would soon be harder to trail. He had to find him before that. He had to find him before he got away. T.D. knew this mountain. He would know how to escape—if he was able.

Angus stared into the shadows of the dense pines, looking for movement, listening for even the sound of a twig snapping. He heard nothing, saw nothing move. He knew T.D. wasn't armed. He knew that the man had dropped the gun he'd been holding to Jinx's head. Unless he had another weapon on him, he was at a distinct disadvantage that way.

However, T.D. had one very good advantage. He was somewhere ahead, and he had enough of a head start that he could be lying in wait somewhere up there. Angus would be expecting an ambush, but would he get a chance to fire his pistol before T.D. sprung his own trap?

It was still a mystery as to who had shot T.D. and Jinx. The rifle report had echoed across the mountain. He'd thought it had come from behind him, but he couldn't be sure. The gunshot had startled them all—even T.D. Angus remembered the sound of a rider taking off not long after the second shot.

Now as he searched the ground for more blood, he worried about Jinx and his brother. He knew that Ella was with Brick, and Max with Jinx. Help had arrived and they both were getting treated for their injuries. Still, a part of him wanted to turn back even though he knew there was nothing he could do to help them.

This wasn't his job, going after T. D. Sharp. He told himself to let him go as he heard one of the helicopters lift off again. Let the sheriff handle this. Anyway, T.D. might already be bleeding to death up here on this mountain like the wild animal he was.

But Angus didn't turn back. He kept going, stubbornly, not willing to chance that the man might get away with what he'd done. Had T.D. heard the helicopters arrive and now begun to take off again? Would he head for them, choosing medical attention over freedom?

ELLA HELD BRICK'S hand in the helicopter on the way to the hospital. He was in and out of consciousness, but the EMTs had stopped the bleeding and were monitoring his vital signs. They weren't as strong as they would like, they'd said.

She kept thinking about how he hadn't wanted to come to Wyoming. How he'd wanted to go see that woman he liked up by the border. Had he sensed that coming here… She shoved the thought away, telling herself that none of them had known he would be shot. Even with all her intuitiveness, she hadn't known this was going to happen.

Brick opened his eyes. "Angus?" he whispered.

"He's fine," she said, even though she didn't know that for sure. As Jinx was being loaded into the second helicopter, Max had told Ella that Angus had gone after T.D., who'd been wounded. Max said Angus had saved Jinx's life. Then he had climbed in with her and the helicopter had taken off.

Just as Ella's chopper with Brick was about to take off, a man had come running out of the woods saying his arm was broken. The EMTs seemed to know him and called him by name—Travis. They'd let him climb in. Ella knew he was a friend of T.D.'s. He sat away from her, looking scared and avoiding eye contact as if he also knew he had more trouble than a broken arm.

Ella squeezed Brick's hand and prayed for him and Angus. It was just like him to go after T.D. Jinx had been hit but was going to make it, the EMTs had said. Angus had saved Jinx, according to Max. So why hadn't he waited and let the sheriff handle T.D.?

Because he was worried the man would get away and go after Jinx yet again, she thought. He was probably right.

JINX DIDN'T REMEMBER much of the helicopter ride to the hospital. Max had been there, telling her everything was going to be all right. She knew better than that.

Now she watched the nurse and doctor moving around the ER as she lay on a gurney in a daze. Max said Angus had saved her. She just remembered T.D., his arm around her neck, stars dancing before her eyes as he cut off her oxygen, and a gun to her temple. He'd said he was going to kill her, and she hadn't doubted that he would before Angus had appeared on the mountainside above them.

She'd thought at first that Angus had fired the shot. But she swore it had come from another direction. She'd felt the bullet graze her temple and hit T.D. He'd shuddered behind her, loosening his hold on her throat and then letting her go.

Close to blacking out, she'd dropped to her knees, gasping for breath. As Angus had rushed to her, she'd seen Wyatt Hanson in the trees. He was holding a rifle, the barrel pointed right at them and then, as if realizing he'd been seen, he'd taken off on his horse.

The rest was a blur except for Angus's handsome face above her, his look of concern in those blue eyes and then his smile when he realized she was going to be all right.

She'd looked down to see the blood, unsure how much of it was hers and how much of it was T.D.'s. And then Max was there, telling Angus to go after T.D. She'd wanted to stop him, but everything seemed to be happening too fast.

Now her heart ached with worry for Angus. He'd gone after T.D. and as far as she knew, no one had seen him since.

When the elderly doctor she'd known her whole life came into her ER room, she asked him if anyone else had been admitted. He shook his head as he checked her pulse. "Angus Savage?"

"Brick Savage is on his way to surgery. I don't believe Angus Savage has been brought in."

"T. D. Sharp?" she asked.

The doctor shook his head. "The sheriff is here, though. Are you up to answering a few questions?"

She nodded. She kept remembering being shot up on the mountain and Max saying, "The helicopters are here. They're setting down in the meadow now. It's going to be all right."

But Jinx had known that nothing was going to be all right. Angus was still up in the mountains chasing T.D.

and she was here. She mouthed a silent prayer for both Brick and Angus.

The sheriff was beside her bed, holding her hand, and she was crying hard. "It's all my fault," she kept saying in between her racking sobs. "All my fault."

Harvey tried to tell her that it wasn't, that he had to check on the others and would be back.

As he started to leave, she grabbed his hand again. "T.D. is still up there. Angus Savage went after him. You have to find them."

"We will," he promised.

"Please don't let anything happen to Angus."

The sheriff smiled and squeezed her hand. "Don't worry."

But all she could do was worry, head pounding. She thought of that young cowboy whom she'd shoved out that barn loft window. She'd almost gotten him killed that day on the Cardwell Ranch when they were little more than kids and here she was again jeopardizing his life. She thought of Angus, his handsome face glowing in the campfire light. The man was likc granite, solid and strong.

She clung to that. She had to believe that no matter what happened up on the mountain, Angus would survive. He had to, she thought, her heart aching.

ANGUS MOVED CAUTIOUSLY through the pines, scanning the terrain ahead for movement. He'd seen the red marks on Jinx's throat along with the tiny specks of blood splattered there so he'd known what had happened, even if he hadn't seen T.D. holding her in a headlock, a pistol to her head.

What he didn't know is who had taken such a dangerous shot. Jinx could have been killed. As it was, the bullet had only grazed her temple. But just one wrong move by her or her shooter…

But that hadn't happened, he reminded himself, pushing away the image that lodged in his brain. Instead, Jinx had gotten lucky. She was alive. T.D. had taken the bullet and once Angus found the man, he'd put an end to this.

That was if T.D. was still alive. His hope was that he would come upon the man's body lying in the dried pine needles. He didn't want to kill him, but he would if it came to that.

Ahead, he saw movement and quickly stepped behind a tree. He could hear something busting through the underbrush on the side of the mountain.

He frowned. Too large for a man? He peered around the tree in time to see several moose that had been spooked out of their beds. He glanced in the direction they'd come from, knowing that was where he would find T.D.

Chapter Seventeen

Wyatt couldn't stop shaking. The ride down the mountain had been at breakneck speed. He'd practically killed his horse and himself. But all he'd been able to think of was getting to Patty. He didn't want anyone else telling her what had happened.

He'd heard the helicopters but had stayed in the trees hoping no one saw him. Not that it would make any difference. There was always the chance that the sheriff could tell which rifle had fired the shot. That was why the only stop he'd made was to drop his rifle into an old mill shaft at the edge of the mountain. He'd thrown in a bunch of rocks to cover it, before getting back on his horse and riding the rest of the way to the corral where he kept his horse.

Wyatt knew there was no way to cover the fact that he'd been up on that mountain. Too many people knew he'd been there. Even if he said that he'd left before they'd gone up to Jinx's camp, there was one person in particular who knew better. The person who'd seen him after he'd fired the first rifle shot. T.D. T.D. knew that he'd shot him. T.D. probably even knew that he'd fired a second shot, trying to finish him off.

That thought rattled him clear to the toes of his boots. He told himself it had been an accident. That he'd been trying to kill Jinx. Or had he, at the last minute, lifted the rifle just a little? Had he seen T.D. in the crosshairs of his scope? Had he realized Patty would never be free as long as T. D. Sharp was alive? Is that what made him take the shot? Or had it really been an accident, his arms fatigued from holding the rifle up for so long, his finger on the trigger jittery at even the thought of what he was about to do?

It was a short walk from the corral to Patty's. He stumbled up to her door after leaving his horse at a ranch on the edge of town. As he tried to catch his breath and still the trembling inside him, he knocked, then knocked louder. He couldn't help looking around as if any minute he expected to hear sirens and turn to find a SWAT team with their weapons trained on him.

The door finally opened. "I shot them." Wyatt pushed his way into her apartment, practically falling in, his legs were so weak.

"Them?" Patty said.

He realized he hadn't meant to say that. But he had. "I shot Jinx. And T.D."

"You *what*?" Patty cried. "Is T.D....dead?"

"I don't know. I didn't mean to. It was an accident. I swear. I was doing what you asked me to. T.D. had Jinx by the throat. She was struggling..."

"Is Jinx dead?"

"I don't know. It all happened so fast." He rushed into the living room and dropped onto the couch. "She was on the ground. There was so much blood. And then I saw T.D. He was holding his chest and there was blood everywhere. That's when I hightailed it off that mountain. It was horrible."

Wyatt dropped his face into his hands and broke down in tears.

"Tell me what happened," Patty said, her voice cracking. When he didn't respond, she came over to the couch and sat down beside him to shake his shoulder. *"Tell me what happened."*

He took a gulp of air and tried to still his sobs. This was not the way he'd wanted Patty to see him. But he couldn't help himself. He was terrified of what he'd done and the price he would be forced to pay.

"Wyatt," she said as if talking to a child. "Pull yourself together and tell me what happened."

He nodded. After a moment he stopped crying, wiped his face with his sleeve and swallowed as he saw that all the color had left her face. She now stared at him as if in shock.

Wyatt cleared his voice and began. "T.D. said we were going to stampede the cattle, but they were waiting for us. They'd set up these booby traps and I heard Travis get caught in one. I think Cash and Royce did, too." His voice cracked. "I think they might be dead." He started to put his face back into his hands, but Patty grabbed one hand and, shaking her head, said, "Tell me how T.D. got shot."

"He never planned to go with the others," Wyatt said. "He sent them in the way he figured Jinx would be expecting the attack. He and I went in the back way. T.D. double-crossed the men with him. He had no intention of stampeding the cattle. He was only after Jinx. Patty, he would never have stopped going after her. *Never.*"

PATTY STARED AT the man, wanting to scream at him, but her throat had gone dust dry. She was shaking inside, afraid she knew what the fool had done. Her worst fears had been realized. What had she been thinking asking Wyatt, of all people, to take care of this for her?

"You fired the shot?" she asked, trying hard to keep her voice level.

"I told you. It was an accident. I was trying to hit Jinx."

"You did hit her, right?" He nodded, looking down as if unable to meet her gaze. "And T.D.? You wouldn't have meant to shoot him. He's your best friend."

His head came up, his eyes full of tears and he nodded quickly. "T.D. had Jinx in a headlock with his pistol to her head. They must have moved when I fired."

"But you don't know how badly either of them was hit, right?"

He shook his head. "I panicked. I just had to get out of there."

He'd killed both Jinx *and* T.D.? Her hand itched to slap him until he quit his stupid blubbering. But she knew she was partially to blame for this. She'd known the man wasn't strong.

She hadn't expected him to do something so stupid as to kill T.D. Not T.D. She fought her own tears at the thought of him being gone. For so long, she dreamed of the day that she and T.D. would be husband and wife. They'd have kids, buy a house, maybe take a trip to Disney World.

That dream burst like a soap bubble. Even if T.D. wasn't dead, he might be lost to her.

"You're a good shot, aren't you?" she asked. "I mean, you beat T.D. and Travis every time at the state fair. You always get your elk and deer every year, killing them in one shot, not spoiling any meat. Isn't that right, Wyatt?"

He nodded, but couldn't hold her gaze. She felt her heart drop. What had the man done?

Patty placed her hand on his thigh. He sniffed but was no longer crying. He wiped his face on his sleeve again and looked over at her as if the sun rose and set on her. "You say T.D. went after Jinx?"

He nodded and she listened as he told her how T.D. had been drinking and getting more angry every hour. The herd was almost to the summer grazing range. They were running out of time.

"You know how he gets when he drinks," Wyatt said, his voice hoarse. "He was crazy. There was no talking him out of it." She patted his thigh and told him to continue. "He and I went in through the camp, but then he found Jinx and started dragging her down the mountain away from the others.

"Travis got hurt first. I heard him scream. Through the trees I could see that he'd been knocked off his horse. I heard him say his arm was broken. Then I think Cash and Royce got caught. That's when I heard a gunshot, then another. I didn't know what was going on. I don't know who all were killed."

"Because you were following T.D. so you could get a good shot at Jinx," she reminded him.

He nodded and swallowed, looking guilty. "I was watching them through the scope on my rifle." He met her gaze. "I was just doing what you asked me to."

Patty removed her hand from his thigh. She could see that was exactly what he would tell the sheriff. That she'd made a deal with him to kill Jinx. She had no doubt that under pressure, he would break down. He would tell the sheriff that it had been her idea. Knowing Wyatt, the fool would probably even tell the sheriff what she'd promised him if he killed Jinx for her. She could deny it, but she feared that Wyatt would be the more believable one, especially if it went to trial.

Panic rose in her, but she tamped it back down. If T.D. was dead, what did she care if she went to prison? Her life would be over without him. But maybe he wasn't. Maybe all of this could be saved.

She tried to think. "Where is everyone now?" Wyatt was sobbing again into his hands. She shook his shoulder again. "Where is everyone now?"

He lifted his head, wiping his face with his sodden sleeve as he tried to pull himself together again. "I saw helicopters. Two of them. The medical ones. I guess the injured are at the hospital by now. I had to get out of there before they saw me."

So whoever had survived this fiasco had gone to the hospital—or was still up on the mountain. "You should stay here," she said. Wyatt brightened. "I'll go to the hospital and find out who all made it." He nodded, looking miserable again. "I'll be back. You should get some rest. Whatever you do, don't leave, okay?" He nodded. "Don't talk to anyone. I mean *anyone*. This is just between the two of us." He nodded again, looking hopeful.

She told herself that if she played this right, she might be able to save herself. If not, it would be her word against Wyatt's. She didn't even have to guess which the sheriff would believe since he'd known them both since they were kids. Which meant she was going to have to get Wyatt to lie. With a sigh, she knew what she'd have to do in that case.

Patty dressed quickly. If T.D. was alive, then he could be one of those brought out by helicopter. She imagined him in the hospital, injured, but alive. She refused to even consider that he was dead up there on the mountain along with all of her dreams.

T.D. was strong and smart and determined, she assured herself. He would survive—he had to. Once she saw him, she'd have to deal with Wyatt. That prospect had little appeal. If only he'd done what she'd asked. He'd said he'd seen Jinx on the ground. He'd said he'd seen blood. Maybe the shot he'd taken had passed through her and hit T.D., barely wounding him. That was possible.

She hung on to the hope that Jinx was dead and T.D. merely injured. Still, she wanted to throttle Wyatt. The damned fool. Why would he take a shot when T.D. was struggling with Jinx?

Because she'd asked him to kill Jinx.

Unfortunately, she feared that wasn't all that was going through Wyatt's mind during that instant when he'd pulled that trigger. The man was too good a shot to do something so stupid. So reckless. So dangerous. But if she was right, then that, too, would be her fault.

Her blood ran cold at what she might have done— signed T.D.'s death warrant. But maybe it wasn't too late. Maybe T.D. was still alive. Maybe it wasn't too late for her, either. Maybe she could cover her tracks.

Then there was Wyatt. Would the sheriff be looking for him? Not yet. She had time.

She drove to the hospital on the edge of town, trying to remain calm. But the moment she pushed in through the emergency entrance, she saw people scurrying around and felt her skin turn clammy. Spotting a young blond-haired, green-eyed woman in soiled Western attire, she stepped to her.

"Were you with the McCallahan Ranch cattle drive?" she asked.

The woman nodded.

"Can you tell me who was brought into the hospital?"

Just then the sheriff walked out of one of the ER rooms. He headed straight for her.

"Thought I might find you here, Patty." Sheriff Bessler was looking at her as if all of this was her fault.

She bristled under his gaze, but held her temper. There was only one thing she wanted to know. "Is T.D....?"

"I don't know any more than you do at this point except that your boyfriend had no business up there and now I've got two gunshot victims." He pushed past her. "Go home, Patty," he said over his shoulder. "If your boy is alive, he's going to jail."

"What about Jinx?" she asked, making the big man stop in his tracks and turn back to her.

"No thanks to T.D. she's going to be fine," the sheriff said, his face set in stone. "She was treated and released. If you see T.D., Patty, you call me or I'll slap you with assisting and abetting a wanted man. You don't think I will? Try me." With that he turned and walked away.

Patty couldn't believe the injustice. Jinx was fine. But T.D. was wounded somewhere up on that mountain? She turned around and saw the young woman wrangler. "Please, you were up there with them. Can you tell me if T.D. is okay?" she asked, hating the panic in her voice.

ELLA CONSIDERED THE woman the sheriff had called Patty. From what she'd gathered, this was T. D. Sharp's girlfriend. Right now all she could think about was Brick and Angus. Brick was up in surgery. She had no idea where Angus was or if he was still alive.

But she couldn't ignore the pain in the woman's voice. "I don't know. I heard he was wounded. That's all I can tell you." Patty started to turn away. "What I do know is that because of T.D., my cousin is fighting for his life and his brother could be, as well, up on that mountain. He'd gone after your boyfriend."

"But T.D. was alive?"

Ella heard no compassion in the woman's voice for the people T.D. had hurt and had to turn away, her sympathy for the woman waning. She walked back down the hall to wait, too worried about both of her cousins to deal with T.D.'s lover.

She told herself that both Brick and Angus were strong. They were fighters. Which meant that Angus wouldn't give up until he found T.D. and finished this. Her heart ached at the thought. T.D. could kill him up there on the mountain and they might never find him.

While she tried to concentrate on thinking positive, she was exhausted. Her senses seemed dulled down to nothing but static. Worry made her heart ache. She told herself they would both be fine, but she didn't feel it in her soul and that terrified her.

Dropping into a chair in the hallway outside the ER rooms, she closed her eyes and prayed. She thought of Brick in surgery. In the helicopter, he'd come to long enough to tell her what had happened on the mountain— how Royce had shot him after Brick had captured him and bound his wrists. Either he or Cash had had a second gun that he'd missed.

The EMTs tried to get Brick not to talk, but he seemed determined to get the words out. "I killed him. I didn't even hesitate after he shot me. I just pulled the trigger." Brick had closed his eyes. "I killed him."

"Only in self-defense," she'd assured him.

She'd heard the anguish in his words as he repeated them. *"I killed a man."*

And then the alarms had gone off and the EMTs were fighting to save Brick's life as the helicopter set down next to the hospital and he was rushed to surgery.

She said another prayer for him, terrified that she would lose both of her cousins. *Please, let them be all right*. Ella needed both men in her life. She couldn't do without either of them. And she didn't even want to imagine what Dana would do if she lost her boys.

Chapter Eighteen

Back home, Jinx felt as if she was going crazy with worry about Angus and Brick and now Max. Earlier when the doctor finally came back in her room before releasing her, she'd said, "I know you said I have a mild concussion so that could be the problem, but I swear I haven't seen Max since I was brought in."

Dr. Kirkland had nodded solemnly, making her heart drop. "I've admitted him. Now, don't get excited," he'd said quickly before she could panic. "He was having some chest pain. Nothing to worry about, but I wanted to keep him overnight for observation. I want to do the same with you."

"I want to see him," she'd said and started to get up off the gurney, but he'd laid a hand on her arm and shaken his head.

"Max is resting. Seeing your concern will only agitate him. I've assured him that you are fine. Now I've assured you that he is fine. Both of you just need rest. You've been through a lot. You can see Max tomorrow. Now please stop fighting me."

She'd lain back but was too restless to stay there. Sitting up again, she'd said, "Please let me go home. I'm going crazy here. And you know I'll sneak up and check on Max if I'm forced to stay here overnight."

Dr. Kirkland had chuckled and given her a look of disbelief. But he'd known her long enough—since the night he delivered her—that he knew her well. "I'd like you to stay, but your concussion is very mild. I see nothing in your vitals to be concerned about. The bullet wound will heal, but you'll have a scar."

She'd thought of Angus's scar—the one she'd basically given him. "I don't mind." It was the scars you couldn't see that bothered her.

The doctor had studied her. "I suspect you have a terrific headache, am I right?"

"It's not bad," she'd lied. "Please, Doc. I'd feel better at home." But she'd known she wouldn't feel better until Angus was found alive and safe and Max was back at the ranch. "Is there any word on Brick Savage yet?"

"He's still in surgery. He had a really close call. Surely there are even more things you need to worry about." He had no idea—or maybe he did.

Dr. Kirkland had finally agreed to discharge her if she promised to take it easy at home. He'd said he'd see to the paperwork.

"I'd feel better if she stayed here," the sheriff had said as he pushed aside the curtain in her ER room.

"You two work it out," Dr. Kirkland had said as he left.

"Have you heard anything?" she'd asked Harvey.

He'd shaken his head. "Since you feel good enough to go home, I'm sure you're up to some questions."

"Shouldn't you be up on the mountain looking for Angus?"

"I have deputies up there right now searching for both Angus and T.D. Anyone else I should be looking for?"

"Cash and Royce were up there. Wyatt and Travis."

The sheriff had nodded. "Travis is getting his arm cast as we speak and from what I heard, Royce is dead.

A chopper will be taking me up to the mountain soon, so why don't you tell me what happened. I've already gotten the story from others who were brought in, except for Brick. He's still in surgery."

She had given him a shortened version. When she finished, he asked, "Booby traps?" and shook his head. "You say you don't know who shot you and T.D.?"

"No, but I saw Wyatt Hanson with a rifle and he rode away right after the shooting stopped."

The sheriff had mumbled something under his breath. All she caught was "wouldn't blame one of his own for taking a potshot at him," before he said, "What the hell was T.D. thinking, going up there after you?"

"Like I know what makes him do what he does. As I told you, he started a grass fire, trying to stampede my herd, but we got that put out. We knew he'd hit again so we made some booby traps to slow them down."

His gaze had saddened. "He tried to rape you."

"But he didn't. Angus stopped him and so did whoever shot him."

Still, the sheriff had looked distraught. "I wish I could have been able to stop him from going up there. Unfortunately, there is no law against riding up into the mountains. But you could have called when you saw him. Even if I hadn't been able to arrest him…"

"What would you have done? We had no proof that T.D. had started the fire. He hadn't gotten anyone killed at that point. He hadn't even gotten close enough to me to arrest him for breaking the restraining order."

"Fortunately, Ella Cardwell climbed a tree on top of the mountain and was able to reach 911 for help. Smart woman."

Jinx had mugged a face at him. "What do you want me to say? That I should have sold my cattle at a loss and never gone up on that mountain?" She'd felt a sob climb her throat. "I wish I had."

The sheriff had laid a hand on hers. "None of this is your fault. This all falls on T.D. and those fools he got to go along with him." Harvey's radio had gone off. He'd checked it and said, "I have to go. They have a helicopter ready to take me up there. Anything else I should know?"

"Just find Angus, please."

"And T.D.," he'd added pointedly. "Until he's behind bars, you won't be safe. Which is another reason I'd like you to stay here tonight."

She'd shaken her head. "He's up on that mountain somewhere wounded. I'm not worried about him. You're going to find him anyway and lock him up." She'd smiled at the sheriff. "I'll be at the house. I have my shotgun loaded by the door."

"Great. We love it when private citizens take the law into their own hands. Nothing can go wrong with that."

"If he so much as steps on my porch, I'm going to shoot him," she'd said with a fierceness that she could see even surprised the sheriff. "He is never touching me again."

The sheriff had looked at her for a long moment before he'd drawn her to him and hugged her. "I'd send a deputy out to your house but—"

"You need them up on the mountain to find Angus and T.D. I'll be fine."

He hadn't looked convinced of that. "I'll call as soon as I know something."

"Promise?"

"Promise."

ANGUS COULD SEE a rock rim ahead. He slowed, feeling the air around him seem to still. The sun was golden against a blue sky studded with puffy white clouds. The morning was cold and crisp and completely still now that the helicopters had left.

But he knew that the sheriff could be arriving soon to search for T.D., pick up Royce's body and investigate the crime scene. The cattle had scattered with the landing of the urgent care helicopters. It was just one more thing Jinx would have to worry about. Angus was determined that T.D. wouldn't still be on that list.

The silence on the mountain took on an eerie feel that made the hair on the back of his neck prickle. He felt as if he and T.D. were the only ones left on the planet. He figured they were the only ones still alive left on this mountain.

Angus studied the terrain ahead of him. He saw no movement, heard nothing for a long moment. A squirrel began to chatter at him from a nearby tree. A jet left a contrail in the sky overhead.

He knew he should turn back and wait for the sheriff. This wasn't his job. But all his instincts told him that he was close and that if he didn't stop T.D., he would get away. Even if he didn't go after Jinx right away, he would always be a threat to her. She would have to be on constant guard, waiting for the other shoe to drop, waiting for him to suddenly appear. When he did...

Angus knew that was why he had to find T.D. and end this. His pistol ready, he moved into the pines beneath the rock rim, knowing that if T.D. was going to hide somewhere, the rocks under the rim would be the perfect place.

He'd expected an ambush. He'd expected gunfire when he got close enough. T.D. had dropped his pistol, but that didn't mean he didn't have another weapon. Angus hadn't seen any blood on the ground for a while now. T.D. wasn't mortally wounded. That meant he was even more dangerous since even if he wasn't armed, he could launch himself from a tree or a rock. T.D. would have the element of surprise.

Angus reached an open area and stopped beside a tree. A slight breeze moaned in the tops of the tall pines. He listened for a closer sound. Movement through the grass as someone approached. The snap of a twig under a boot heel. A stumble overturning a rock.

Hearing nothing, he spotted an object caught on the tall grass in the middle of the clearing. It appeared to be a blood-soaked bandanna.

Angus moved toward it, watching the tree line ahead as he did. When the warning came it was too late. He heard a rumble like thunder and looked up the mountainside. The rocks T.D. had dislodged were bounding down the steep slope directly toward him. The man had left the bandanna on the tall grass knowing Angus would see it and believe he'd crossed the clearing. T.D. had known he was following his blood trail.

The ruse had worked. Angus had only a few seconds to decide which way to run—forward or try to double back. The rocks had dislodged other rocks and started a landslide that filled the clearing above him.

Angus realized belatedly that the clearing was an old avalanche chute. There was nothing to stop the landslide now barreling down the mountainside toward him.

In those few seconds he had, he made up his mind. He sprinted forward, hoping to get to the trees before the landslide caught him up in it.

The damp, dew-soaked new grass was slick, his cowboy boots slipping and losing purchase. Once, he almost fell when his feet threatened to slide out from under him. He ran as hard and fast as he could. His legs ached from the sudden intensity of his effort. His lungs burned. He could hear the low rumble getting louder and louder, so close he could feel the air it displaced as it roared down the mountainside.

He was almost to the trees. Just a few more yards. A large rock appeared in front of him, careening past. Then another. He tried to dodge the next one. It clipped him in the leg, knocking him to the ground.

He rolled, the shelter of the trees so close he could almost reach it. A rock hit him in the side, knocking the breath out of him as he pulled himself up on all fours and launched himself into the trees. A fist-size rock bounced just as he threw himself forward. It smacked him in the head.

The lights went out before he hit the ground.

Chapter Nineteen

T.D. stared down the mountainside. He'd seen the wrangler get hit a couple of times by the rocks tumbling down the slope. Now all he could make out was the cowboy's boots, still visible, protruding from one of the pines along the side of the clearing.

Was the man dead? Pretending to be dead? T.D. pressed his glove over his wound. He'd gotten it bleeding worse with the effort of pushing off the rocks to get the landslide started. But it had worked. The cowboy still hadn't gotten up.

He waited, unsure what to do. Go down and check to make sure the man wouldn't be after him again? Take the man's gun and finish him? Or just get the hell out of Dodge?

He felt light-headed from loss of blood. He knew he needed a doctor. Fortunately, there was someone who was fairly close to a doctor who could patch him up and would without calling the sheriff. All he had to do was get off this mountain. He was pretty sure the bullet had gone clean through his chest just below his left shoulder. With luck, he would live.

The wrangler still hadn't moved. He knew he probably couldn't trust his thinking since he suspected he might be in shock. He wouldn't have minded finishing the bastard off. The cowboy had come to Jinx's rescue not once, but again last night. He'd seen them together. He knew that look of Jinx's.

Just the thought made his blood boil. The sound of another helicopter made up his mind for him. He took one last look at the cowboy still lying at the edge of the pines unmoving and then he turned toward the game trail that he knew would lead him off this mountain to a ranch where he could get the help he needed.

He hadn't gone far when he saw a saddled horse standing in the middle of the trail. He recognized the mount as Royce's and couldn't believe his luck. The mount was dragging its reins as if it had gotten spooked and come untied. He wondered where Royce was, but the thought was a quickly passing one.

T. D. Sharp wasn't going to look a gift horse in the mouth, so to speak.

JINX WILLED HER phone to ring. The sheriff had promised he would call her the moment he knew anything about Angus Savage as well as T.D.

She knew Harvey would do as he promised. Which meant he hadn't found Angus or T.D. Just the thought of all that country up on that mountain… The men could be anywhere. T.D. was wounded, but that didn't mean that he couldn't be dangerous. Angus had come all this way to help her and now he could be dead.

She found herself pacing the floor even though the doctor had told her to take it easy. She said she would or he wouldn't have released her from the hospital. Her temple felt tender under the bandage and her head ached. She'd been going crazy at the hospital. She hated feeling like an invalid on an emergency room gurney when she hadn't been injured that badly. Worse, she hated feeling helpless.

The sheriff was right. She liked to believe she could take care of herself. She'd never liked asking for help, especially after she'd kicked T.D. out. She'd wanted to show everyone that she could handle all of this—the ranch, her father's death, T.D. and the divorce.

But as strong as she knew she was, she'd needed help. She didn't know what she would have done without Angus, Brick, Ella and Max. Her eyes filled with tears. Her stubbornness had put them all in jeopardy.

Picking up her phone, she called the hospital to check on Max and Brick.

"Both are sleeping comfortably, Jinx," the nurse she knew told her. "Ella Cardwell is on a cot in her cousin's room. Everyone is down for the night. Just like you should be."

She knew the nurse was right as she touched the bandage on her temple. Her head still ached, but it had dulled. She hung up, thinking of the scar she would have, which made her think of Angus's small one on his chin. She wished she were in his arms right now. She closed her eyes as she remembered the heat of their kisses. Stolen kisses and one of the few things she would never regret.

You're falling for him. Her eyes flew open. No. True or not, she couldn't trust her heart. Not now. Not with the divorce and knowing she was losing the ranch. Anyway, how could she possibly trust something that had happened so quickly? She couldn't. She'd leaned on Angus. He'd come to her rescue. He'd saved her life.

Of course she felt something for him. But love? She shook her head even as her heart drummed in her chest at the thought of the man, and worry nagged at her. He had to be all right. He just had to. She couldn't bear the thought that T.D. might kill him. That she might never see Angus alive again. Her heart ached with worry.

Why hadn't the sheriff called? Hours had gone by. Maybe he hadn't found either Angus or T.D. Or maybe he'd found them both. She knew Harvey. He'd never tell someone over the phone about a death of a loved one. That was something he did, hat in hand, head bowed, at the person's door.

Chapter Twenty

Angus surfaced to the sound of a helicopter. He opened his eyes. How long had he been out? Not that long, he told himself as he found the sun still glowing in Wyoming's big sky. But he had lost some time.

He tried to sit up, his head swimming. He gingerly touched the spot where the last rock had clocked him. It was painful. He looked around, blinked. T.D. Where was the man? Turning carefully, he glanced back up the mountain. Why hadn't the man taken advantage when he was out cold and finished him? Because T.D. wasn't really a killer? Or because he wanted to get off this mountain as fast as he could?

Pushing himself to his feet, he glanced down the mountain to where the helicopter was hovering before setting down. He headed in that direction although he felt dizzy, his head aching and his footsteps unsure. When he heard the rotors on the helicopter finally stop, he pulled his pistol and fired three shots into the air.

His call for help was answered by a returned three reports, one after the other. He holstered his gun and kept walking in the direction of the chopper. By now, this mountain had to be crawling with cops. Was it possible they'd caught T.D.? He couldn't bear to think the man had gotten away.

Ahead, he could make out the helicopter through the trees. It had landed in a clearing. Before he could reach it, a deputy sheriff intercepted him, demanding to know who he was.

"Angus Cardwell Savage," he said, feeling light-headed.

"Mr. Savage, are you aware that you're bleeding?"

He never got to answer because he'd seen the sheriff coming through the pines toward him and then darkness closed in again.

PATTY KNEW SHE should go home, but Wyatt was there and she wasn't ready to deal with him yet. She pushed into the bar and headed for a stool. It was early enough in the afternoon that the place was almost empty. Just the way she liked it when she was feeling the way she was.

Marty came down the bar. He looked surprised to see her. She still felt bad about what she'd said to him before. "Cola?"

She shook her head. "Whiskey. Straight up." Her voice broke and she was glad when he merely nodded and went down the bar to get her drink. She was in no mood for small talk, let alone anything deeper. She didn't need to be told again what everyone thought about her and T.D.

Just the thought of T.D. brought tears to her eyes. He couldn't be dead. Wouldn't she know it in her heart if he was? And what was she going to do about Wyatt?

Marty set a shot glass full of whiskey on a napkin in front of her and put down the bottle next to it. "Thought I'd save myself the walk back," he said.

She could tell he was waiting—just in case she wanted to talk. She picked up the shot glass and threw back the whiskey. It burned all the way down. Her eyes watered again, this time from the alcohol. "I'm sorry about—"

He waved that off. "Bartenders are just supposed to listen. No one with a lick of sense would take advice from one." He started to turn back down the bar.

"Marty," she said and reached out to touch his forearm to stop him. "I don't want to be me," she said as she removed her hand from his arm. "I hate the person I've become but I don't know how to change."

"Everyone has days like that."

"No, not like this one," she said and poured herself another shot. For a moment she merely stared at the warm golden liquid. "I'm going to have to do something I'm going to regret and yet, I don't have a choice, you know?"

Clearly, he didn't. He studied her openly. "Don't take this wrong but maybe you want to do whatever it is sober."

She laughed. "Not a chance." And threw down another shot.

JINX HAD THOUGHT she would feel better at home instead of in the hospital, but she'd been wrong. She found herself walking through the house as if lost as she kept reliving what had happened on the mountain.

She touched her throat, shuddering at the memory of T.D.'s arm locked around it. He'd cut off her air supply to the point that she'd almost blacked out. When she saw Angus appear, she'd thought she was dreaming. She'd seen the gun in his hand but thought he'd put it down. Had he fired the shot that had hit her and T.D.?

She still felt confused. Where had the shot come from? All she remembered was feeling something hit her in the head. T.D. had jerked, his arm loosening on her throat, as he stumbled back. She'd dropped to the ground, weak from lack of oxygen, blood dripping in her eyes. Hadn't there been another shot? She recalled turning to see T.D. holding a spot high on his chest.

He had looked confused as if like her, he hadn't known where the shots had come from. Then his expression had changed as if he saw something…someone in the distance. She'd followed his gaze and seen Wyatt holding a rifle and looking in their direction before jumping on his horse and taking off.

Wyatt had to have been the one who'd fired the shot— just as she'd told the sheriff. And yet, it made no sense. He was T.D.'s best friend, often his only friend. She frowned. Things had gotten so crazy up on that mountain, they might never be able to sort it out.

She just remembered that after she was shot, everything had happened so fast. It now felt like a blur. Angus she recalled had thrown his body over hers to protect her from further gunfire, flattening them both against the ground before Max had appeared and told Angus to go after T.D.

She could understand why both men wanted T.D. stopped. Hadn't she told the sheriff that she would kill him the next time he showed up here at the ranch? But all this waiting, all this worrying.

She pulled out her cell phone and called the sheriff to see if there had been any word. It went straight to voice mail. She reminded herself that Harvey had promised to call the moment he heard anything. He'd always been good to his word. He would call.

Or he'd show up at her door, she thought with a stab to her heart.

Walking to the window, she looked out. It was dark outside. She blinked in surprise. Exhaustion pulled at her. She knew she needed sleep because she couldn't account for the missing hours. Had she been pacing the floor all this time?

As she started to turn from the window, she heard the wind howling along the eaves. One of the fir trees scraped against the outside of the house as the others bent and swayed against a darkening sky. Another thunderstorm?

Jinx hugged herself, suddenly chilled. T.D. was still out there. For all she knew he was dead. But then again, she knew the man. He could be determined to the point of obsession when it was something he wanted.

If he could, he would survive and when he did, he would come after her.

Jinx shivered, hugging herself as she looked out into the darkness. Was Angus still up on the mountain? Why hadn't she heard anything? Just the thought of him made her heart ache. He'd gone after T.D. because he'd known—just as she had—that T.D. wouldn't stop. Not until she was dead.

She assured herself that by now half the county had gone up into the mountains looking for T.D. They'd find him. They'd find Angus. Angus would be all right. They would find T.D. alive. He would be arrested. This would end and when it did...

That was the part, though, that she didn't have figured out yet. But she wasn't going to get it figured out tonight. Her head ached and she felt weak and sick with worry.

She'd never felt more alone. She kept remembering that her stubbornness had causes this mess. If she'd just sold the cattle, taking a loss, and given the money to T.D.... She knew that wouldn't have been enough for him. He wanted more than money. He wanted vengeance.

But at least she might be divorced from him by now. No longer his wife. No longer his. As long as they were husband and wife, he thought he could do anything he wanted with her. Right now she would gladly give him the ranch just to get him out of her life.

Just to know that Angus was all right.

Had Angus found T.D.? She knew T.D. would never fight fair. What if he'd seen Angus tracking him? What if he'd waited in ambush and killed him?

She turned away from the window, telling herself she had to have faith that Angus was all right. She had to because he'd made her want to go on when she'd felt like quitting, not just ranching, but life.

Max was getting too old for this. She knew that he wouldn't quit as long as she needed him. She thought about calling the hospital again, but knew she'd get the same report. She needed rest. If she could escape for even a little while in sleep…

Her cell phone rang, making her jump. She saw it was the sheriff and quickly picked up.

"Angus was found," he said quickly. "He's going to be fine. He was admitted to the hospital and no, you can't see him tonight. He has a concussion. Was hit in the head, but as I said, Doc assured me that he will be fine."

She felt a flood of relief that brought tears to her eyes. "And T.D.?"

Harvey was silent for a moment. "He got away. That's why I'm sending a deputy out to your place as soon as the shifts change. Most everyone has been up on the mountain looking for him."

"You don't need to send a deputy out here."

"Don't tell me how to do my job, young lady. I'm worried about you. The deputy will just sit outside your house. He won't bother you."

"You sound tired," she said, touched by Harvey's concern for her.

"I am. You sound tired yourself. I thought the doctor said you could go home but only if you rested."

She smiled to herself. "I was just heading to bed. Thank you for letting me know."

"Sleep well."

"You, too." She hung up and headed for her bedroom. Now that she knew Angus was all right, she might be able to get some sleep, she thought as she turned out the lights as she went.

She'd reached her bedroom door and fumbled in the pitch-black room to flip the light switch. Nothing happened. *The overhead lightbulb must have gone out,* she thought. She was working toward her nightstand next to the bed to turn on that lamp when she heard a sound that stopped her cold.

Someone was in the room. In the room waiting for her in the dark. Her blood turned to slush as she said, "Who's there?" fearing she already knew.

Chapter Twenty-One

Jinx let her hand drop to the nightstand drawer. "I know you're there," she said as she eased it open and felt around for the pistol.

It was gone.

The lamp on the nightstand across the bed snapped on, illuminating Patty Conroe sitting in the chair beside the bed. She was holding the pistol from Jinx's bedside table.

"Patty?" She felt confused to see the woman for a moment. She'd been expecting T.D. But as she looked at her husband's lover, she knew she should have been anticipating this visit for some time. "What do you want?"

"What you've taken from me," Patty said.

"What I've taken from *you*?"

Patty's once pretty face showed the road map her life had taken since the two of them were in high school together. "T.D. was mine first."

"You can have him." She noticed the way the woman was holding the gun. Patty knew how to use it.

"How's your head?" Patty asked offhandedly.

"Not fatal."

"That's too bad."

"Patty, where did you leave your car? I didn't see it when I came home."

"I left it behind that old barn on the way in so you

wouldn't see it. I wanted to be here waiting for you the moment I heard you were being released from the hospital. The nurse was so helpful when I called."

"How did you get in here? I know the door was locked."

"I used T.D.'s key. You need to know the truth," the woman snapped. "T.D. came to me when he wasn't getting what he needed from you. I didn't lure him away from you."

"It doesn't matter," Jinx said with a sigh. "I'm divorcing him. He's going to be all yours."

"If he's not dead because of you." Patty sniffed, the pistol wavering in her hand.

Jinx smelled alcohol. She should have known that Patty wouldn't have come out here unless she had been intoxicated. In that way, she was a lot like T.D. And that made her more dangerous. "He's not dead."

"You can't know that," she cried.

She heard such heartbreak in the woman's voice. Had she ever cared that much about T.D.? Not even when she'd married him. She hadn't known then what it felt like to really be in love with anyone, she realized. Her own heart was breaking at the thought of Angus injured and at the hospital because of her.

"Patty, put the gun down and go home. Your fight isn't with me."

The woman let out a bark of a laugh. "Are you serious? T.D. wouldn't be wounded and up on that mountain, possibly dead, if it wasn't for you," she said, her voice hoarse with emotion.

Jinx thought at least that might be true. "He's the one who followed me up there. You blame me for that?"

"You made him crazy. You have his blood on your hands."

"Enough. Go home, Patty. This is getting us nowhere."

Patty pointed the pistol at her heart. "You ruined my life and T.D.'s. You have to pay for that, Jinx."

"I TOLD YOU going to Wyoming was a bad idea," Brick said weakly as he gave Ella a lopsided smile.

Ella started on her cot next to his hospital bed. Tears instantly flooded her eyes as she shot to her feet to take his hand. "You had me so scared," she said, never so happy to see that grin of his.

"Angus?" he asked, his voice hoarse with emotion and no doubt pain as he looked around the hospital room. Of course he would know that Angus would be right here beside his bed, as well—if he could. "Ella?" There was a worried edge to her cousin's voice.

"He's going to be fine. He went after T.D., got hit in the head, but the doctor said other than a concussion and a few scrapes and bruises, he'll be fine. He's here in the hospital. You'll get to see him soon."

Brick seemed to relax. "I knew something had happened. I had this dream…" He seemed to shudder. He met her gaze. "I almost didn't make it, didn't I?" She nodded and swallowed the lump in her throat. "And T.D.?"

"He was wounded but got away."

"Jinx?"

"She was given medical attention and released. You'll hear all about it, once you've had some rest."

Brick closed his eyes. "I remember you and a helicopter?" he asked, opening his eyes again.

She nodded. "I was able to get cell phone service and called for help. You and I were flown to the hospital. Max rode with Jinx."

"Is Max okay?"

"He was admitted to the hospital for observation. The

doctor doesn't think he had a heart attack but wanted to monitor him."

"T.D. got away?"

"Half the county is up on that mountain looking for him. They'll find him."

"I hope you're right." He reached for her hand and squeezed it. "When you see Angus…"

She nodded, tears burning her eyes. "I'll tell him that you miss him."

Brick smiled. "Tell him that I love him, okay? I'll deny I said it." He shrugged.

She had to smile, knowing he was telling the truth. "Your mother just went down the hall to get some coffee. Your dad flew down to Jackson Hole to see if he could help find T.D. since there was nothing he could do here but wait."

"That sounds like him. How's Mom?"

"Worried but you know Dana. She's as strong as they come. The rest of the family has been in and out. They're going to be delighted to hear that you're conscious and your old self."

Brick met her gaze. "I don't feel much like my old self right now. But it's so good to see you." He frowned. "Ella, what aren't you telling me?"

"You just worry about getting out of this bed and back on your feet."

"Ella?"

"It's my mother." She shook her head. "It's just this feeling. I'm sure it's nothing. Dana said she's minding the ranch while everyone else is down here."

She could see that he was drowsy and struggling to keep his eyes open. "You rest. Everything is fine now." And yet she couldn't shake the feeling that her mother was in some kind of trouble.

"TELL ME YOU found him," Angus said as the sheriff stepped into his room. He could see that the lawman looked exhausted.

"I'm afraid not," Harvey Bessler said as he removed his hat. "We'll resume the search in the morning."

Angus swore, making his already aching head hurt more. He'd been so hopeful when he'd been told how many were up on the mountain looking for T.D., his own father included. "You know Jinx won't be safe until T.D. is caught."

The sheriff nodded. "I just talked to Jinx before I came in to check on you. She's fine. I'm sending a deputy out there to keep an eye on her. Now, get some rest and quit worrying."

He watched the sheriff leave, wishing he could quit worrying. Common sense told him that T.D. was wounded and probably still up there on that mountain. Even if he'd gotten off it, he was in no shape to be going after Jinx again. The sheriff was right. He shouldn't worry.

But he did. Glancing around his hospital room, he spotted two things that helped him make up his mind about what to do about his worry. He saw his dirty clothing piled up on a chair by the bathroom door. He also saw his mother's coat and purse. Earlier, she'd been sitting next to his bed before going to check on Brick.

Angus quickly rose from the bed. He had to stop for a moment until the light-headedness passed. Struggling into his clothing, he questioned what good he would be to Jinx if his instincts were right and T.D. had somehow gotten off the mountain and headed for her ranch.

In his mother's purse, he found the keys for the rental car she'd told him about. He felt a little stronger. At least he told himself he did as he quietly opened the door and peered out.

It was so late that the hallway was empty. He headed for the exit sign, knowing he couldn't rest until he made sure Jinx was all right.

"PATTY, WHY WOULD you kill me?" Jinx demanded, seeing the gun waver in the woman's hand.

"Because someone has to do it!" she cried. "Otherwise, T.D. will never be free of you, and you know it."

Jinx thought of Wyatt Hanson in the trees, holding his rifle before riding away. Who had he been trying to shoot? Her or T.D.? "You think shooting me is going to free him for you? You'll be in prison." So would T.D., though she didn't mention that. "What happens when he comes off that mountain and finds out that you're in jail for shooting me?"

Tears filled Patty's eyes. "You really think he's alive?"

"Knowing T.D., I would count on it," she said truthfully.

The gun seemed to grow heavy in Patty's hand. "I don't want to live without him."

"You won't have to, unless you shoot me," Jinx told her. "Don't throw away your future." She could see that this had been a flawed plan of Patty's to start with. The woman wanted Jinx out of her life badly enough that she thought she could shoot her. Jinx understood that on some level. She wanted T.D. out of hers just as badly.

"Put the gun down, Patty." The male voice at the door made them both jump. Startled, Patty pulled the trigger, the pistol bucking in her hand. For the second time that day, Jinx felt a bullet buzz past her head. This one, though, didn't break the skin.

T.D. swore, his bellow almost drowned out by the report of the gun. He moved quickly for a man who was injured, grabbing the pistol and backhanding Patty, sending her flying to the floor at the corner of the room.

"I wasn't going to kill her!" Patty cried as T.D. turned the gun on her.

Without thinking, Jinx started to rush T.D. as if she thought she could stop him from killing the woman.

He swung the barrel of the pistol in her direction as he said, "I wouldn't if I were you." She froze where she was. She could tell that T.D. was weak from his gunshot wound even though he'd apparently gotten some sort of medical help. She could see part of the bandage sticking out of the collar of his shirt. But Jinx wasn't fool enough to think that would even the odds if she rushed him.

"Okay," he said, sounding as exhausted as she felt. "Now, tell me what the hell is going on here."

Patty was crying, still on the floor. "I just wanted to free you of her. I thought if she was dead..."

T.D. nodded, not taking his eyes off Jinx. "I stopped by your apartment before I came here," he said, without looking at Patty. Jinx heard the woman let out a cry as if he'd kicked her. "Had a little talk with Wyatt." Patty began to sob, her words lost in her tears. Jinx heard enough, though, to know that the woman had put Wyatt up to killing her up on that mountain. Now T.D. knew it, too.

"Did you really think that if you got Wyatt to kill Jinx that I would want anything to do with you?"

"We could get married," Patty said between sobs. "I would make you happy. You know I could."

"No, Patty, you and I are never getting married, especially after you almost got me killed. I will never love you the way I did Jinx. Never. You need to leave now, Patty. I don't think you want to watch what happens next."

Patty quit crying and wiped her face. "What are you going to do? You're in enough trouble. You can't kill her."

"Oh, I'm not going to kill her," he said, narrowing his

eyes at Jinx. "Though she might wish I was when I'm through with her. Now, get out of here."

Patty got to her feet, hesitated and then rushed out the door.

T.D. hadn't moved. He seemed to be waiting until he heard a car engine to make sure Patty was gone before he said to Jinx, "Take off your clothes."

ANGUS DROVE UP the road to the Flying J Bar MC Ranch as fast as he dared. It had only been a few days since he and his brother and cousin had driven up this road. So much had changed in that time.

He pulled in behind the sheriff's department car and got out, telling himself this was probably a fool's errand. Just as the sheriff had said, there was a deputy watching the house.

But as he came along the side of the car, his heart began to pound. The deputy would have seen him drive up. He would have gotten out of his car to see who it was. That was if he could.

As Angus reached the driver's side, he saw the deputy slumped over in the seat and swore. His first instinct was to race into the house. But he was smart enough to know that in his physical state, he might need all the help he could get. He eased open the deputy's car door, grabbed the car radio and called it in. Once the dispatcher told him that help was on the way, he headed for the house.

JINX LOOKED ACROSS the expanse of her bed at T.D. "You know I'm not taking off my clothes."

He chuckled. "It was worth a try." He put the pistol down on the nightstand. As he did, she bolted for the door. Of course he beat her to it, knowing exactly what she would do. Grabbing a handful of her hair, he dragged her back into the room and threw her on the bed.

She could tell the effort hurt him, just as she knew it wouldn't stop him. He knew this was the very last thing she wanted from him so he was more determined than ever. He climbed on top of her, and holding her down, began to rip off her clothing as he told her—as he had on the mountain—all the things he was going to do to her. Only this time, there was no one to stop him.

Even with him injured, she was no match for him. She knew she should just submit, just as she knew she wasn't about to.

The sound of the gunshot startled her. She looked up into T.D.'s sneering face as she felt his hold on her lessen. The second shot made him jerk. The third crumpled him on top of her.

Jinx felt his warm blood spreading over her chest. She pushed him off and leaped up from the bed to see the shooter standing in the shadowed doorway of her bedroom.

"Patty?" she whispered, seeing the glazed-over look in the woman's eyes and the gun still clutched in her hand, the barrel now pointed at Jinx.

"The two of you didn't even notice me come back into the room," the woman said. "The two of you were so busy that you didn't even see me pick up the gun."

"You know I wanted none of that," Jinx said, and saw something in the woman's expression that turned her blood to ice. "Don't make this worse, Patty."

"How could it be worse?" she asked on a sob. "I loved him. I would have done anything for him. Anything. But all he wanted was…you." She raised the gun to heart level and pressed the trigger.

ANGUS HAD BEEN moving stealthily down the hall toward the sound of voices when he'd heard the first gunshot. By the second gunshot, he was running. By the third, he'd reached the woman standing in the doorway of the bedroom.

Before she could pull the trigger again, he slammed into her. The report was like an explosion to his already pounding head. The woman went down. He went down with her as he fought to get the pistol out of her hand.

"Let me kill her!" the woman was screaming. "Please… You don't know what she's done. She ruined my life." She'd broken into sobs but was still fighting for the gun as they wrestled on the floor.

Normally, Angus could have easily disarmed the woman, but his head injury had left him weak and slow as if he was moving through quicksand.

Out of the corner of his eye, he saw Jinx and was instantly thankful she didn't appear to have been shot. She stepped down on the woman's hand holding the gun, grinding her boot heel in until he heard a cry and Jinx kicked the gun away.

He sat back against the wall, the gun at his side, as Jinx dropped to the floor next to him.

"What are you doing here?" she demanded. "You should be in the hospital."

Angus could only smile because he had to agree. "I was worried about you."

"Oh, Angus." She cupped his face and bent to kiss him. The sound of sirens filled the air, drowning out at least some of Patty's sobs. The woman had climbed up on the bed and now had T.D.'s head cradled in her lap. She was smoothing back his hair and telling him about a dream she had that involved Disney World.

Chapter Twenty-Two

"What's the plan now?" Marshal Hudson Savage asked from the head of the huge family table in the dining room at Cardwell Ranch.

"Don't cross examine them, sweetheart," Dana said sweetly but strongly. "They've been through enough without having to decide their futures at my dinner table right this moment. Have some more roast beef," she said to her twin sons seated across from her.

"I'm going back to Wyoming to help Jinx get everything ready for the sale of her ranch," Angus said, passing on more roast beef.

Brick took some, though, thanking their mother. "Mom, everything is delicious," he said after chewing and swallowing. His recovery was going slowly, making them all worried about him.

She smiled. "Thank you, Brick. You know you both gave us a scare. I'm just so glad that you're home."

"But for how long this time?" Hud asked, not to be deterred. Brick hadn't looked up from his meal, eating quietly as if lost in his own thoughts.

"I shouldn't be gone for more than a couple of weeks," Angus said. "Then my plan is to come back and go to work here on the ranch." He said this to his mother. "That's if you'll have me."

His mother's eyes filled with tears. "Really?"

"Finally," Hud grumbled. "You boys are going to be the death of me."

"Are you coming back…alone?" she asked, pretending interest in the small portion of mashed potatoes on her plate.

Angus laughed. "You are so subtle, Mom."

"Like a sledgehammer," his father muttered under his breath.

"Well?" she asked, clearly ignoring her husband.

"Alone, Mom. At least for now. Jinx and I both need some time."

"What about you?" Hud asked Brick.

"I've actually been thinking about what I might want to do once I'm healed," he said, motioning to the sling that had his mother cutting his meat up as if he was five. Angus could tell that his brother didn't mind. Like him, Brick seemed to be glad to be home. "I heard you might have an opening for a deputy marshal."

His father looked up from his meal in surprise. "Are you serious about this?"

Brick nodded. "I am."

"You have to go to the law academy, but if this is something you want…"

Angus could tell that their father was delighted at the prospect that at least one of their sons might be interested in law enforcement. Their older brother Hank lived on the ranch with his wife, Frankie, and Mary did the ranch's books. It had looked like they all might be involved in ranch work in this family.

He looked over at their mother. Clearly she'd prefer Brick not become a lawman, but she only took her husband's hand and smiled at Brick. "It will be nice to have you boys home," Hud said.

"I'll get dessert," Dana said and got up to hurry into the kitchen. Angus could tell that she was thinking about all the meals the family would be having at this table in the future. Tonight she'd wanted it to be just the four of them. But he knew they were in for a lot of big family celebrations at this table.

When his mother returned with a three-tiered chocolate cake, he said, "By the way, I thought Ella was going to be here tonight."

Dana shook her head as she began to cut the cake. Brick already had his fork ready and was saying how much he'd missed his mother's cooking, making her beam.

"Ella?" she said. "She wasn't around. Hank told me that he saw her leave." She stopped cutting to look up at him. "I think she's gone to look for her mother."

"Stacy?" Brick said as he took the slice of cake his mother handed him. "Where's she off to?" he asked and took a large bite of the cake and thick fudge-like frosting, one of his mother's favorite recipes.

"That's just it," Dana said. "We don't know. Stacy just left." She looked to her husband, who shook his head. "Maybe she just needs a break from all of us."

"Maybe," Angus said, but he could tell that his mother was worried about her sister.

"Ella will find her," Brick said. "That woman is like a bloodhound when she gets something in her head."

"I hope you're right," their mother said as she handed Angus his cake. "Now, tell me about Jinx. I want to know everything."

ON A BEAUTIFUL fall day, JoRay "Jinx" McCallahan drove into Cardwell Ranch in her pickup, pulling a horse trailer with her favorite horse inside. She slowed as she crossed the bridge over the Gallatin River to look down. The water was incredibly clear, a pale green that made the granite rocks along the bottom shine as if pure gold.

She breathed in the fall air scented with the river and the pines and looked up at the towering mountain with its rock cliffs before letting herself take in the ranch. The house was two stories with a red metal roof. And there was the large old barn that she recalled as a young girl.

Jinx smiled, thinking how strange life was that she was here again. Only this time, she couldn't wait to see that cowboy she'd pushed out that barn window all those years ago. Time heals all wounds, her father used to say. To some extent that was true. She still missed her father just as she missed the Flying J Bar MC Ranch she'd grown up on.

But it was a dull ache overpowered by the excitement she felt to be on the Cardwell Ranch again. She actually had butterflies flitting around in her stomach at just the thought of seeing Angus after these months apart. They'd talked on the phone for hours every day about everything but the future. Angus had left the door open.

"I'll be here if you ever want to come north again," he'd said. "I'll be waiting."

ANGUS WAS IN the barn when he saw the truck and horse trailer coming up the road. He stepped out, pulling his Stetson down to shade his eyes. He couldn't see who was behind the wheel. His heart leaped anyway. He'd been waiting for this day for too long not to know it had finally come.

As Jinx pulled up into the yard, he strode toward her truck, trying hard not to run. She opened the door and stepped out. Her beautiful copper hair caught the autumn sun. She reached back into the pickup for her straw hat and putting it on, looked in his direction.

By then, he was closing the distance between them, running toward their future. When he reached her, he grabbed her, wrapping his arms around her and lifting her into the air. She laughed, a sound that filled his heart with joy. Slowly, he lowered her back to the ground and looked into her beautiful freckled face. Now he would have all the time in the world to count every one of them, he thought and glanced into the warm honey of her eyes.

"Jinx," he said on a breath as light as a caress.

"Angus." She smiled, those eyes glinting. "You said to just drive up when I felt like it. I felt like it."

He laughed as his heart swelled to overflowing. "I'm so glad. Wait until you taste my biscuits."

She laughed. "You still have that bet going with Max?"

He nodded. "He promised to come up to the ranch." Angus looked into her eyes and knew that if he'd had a preacher standing by, he'd have married this woman right here and now. Looping his arm around her waist he pulled her to him and kissed her as if there was no tomorrow.

At the sound of the front door of the house banging open, he let her go. "Two seconds from now we are going to be mobbed by my family. Before that happens, I need to tell you something. I love you."

She nodded. "I love you, Angus."

"That's good because I don't have to look over my shoulder to know that the woman hurrying this way is my mother. She's going to want to know when we're getting married. I don't want to rush you but…"

Jinx looked over her shoulder, then back at him, grinning. "If that's a proposal—"

He dropped to one knee, pulled out the small velvet box he'd been carrying around for months. "It certainly is. Say yes. Please. The engagement can be as long as you want, I promise."

She laughed and nodded. "Yes."

He opened the box, took out the ring and slipped it on her finger. He heard his mother's cry of glee behind him.

"It's beautiful, Angus," Jinx said and kissed him as he rose to his feet again. "I don't need a long engagement since I've known for a long time I want to spend the rest of my life with you."

"Oh," Dana cried. "That is so beautiful." Then she was hugging the two of them as more family members began to show up.

Angus introduced his large family and extended family until the yard was full of Cardwells and Savages. It was as if they'd known today was the day to be on the ranch. He wondered if his mother had anything to do with this.

"I should have warned you about my family," Angus whispered to Jinx. "You can still change your mind."

Jinx shook her head. "Not a chance, cowboy."

"I'd like to tell you that it won't always be like this," he said.

"I love it." She looked around at all of them, most talking over the others as if her arriving had turned into a party. "I remember you telling me about your mother wanting all of your boots around her big dining room table. I want my boots under that table."

"You're killing me, Jinx," he said as he pulled her to him again for a kiss. "I can't tell you how long I've wanted this with you."

She nodded, her eyes bright with tears. "It's strange but I feel as if I've always been headed back here. I know it sounds crazy, especially knowing how hard it was for me to sell my family's ranch, but driving in just now, I had the strangest feeling that I've come home."

Angus pulled her closer. "Welcome home. Trust me, now that you're going to be a part of Cardwell Ranch, you should know it's going to be a wild ride."

* * * * *

MIDNIGHT ABDUCTION

NICHOLE SEVERN

I have enough self-awareness to know I worked damn hard on this book, so I'm dedicating it to me.

Prologue

They warned him not to go to the police.

He couldn't think. Couldn't breathe.

Forcing one foot in front of the other, he tried to ignore the gut-wrenching pain at the base of his skull where the kidnapper had slammed him into his kitchen floor and knocked him unconscious. Owen. Olivia. They were out there. Alone. Scared. He hadn't been strong enough to protect them, but he wasn't going to stop trying to find them. Not until he got them back.

A wave of dizziness tilted the world on its axis, and he collided with a wooden street pole. Shoulder-length hair blocked his vision as he fought to regain balance. He'd woken up a little less than fifteen minutes ago, started chasing after the taillights of the SUV as it'd sped down the unpaved road leading into town. He could still taste the dirt in his mouth. They couldn't have gotten far. Someone had to have seen something…

Humidity settled deep into his lungs despite the dropping temperatures, sweat beading at his temples as he pushed himself upright. Moonlight beamed down on him, exhaustion pulling at every muscle in his body, but he had to keep going. He had to find his kids. They were all he had left. All that mattered.

Colorless, worn mom-and-pop stores lining the town's main street blurred in his vision.

A small group of teenagers—at least what looked like teenagers—gathered around a single point on the sidewalk ahead. The kidnapper had sped into town from his property just on the outskirts, and there were only so many roads that would get the bastard out. Maybe someone in the group could point him in the right direction. He latched on to a kid brushing past him by the collar. "Did you see a black SUV speed through here?"

The boy—sixteen, seventeen—shook his head and pulled away. "Get off me, man."

The echo of voices pierced through the ringing in his ears as the circle of teens closed in on itself in front of Sevierville's oldest hardware store. His lungs burned with shallow breaths as he searched the streets from his position in the middle of the sidewalk. Someone had to have seen something. Anything. He needed—

"She's bleeding!" a girl said. "Someone call for an ambulance!"

The hairs on the back of his neck stood on end. Someone had been hurt? Pushing through the circle of onlookers, he caught sight of pink pajama pants and bright purple toenails. He surrendered to the panic as recognition flared. His heart threatened to burst straight out of his chest as he lunged for the unconscious six-year-old girl sprawled across the pavement. Pain shot through his knees as he scooped her into his arms. "Olivia!"

Chapter One

"Congratulations, Ramirez." Director Jill Pembrook swiped her index finger across the tablet's screen in her hands, and the entire network of monitors embedded into the conference table came to life. "You've got your next assignment."

A new case? It had been so long she was starting to think her past mistakes had caught up with her and negatively impacted her profile with the team. Agent Ana Sofia Ramirez bit back her smile as exaggerated congratulations and clapping from two other agents on the team filled the conference room. Her leather chair groaned as she leaned back to study the main screen behind the director, her fingernails skimming the table's surface. "What's the case?"

"Abduction of a six-year-old boy," the director said.

The room quieted, the silence almost a physical presence as the tendons between Ana's shoulders and neck tightened. Drawing a deep breath, she focused on the monitor in front of her. This was what she'd been trained for—finding the missing—but not a single agent around this table would volunteer for an assignment like this. "Timeline?"

"We've been given twenty-four hours. The father

is adamant no one but the agent he requested can get involved in the recovery, but the clock is already ticking, and we're going to use all available resources we have whether he likes it or not. That's where you come in." Director Pembrook turned to the largest screen at the head of the conference room, pulling up a map pinpointing a small section of private property a little outside Sevierville, TN. The petite, graying woman with sharp features at the head of the room had been a force to be reckoned with within the Bureau for nearly forty years. She wasn't a woman to disappoint, and Ana didn't plan on testing that theory. The director tossed a manila envelope across the table. "You'll go undercover as a former lover who's in town visiting and has heard the devastating news his son has been taken. I want you to get close to the father and find out what he could possibly gain from this abduction by keeping us in the dark. Agents Cantrell and Duran will provide support from this location until you say otherwise."

Maldicion. Damn it.

"If this is a targeted abduction, the kidnappers will have done their research. They might've already sifted through the people in the boy's life." Ana lifted her gaze to the men across the table from her. Agent JC Cantrell handled surveillance, Evan Duran worked hostage negotiations and Ana did whatever it took to find the missing. Together they made up only part of the Tactical Crime Division, and it looked like they were headed to Sevierville, TN, the last place she'd intended to set foot again. Too many memories. Too much pain. But the thought of passing on this case, when she'd battled so hard to make up for the past, built pressure behind her sternum. "What's the guarantee my cover won't be blown the instant I come into contact?"

"That won't be a problem during this investigation," Director Pembrook said.

While the FBI had massive resources and vast intelligence relating to criminal activity, they were headquartered in DC. The Bureau had regional field offices in major cities across the country to assist local police when needed, but that left smaller or rural towns with sparse populations without rapid support. More and more, agents and federal law agencies mobilized to remote locations to address large-scale crime scenes and criminal activity. Terrorism, hostage situations, kidnappings, shootings. But with the growing concern and need for ever-increasing response times to these criminal events, the Bureau saw the need for a specialized tech and tactical team, combining specialists from several active units. Together they made up Tactical Crime Division.

"How long has the boy been missing?" As one of the most successful hostage negotiators in Bureau history, Agent Evan Duran saved hundreds of lives over the course of his career by getting more information out of a suspect with as little commitment as possible on his part. If the kidnappers had made any kind of demand, Ana trusted him to mine for the intel she needed to find the victim. "Any demands?"

"Six hours." Director Pembrook took her seat at the head of the table. "And, no."

"There hasn't been a ransom call?" Ana swiped through the file directly from the monitor in front of her. Every forty seconds a child went missing somewhere in the United States. More than 460,000 children were reported missing each year. Of those missing children, almost 1,500 of them had been kidnapped, with most of those reports narrowing the suspect list to a parent or close relative as the abductor. There was a chance the boy's mother was responsible, which would account for the lack of demands or ransom. Or… Ana froze, paralyzed as she read the father's name on the police report. "Benning Reeves."

The boy who'd been kidnapped was Benning's son, Owen.

"He asked for you specifically, Ramirez." The weight of Director Pembrook's attention crushed the air from her lungs. She was the agent Benning had requested. Was that why she'd been given the lead on this case? Not because of her experience in recovering the missing but because she'd actually been intimate with the man keeping the FBI at arm's length during his son's kidnapping investigation.

The director was right. Her cover wouldn't be a problem during the investigation.

It was the truth.

Ana swiped her tongue between dry lips. "What about the girl? Olivia."

"She was taken, too, but local police recovered her minutes after the abduction." Relief coursed through her as the director's gaze narrowed, but Ana didn't have time to crumble under the pressure of Pembrook's study. Someone out there had taken Benning's son, and time was running out to get him back. The question was why. As far as she knew, Benning had kept his job as a building inspector for the city all these years, wasn't in debt and wasn't the kind of man to get himself mixed up in criminal activity. Assuming this was personal, why would someone target Benning through his children? "They believe she escaped her kidnapper's vehicle while in motion, but it's impossible to know for sure until her medical team lets law enforcement interview her. You need to be there when she wakes up and find out what she remembers to help recover the son. Whether the father wants the TCD officially involved or not."

She nodded. They could at least exclude the twins' mother from their list of suspects. Lilly Reeves had passed away giving birth to them six years ago. Ana struggled to control the racing pulse at the base of her skull. Benning had asked for her help with this case, but given the last time they'd been in the same room— the same bed—she didn't understand why. A single phone call had changed everything between them, and he'd moved on. He'd married a woman in town and had children not long after Ana had left. Now she was expected to reinsert herself back into his life in order to find his missing son.

There were far more qualified agents to handle this investigation, agents who hadn't put their entire career at risk because of one wrong decision. Agents who didn't have a personal connection to the case. What was she supposed to say to him after all these years? They hadn't spoken since that night, despite the small part of her that'd urged her to reach out, to reconnect with the only person she just couldn't seem to detach herself from. She swallowed through the tightness in her throat. No matter what'd happened between her and Benning, she couldn't let emotion cloud her judgment this time. A little boy's life was at risk.

"I'll look into the traffic cameras." Agent JC Cantrell shoved to his feet, locking light green eyes on her as he stood. Specializing in surveillance operations, the former soldier led most of TCD's surveillance ops, but whether those ops were completely legal was another question. Right now Ana didn't care. There was a six-year-old boy out there—alone and afraid. This was what their division had been trained for, what she'd been trained for. She wouldn't make the same mistake with this case as she had when Benning had been in her life the first time. JC headed for the door, Duran at his side. "With any kind of luck, I'll have a license plate for you and a location of the getaway vehicle in the next hour."

"Keep me in the loop and stay close to your phones. I'll call you if I need you." Ana pushed away from the conference table to stand, her long, dark hair inherited from her Hispanic father sliding over her shoulder in front of her. Sevierville wasn't far, only thirty miles southeast of TCD headquarters here in Knoxville, but if she wanted to interview Benning's daughter before the girl's medical team gave permission to local PD, she had to leave now. With a nod toward Director Pembrook, she pushed her chair into the edge of the table. "I'll brief you as soon as I'm finished interviewing Olivia Benning."

"Be careful, Ramirez." The director's voice carried across the conference room, stopping Ana in her escape toward the double glass doors. The weight of those steel-gray eyes drilled straight through her. "I assigned you this case because you have a connection to the victim's father and he's made it clear he won't play nice with anyone else, but don't let your emotions and that connection get in the way of doing your job." Pembrook's voice softened. "We can't afford to lose anyone else. Understand?"

The hairs on the back of her neck stood on end, but she couldn't turn around. She couldn't face the reality of Jill Pembrook's warning. Gravity increased its natural pull on her body. The backs of her knees shook as a fresh wave of memories penetrated the barrier she'd built over the past seven years. She curled her fingernails into the centers of her palms, and just as quickly as they'd charged forward, she closed the lid to the box at the back of her mind. She'd gotten good at that. Compartmentalizing, detaching herself from feeling the things she didn't want to admit to herself. Especially when it came to Benning Reeves. But underneath the numbness and denial, Ana understood the director's advice. Getting Benning's son home to his family would be her last chance to save her career. She'd failed a victim once. She wouldn't let it happen again. "Yes, ma'am."

BENNING REEVES CROSSED the small room for the eighth— or was it the ninth?—time in as many minutes. It'd been almost five hours since he'd woken in the middle of his house, his children gone. And Olivia… He slowed at the side of her hospital bed. Her small body nearly disappeared in the heaping of pillows and blankets he'd packed around her as her chest rose and fell in smooth, rhythmic breaths. The sedative the nurse had given her would keep his daughter unconscious for the next few hours. It was the only way to ensure her brain would get the rest it needed. He smoothed her short brunette hair away from her face. Truth was, the doctors had no idea if her memories would come back. Something about trauma-induced amnesia. Dissociative? She'd barely remembered her brother's name when she'd been questioned, let alone what'd happened to him after she'd escaped the SUV.

Tremors racked through his hand, and he forced himself to back away for fear of waking her. The kidnapper should've made contact by now, given him further instructions or proof of life. His ears rang. He needed to be out there looking for his son, but he didn't dare leave Olivia here on her own, either. Not after what she'd been through. Heat built in his chest. Someone had broken into his home, knocked him unconscious and taken his children. All because of what'd he found on that construction site.

The fire spread under his skin, and he closed his eyes as the all-too-familiar feeling of instability he'd kept in check all these years clawed for release. Benning unpocketed his phone, the sight of the photo behind the shattered glass immediately drowning the ringing in his ears. His pulse evened as he studied his twins' smiling faces as they tackled him from behind on the screen. He'd get Owen back. He'd already lost too many people in his life. He couldn't lose his kids, too.

A surge of awareness hiked his senses into overdrive, and Benning followed it to the hospital room door. Brown eyes ringed with green centered on him, and the world dropped out from under him. She'd come. In the minutes following Olivia's arrival at the hospital, he hadn't known who else to call. Or if she'd come back to Sevierville. The kidnapper had warned him not to involve law enforcement before knocking him unconscious, but Ana Sofia Ramirez wasn't just a federal agent. She'd been everything to him. Before she'd ripped his heart from his chest in the middle of the night without warning.

Her flawless Hispanic heritage intensified the angles of her cheekbones and nose, silky dark hair reflecting the fluorescent lighting from above, just as he remembered. Pressure built behind his sternum—had been for the past seven years—and he wanted nothing more than to close the distance between them in an attempt to release it. "Ana."

"I came as soon as I heard the news." She rushed toward him and dropped a duffel bag at her feet. Wrapping her arms around his waist, the woman who'd walked out of his life melted into him, and everything inside him quieted in an instant. The insecurity, the rage, the fear and the failure. Now there was only calm. Clarity. Hints of her perfume—something light and fresh—tickled the back of his throat as he buried his nose against the crown of her head. At five foot five, she fit perfectly against him. Toward the end of their relationship, he'd even believed she'd been made specifically for him. Skimming her chin along his shoulder, she set her mouth at his ear, eliciting a shudder from his spine, and lowered her voice. "The kidnapper could be listening. Pretend we're two friends randomly coming back into contact, and my team and I will do whatever it takes to get your son back."

His insides tightened. Right. Her team. The hug hadn't been personal, simply a way to get her message across. She hadn't come because he'd called in a personal favor. She'd come to do her job. But given the fact his kids had been targeted in order to get to him, he'd do whatever the hell she instructed. He just wanted his son back. No matter the cost. He increased the space between them, shutting down the internal reaction to her proximity exploding through him, and cleared his throat. "What are you doing here?"

"It's my parents' fortieth wedding anniversary. My brothers and I are flying in to surprise them, but then I heard about what happened, and I wanted to make sure you were okay." Weaving truth in with the lie. He'd read about that, how law enforcement officials, especially those assigned undercover work, trained to remember their stories by inserting bits and pieces of their own lives into their cover stories. Ana did have brothers. Three of them. But as for the wedding anniversary and wanting to check up on him, Benning was sure she'd improvised. Ana pulled her hair back in a tie and turned toward Olivia still asleep in the bed. Her knees popped as she crouched to unzip the duffel she'd brought. In his next breath she straightened with a small black box in her hand and moved toward the bed with the device raised out in front of her. Pulses of green light strengthened on the screen as she moved around the room. "How is she? Any news about Owen?"

She believed the kidnapper was listening. That was what she'd said. Waiting for him to see if he'd call the police? But unless the man who'd broken into his home knew Olivia would escape the SUV and which hospital room she'd be assigned when she arrived, Benning didn't see how it was possible after Olivia had been checked in. He'd been by her bedside the entire time, only her nurses and doctors coming in and out of the room. "Nothing yet. Olivia suffered a concussion when she escaped the SUV. Doctors aren't sure if the damage goes deeper than her short-term memory, but they'll—"

A red light flashed on the device in Ana's hand, and she stilled. With a quick glance over her shoulder toward him, she reached behind the faux wood head-board of Olivia's bed and detached something from the back. Swinging her hand toward him, she stepped away from his daughter and held out the miniature circle-shaped piece of metal. She extended her index finger of her other hand in a spiral motion to signal him to keep talking.

Someone had installed a bug in his daughter's hos-pital room. Either they knew she'd wind up in this hos-pital room or—Benning curled his fingers into tight fists as he ran through a mental list of people who'd stepped foot inside this room—one of the people on Ol-ivia's medical staff had placed the bug while attending to her injuries. He swallowed, tried to keep his voice even as Ana stared up at him. "They'll run more tests once she's awake."

"How are you doing?" She nodded before maneu-vering past him to the other side of the room. Dropping the bug into the glass of water at Oliva's bedside, she searched the rest of the room, not seemingly interested in his answer.

"It's been a long night," he said.

The light on her detector remained green. Physical relief smoothed her expression as she pocketed the black box into her knee-length coat when she was finished, and a hint of the woman he remembered returned. "The rest of the room is clear. They won't be able to hear any-thing now. I'll be sure to get the bug to one of the agents on my team. There's a chance we can trace it back to its owner and find out who took your son."

And there she was. The federal agent he'd fallen for the instant she'd walked onto that construction site seven years ago interviewing anyone on his crew who might've known about the disappearance of a local teenage girl. Benning latched on to the handrail of his daughter's hospital bed in an attempt to keep himself in the moment. "Assuming the man who took him is the same one who planted that bug."

But what were the chances the two weren't connected?

"Yes." She nodded toward him, her voice flat, unemotional, and his gut clenched. "You're bleeding. Has someone looked at that cut on the back of your head? I can stay with her—"

"I'm fine." It was a lie, but he wasn't about to leave Olivia's side. She'd already been through so much; he didn't want her waking up without him in the room. He tracked Ana's every move with an awareness he hadn't experienced since the night she'd left Sevierville all those years ago, noted the slight bulge beneath the left side of her jacket. Her service weapon. He'd imagined confronting her so many times, memorized what he'd say, how she'd react. None of it included him asking for her help, her armed with a gun or one of his children missing.

She'd made her choice. She'd decided her career was more important than what they could have together and had run off to save the world. He'd stayed here, and in the wake of losing her, he'd made the stupidest mistake of his life. He'd rebounded. When Lilly told him about the pregnancy, he'd married her, worked at building a real family together for the sake of their twins, despite the lack of love between them. It'd been nothing more than a one-night fling the night he and his late wife had gotten together, but that one night had changed the course of his life. Benning tucked his hands in his jeans. "Ana, I know why you left, but—"

"All that matters right now is getting your son back." Moving around the end of the bed, she hauled the duffel bag into an empty chair, her bangs hiding the dark shadows in her eyes. "That's why you requested me to work this case, isn't it? This is what I do."

Right. He'd read the articles splashed on the front page of *The Mountain Press*, watched the interviews on the major news channels. According to the media, her recovery rates were the highest in the Bureau. When it came to finding the missing, Agent Ana Sofia Ramirez was the best. Right now he needed the best to find his son. He'd shut down the urge to reach out to her over the years, telling himself she'd left for a reason and he was the last person she wanted to hear from, but as far as he was concerned, she would always be unfinished business. "The guy who broke into my house, the one who took my son. I think he's tied to one of the construction sites I inspected—"

A red dot centered over her heart, and Benning lunged.

A gunshot exploded overhead.

Broken glass hit the bottom of Olivia's bed and sliced across the exposed skin of his arm. Pain shot up his wrists as they landed hard on the cold tile. Her sharp exhale rushed across the sensitive skin under his chin and beard, and his heart shot into his throat.

Rolling him off her, Ana pushed to a crouch, her service weapon already in hand.

A familiar scream pierced through the settling silence.

"Olivia." He crawled toward the bed, trying to keep

as low as possible. Sunlight reflected off bright blue eyes matching his own as he leveled his gaze with the mattress, and he wrapped his hand around hers. The bruising along his daughter's wrists and arms had darkened over the past few hours, but even more terrifying: someone had taken a shot at them. "It's okay, baby. I'm here."

"Daddy." Her whisper tore through him.

Ana pressed her back against the wall beside the window, then straightened to crane her head around the windowsill. "We have to get out of here."

"I'm not leaving her." His phone vibrated in his pocket. He extracted his cell as Ana turned hazel-green eyes onto him. The number was blocked. Warning tensed the muscles across his shoulders. This was it, the call he'd been waiting for. Locking his gaze on Ana's, he tapped the screen to answer, then put the call on Speaker. "Who is this?"

"I warned you about involving law enforcement, Mr. Reeves," an unfamiliar voice said. "Now your son is going to pay the price for your mistake."

"Let me talk to him. Let me talk to my son." No answer. Benning tightened his hold on Olivia's hand, his breaths coming shorter and faster. "Let me talk to my son!"

The call ended.

Chapter Two

No payment demand or instructions. No proof of life. Whoever'd taken Benning's son wasn't following typical patterns for an abduction. Which meant this was more than a simple kidnapping. They wanted to hurt Benning, manipulate him. Or they wanted something from him. The question was why.

Ana scoured the parking lot two more times. A gunman couldn't fire a shot into a hospital without exposing himself, but there was no movement. Nothing to give her an idea of who'd pulled the trigger, or if they were still out there. She locked her grip around her weapon and turned toward Benning. Either way they were sitting ducks in this room. "Get her out of the bed. We've got to move."

He shook his head. "Olivia's not going anywhere. She needs rest. Her head—"

"You see these bruises around her wrists? How thin they are?" She closed the distance between her and the side of the bed opposite him. Ana flipped his daughter's hand over as gently as she could. "There's not enough skin damage for them to be caused by a rope or handcuffs. These are from zip ties, Benning. Someone bound her wrists while she was in that SUV, and she tried to get free, but she's not strong enough to get out of them herself."

He took a step back. "What are you saying?"

"I'm saying he let her go." She steadied her attention on him, tried to keep the warning out of her voice as much as possible. Benning was a smart man, but sometimes the fear of losing a child hazed over a parent's ability to string reality together. "Whoever took her, whoever took Owen? They wanted Olivia to be found. They wanted you in this room and planted the device we found to ensure you followed whatever instructions they'd given you the first time they contacted you." She studied his expression for any hint she'd hit the nail on the head, and her heart rate spiked as he flinched against the accusation. She was right, and the phone call he'd received seconds ago confirmed it. The kidnapper had warned him not to involve law enforcement, on threat of harming his son, because they weren't finished with Benning. "They knew exactly where to find you. Do you really want to put Olivia's life in more danger by staying here, or do you want to save both your daughter and your son?"

One breath. Two. Benning grabbed the near-empty IV bag, then scooped his daughter gently into his arms. Olivia's small body fell limp against his muscled chest as she continued to combat whatever sedative her doctors had put in that IV. He rounded the end of the bed, those bright blue eyes settling on her. Warmth shot up her neck and into her face as the veins in his sinewy arms fought to break through skin. He hadn't changed much over the years since she'd last seen him, but there was a new roughness to him, a strength that hadn't been there before and she couldn't look away. "Do whatever it takes to get her out of here. Okay? She's the only one who matters."

"I'll get you both out of here. I give you my word." The adrenaline rush increased her focus. She'd memorized the layout of the hospital before she'd left Knoxville. There were three exits from the second floor, not including the windows, but they'd take the stairs at the back of the building in case the shooter had stuck around. She headed toward the door and intercepted his path into the hallway. Adjusting her grip on her weapon, she pulled open the door a crack and studied both ends of the hallway. Lucky for them, Olivia's room was positioned in the corner, the closest to the stairs. Somehow, her kidnapper had gotten access, left the listening device and escaped without notice. Which meant they weren't dealing with an amateur. "Stay behind me. Use me as a shield if you have to."

"Okay." His voice dropped into graveled territory, as though he was fighting to keep the inflection out of his words.

She twisted her chin directly over one shoulder. "As soon as we're safe, you're going to tell me why someone would target your kids to get to you and who exactly was on the other end of that phone call." Because unless he trusted her, his son might not make it home alive.

She moved into the hallway, shouts hiking her nerves into overdrive. The officers assigned to sit on Olivia Reeves until she woke up would've heard the gunshot, but she and Benning couldn't wait around to give their statements. There was no telling how far the abductor would go to ensure they weren't connected to attempted murder and kidnapping charges. Or how many people they'd hurt along the way. She cleared the hallway, the lights reflecting off the white tile bright. Nodding toward the exit to their left, she maneuvered Benning and Olivia past her. "Stairs."

She followed close on his heels through the door as uniforms came around the corner down the hall. Carefully closing the stairwell door behind them, they descended the stairs and pushed through the maintenance exit on the first floor until crisp winter air brushed across the exposed skin of her neck. Swinging her weapon up, she swept the parking lot. No movement. Nothing to suggest an ambush, but she wouldn't let her guard down until Benning and his daughter were safe. "Black SUV five stalls back. Go."

They crossed the parking lot at a jog, but every cell in her body screamed warning as movement registered off to her left. She had only a moment to react. Ana shoved Benning and Olivia behind the nearest car with everything she had. Gunfire ripped across the asphalt. A bullet cut through the thick fabric of her coat as she fired back at the masked shooter taking cover behind a vehicle two rows over. Once. Twice. Olivia's scream pierced through the thud of her pulse behind her ears, but Ana couldn't focus on that right now. Both hands around her weapon, she centered herself behind a parked vehicle between her and the shooter and pulled the trigger three more times, but it was too late. The shooter was already climbing behind the wheel of a black SUV. Maybe even the same vehicle used to abduct Owen and Olivia. In the span of two breaths, he fishtailed out of the parking lot and disappeared down the street.

Hijo de...

"I think it's safe to say my cover is blown." Her exhales crystallized in front of her mouth as she turned back toward Benning and his daughter, the girl's hands locked over her ears. Her fingers tingled with the urge to comfort the six-year-old, but Ana chose to reholster her weapon and positioned her coat over the fresh wound in her side before Olivia saw the blood. The girl had already suffered so much. She didn't need more material for her nightmares. "Let's get her in the car. We can't wait around for the shooter to come back and finish the job."

Hauling Olivia into his chest, Benning straightened and secured his daughter in the back seat of the SUV. His mountainous shoulders and arms were massive compared to the girl's small frame as he brushed something from Olivia's chin, his whisper inaudible to Ana less than two feet away. He was careful of his daughter's injuries, caring, and Ana fought against the sudden tightness in her throat. There'd been a time she'd imagined him treating their future children's scrapes and bruises like he'd done with Olivia. Her throat threatened to close, and she turned away from the visual to dislodge the string of thought. She'd buried that future the second she'd snuck out of his room that night.

"Are you okay?" Benning closed the door, his focus on Ana, and her entire body heated as though he'd physically trailed a path down across her clavicle bone. He closed the small distance between them, reaching out, but she dodged his attempt to touch her. His expression fell, his hand falling to his side. "I thought you'd been hit."

"I'm fine." Lie. The pain crushed the air from her lungs. She'd most likely need stitches—maybe a surgeon—but she couldn't worry about that right now. They were vulnerable out here in the open. Targets.

Blood trickled into the waistband of her slacks, the ache the only thing keeping her in the moment. He had every reason to hate her for what she'd done, but right now the way he looked at her, as though she were the only woman in the entire world, weighed heavy on her chest.

It'd be so easy to fall back into old habits with him, to remember the way his entire face lit up when she walked into a room, the promises of forever he'd whispered into her ear from between the sheets, how happy they'd been simply curled up in front of the fireplace. It'd be easy to become attached to the man she'd walked away from, but she'd come back to Sevierville for one thing: to find Owen Reeves.

She couldn't do that without the truth.

Ana clamped her hand to her side, awakening her pain receptors all over again, and wrenched open the driver-side door. Every minute they wasted out here was another minute Owen was in the hands of his kidnapper. She wanted to bring him home. *Needed* to. "Get in."

Benning rounded the back of the SUV as she settled into the front and pushed the ignition button to start the engine. The interior filled with his wild, pine-and-dirt scent as he climbed inside, and she breathed a bit deeper, held on to it as much as she could in an attempt to dull the pain in her side. She'd missed that smell, a combination of soap and outdoors. Missed him.

"You can't go back to your house. The shooter could be waiting for you there." She maneuvered the SUV out of the hospital parking lot as sirens echoed down the street. The officers who'd been stationed to watch Olivia had called in backup, and while Owen Reeves's kidnapping fell under federal jurisdiction, they'd need all the help they could get. Ana hit the call button on the steering wheel, the line connecting almost instantly.

"Calling for help already?" JC asked. "This wouldn't be about Sevierville PD reporting shots fired at LeConte Medical Center, would it?"

"You read my mind. We've got an unknown shooter in a black SUV, no plates and local PD closing in on the scene." She pressed her foot against the accelerator, the weight of Benning's attention increasing as they sped from the hospital. "Think you could take care of that for me?"

"I live to serve." JC's laugh fought to lighten the tension tightening down her back, but Ana had a feeling that as long as Benning was involved, nothing would help. "I checked the traffic cams around the time of the kidnapping. There's no sign of the getaway vehicle. I've got IT working their magic, but someone brought down the cameras beforehand or knew where they were positioned so they could stay clear. We've got nothing."

Which meant the kidnapping had been premeditated. This was the work of a professional.

Benning ran one hand through his hair, leveraging his elbow on the passenger-side door. Frustration played clearly across his expression, and in that moment her instincts said there was more to this investigation than a simple kidnapping.

"Thanks, JC. Sevierville PD is about to bag a listening device I found attached to the back of the girl's hospital bed. I need you to see if you can trace it back to its owner. Call me if you find something." She ended the call, checked the rearview mirror for any vehicles behind them, then slammed her foot against the brakes.

The seat belt pressed into her chest as her body weight shifted forward from momentum.

"What are you doing?" Benning straightened, braced against the dashboard. Pushing his dark, shoulder-length hair behind one ear, he turned on her. "The shooter could be following us."

"You brought me into this investigation by requesting me specifically, but I can't do my job if you're keeping information from me. I think now's a good time to tell me who took your son, don't you?" Heated rubber filled her lungs, clearing his scent from her system. She faced him. "The kidnapper contacted you before that call in the hospital, didn't he? He warned you not to involve the police, so you thought if you reached out to a former acquaintance who happened to be an FBI agent, he wouldn't know. The listening device, the rifle shot through the window... This guy is a professional, Benning, and he has targeted you. What does he want?"

He stared out the windshield. Seconds ticked by, a minute. Pressure built behind her sternum the longer he took to answer, but when he turned that bright blue gaze to hers, her gut said she wasn't going to like the next words out of his mouth. "He wants the skull I found."

"A HUMAN SKULL?" she asked.

Snowflakes drifted across the windshield. January temperatures tunneled through his shirt, but the memories of what he'd found—evidence of what a killer had done—generated enough heat to haunt him for the rest of his life. Someone had kidnapped his twins and taken a shot at Ana through the window of his daughter's hospital room. Because of him. He couldn't keep the truth to himself any longer. "A woman approached me two weeks ago on the site of one of the buildings I was inspecting. She offered me fifty thousand dollars to give a residential project the go-ahead, but the crew had cut too many corners. There were sections of framing missing. The plumbing wasn't up to code." Benning smoothed his palms down his jeans, blood crusted on the underside of his fingers. Olivia's. Glancing toward his daughter in the back seat, he studied the perfect curve of her mouth as she slept—anything to distract him from the fact he'd almost lost her less than six hours ago. And that her brother had been taken. "I couldn't ignore any of that, so I said no. Told her I suggested she hire a new crew to do the job right before the city came in with a lawsuit."

Ana's uniquely enthralling eyes—the ones he'd dreamed about for years—softened. "What happened after you gave her your answer?"

"I couldn't get past the thought that she'd bribed inspectors before. She seemed…comfortable with the approach, so I started looking into the company's past projects." He shook his head. "I found settlement paperwork between Britland Construction and tenants who'd been injured or left homeless because their buildings weren't up to code. Years' worth, with millions of dollars at stake, but the problems were only getting worse, and somehow their projects kept getting approved by the city. I wanted to know why."

"You started investigating on your own." Ana leaned back in her seat, her expression smooth. How was that possible? How could she pretend nothing had happened between them—that she hadn't torn his life apart—and keep herself so…detached?

"I went to the police. They brought the woman in

for questioning, but there wasn't enough evidence to prove Britland had sent her to bribe me. Her lawyer threw around so much weight, the investigating officers couldn't even verify she worked for them. Dozens of families were being hurt every year because of this company's negligence and greed, and I couldn't let them get away with it. I'm the only inspector the city has, so when Britland needed another project across town inspected, I added the job to my afterhours schedule last night. I ripped open one of the main walls to check the electrical." He dug his phone out from his pocket and swiped to a photo he'd hidden in the cloud. "That's when I found this."

Ana took the phone from him, her fingers brushing against his, and everything inside him fired in a heated chain reaction. She'd always had that effect on him; had always been able to take total control of his body with a single touch, but despite the fact he'd been the one to bring her back into his life, he couldn't give in to those feelings now. Now he had to get his family back. That was all that mattered. "That's most definitely a skull." She brought the screen closer to her face. "We won't be able to narrow time or cause of death without my forensics team getting their hands on it, but that hole in the frontal bone looks like a gunshot wound."

He'd thought so, too.

"I called the police as soon as I found it, but before my call connected, someone shouted at me from behind. I turned around to find a gun and a flashlight pointed at my face. I thought the guy was site security, so I explained who I was, and why I was there and offered to show my work order, but when my eyes adjusted, I noticed the ski mask." His heart rate picked up as a fresh wave of adrenaline dumped into his veins. "He said he'd wished I hadn't found the skull, and that he was sorry. He had his finger on the trigger, and I knew then he was going to shoot me for what I'd seen, but then an actual security guard ordered him to lower his weapon. The shooting started, and I just grabbed the skull and ran."

"You said he was wearing a mask. Did you pick up on any other characteristics? Anything we can use to identify him?" she said. "An accent, tattoos, scars, clothing, the color of his eyes?"

"No, none of that." He shook his head.

She handed the phone back, seemingly determined to avoid physical contact this time. "Where's the skull now?"

"Safe." He hit the sleep button on the side of his phone. "At first, I didn't think Britland could be responsible. It'd be too obvious. There was a paper trail linking the payoffs to the victims, and the skull I found had been drywalled inside their own building, but as soon as I left the site, I knew I couldn't go home. At least not right away, in case the guy in the mask decided to follow me." Rage burned through him. He should've been more careful. Should've taken the skull straight to the police. He cleared his throat as his eyes burned. "My nanny—Jo West—was supposed to drop the kids off for a sleepover at a friend's house, but she called me saying Owen had been sick for the past few hours, and he wanted me to come home." Now his nanny was missing. "When I got to my house, I hid the skull in an old, unfinished brick fireplace my dad had started building when I was a kid, but when I got inside the bastard was already in my house. I fought him off as long as I could, but I couldn't stop him. He hit me from behind almost the second I walked through the front door. When I woke up, my phone was vibrating in my pocket, the house was quiet and Jo and the kids... They were gone."

Now the SOB had his son.

"He warned me if I involved the FBI or police, I'd never see my kids again, said I had twenty-four hours to turn over the skull before he'd start hurting them." He hadn't been fast enough, strong enough. But with the evidence he'd recovered, he was going to expose them all. He'd make sure they never hurt his family again, never hurt anyone's family again. "I know what I'm asking you to do, Ana. I know you don't want to be here, but these people went after my family. You're the only one who can help me find my son before it's too late."

Pain throbbed at the base of his head in rhythm with his racing heart rate.

"Then it's a good thing I came into town for my parents' surprise wedding anniversary." The hardened exterior she'd hidden behind the moment she'd stepped into his daughter's hospital room cracked as one corner of her mouth lifted into a smile. She put the SUV back in gear and pulled into traffic. "There's a safe house the FBI has secured outside of town. You and Olivia can stay there while I collect your bodiless friend from the fireplace. After that, our forensics unit can run dental and DNA for an identification and hopefully trace the victim back to the kidnapper. If he wants the evidence so badly, there's a reason. I'm going to find out what that reason is so we can get your son back."

Water and snow kicked up alongside the SUV as they headed out of the city, Main Street passing in a blur. In this quiet, Smokey Mountain town of less than 20,000 residents, there wasn't much in the way of scandal and crime, but when it hit, it hit hard and left a wake of grief behind. Plowed streets disappeared under a new layer of snow, the trees growing thicker as they headed southeast along the highway. Oliva's soft snores and the high-pitched clearing of slush beneath the tires coaxed him to relax, but he couldn't ignore the strained silence between him and the woman who'd amazingly put herself in harm's way for his daughter. "Thank you for taking the case. I didn't know who else to call."

"No need to thank me." Thin lines around her eyes deepened as though she was in the middle of an internal battle of some kind. "This is my job. This is what I'm trained for."

Was that all this was to her? A job? His gut clenched. He should've known better; should've realized reaching out to her wasn't going to change anything. He should've had enough sense to let the past die, but he hadn't been able to stop the loop of what-ifs since that morning he'd woken alone in his bed. Until he caught sight of the stain of blood pooling on her slacks. Benning jerked forward in his seat. Hell. She'd gotten shot, her wound had been bleeding this entire time and she'd kept it to herself. "Damn it, Ana, you're hurt. Pull over."

"I said I'm fine. It's been six hours since your son was taken. If we get stuck out here, we're not finding Owen before the deadline." The muscles along her throat worked to swallow. Her left arm hung limp at her side, her free hand gripped so tight around the steering wheel her knuckles threatened to split the translucent skin. "Besides, I've survived a lot worse than a bullet wound. Tell me about Owen."

A lot worse? What the hell did that mean?

Hesitation gripped him hard, but he couldn't argue with her logic. Every minute they were on the run was another minute his son didn't have. "He hates peanut butter. Won't go near the stuff. All he wants to do is sit on his tablet and watch those stupid videos online of other kids playing with toys, but I let him because it makes him happy." Adrenaline from the shootout at the hospital drained from his veins the longer he talked about Owen. "The kid can't go anywhere without the blanket I bought for him while Lilly was pregnant with them. Sleeps with it every night, takes it with him wherever he goes. Except school. That's where I had to draw the line."

That damn blanket was still right where Owen had left it in the middle of the living room floor during the abduction. His son must've dropped it when the kidnapper had rushed him out the door. Only now Benning wished he would've brought it with him, had something to hold on to of his son's. A minute passed, maybe more.

"I'm sorry about Lilly. I wanted to…reach out, but I wasn't sure after what'd happened between us…" She cleared her throat, redirected her attention out the driver-side window. "Has it been hard? Not having her around?"

He let her words settle, focusing on the topic of his late wife.

"At first." He couldn't really remember single moments of the first few months of the twins' lives. It'd been a blur of diaper changes and spit up, of having to take a leave of absence until he'd found the right nanny to take over, of trying to make sense of being a single father. Of trying to forget about the rookie federal agent who'd extracted herself from his life as quickly as she'd appeared. He studied the snow as it melted against the hood of the SUV. "My entire world got turned upside down. I had to start thinking of things like formula temperature, not being able to sleep for more than an hour at a time and which diapers worked better for girls compared to boys. To be honest, I still don't know what I'm doing or if I'm making the right choices for them." He scratched at the spot of dried mud on his jeans as heat flared into his neck and face. "Guess I should be grateful I got to do any of that stuff… Lilly didn't."

"I'm sorry." Sincerity laced her words. "I didn't mean—"

"No, it's okay." He'd healed from that wound a long time ago. "Lilly and I both knew what we were getting ourselves into, and we'd both accepted the possibility that we might not be able to make it work. We agreed what'd happened between us was a mistake, but I can't say I regret what came out of it. I wouldn't have Owen or Olivia if it wasn't for her." He twisted toward Olivia. "What about you? Got someone waiting for you when you head back to Knoxville?"

The idea she'd found happiness with another man— someone other than him—built pressure behind his sternum, which didn't make sense. She'd been the one to drive the wedge between them. What she did with her life after that shouldn't have even crossed his mind, but there she'd been, always emerging when he failed to distract himself or had a few minutes alone.

"No. The cases I work, the things I've seen…" Ana shifted in her seat, flinched against an invisible pain he couldn't see. She slowed the SUV on approach to one of the side roads off the highway up ahead. She turned that hazel gaze onto him for a moment as she maneuvered the vehicle up the long, winding drive to a cabin set a little less than an eighth of a mile back on the property. In an instant he was the man completely smitten with the rookie fresh from Quantico who'd been working her first missing persons case in Sevierville. "It's impossible to find the light when I have to spend all my time walking through the dark."

Chapter Three

Trees surrounded the property from every side, cutting them off from civilization. Ana climbed the short set of stairs leading up to a covered porch, old wood protesting under her boots. Nobody would be able to find them out here, and with the Smokey Mountains interfering with cell signals and transmitters, she, Benning and Olivia would be completely on their own.

Using the key she'd been given by Director Pembrook before leaving Knoxville, she pushed her way inside. Met with a spacious living room, pale stone and open ceilings, she dropped her duffel at her feet. The alarm panel to her right screamed for attention. She keyed in the code, also provided by the director, and moved to shed her coat. Pain registered as she pulled the heavy fabric from her shoulders, her T-shirt crusted to the wound. Securing the property—that was all that mattered right now. Then she could worry about digging the bullet from her side and recovering the evidence Benning had removed off that construction site. Heat brushed across her arms and neck as Benning carried his still-sedated daughter and her IV through the door. "You can put Olivia in one of the bedrooms over here. The fridge is fully stocked if you're hungry. I'll have someone on my team check in with her doctor about the head trauma protocol."

The girl had lost a lot of color in her face, her elvish features more gray now. Abducted, hospitalized, shot at. Ana could only imagine the nightmares coming when Olivia drifted off to sleep, and her heart lurched in her chest. To go through so much pain, at such a young age… It'd stay with her the rest of her life. Just as it'd stayed with Ana since she was that age.

But she had the chance to make sure that pain didn't tear Benning's family apart as it had her own.

"Thanks." He moved past her, the muscles along his neck and back flexing with every step as he headed around the short wall separating the entryway from the hallway. Smells of cinnamon and apples filled the space, but it would take a lot more than a few air fresheners to clear Benning's naturally intoxicating scent from her lungs. She'd been wrapped in a protective bubble with him for the past two hours inside the SUV. She wasn't sure if she could ever get him out from under her skin, but she'd keep her distance. His son's life depended on it.

Infierno. She forced herself to focus on the injury, peeling back the thin fabric of her T-shirt. To prove he didn't have this gripping hold over her. The bleeding had slowed, but the risk of infection out here was high. They were miles from any hospital, and with the bullet still inside, every move on her part only caused more damage. She had to secure the perimeter before arming the alarm system, then she could worry about the hole in her side. Sliding one arm back into her coat, she hissed as the pain increased.

"Where are you going?" That voice. His voice. Even

after all these years, it hiked her pulse higher and heated her insides. How was that possible? She'd buried her feelings for him a long time ago. She'd moved on, healed. Four words out of his mouth shouldn't leave her wanting more.

"I need to make sure the security measures are up and running." A wide expanse of floor-to-ceiling windows revealed miles of wilderness, mountains and snow. If anyone had tracked them here, those trees would be the perfect cover, but safeguards had been put in place once the FBI had seized the cabin from its last owner. Cameras, motion-activated lights, heat sensors. All of it could've been compromised over the past few weeks of heavy snowfall. She'd check every single one of them before leaving Benning and Olivia on their own. They would be safe here, but the tension tightening the tendons between her neck and shoulders hadn't lessened. It was one thing to come back to Sevierville to find a missing boy. It was another to hole up in a safe house with a former fling for as long as it took to find that boy. More than that, she needed distance, needed to clear her head—of him. Dropping the magazine from her weapon, she counted her remaining rounds and slammed it back into place. She holstered her gun. "Shouldn't take too long. I'll brief my boss while I'm out. I should be able to get a team to the scene at your house in the next hour or so."

"Ana, wait." Her name whispered from his mouth, but she couldn't look up at him, couldn't allow him to see the battle she forged to keep her expression smooth. "I need you to understand something."

Six words. That was all it took for that small glimmer of hope she'd held on to to burn through her, but she couldn't afford to give it oxygen. It infiltrated the invisible barrier she'd built over the course of the past seven years, uninvited, and threatened to break through her control. Their relationship—however powerful it'd been—was over. She'd made sure of that when she'd transferred back to Washington, DC, without telling him.

"My kids are all I have, and I will do whatever it takes to protect them and to get my son back." One step. Two. He shortened the space between them until that hint of pine teased her senses again. "Even if that means throwing a wrench in the FBI's investigation."

What the hell did that mean?

"You requested me to work this case, Benning, to recover your son. That's exactly what I'm going to do, but if you want the person who took him to pay for what they've done, you're going to have to trust me." Turning toward the front door, she huddled inside her coat to head back out into the cold. Where she belonged, an outsider looking in. Not with Benning. Not with his daughter. This was just another case. Once upon a time, they'd talked about having a family of their own, but this one wasn't hers. They never would be. She'd meant every word during the drive out here. She'd dedicated her life and her career to finding the missing and that decision had ended their relationship. Attachment to each and every victim and their families was only a distraction to that cause. She'd learned that the hard way. Seven years ago she'd let those emotions get the best of her. She'd made a mistake, and a victim had paid the price. "You should get some rest. You and Olivia have been through a lot."

A wave of dizziness directed her shoulder into the nearest wall.

"You're not going anywhere." A strong hand threaded between her arm and the uninjured side of her rib cage and spun her into a hardened wall of muscle. She pressed against his chest, but Benning's massive body wouldn't budge. He'd put on more muscle over the years, the ridges and valleys fighting to escape his long-sleeve T-shirt. She imagined it'd partly been due to the fact he lived on the outskirts of town, on the property he'd inherited after his parents passed away. Calluses on his palms spoke of working the land with his bare hands. He was so much bigger than she was at over six feet; stronger, too, but he'd never used that strength to intimidate her. It wasn't part of his genetic makeup. He released his hold on her, giving her a chance to retreat, but she was paralyzed. Frozen in place with him so close. "You're bleeding through your coat."

"Comes with the territory of getting shot." Pain lightened through her nerve endings as though reminding her she had yet to pull the slug from her side. Right. With the rush of adrenaline from the shootout and every cell she owned tuned to every cell in his, her body's priority had been pushed to the back of her mind. Then again, she wouldn't be able to do her job if she bled out in the middle of the safe house.

He maneuvered her toward the dining room table. "You got a first-aid kit somewhere in this place?"

"Should be under the kitchen sink." She pulled one of the chairs away from the table and collapsed into the seat, hand clamped to her side. Sweat slid down her spine, her heart pounding at her temples. It'd been two hours since she'd been shot. Looked like her body had decided it wasn't going to be ignored any longer.

In seconds Benning returned with the red-and-white box, set the case on the table and settled into the chair beside hers. "Get rid of the shirt."

"I can stitch myself." She reached for the needle and thread inside the kit.

"I know you can, but you took that bullet for me and Olivia." He took the supplies from her hand. "The least I can do is help get it out of you before you lose consciousness."

"Do you know what you're doing?" At this point she wasn't sure she cared.

"Owen needed stitches last year after running head-first into that old fireplace on our property I should've knocked down years ago. My sewing skills seemed good enough for him." Cold worked across her skin as he cleaned away the excess blood with alcohol pads in efficient strokes.

"Do six-year-olds usually have strong opinions about head wounds?" she asked.

"He was more concerned about the fact the gash would leave a scar." Silence descended between them, every move made, every brush of his fingers against her skin, every breath he took, pinging on her radar. Loose strands of hair hid his face, but she didn't have to see him to know what was going through his head right now. She'd memorized his tells a long time ago. "Why did you come back here?"

"You don't remember? You requested me to work this investigation." She studied the deep lines set around his mouth. Not much had changed about him over the years. He was still handsome as ever, but there was a heaviness in the set of his eyes now. The same man she'd left behind sat mere inches away, but the past few years had left him weathered, battle torn. Rugged. He'd taken on the sole responsibility of raising his children and keeping his inspection business afloat. She couldn't imagine the amount of pressure that'd been thrust onto his shoulders practically overnight when he'd lost Lilly and ended up with two small newborns to care for alone. But the way he was looking at her now, the way her body responded to his touch... It was just the two of them. The investigation, their shared past, it all fled to the back of her mind. "Or did the man who broke into your house hit you harder than you thought?"

"You could've handed it off to one of the other agents on your team. The FBI has an entire division dedicated to this kind of thing." Benning discarded the bloodied wipes, then opened a fresh package and cleaned the oversize tweezers he'd set out a few minutes ago. Standing, he unbuckled his belt, bringing her attention to those powerful thighs wrapped in denim. "But you took this assignment anyway." He handed her his belt. "Here, bite down on this."

Ana clenched the leather between her teeth as he pried at the edges of the wound with the head of the tweezers. She forced herself to keep her body relaxed, but the pain got the best of her after a few seconds. Ana screamed against the fire scorching through her side as he fished the bullet out of her. In seconds Benning discarded the slug onto the kitchen table. She shut down the primal urge to lean just a bit closer, to touch him for some warped sense of comfort, and spit out the belt.

"Does it matter?" Deep down she knew the answer. Why she'd taken the case when she could've pushed it off onto another agent. It had nothing to do with re-demption. "Finding victims is what I've been trained for, and I'm going to do whatever it takes to get your son back."

He nodded, threading the needle from the kit. After stitching the edges of her injury together in quick rows, he taped a fresh piece of gauze to her side and cleaned up the bloody mess she'd left behind. He stood over her. Bigger, more intimidating than he'd been a minute ago. "I know you will. Because if you can't, the bastard who took Owen is going to wish he'd killed me last night."

HE SMOOTHED THE backs of his knuckles across Olivia's forehead. The swelling where she'd hit her head—presumably when she'd jumped or been pushed from the kidnapper's SUV—had gone down, but she was still fighting against the sedatives the doctor had given her. Red flannel and pale bedding surrounded her small form on the queen-size bed. The saline bag attached to her IV had been emptied within the last hour, and he carefully unscrewed the connection, then wrapped her hand—needle and all—with gauze at the direction of her doctor's message. With only two beds in the massive cabin, he and Olivia would be bunking together, but he couldn't sleep. Not with Owen still out there. Alone. Afraid. His eyes burned as thoughts of how this investigation could end filled his head. If Benning handed over the skull he'd found in that building, what were the chances his son's kidnapper would let Owen go free? What would stop them from ripping Olivia's brother from her life?

"Can't sleep?" Her voice slid through him, stretching into the deepest parts of his mind to chase back the uncertainty clawing at him from inside. Ana's boots echoed off the hardwood floor as she closed the distance between her and the end of the bed. She'd gotten rid of the stained clothing, her shoulder holster and weapon stark against her white T-shirt, and in an instant, he had his answer. Ana. Ana would stop them from tearing his family apart. Just as she stopped so many others. She studied Olivia in the bed, then handed him a steaming mug of dark liquid.

"She's hogging the bed." The ceramic burned the oversensitized skin of his palms, but he only held the mug tighter. To keep him in the moment, to feel the pain. To remind himself that no matter how she still might affect his biological reactions, Ana was here to work this case and nothing more. He took a sip of his coffee. Decaf. "Unless you're willing to share?"

The idea drilled down through his core, eliciting too many tempting visuals.

"I think you felt me up enough getting the bullet out of my side." Her smile—the one he hadn't been able to forget after all these years—flashed wide, and his nerve endings caught fire. This right here. This was one of the reasons he'd fallen for her in the first place. The quick banter, her jokes. No matter how dark the situation, she'd always had the ability to lighten the mood, and the hollowness that'd carved straight through him the moment he'd learned she'd left him ebbed for the first time in years. Maneuvering around to his side of the bed, she pulled up a chair. The lamp beside his daughter's bed reflected the natural sheen of Ana's long, dark hair as she rested her heels on the edge of the mattress beside his. Would it still be as soft as he remembered? "I briefed TCD on the latest developments of the case.

The director is sending two agents to your property to oversee processing the crime scene. Good agents, who know what they're doing. With any luck, they'll have something we can use to identify the man who took your son and where he's keeping Owen."

He didn't have to look at his wrist to see how many hours were left until the deadline the kidnappers had given him. It was as though the countdown clock had become part of his consciousness. Always there. Always ticking off the seconds one by one. Owen had been taken close to nine hours ago. The man who'd broken into his house had given him twenty-four to hand over the skull and any other evidence he'd uncovered before his son paid the price for his mistake. Would the agents sent by Tactical Crime Division be able to process the scene at his house before time ran out?

That all-too-familiar sense of instability rocked through him.

"I need to hand over the evidence." Benning shoved to his feet, his entire body buzzing with the need to take action. He should be out there looking for his son, doing whatever it took. Not holed up in some safe house imagining all the ways this investigation could go wrong. Placing the coffee mug on a side table, he scraped his fingernails across his scalp, shoulder-length hair caught between his fingers. Long stretches of trees and mountains on the other side of the massive floor-to-ceiling wall of windows increased the isolation growing inside. The sun had started dipping behind the Smokey Mountains. They were running out of time. Everything—the kidnapping, the shooting—it was all on him. "None of this would've happened if I hadn't started looking into Britland Construction. I should've left it alone. I'm the one who's supposed to be responsible for him. I promised him I would always keep him safe, and now Owen's out there in the hands of a possible killer because I wanted to play detective."

"You and I both know once you hand over that evidence, the person responsible for taking your son won't let you or your family walk away. You're too much of a risk." Her voice dipped to soothe the rough edges of anxiety tearing him apart from the inside. Movement registered from behind, and he turned to find her setting her own mug on the end table beside the bed. She closed the empty space between them without a single sound, taking special care not to wake Olivia. She motioned toward the bed with the crown of her head, but he couldn't look away from her, couldn't ignore the sudden shift in her expression. "Do you see that beautiful little girl there? She's alive because of you, Benning. You protected her from getting shot in that parking lot, and you tackled me to the floor in her room before the shooter could take me out. Neither of us would be here if it weren't for you."

She was right. Turning over the evidence wouldn't guarantee Owen's release, but his insecurity—the need for action—pricked at the back of his neck. "I want to be the one out there, looking for him."

"I know, and I know it doesn't feel like you're doing much, but I promise you, you are exactly where you need to be." Raising her hand, she settled it on his forearm. Heat and electricity coiled together in a dangerous combination that traveled down his spine. Tantalizing hints of her perfume nudged at the raw memories he'd tried to forget, and it took everything inside him not to give in. "We're going to get your son back. Together."

Her confidence, combined with her hand still on his arm, slowed his racing heart rate, and suddenly he was more aware of her than ever. Aware of the way her bangs settled along the curve of her cheeks, the way the swell of her lower lip was slightly fuller than the top and how the brown in her eyes had seemingly deepened over the past few minutes. She was a strong, intelligent, confident woman who'd committed herself to saving the lives of strangers on a daily basis, not to mention she was one of the most intense people he'd ever met. Admirable. Honest. Observant. Everything he thought he'd wanted in a life partner. Gravity pulled his gaze to her dark red fingertips resting against his skin. Until she'd left without a word. "Tell me why I had to find out you'd requested a transfer to Washington after you'd already left."

She let her hand slip away, the burn of her touch chased back by the cold penetrating through the wall of windows on his right. Diverting that mesmerizing gaze of hers toward his daughter in the bed, she took a step back. "Benning, we don't have to do this now."

"I was afraid you were dead." The admission tore from him. The hollowness he'd struggled to fill had been increasing every second since the moment she'd walked into that hospital room, and he couldn't take it anymore. "I called the police, the hospitals, the FBI, anyone who might've been able to tell me where you were or what'd happened to you. I looked for you for three days, Ana, with no phone calls, no messages, no emails or texts." He forced himself to take a deep breath before their conversation woke Olivia. "I woke up, and you were just…gone. I want to know—"

"Because my partner found her body." A hardness

etched into her expression, her voice dropping into level territory. No emotion. No infliction. In an instant, the woman who'd joked with him a few minutes ago disappeared. Nothing but the cold, distant, detached federal agent he'd believed her capable of being all these years.

Confusion gripped him hard. "Whose body?"

"Samantha Perry," she said.

He'd heard that name before. Why did it sound so familiar? Somberness overcame him, his hands relaxing at his sides. Recognition flared as snippets of memory of his and Ana's first meeting rushed to the front of his mind. The first time he'd set eyes on her, she'd been partnered with another agent, but while Benning couldn't remember her partner's name, he could never forget Samantha Perry. Hell. "The teenage girl you'd come to Sevierville to find."

"They found her in the corner of an alley between two restaurants in Knoxville, discarded like a piece of trash three months after she disappeared." Her eyes remained steady on his, but almost absent, distant in the way she never blinked. "I was assigned to find her. I promised her family I would find her. She was an innocent fifteen-year-old girl who'd been taken from school by a janitor named Harold Wood who worked there, but we couldn't prove it. We searched his house, his car, the entire school. There was no sign of her, of her clothing, DNA, nothing, but her best friend swore she'd seen him on campus the day she went missing. The only proof that could've nailed that bastard to the wall was if her body turned up, but that wasn't good enough for me. I needed to find her alive, but I was too late. I failed her." Ana unfolded her arms, her gaze suddenly alive, the muscles across her shoulders hard. "She died because I let myself get distracted. With you."

His stomach dropped. A distraction?

"The minute I got that call from my partner, I swore to myself I would never let my emotions cloud my judgment again. So yes, I requested the transfer, and as soon as I got it, I left." She took a single step toward him. "Because every minute I wasn't focused on finding Samantha Perry was another minute she'd been tortured, violated and alone." Her expression smoothed as though she couldn't hold back the exhaustion and effects of blood loss anymore. Defeated. "I can't live with the weight of another life on my shoulders, Benning. Even for you."

Chapter Four

She strengthened her grip on the splintered wood railing off the cabin's back patio, staring out into nothing but darkness. Snowflakes clung to her hair and T-shirt as January temperatures dropped with the setting sun, but her heart rate hadn't slowed yet. Of all the people she'd been forced to discuss her part in that failed investigation with, she never thought Benning would be one of them. Then again, she never thought she'd have to come back here.

Her cover story hadn't been all that far off from the truth. Her parents were still living out their happily-ever-after, only not here. They'd relocated back west a few years ago for the warmer temperatures and open desert. As far as she knew, her three older brothers were still assigned to their respective law enforcement agencies, but it'd been years since she'd talked to or seen any of them, and right now she ached for that anchor. For something—someone—to keep her from getting dragged below the crushing weight she'd carried for the past seven years. Her family had tried to keep her head above water, but in the end, they'd realized there'd been nothing they could do to convince her Samantha

Perry's death wasn't her fault. She'd have to live with that for the rest of her life.

It wasn't until Director Pembrook approached her in Washington a year ago—offered to give her a chance at redemption—that Ana had considered coming within one hundred miles of Sevierville. Because the truth was, leaving Benning had been one of the hardest decisions she'd ever had to make, even if it had been for the right reasons. Which didn't make sense. They'd only been seeing each other for a few months while she'd worked the Perry investigation, not nearly long enough to develop anything lasting. But she couldn't deny those short few months had changed everything.

The sliding glass door protested against the metal track from behind, but she didn't have the energy to face him yet. Forcing herself to take a deep breath, she studied the patterns her exhales made in front of her mouth. No matter what'd happened between them or how close to the surface her emotions seemed to get when he was near, she still had a job to do. Protect him and his family against the threat and get his son back. That was all that mattered. "You shouldn't be out here or anywhere close to the windows—"

"Are you a spy?" a small voice asked.

"What..." Ana turned to find Olivia huddled in one of the flannel blankets from her bed barefooted, a few feet away. Perfect ringlets of brunette hair framed round cheeks and bright blue eyes. Snow melted around the girl's purple-tipped toes, and she crouched low to level with the girl's gaze. She reached out, rubbing her hands up and down the girl's arms over the blanket to generate some semblance of heat, but with the light sheen of sweat clinging to the girl's face, Ana had a feeling the cold would have a hard time penetrating through. Curiosity bled into Olivia's wide-eyed expression. "What are you doing out here? You're going to freeze to death."

"Deflecting direct questions." The girl cocked her head to one side, suddenly seeming so much older than her six years of age. "That's exactly what a spy would do."

"I'm not a spy." Ana couldn't hold back the laugh escaping past her lips and reached into her back pocket for her credentials. Showing the girl her ID, she smiled as Olivia's small fingers smoothed over the plastic protector of her thin wallet. "I'm a federal agent. See?"

"Agent Ana Sofia Ramirez of the FBI." Olivia's smile stretched wide across her bruised face. "Cool! I've never met a federal agent before, but I read about them all the time. Detectives and private investigators, too."

"Yeah? Do you have a favorite?" Ana asked.

"There's a whole series about a girl Sherlock Holmes who solves crimes, but she's pretending to be a boy so the police don't know it's her." Animation chased back the dark circles from beneath Olivia's eyes, followed by pride. "I've read all the books six times."

"Wow. You must really like reading." Sliding her wallet back into the rear pocket of her jeans, Ana winced at the loud growls coming from her stomach. "You know what? I haven't eaten in a while, and I was thinking of making some chocolate chip cookies. How about I make the cookies, and you tell me about all the other books you've read?"

The girl nodded, then dragged her oversize flannel blanket edged with melted snow back into the cabin. Closing the sliding glass door behind them, Ana scanned the main floor, but didn't see any sign that Benning was aware his daughter had escaped her room. She wasn't a doctor. She didn't have the deciding power as to how long Olivia needed rest or if she should be out of bed at all. But Benning did, and the last thing she wanted was to step over the parenting line. Tensions between them were strung tight enough. "Do you think your dad would like some when we're done?"

"He's in the shower." Olivia climbed to the top of one of the bar stools at the counter's edge, the blanket falling from her small shoulders. Bruising darkened in thick patches across the girl's pale skin, the stitches across the laceration in her head somehow more pronounced now. It'd been ten hours since Olivia and her twin brother had been kidnapped. Leaving only fourteen to get him back. "He doesn't know I'm awake, but I didn't want to sleep anymore."

"I see." After pulling the dry ingredients from the pantry, a few eggs and butter from the fridge, Ana set them out on the granite-topped island. Offering Olivia a whisk, she set about measuring the ingredients into a large bowl. "Well, I won't tell him you're out of bed when you're supposed to be resting if you don't tell him how much of this dough will actually be made into cookies. Deal?"

"Deal." Olivia took the whisk from her and attacked the ingredients as fast as she could. Flour, egg and sugar flew over the edges of the bowl onto the countertop, her laugh rising over the sounds of the metal whisk scraping against the bottom of the bowl.

"Okay. Take it slow. Slower." Ana automatically shot her hands out to save what was left of the batter. But after a few seconds nearly the entire contents of the bowl were spread across Olivia's stained pajamas, the countertop, and flecked into Ana's hair. Just witnessing the brightness in the girl's eyes after she'd had to suffer so much hurt lightened the persisting knot coiling tighter at the base of Ana's spine. In the next second the girl pulled the whisk up straight, big globs of unmixed ingredients dripping over as her smile flashed wide. Warning exploded through Ana's system. "No, no, no, no. I don't think so. Olivia, I swear, if you fling that at me, you're going to be in so much trouble—"

With a flick of Olivia's wrist, the batter flew straight across the island.

Gooey pieces of egg and dried blobs of batter slammed into Ana's face, then dropped down onto her clean shirt and the floor. *Santa madre de…* An exaggerated growl tore from her throat as she dashed through the kitchen to the other side of the counter. Feigned seriousness tainted her words. "I'm going to get you for that. I just changed into this shirt!"

Faster than she thought possible, Olivia jumped from the stool and ran to escape, the whisk still in her hand. Grabbing a spatula from the countertop, Ana scooped a chunk of cookie mix onto the utensil, then flung it across the kitchen. Olivia froze, her eyes and mouth wide. "Bull's-eye."

The next few minutes passed in a blur of flying cookie dough and laughs until both of them were too tired to move. Settling onto the floor, their backs against the island cabinets, Ana positioned the bowl of finished dough between them with two spoons. She fought to catch her breath. Over eight hundred hours of physically demanding firearms training and tactical operations, and she'd been worn out by a six-year-old with a penchant for mystery novels. Chunks of dough fell from cabinets across from them, but there would be plenty of time to clean up. Later. Right now they'd enjoy the sugar rush. The stitches in her side ached as her lungs struggled to keep up with her heart. "Whew. You, my friend, are a worthy opponent. I think you hit me way more times than I hit you."

Olivia scooped a spoonful of dough into her mouth. "I always win when me and Owen play Nerf guns. I'm a way better shooter than he is."

Ana set down her spoon. She'd been trained in child forensic interview techniques, the protocols running through her head. When it came to questioning children who'd been part of a crime or witnessed a crime, it was best to take it slow. She'd already developed a rapport with the girl, but there was a chance that not only wouldn't Olivia want to remember what'd happened to her brother but also couldn't because of the head trauma she'd sustained. Just as her doctors had diagnosed. "Can we talk about your brother? About what happened after that man took you away from your dad?"

The girl's chewing slowed, those bright blue eyes that matched her dad's losing a bit of light. Sliding her heels toward her rear, Olivia went back in for another scoop of dough, but something had changed. Could she have remembered something? Hesitation and nervousness played strong across her expression. Her heart-shaped lips rolled between her teeth. "I don't remember anything."

"Okay." But it certainly looked like Olivia was keeping something to herself. "But you know not even your favorite Sherlock Holmes can solve a case unless she has all the information she needs. I would really like to find your brother for you, Olivia. For you and your dad. Isn't that what you want?"

"No!" The girl shoved to her feet, throwing the spoon as hard as she could across the kitchen. Those ringlet curls bounced off her shoulders as she dashed across the house.

"Olivia, wait!" Ana ran after her.

"Olivia, what are you doing out of bed?" Benning's soothing voice preceded the rest of him. His damp, glistening bare chest reflected the droplets of water dripping from his shoulder-length hair. He lowered into a crouch to catch his daughter around the waist, dressed in nothing but a pair of jeans, and Ana's heart threatened to beat out of her chest. Familiar blue eyes, immediately darker in that instant, locked on her. "What's wrong? What happened?"

Sobs racked through Olivia's body as the girl buried her head between Benning's neck and shoulder, and Ana could do nothing but watch. Every moment of the fun she and Olivia had had together vanished in the span of a few words. "I don't want to remember!"

BENNING CLOSED THE door to his and Olivia's room behind him. He'd calmed her down enough to quiet her sobs, but nothing would settle the fear hooking deep into her head. She didn't want to remember what'd happened when she and her brother had been taken, and he couldn't blame her. There was nothing he could do—nothing he could say—to make his six-year-old daughter believe she wasn't responsible for what'd happened to Owen, even if she had been able to remember something that would help find him. And he wasn't about to push her fragile mental state more than he already had.

Abducted, suffering head trauma, being shot at... Olivia had been through more in the past ten hours than most children experienced in their entire lives. How much more could he honestly expect her to take before she broke?

Fisting the T-shirt he'd discarded before hitting the shower, he headed back toward the kitchen barefoot. Even with the self-imposed distance between them and the outburst from his daughter, he couldn't get Ana's words out of his head. She blamed herself for the death of that girl, the teenager who'd gone missing seven years ago. But deeper than that, she blamed him. Isn't that what she'd meant when she'd sworn not to let her emotions cloud her judgment again? That the feelings they'd had for each other had caused her to lose focus? It'd taken both of them jumping into that relationship with both feet, and that made him as much responsible for her imagined failure. He and Ana had only been together for a few months, but those few months had been the most intense days of his entire life. He remembered every second of them, and the fact that Ana was trying to forget—to discount everything between them— knotted his gut tighter.

Every cell in his body froze as he stepped directly in a wet pile of what he hoped to hell was raw cookie dough. The island in the center of the kitchen was a mess. Flour, egg shells, sugar and random land mines of chocolate chips scattered over the countertop. Bowls, whisks, measuring cups. The place resembled a battlefield, and there, in the center of it all, Ana attempted to clear the casualties from the cabinets. He couldn't help but smile at the combination of small bare footprints and larger boot prints dusted into the floor. "Did you at least win?"

"Not even close. But to the loser go the spoils." Turning, she pushed her bangs out of her face. She held up a half-eaten bowl of unbaked dough, specs of flour and butter crusted into her hair, as she spooned a mouthful of sugar and butter past her lips. His heart jerked in his chest. In that moment she wasn't the federal agent assigned to recover his son. Right then, she was the woman who'd gotten his daughter to laugh. That sound, the sound of Olivia's exaggerated screams, had pulled him from the shower, but what he'd seen would be burned into his memories forever. Ana chasing his daughter around the counter with a spatula. Olivia's wide smile that he feared he'd never see again after what she'd witnessed. For those gut-wrenching seconds, the kidnapping, the evidence he'd stashed on his property, the reason for Ana coming back into his life… It'd all disappeared. In a matter of minutes he'd gotten a real-life glimpse into the fantasy he'd constructed in his head. A family—his family—complete. Happy.

"That right there makes losing worth it. I'd offer to share, but I don't want to." Speaking around her mouthful of dough, she studied the stains across her shirt, the dish towel still in one hand, and Benning couldn't help but follow her gaze across the long, lean muscle running the length of her body. Heat speared through him as the past rushed to meet the present. The feel of her skin against his, how he'd memorized every scar, every mole, with his hands. She hadn't changed a whole lot over the course of the few years. If anything, Ana Sofia Ramirez had only become more beautiful, more…

tempting. "Although, I'll admit I didn't think she'd destroy me this bad."

"You got hustled." He hobbled to the kitchen sink to clean the dough off his foot. Trying to focus on the raw egg stuck under his heel instead of the reaction his study of her had ripped through him, he gave in to the laugh rumbling in his chest. "That girl asked me to teach her how to shoot my rifle when she was four years old so she could help the police solve crimes. The only way I can ever get her to calm down during a temper tantrum is to promise to let her listen to an episode of a true crime podcast. She loves the idea of saving lives and catching bad guys and has better aim than anyone else I know. She's not afraid to show it, either. Next, she'll want me to take her to the police station to ask if she can help solve one of their cases."

"Well, maybe I can give her a tour of TCD headquarters in Knoxville one day. You know, give her a chance to see what federal agents really do on the job." Ana stilled, the weight of her attention pressurizing the air in his chest, but he didn't miss the assumption there would be a *one day* for them. That she wouldn't disappear from their lives after Owen came home, and his blood pressure spiked. She cleared her throat as though she'd caught herself making promises she might not be able to keep. Just as she had with Samantha Perry's family. "You must be proud. She's going to make a hell of an agent one day."

"That's her plan, and probably why she opened up to you the way she did. I can tell she admires you, what you do." Benning straightened, echoes of their earlier conversation replaying in his head on a nonstop loop. He tossed the paper towel he'd used to clean his foot in the trash beside the island. "So do I, to be honest. The work you and your team do saves lives. I know I already said thank you, but I meant it."

"Like I said, you don't have to thank me." She dropped that mesmerizing gaze to the counter, sweeping the spread of flour into the sink set into the island with one hand, and swiped beneath her nose with the other. Touching her face had always been a nervous habit. "All part of the job."

"Is that what this is for you, Ana? Just another job? Because this case is definitely a lot more personal to me." Benning maneuvered around the counter, his bare chest nearly pressed against the exposed skin of her arm. He set his hand over hers on the granite, her quick gasp searing through him. Her warmth penetrated past skin and muscle, deep into his bones. "After what you told me about the Samantha Perry case, I realize now how hard it must've been for you to come back here, and you're standing there as if none of it affects you. But is that how you really feel?"

He wanted—no, *needed*—to know. Was this going to play out exactly as it had between them the last time? Had he made a mistake requesting her to work this case?

Her mouth parted. "I…"

Skimming his fingers along the back of her hand, he trailed a path up her arm to her jaw, and all of his thoughts burned away. There was only the two of them. The softness of her flawless skin and hardness in her invisible guard. After everything that'd happened, after everything they'd already been through in the short span of time she'd walked back into his life, he'd struggled to keep the uncertainty, the rage, the fear, at bay so he could stay strong for Olivia. To prove that he could protect her from any threat, be the father she and her brother deserved. But Ana...stripped him of all of that. With her, Benning felt raw, exposed, bare. She was real. She was here. Not a memory—a fantasy—anymore, and it took everything inside him to pull himself away from her. "You had some cookie dough on your chin."

She'd left because she believed her emotions clouded her judgment on the Samantha Perry case, and he wasn't about to complicate anything else between them. Not when it was his son's life at risk this time. Ana turned her gaze up to his, a small tremor crossing her shoulders, and an invisible anchor settled inside his chest in the dark, watery landscape of this case. No matter what happened, Ana would bring his son home alive. He had to believe that. He had to believe in her. Otherwise, he'd have nothing left. "Thanks."

A soft trill broke the silence spreading between them, but she didn't move.

"I think your phone is ringing." He cleared his throat, trying to drown the surge of awareness burning through him, and stepped away. It was for the best. Because anything that happened between them would only take away from their focus on finding his son, and that wasn't a risk he was willing to take.

Ana pulled her phone from her back pocket, running one hand through her hair, but only ended up streaking more flour into the soft strands. Tapping her cell's screen, she answered the call and pressed Speaker. "What do you have for me, JC?"

The agent she'd called from the car. The muscles down Benning's spine contracted as every sense he owned homed in on the voice on the other end of the line. Had the team dispatched to the crime scene at his house found something that could tell them where Owen was being held? He hiked his T-shirt over his head and shoved his arms through.

"Sevierville PD is still working the scene, but I can tell you right now, it's not looking good," JC said. Tension replaced the rush of sudden desire throughout Benning's body. What the hell did that mean? Static cut through the line, but given the cabin's proximity to the Smokeys, it was a miracle they'd received the call at all. They were two hours out of town, with nothing and no one around but trees, the mountains and wildlife.

Three distinct lines deepened between Ana's dark eyebrows. "What are you talking about?"

"We searched the property and found the old outdoor fireplace a few hundred feet from the house you'd told us about. Kinda hard to miss seeing as how the entire thing was on fire. Bad news is, that skull you sent the photo of with the gunshot wound wasn't inside," JC said.

"How is that possible?" Benning didn't understand. "No one knew that's where I hid it."

"That's not all," JC said. "We might not have the skull you wanted, but the coroner did pull an entire set of bones from the fireplace once we got the fire under control, and, Ana, the remains… It's going to be nearly impossible to identify them now."

THE BASTARD HAD used an accelerant.

The odor of gasoline burned Agent JC Cantrell's nostrils, even with his nose and mouth buried in the crease of his elbow. Crime scene techs and the coroner carefully removed the charred remains one by one from the brick fireplace hidden back on Benning Reeves's property as he disconnected his call with Ramirez.

Hell, the only reason they'd found the fireplace had been because the whole damn thing had been on fire, which meant their UNSUB—unidentified suspect— hadn't just taken Benning Reeves's kids last night, he'd also come back to clean up his own mess. Assuming it was the same perp behind both crimes. Black smoke still lingered in the air and irritated his eyes. It was a miracle the flames hadn't started a wildfire, but whoever'd lit the match most likely hadn't even thought about the possibility. They'd been too busy trying to cover up a crime by destroying evidence. Which, from the looks of the blackened bones currently being sealed into evidence bags, had done a damn fine job.

He followed the pattern of scorch marks scarred into the dim red bricks. Gasoline burned upward of five hundred degrees, but add in the fact those bricks held on to that heat and the metal inside the fireplace, there was a good chance dental records, fingerprints and DNA had all been burned away. Without an ID on the body, the chances of that six-year-old boy coming home only got smaller. "Damn it."

Sevierville PD had taped off the target scene with a wide perimeter through the trees at JC's instruction, the entire property in controlled chaos. Local PD had already searched and processed the house, but out here it'd take days—weeks—to filter through what qualified as evidence. Small towns like this saw a few instances of violent crime, but this case was about to blow Sevier- ville's crime stats through the roof. Someone had used the fireplace out of convenience, knowing the remains would be found, but they hadn't wanted the victim to be identified. That was where the accelerant came in. With any luck and depending on how long the fire had been going, the forensic lab might still be able to put a rush on pulling DNA from the bone marrow of the victim and nail this killer to the wall. JC would be there when they did.

He noted the shortened bones of the hand the coroner was in the process of securing. He faced Evan Duran, hostage negotiator extraordinaire, crouched a few feet away, and dropped his arm away from his mouth and nose. "Looks like our UNSUB went out of his way to ensure pulling fingerprints were out of the question. Cut the tips of the victim's fingers clean off before lighting the match."

"The guy knows what he's doing, that's for sure. That's why we couldn't trace the bug he planted in Olivia Reeves's hospital room and couldn't get any surveillance of the getaway vehicle the night of the kidnapping. I'd say our suspect has at least some knowledge of crime scenes or forensics given he chose to toss in the gasoline." Duran straightened, gaze to the ground as he moved farther from the epicenter of the crime scene. This case had the entire Tactical Crime Division team on edge. Hell, JC couldn't even imagine what was going through Ramirez's head right now having to partner with a former lover to find the guy's son, but for Duran, this investigation hit a little too close to home. The hostage negotiator's little sister had been taken from right in front of their apartment building when he was only ten years old, too small to do anything but watch, but it was that moment that drove Duran's attention to this case now. He would do whatever it took to bring Owen Reeves home. They all would. Shadows darkened Duran's Latino features as he nodded to the trail carved through the mud. "But he wasn't careful enough."

"What do you got?" JC arced his path out from his teammate's to avoid contaminating whatever Duran had found. Slowing, he caught sight of the deep grooves carved into the snow and mud—most likely drag marks from his victim's heels—coming from the house and snapped a pair of latex gloves over his hands. Cold worked past the thick layer of his coat the longer they searched the scene, but the sight of a silver or white gold piece of jewelry partially uncovered in the dirt froze him straight through. A charm in the shape of the scales of justice with the eyelet spread wide as though it'd been torn from a necklace or bracelet. He swiped up on his phone's screen and took a photo before digging for an evidence bag from his jacket. He pinched the metal between his index finger and thumb and dropped it inside.

"Might help us identify the victim," Duran said.

"The coroner would've mentioned if there'd been evidence of jewelry melted to the bones. Gasoline burns hot, but not hot enough to evaporate silver or white gold." JC pushed to his feet, studying the charm still in his hand. Sunlight pierced through the trees, reflected off the tarnished metal. His lungs still burned with the smell of gasoline and dropping temperatures. They were losing daylight. In another hour Sevierville PD would have to pull out the spotlights, making it that much harder to search the scene. "Which means it came from somewhere else."

From someone else. Another victim? Were they about to find more bodies out here? JC messaged the photo he'd taken directly to Ramirez. Scanning the trees around them, he couldn't shake the feeling every piece of evidence they recovered, every move they'd made out here, was being carefully curated and watched. The vibration of his phone snapped him back into reality, and he answered Ramirez's call. "You get the picture I sent?"

"Where did you get that charm?" A combination of tension and panic tinted her words, and everything around JC slowed. Ramirez wasn't the kind of agent to wear her emotions on her sleeve, but something about this charm had obviously rattled her.

"You recognize it." Not a question. He leveled his gaze with Duran's, the hairs on the back of his neck standing on end.

One second. Two.

"Ramirez?" JC checked the screen. The call hadn't been dropped.

"Yes. I recognize it. It belonged to a fifteen-year-old girl whose body was found a few months after she went missing from Sevierville. Her name was Samantha Perry," Ramirez said. "I was one of the agents assigned to find her."

Chapter Five

It wasn't possible. Samantha Perry's charm shouldn't have been at that crime scene. Not unless… The edge of her phone cut into her hand, her gaze rising to meet Benning's. "Search the rest of the property. I need you to find that skull and get me an ID on the victim. Now," she ordered JC.

She disconnected the call, the entire floor shaking beneath her as though a high-magnitude earthquake had rolled through Sevierville. Or maybe the possibility of a familiar killer had her senses on the edge of an unknown precipice. She didn't know. Didn't care. The FBI had been hunting Samantha's murderer for seven years with no leads, no evidence, no crime scene left behind. Nothing. Until now. Couldn't be a coincidence. She fought to control her breathing, an acidic bite on her tongue, but gravity had drained the blood from her upper body too fast.

"Ana?" Her name on his lips, that seductive combination of a growl and concern, pushed at the barriers she'd set between her and the rest of the world. "Tell me what happened."

"Have you seen this charm before? Could it be Olivia's or one of her friends'?" Swiping her tongue across her dry lips, she angled her phone toward him, the screen bright with the photo JC had sent.

"No. The only piece of jewelry Olivia has is a beaded necklace she made herself." He shook his head. "I don't let her or the kids' friends go that deep into the woods. Not after Owen cut open his head on that fireplace."

"Agents Cantrell and Duran found this bracelet charm near the crime scene on your property after the coroner pulled an entire set of remains from that same fireplace. The girl who went missing when we were… Samantha Perry." No. Now wasn't the time to fall back into the past, no matter how much she wanted to sink into the familiar cage of his body around hers. There were too many similarities between then and now, but she couldn't afford to let the past dictate the present. "She had one exactly like it. She and her best friend had a matching set. Only Samantha's wasn't recovered with her body. They found her bracelet, but the charm had been torn off."

He took the phone from her, his calluses catching on the side of her hand, but where her body had instantly warmed at their brief contact mere minutes ago, the hollowness inside only tore through her now. "Justice scales?"

"It's the zodiac sign for Libras. Both girls shared the same birthday. They were friendship charms." What were the chances another charm like that would surface now, right when Ana had come back to Sevierville? "My partner and I theorized Samantha's killer kept it as a trophy, but we couldn't prove it. Harold Wood disappeared off the FBI's radar. He quit his job at the school, wasn't seen by any of his neighbors or his family in the area. No one has been able to find him for seven years."

"But now the charm's surfaced, and someone burned a body on my property." He handed her back the phone, but the numbness spreading through her was all consuming as he stumbled backward. Color drained from his face, his wet hair leaving pools of dampness across his shoulders. "You think the man who killed Samantha Perry has something to do with Owen's kidnapping?" He ran his hands through his hair, fisting the dark strands. "What about the victim they found? Was it... Could it be—"

"No." She rushed toward him, her hands gripped around his muscled arms to keep him upright. *Infierno.* His skin was hot. She battled against the possibility of his six-year-old boy being held by a vicious killer, but she couldn't discount anything at this point. That charm had been discovered on Benning's property, mere feet from a fireplace that contained human remains. The chances that specific piece of jewelry had turned up in not one but two of her investigations were slim, but the idea Owen Reeves had been taken by the same monster who'd killed Samantha Perry... Nausea churned in her gut. She sought his gaze and put every ounce of confidence she had left into her voice. "It wasn't your son, Benning. Agent Cantrell said the remains belong to an adult. Owen is still out there. He still needs our help."

"Someone took the skull and stuffed another body in there?" Mountainous shoulders rose and fell in rapid succession as he leveled bright blue eyes with hers. "You said you needed an ID on the victim they found right away. You already have an idea of who the victim is."

She nodded. After all these years, how could he still read her so easily? How could one look from him make her forget why she'd left in the first place? She swallowed hard against the urge to lean a bit closer, to confirm the unsettling pressure inside was nothing more than biology in a stress-induced situation and had nothing to do with the man standing in front of her. Ana forced her fingers to unwrap from around his arms, the heat sliding past her defenses too familiar, too comforting. Too tempting. "You said your nanny should've been there with the kids when you got back home. The killer might've gotten to her first and taken advantage of the fireplace to get rid of her body. Or... Samantha's best friend owned the same charm bracelet. She would be an adult now, but if it doesn't belong to Samantha, then, given the fact her best friend is the one who led us to him as a suspect, there's a possibility he resurfaced here in Sevierville for another victim. For Claire. Either way, there's a chance whoever took your son has the skull, too."

The rush of his exhale swept across her neck and collarbones. "You make it sound like this guy is a serial killer."

"Somebody drywalled that skull into one of Britland's construction projects, used your kids as leverage because you found it, and is now trying to tie up loose ends by destroying the evidence." In her experience, that didn't sound like the plan of a serial killer. Not with the seven-year cooling-off period and differences in MO between the victims. But Ana couldn't ignore the number of victims missing in this investigation or the charm found on Benning's property. No. The random—almost chaotic—moves this killer had made spoke of something much more dangerous. "I think whoever we're dealing with is desperate to hide what they've done. No matter who gets in their way."

"Just tell me what I need to do to get my son back," Benning said.

"We start where this all began. Finding the skull. If we can pinpoint how and why the victim ended up in that wall, we'll find who put them there." Her phone vibrated from another incoming message from JC. Crime scene photos. She scanned through the shots her teammate had taken of the remains as the coroner sealed each bone into individual evidence bags. How the rest of the bones had gotten there, she didn't know. She had to assume whoever'd started the fire had tried to destroy the evidence all at once. She wanted to be there, wanted a firsthand look at the scene, wanted to do something that would help the investigation and not make it so she didn't feel so…helpless, but as long as Benning and his daughter were in danger, Ana would stay. She'd do for them what she hadn't been able to for Samantha Perry. She'd protect them.

She studied the photos. The fire had most likely burned away any chance of comparing DNA from the remains, so it'd be almost impossible to identify the victim, but the slight discoloration on a few of the skull's fragments—different than the rest—held her attention. Evidence of blunt-force trauma. The photo Benning had taken of the skull he'd recovered flashed across her mind. The owner of the skull from the construction site had been shot in the head. Not hit from behind. Another difference in MO. "The skull you found. What did it look like when you pulled it out of the wall?"

He moved to her side. "You mean aside from the fact it wasn't attached to the rest of the body?"

"I mean was there evidence of blood, mold?" She wasn't trained in forensics, but even the smallest clue might help them date how long the remains had been sealed behind the drywall or where the victim had died. "Was there a distinct odor?"

"Actually, it seemed like it'd been there for a while." He rubbed his hand across the back of his neck. "The building I found it in is one of Britland Construction's oldest ongoing projects. I found out construction has been on hold for almost five years because of all the settlements the company is dealing with."

"So it could've been sealed behind the wall anywhere from a few months to years." Decaying bodies emitted gases as bacteria broke down cells over time. Whoever'd hidden the remains had to have used something to cover up the odor. They'd had access to that building and hadn't expected anyone to find that head for years, if ever, but then Benning had started investigating Britland. He'd put a target on his back by getting too close to the truth, and the killer had known the moment he'd removed the remains and lashed out to keep their secret. But none of that explained the possible connection to the Samantha Perry case.

"I'll start by looking into employment records for Britland and run background checks on their personnel. If this is tied to them, that should give us what we need so I can narrow our suspect list down to the man who took your son." And find out how that charm had ended up at the crime scene on Benning's property. She tucked her chin to her chest as awareness of how close he'd gotten rocketed through her. Stepping away, she pocketed her phone, her insides cooling instantly with his lack of body heat adding to hers. She fisted the dish towel she'd been using to clean up after her and Olivia's cookie dough fight in an attempt to lock down her body's visceral reaction, and tossed it into the kitchen sink with the dishes. In vain.

In the short few hours she'd been back in Sevierville, the time that'd kept them apart, the distance she'd wedged between them, the complete and utter focus on her cases... It'd all faded. As much as she hated the idea he could still affect her after all this time—after everything she'd worked to bury—that deep, lingering attraction held tighter than ever before. But she couldn't risk giving it more power over her than she already had. Not when it jeopardized her ability to do her job. "With any luck, the medical examiner will have an ID and cause of death on the victim from the fireplace in the next couple of hours, and we can connect the two to get your son back."

She headed for the duffel she'd dropped at the front door with her laptop inside. Running through Britland employment records. Identifying the victim who'd been burned in the fireplace on Benning's property. Finding his son. Nothing else mattered. They'd already wasted so much time. She didn't dare give in to any more distractions.

"Ana, wait." Callused fingers slipped around her arm, swinging her into a wall of muscle. He didn't move, her exhales mingling with his. Her brain locked on to the fact his free hand had drifted to her waist, and she couldn't think beyond the searing heat seeping past her skin. "I just..." Hesitation lightened his hold on her as a darker shift deepened the color of his eyes.

Then he crushed his mouth to hers.

HER SPINE OF steel hardened under his touch, triggering every cell in his body into mind-numbing protest.

But instead of pulling away, the woman who'd walked out on him years before sighed against his mouth. That sound, so small, so vulnerable despite her toughened exterior, only added fuel to the raging desire burning through his veins. She was everything he remembered and more. Soft but strong, unapologetic and honest, confident yet afraid of failure. Ana was the kind of woman if threatened with battle, she brought an entire war, a warrior who never backed down and never gave up. And there wasn't a damn thing he'd been able to do over the years to get her out of his head, no matter how many times he'd tried. Now, with her here, fighting to save his family, he wasn't sure it was possible. Or if he wanted it to be.

He penetrated the seam of her lips, memorizing her all over again as she arched against him. Her fingernails scraped against his scalp as she threaded her hand through his hair, and in an instant he was lost. In her. In the way her heart beat hard at the base of her throat, in her light sultry scent, in the way she'd managed to make him forget years of uncertainty and isolation with a single smile. Lean muscle flexed and released as he explored the smooth skin along her back. Things had changed between them. They'd gone their separate ways in an attempt to move on, to forget what'd happened between them, but this—the feel of her skin against his, the taste of her in his mouth—he'd missed this. Missed her. He'd given everything he could to make his marriage to Lilly work, loved his children more than he'd imagined possible, but the damage Ana had carved through him when she'd abandoned him had only torn deeper over time. Had left him hollow. Until now. "Ana—"

"We…" She pressed her hand against his chest, directly over his pounding heart. Hazel-green eyes lifted to his as she swiped something from his bottom lip with the pad of her thumb, sensation spreading across his face and down his neck. One word. That was all it took to bring him back to reality, to remind him of what was at stake if they took this any further, to remind him that there were lives at risk. His son's life was at risk. She sank back onto the four corners of her feet and increased the empty space between them. She pressed the back of her hand against her mouth, a combination of regret and horror contorting her smooth expression that pierced straight through him. Shaking her head, Ana dropped her gaze to the floor. "We can't do this, Benning."

"I know." Dread pooled at the base of his spine. She was right. They couldn't do this. Because of the case. Because she blamed herself—her feelings for him—as the cause for that girl's death, and he didn't know what the hell had come over him other than he hadn't been able to keep his distance from her for even another fraction of a second.

For years he'd kept himself in check. He'd buried his feelings for her at the back of his mind and tried to forget the rookie FBI agent who'd turned his entire world upside down. He'd thrown himself into taking care of his kids and building his company, but the moment he'd caught sight of her running around the kitchen island, chasing after his daughter with a spatula full of raw cookie dough, he'd realized it'd all been for nothing. Every minute they'd been together for those short few months had left an undeniable mark.

All this time he'd been turning down dates, offers of

coffee, or grabbing lunch in the name of protecting his kids from losing yet another feminine influence in their lives. Protecting himself from getting too attached— from getting hurt—but when it came right down to it, he'd been holding out for her to come back into his life. Now here she was, more out of reach than ever before, and all he could do was laugh. "You're right, and I'm sorry. You've made it perfectly clear you don't have feelings for me."

"You say that like I didn't feel anything for you when we were together," she said.

He pulled his shoulders back. "Did you? Because you certainly made walking away in the middle of the night look easy."

Her fingers curled into fists at her sides, as though she was preparing for battle, and hell if he wasn't ready for it. Shadows smoothed the emotions from her features, every detail of her face guarded in an instant. "My job is saving lives, Benning. I'm trying to bring as many victims home to their families as I can, and letting what happened between us distract me from finding your son only makes it harder—"

"Damn it, love isn't a distraction, Ana." He hadn't meant his admission to roar past his defenses, but there it was. Out in the open. His heart threatened to beat straight out of his chest, lungs fighting to catch up with his fight-or-flight response. He understood the importance of her work, why she'd dedicated her life to bringing home the missing, why her brothers had all chosen law-enforcement careers, and he needed that cause now more than ever. But there had to be a point where she couldn't blame herself for the actions of the monsters she chased. She deserved more than taking on one assignment after the next with nothing to gain. Didn't she realize that? All she had to do was face that truth. Her little sister, Samantha Perry, all of the victims she hadn't been able to find over the years? They weren't coming home, and closing herself off from feeling that loss—or much of anything else—would only destroy her from the inside.

"Love?" The single word struggled past her kiss-stung lips. Her gaze connected with his. "Benning, I wasn't... We didn't—"

"I was in love with you." He shortened the distance she'd wedged between them as the sun disappeared behind the ridge of the Smokeys through the windows. Worn wood flooring protested under his weight, the only break in silence settling throughout the cabin. Benning locked his jaw against the urge to touch her, straightening as he lowered his voice. "Listen, I know why you're out there saving lives. I know why you push yourself so hard and why you've detached yourself from connecting with the people around you. But now it's my son who's been taken, and I need you to care. I need the woman I fell in love with seven years ago working this case because she's my only chance of getting him back. Not the empty shell she's trying to become."

He didn't wait for her response. Turning on his heels, he headed for the cabin's front door and didn't stop until he'd disarmed the alarm and stepped into the biting cold. Silent flakes fell around him as he stared out into the trees from the front porch. He could still taste her on his mouth, the slight hint of chocolate mixed with sugar and butter from the cookie dough on the back of his tongue. What the hell had he been thinking, kissing her while his son was out there in the hands of his abductor? That was the problem when it came to Ana. He couldn't think. Couldn't remember to breathe. Logic and self-preservation didn't exist when he got close to her, but knowing now that she hadn't felt the same way toward him as he had for her, that cleared up a lot of confusion. Back then he'd wanted, he'd taken, and he hadn't given a damn about the consequences. Only now he had Owen and Olivia to think about, and his son would be the only one to pay the price if he let himself slip again.

He forced one foot in front of the other down the steps. Benning kicked through the six inches or so of snow toward the remains of a tree stump and pile of firewood along the side of the cabin. Wrapping his stiffening fingers around the handle of an ax embedded in the stump, he pulled the blade free. Muscle memory kicked in as he used the weight of the ax head to slide his hand lower on the handle and centered a log upright on the stump. Calluses from the thousands of times he'd chopped wood on his own property frictioned against the wooden handle. He'd lived his entire life in Sevierville, taken over his father's inspection business and worked the twenty acres of land he'd inherited from his parents with his own two hands. No matter what'd come his way, he'd found a way to keep his family's heads above water and food on the table, but he couldn't fix this. Couldn't make Ana feel something she didn't want to feel.

"Seven years." He rotated his shoulder as he swung the ax blade back and around. The crack of wood filled his ears as the log split down the middle and fell to either side of the stump. The breath he'd been holding rushed out of him, instantly freezing just beyond his mouth. The sun had gone down, the cabin's motion-detecting lights washing over him and the snow around him, but the weight of being watched never surfaced. Ana had most likely gone to do exactly what she'd said she would. Run background checks on Britland Construction employees and shut out everything that didn't matter to the investigation. Including him. Sweat built at the base of his spine as he swung again. And again. Exhaustion, exertion, guilt. Fatigue worked through his muscles after a dozen swings, but he wouldn't stop. Not until he got his head back on straight. Although one thing was certain now: as soon as he and Ana brought his son home—ended this nightmare—he'd be the one to walk away.

Yet, for a brief moment she'd kissed him back.

A twig snapped somewhere beyond the tree line to his right, and Benning slowed the ax's next arc. The blade swept across his pant leg as he scanned the darkness ahead for the source. Out here, this far up against the mountains, outlined black bear territory. He tightened his hold on the ax between both hands as the hairs on the back of his neck stood on end. Taking a step back, he listened for any other sign of movement.

Then pain exploded across his head from behind, and the world went black.

Chapter Six

Her middle finger hung poised above her laptop keyboard as she forced herself to read, for the third or fourth time, each and every Britland Construction employee name TCD had forwarded on, but none of the names registered. She couldn't focus. Couldn't ignore the bright warning of motion-sensor detection from the south side of the cabin on the right side of her screen. Benning had stormed out so fast, she hadn't gotten the chance to disarm the sensors, but from the soft rhythmic thumping coming from outside, she imagined he'd found the firewood and ax.

She'd confirmed his retelling of events with a digital copy of the Sevierville police report filed last night. Site security had called police after shots had been fired by an unknown shooter in a black ski mask, who'd escaped before officers arrived, but they hadn't gotten a clear look at the man who'd been on the other end of the barrel before he'd run. Benning.

I need the woman I fell in love with... Not the empty shell she's trying to become.

He'd fallen in love with her. Ana gripped the edges of the countertop until her knuckles whitened against the translucent skin there. Hints of dropping temperatures bled through the windows, but it was the cold sliding through her insides that kept her cemented in place. Benning had fallen in love with her seven years ago, but he didn't think she was capable of feeling anything for him. Didn't think she cared about the little boy he'd asked her to find. Isn't that what he'd said? That she'd made disappearing in the middle of the night look easy. Because she was just an empty shell.

The kitchen lights flickered above, then died. Ana raised her gaze to the ceiling, her attention sliding down the walls toward the front door. The familiar LED light on the alarm panel on the wall blinked rapidly. The cabin's previous owner had programmed a backup generator to automatically kick on when the property lost power, a necessity considering how far they were from civilization. But after a full minute, the lights remained dark.

And the thumping from outside had stopped. "Benning?"

Warning skittered up her spine, raising a trail of goose bumps across her shoulders. Ana unholstered her weapon but kept it at her side as she stepped into the main living space. She heel-toed it slowly toward Olivia's bedroom, old wood groaning beneath her feet. No movement through the windows. Nothing but the sound of her own breathing. Routine blackouts occurred frequently throughout the area, but that didn't explain why the generator hadn't started. She'd checked the fuel levels and connections during her initial perimeter search. The tank had been full. Which meant it had to have been disconnected.

Wrapping her hand around the bedroom doorknob, she shouldered her way inside Olivia's room. Curtains drawn, lights out. It took a few seconds for her eyes to adjust, but the soft outline of Olivia beneath the covers—asleep—brought her racing heart rate down a notch. Ana reached her free hand around the door and twisted the lock before closing it behind her. No matter what happened, nothing would get through this door. She'd make sure of it.

She skimmed her fingers across the alarm panel beside the front door and hit the panic button. No response. Her stomach sank, and she raised her weapon parallel with the floor. Whoever'd cut the power and the generator must've also cut the lines to outside contact. Unpocketing her cell phone, she checked for coverage. Nothing reliable. *"Maldicion."*

As of right now she was all that stood between the threat and Benning and his daughter. She shoved her phone back into her pocket. After dropping the magazine from her service weapon to double-check the rounds left over from the parking lot shootout, she slammed it back into place and removed the safety. Finger beside the trigger, Ana retraced her steps toward the kitchen. Then slowed as cold air brushed against her face.

The sliding glass door hadn't been open when she'd gone to check on Olivia.

A soft protest of wood flooring from behind spun her around just as a wall of muscle slammed into her. The cabin blurred in her vision a split second before her head snapped back onto the floor. Hand tight on the gun, she took aim at the masked attacker, finger over the trigger.

But faster than Ana thought possible, he clamped his hand over the barrel of the weapon and twisted until the sound of crunching bone and splintering pain was all she knew. Her groan drowned the rough inhales and exhales coming from beneath her attacker's mask, but she wasn't down yet. Hiking her knee into his kidneys, she used his own momentum to slam him into the floor face-first. Disoriented, he gave her enough time to latch on to the glass coffee table and shove to her feet.

The bedroom door swung open, and Benning's daughter stepped into the moonlight.

"Olivia, no! Run—" Searing pain spread across her scalp as the bastard fisted a handful of her hair and threw her back into the wall that made up the over-size fireplace. The air slammed out of her lungs, but she didn't have time to recover. She dodged the fist aimed directly at her face as he rocketed his knuckles into the stone behind her. Targeting her shoulder into his midsection, she threw everything she had into hiking her attacker off his feet. She couldn't let him get to Olivia. Her stitches pulled tight. She locked her back teeth against the scream working up her throat but didn't make it so much as a single step forward before a direct hit to her bullet wound knocked her off balance. They both collapsed, both fought for air, but pain-induced nausea kept Ana down.

Her attacker stood over her, a hint of sweat and new car smell working deep into her lungs. This wasn't some run-of-the-mill criminal set on covering up a murder. The way he moved, the way he'd targeted her wound. He was a professional. Former military, or at least trained in advanced maneuvers, and he'd put Benning and his family in his sights. "You weren't supposed to get involved, Agent Ramirez."

"Congratulations, you've done your homework and

figured out who I am." Shaking her head, she clamped a hand over her side and struggled to her feet, only to collapse again. Blood soaked through her cookie dough-stained shirt. *Mierda*. Would she have any clothes left by the time this case was over? She forced her breathing to slow and swallowed the dryness in her throat. Steel resolve pulled her shoulders back, and she settled her gaze on her attacker's. She'd made Benning a promise. She'd given him her word to protect him, protect Olivia and bring Owen home. She wasn't about to fail him now. "What I want to know is who the hell are you? And where's Benning?"

A hollow laugh filtered through the pounding behind her ears. In less than two moves, he dropped the magazine from her service weapon and disassembled the gun. Pocketing the magazine, he tossed the rest, the sound of metal on wood a shock straight to her nerves.

"I know you, Ramirez. I used to be you, so believe me when I say it'd be in your best interest to walk away while you still can." He shot his hand out, gripping her throat and hauling her into his muscled chest. Her heart threatened to punch through her rib cage as he squeezed hard enough to constrict her airway. He cocked his head to one side, revealing a line of flawless skin between the ski mask and his leather jacket. He braced his feet apart as she struggled with both hands around his wrist. "Mr. Reeves took something that didn't belong to him, and now I'm the one who has to clean up the mess, but I wanted to give you a choice. For old time's sake. Give me the skull, hand over Benning Reeves and I'll let you live, or count yourself among the casualties when I'm done."

The skull. He didn't have it. Which meant someone

else had taken it from the fireplace. Not the killer. Not Benning. Then who?

"Give me… Owen, and… I'll let you…live." Her eyes watered, that dark gaze blurring in her vision. Or was it the lack of oxygen making her dizzy? Didn't matter. In another thirty seconds—maybe a minute— none of this would matter. She had to stay awake, had to keep him from reaching Olivia, give Benning and his daughter a chance to run.

"I take it you're declining my offer," he said.

She dug her fingernails into her attacker's skin, drawing blood. His grip faltered, and Ana took advantage. Releasing her hands from his wrists, she struck his knee as hard as she could with her heel, and he dropped. She wrapped her hand and wrist close to his ear and used her weight to slam the side of his head into the floor. Her throat burned as she breathed, the muscles alongside her neck already sore. "I take it you haven't done nearly as much research on me as you should have."

A glint of moonlight off metal was all she noted before pain sliced across her arm. Her body twisted with the swipe of the blade, giving her attacker enough time to close the distance between them. Targeting her midsection, he hefted her off her feet, his arms locked around her waist. Ana jabbed her elbow into the sensitive bundle of nerves at the base of his spine as he pushed her backward. Once. Twice. Pain exploded through her lower back as he rammed her into the is- land countertop, and her laptop crashed to the floor. She blocked the hit aimed for the right side of her jaw, but the second swing came in too fast. She hit the floor. Hard.

"I didn't want it to end like this, Ramirez." His footsteps reverberated off the old wood flooring as her attacker took position above her. "You were one of the good ones until you put your own selfish needs over saving that poor girl."

Samantha Perry? How did he—

Lightning spread through her. Every breath, every movement on her part, taught her a new lesson in pain tolerance. Raising her head, she caught sight of her discarded service weapon. He'd stripped it down, removed the magazine, but she wouldn't give up. The front door swung inward on its hinges, cold leaking into the cabin. Olivia had gotten away, but for how long? Alone, unarmed, unprotected, the girl wouldn't last the night on her own out there in the woods. Blood dripped from her nose, the taste of salt and copper filling her mouth as she reached for her gun only a few feet away. "I'm not dead...yet."

"Then let's get to it, shall we?" Ripping her off the floor, he dragged her toward the floor-to-ceiling windows looking out over the north side of the cabin and spun her back into the glass. The window vibrated along her spine, cracks spidering outward, and her blood pressure spiked higher. "Nothing personal, Ramirez. You used to be a good agent, just not good enough to beat me."

He landed a hard kick to her stomach, and the window shattered, sending her into darkness.

THE CRUNCH OF footsteps in snow pierced through the haze in his head.

Benning pulled his chin from his chest, but his head hit something solid. Pain exploded down his neck. Son of a… Sections of his shoulder-length hair caught in his beard. What the hell happened? His shoulders ached, the cold working into his joints, but that wasn't what was stopping him from moving his arms. He'd been tied against a tree, with rope from the feel of it. Who—

He'd been chopping wood to distract himself after accusing Ana of being nothing more than a shell of the woman he'd fallen in love with. Regret for what he'd said had only served to push him harder, torn open the gaping wound he'd struggled to plug since she'd left. Obviously without success. He'd heard something move in the trees. Then there'd been nothing but darkness. He'd been hit from behind. Someone had knocked him unconscious. Someone knew they were here.

"Your son is running out of time, Mr. Reeves." Motion-detecting lights cast the man in front of him into shadow, a ski mask covering the bastard's face. Snow crunched under heavy footfalls as his attacker crouched in front of him. Gravel coated the man's voice, but instant recognition threw Benning back to the night Owen and Olivia had been taken. It was him, the man who'd pointed a gun at him on that construction site and abducted his son. "I gave you twenty-four hours to hand over what you took from the site, and now you've forced me to do something I don't want to do." The cabin's outdoor lights reflected off a jagged-edged blade, stained with some dark substance along the blade—blood?— and Benning leveraged his feet into the snow. "Where is the skull?"

"I don't have it." Truth. But apparently, neither did the SOB in front of him. Agent Cantrell had been right. Someone had gotten to the skull before the Tactical Crime Division had. Spitting the thick coating in his mouth into the snow, he set his head back against the tree. His head throbbed with his racing heartbeat. He tugged at the ropes around his wrists, but there wasn't any give. "I can tell you one thing. The second I get out of these ropes, I'm going to kill you for taking my son."

Lightning exploded as the bastard's fist connected with one side of his jaw. His eyes watered, blood filling his mouth as the trees, the outline of the man in front of him, everything blurred.

"You know, Ana Sofia threatened me with the same end." His attacker leaned in, the scent of new car smell and soap heavy in the air. "Right before I threw her through a window."

No. That wasn't possible. Ana wasn't dead. Couldn't be. She was a federal agent. She'd been trained to fight, to protect the innocent. Nothing—not even the bastard in front of him or anything Benning had accused her of—could bring her down. Heat spread from behind his sternum as seconds ticked by, the muscles along his jaw protesting. Shaking his head, he let the tree bark bite into the wound from where he'd been knocked unconscious. She wasn't dead. Because that meant... That meant he'd never get to tell her he hadn't meant what he'd said. "You're lying."

"Are you really willing to take that chance? Are you willing to bet your daughter's life on it?" His attacker pressed cold steel against Benning's face, and the muscles across his back tensed. "Because without Agent Ramirez protecting her, there's nothing stopping me from doing to her what I plan to do to Owen once your twenty-four hours runs out." The edge of the blade pierced through the thin skin at his cheek, a drop of blood trickling down from the cut. "The skull, Mr.

Reeves. That's all I want, and you and your kids can go back to your lives and forget I ever existed."

He wasn't part of this world. He wasn't trained in hand-to-hand combat, weapons or negotiation. He didn't come into contact with killers on a daily basis like Ana and the rest of the Tactical Crime Division, but even Benning recognized the lie behind the promise. He forced his fingers to uncurl and plunged them into the snow behind the tree, out of sight. There had to be something—anything—he could use to cut himself free. He just needed more time. His finger brushed against a sharp edge of a rock. Not sharp enough to break skin, but he hoped like hell it would do the job. Setting the rock against what he thought was the thinnest section of rope, Benning worked to cut through the braided fibers as fast as he could. "Tell me whose body the FBI pulled from the fireplace on my property."

"Your new friends at TCD haven't ID'd her yet?" He shook his head. "Pity what had to go down. It was nothing personal, but your nanny took her job a little too seriously, watching those kids."

Jo. Dread fisted in the pit of his stomach. "She didn't have anything to do with this."

"You're the one who brought her into this when you removed the skull from that site, Mr. Reeves. Not me. Her blood is on your hands. Just as Agent Ramirez's, and just like it will be when I find your daughter." His attacker straightened, the weight of those dark eyes pressurizing the air in his lungs. If this guy had beat Ana as he'd claimed, he'd been trained. There was no way Benning could compete with that, but he sure as hell wasn't going to go down without a fight. Not with his daughter unprotected. Not with his son missing, and not with Ana injured—possibly dying—somewhere out here. "You're stalling."

"Yes, I am." Benning cut through the last of the ropes at his wrists and launched forward, taking the bastard by surprise. He aimed to return the hit to his jaw, but his attacker dodged the attack and used his own momentum to unbalance him and slammed another fist into his face. Benning stumbled backward, then shot out another punch, making contact. Bracing his feet apart, he lifted his hands into position as his head threatened to split down the middle. He caught the SOB's wrist as the blade swung down toward him but left his midsection open. One hit. Another. The air crushed from his lungs as the man in the mask took advantage, and Benning had to release his hold on the knife in order to protect himself. The blade sliced down his arm, the sting drawing a gasp from between his teeth, but for a split second, the movement left his attacker open. He wrapped one forearm around the bastard's neck and hauled him back off his feet. Only he hadn't anticipated the elbow straight back into his gut. His grip loosened as pain exploded through his side, and he let the man in the mask free.

The killer caught Benning's wrist and twisted it behind him. His shoulder socket screamed right before a knee rocketed into Benning's face.

His vision went dark. He hit the ground, snow working under his shirt and into his boots. Every cell in his body begged him to stay down, to give up. It'd be easy, but this wasn't how this would end. He wasn't going to leave his kids' lives in the hands of a killer. He wasn't going to let Ana's sacrifice be for nothing.

"You don't know when to give up, do you? But I'll

tell you the same thing I told Ana before I sent her to her death. You can't beat me. I've lost once before, and I'm not about to let it happen again." Movement registered above him, a shadow casting across his face. "Now, I'm going to give you one last chance to tell me where you hid the skull you took from the construction site before I lose my patience and put a bullet between your eyes, just as I did to him."

His breath sawed in and out of his lungs. Leveraging his palms into the snow, Benning struggled to his feet. His vision cleared. Exhaustion and pain tore through him, but he braced his legs wide. Ready to finish this once and for all. "I'm going to keep my word about killing you."

Benning kicked out, landing his boot heel center mass, then struck out with a right hook, followed by a left. Adrenaline dumped into his veins, throwing the pain and exhaustion into the back of his mind where it belonged. His knuckles met bone twice more before the bastard blocked his third attempt. The next fist made contact to the left side of his head, disorienting him. Benning stumbled back and slammed into the tree he'd been tied to seconds before. Sliding down the bark, he battled to stay upright as the man in the mask landed one hit after the other. His head twisted after each strike. He couldn't block the punches. They were coming too fast. Too hard.

"Leave my daddy alone!" The familiar voice sent panic through his system. Blood dripped from one eyebrow as his eye swelled shut, but Benning didn't mistake Olivia's small frame running as fast as her legs could carry her toward him.

"Olivia…" The brutal attack from the man above

him ceased as the bastard turned his attention on his daughter. Suddenly, the physical pain, the exhaustion, the haze closing in, it all disappeared. A growl tore from his throat. "No!"

His son had already been taken from him. Ana had come back into his life only to be ripped away. The SOB wouldn't take Olivia, too. Ever.

His daughter swung the tree branch between both hands at his attacker as hard as she could, but her target stopped the attack before she could make contact. Ripping the makeshift weapon from her hands, the man in the mask advanced. Olivia tripped, landing on her rear, bright blue eyes widening in terror.

"Stay the hell away from her." Benning used everything he had left to get to his feet. The ground threatened to fall right out from under him, but he used the temporary rush of adrenaline to stay upright. "Your fight is with me."

"You're right." His attacker pivoted, keeping both Benning and Olivia in his peripheral vision on either side of him. One second. Two. In the blink of an eye, the shooter withdrew a gun from his low back and took aim at Benning. "It's time to put an end to it."

He pulled the trigger.

Olivia's scream echoed in his head as Benning collapsed to his knees. "Daddy!"

Chapter Seven

The gunshot ripped her from unconsciousness in blinding fury.

A gasp tore from her throat as the reality of what'd happened closed in, second by second. The intruder, the fight, the window. Ana tucked her chin to her chest, trying to sit up. A large piece of glass pierced straight through her thigh. A soft whimper escaped from between her lips as she tested the injury with one hand. *Hijo de perra.* She collapsed her head back into the snow, barely registering her stiff joints and muscles. How long had she been out here, unconscious? She searched the sky, the sun well behind the Smokeys. The only source of dim light came from the motion-detecting spotlights around the corner of the cabin, which ran off batteries instead of the main power or generator. But that gunshot had come from nearby. Tears burned in her eyes. "Damn it, Benning."

No. She swallowed the sob building in her throat. Emotions led to mistakes. Mistakes risked lives. She had to get up, had to find him, find Olivia. Given the fact she was conscious, the glass must not have cut through an artery, but she couldn't take the chance of removing it without cutting off blood supply first—just in case. Okay. She had to use something as a tourniquet, then take care of the wound. Should be relatively easy. She'd been shot less than twenty-four hours ago, and it hadn't stopped her from doing her job. A piece of window in her leg wouldn't slow her down, either. She locked her back teeth in an effort to distract her from the pain. "Get up, Ramirez. You're not finished."

Leveraging her weight into her elbows, she searched her surroundings and caught sight of her SUV parked in the driveway along the other side of the cabin. There had to be something inside she could use. Rope, a bungee cord. Something. Thirty feet. She could make it thirty feet. Her exhales didn't crystallize in front of her mouth, her body temperature dropping too fast, but she couldn't worry about that right now. She had to make it. There were no other options. Not for Benning, and not for his family. She stretched one arm out above her head and slowly rolled onto her side, careful not to nudge the sharp tip of glass that'd cut straight through her. One hand pressing into the ground, she balanced with the other until she'd put nearly all of her weight into her uninjured leg and straightened. A wave of black washed over her vision, gravity doing everything in its power to bring her back to earth, and she had to force herself to breathe through the pain in her side. "Move, damn it."

One step. Then another. Blood slid down the inside of her pants. She only pushed herself harder. The faster her heart raced, the faster she'd bleed out, but she'd take that risk if it meant getting to Benning in time. She wasn't going to deny the ache she'd had to live with since that night she'd slipped from his bed and disappeared. Throwing herself into her work hadn't helped. Making herself numb to emotion or caring about the people around her—the people she saved—hadn't helped. Nothing had. Until he'd kissed her.

It'd been reckless and dangerous and wrong, but she hadn't done anything to fight it. She'd laid out the rules in no uncertain terms when it came to what'd happened between them, but in that moment Benning had broken past the defenses she'd taken so long to build with a single sweep of his tongue past her lips. Just as he'd always been able to do. He'd stirred things inside her she hadn't let herself feel in so long, and there'd been nothing she'd wanted more. In those few seconds she'd been stripped bare, left raw and exposed to the truth. That she... She'd been in love with him, too. She'd denied how she'd felt in the name of saving lives, when deep down the real reason had been festering all along.

She couldn't take the pain of losing anyone else.

Not after losing her baby sister at two years old, not after failing to recover Samantha Perry before her body was found decimated in that alley. She'd ensured she'd never have to feel that grief again by leaving behind the one man who'd undeniably break her into a thousand pieces if given the chance in order to protect herself. Benning.

She wasn't going to die out here. Not until she fulfilled her promise.

Using the exterior of the cabin as a stabilizer, Ana hobbled toward the SUV as fresh snow fell from the sky. Her lungs burned, nausea churning in her stomach. She'd already lost so much blood it felt as though ice sludged through her veins, but the pressure of being exposed—out in the open—took priority. Her attacker had taken her gun and nearly her life. She could only do something about one of those things right now. Twisting her head around the corner of the cabin, mere feet from the SUV, she listened for movement, waited for the next ambush. Only the pounding of her own heart behind her ears registered. Exhaustion compelled her to rest here, to close her eyes and wait until her strength returned, but time was running out. She had no idea who that gunshot had been meant for, if Benning was alive, or if Olivia had gotten to safety. And as long as she was conscious, she'd fight to find out.

"Now or never, Ramirez." She took a few deep breaths, the burn in her lungs a dull piercing now. Blood was still leeching from the wound across her pant leg. It hadn't slowed, which meant the piece of glass wasn't doing a great job holding her together. Benning wasn't the only one out of time. "You didn't come all this way for nothing."

She searched the side of the house one more time. Then ran.

A bullet ripped past her left arm, an inch—maybe two—from her heart as she lunged for the tail of the SUV, but she had to keep moving. Her leg dragged behind her, her toes and calf muscles numb. Two more shots embedded in the side of the cabin and another in the passenger-side door of her vehicle as she took cover. Out of breath and ideas, she pulled her injured leg behind the SUV and closed her eyes as another four rounds exploded through the night. *Hostia*. Bloody hell. She pressed her neck and back into the vehicle's bumper and got to her feet, compressing the hatch's lever. Locked. The breath rushed out of her as she scooped a fist-size rock from the snow and shattered the back windshield. She cleared glass from the bottom track, discarded the rock, and opened the hatch from the inside. Crawling inside, she bit back the urge to scream as the glass shifted in her thigh, and she closed the gate behind her. She was hidden. At least temporarily. It wouldn't do much considering she'd left a trail of blood and glass in her wake, but none of this would matter unless she got the bleeding under control. If she was going to get Benning and Olivia the hell out of here, she had to focus. "Okay, okay. If I were a piece of rope, where would I be?"

Tossing extra raincoats, flares and spare water bottles from the emergency kit, she dumped the rest of the contents into the SUV's cargo space and nearly collapsed back in relief. She grabbed the single bungee cord, still in its package, from the mess. Closing her eyes, Ana set her back against the second row of seats. She prepared herself for the pain that was coming before pinching the glass between both sets of fingers. She sucked in a deep breath. Pressing her heels into the vehicle's floor, she locked her back teeth to keep from giving away her position. "Like a Band-Aid. Nothing you haven't survived before."

She pulled the large piece of glass entirely through her leg with everything she had left, then tossed it aside. Reaching for the bungee cord, she discarded the packaging and wrapped the braided fibers tight around her leg, above the wound. She slammed her head back into the row of seats as pain exploded through her. Tingling sensations shot like lightning down through her calves and toes as feeling rocketed back into her nerves. Darkness closed in around the edges of her vision, but she had to stay awake. Had to get to Benning.

"I know you're in there, Ramirez." Snow crunched

beneath heavy footsteps outside the vehicle. "And from the trail you're leaving behind, it looks like you're not in very good shape."

A knot swelled in the pit of her stomach.

Sifting through the supplies she'd dumped across the cargo space, she gripped a screwdriver. The bright orange head faded in and out of focus as she tried to pry open a hidden storage panel beside the tailgate. The plastic cover finally fell away, and she wrapped her hand around the backup piece she'd stored before she'd left TCD headquarters. Always be prepared. That was what her brothers had taught her from the time she'd been five years old. That, and how to disassemble a gun so it'd fit inside any small storage compartment. She made quick work of assembling the pieces into place and loading the magazine as the footsteps pierced through the pounding in her head. "Only eight more lives left. Don't suppose that means you're going to cut me some slack—"

Gunshots exploded from outside. Blood burst across the tinted side window of the SUV, and the large outline of a man fell against the side of the vehicle. Ana fell back onto her side and raised her weapon. Waiting. Tension stretched across her shoulders as the seconds ticked by. Maybe a full minute. Slower than her instincts told her to go, she unlatched the tailgate and slid out of the vehicle, gun in hand. Her breath shuddered in her chest. She swung around to the passenger side of the vehicle, ready to pull the trigger.

But no one was there. Only a trail of blood—separate from hers—and a larger set of footprints led away from her position and into the trees.

"Ana." Movement registered from behind, and she twisted around and took aim.

At a familiar face.

"Benning." She released the breath she hadn't realized she'd been holding, adjusting her grip around her weapon. Her hands shook, the pain in her leg the only thing keeping her in the moment. She lowered the gun to her side as a sob nearly broke through her control.

Just before she collapsed.

"ANA!" HIS BLOOD ran cold, heart jerking in his chest. Lungs emptied of oxygen as a different kind of pain exploded through him. Benning pushed his legs as hard as he could to catch her before she hit the ground. But he wasn't fast enough. His boots slid across an iced-over patch of snow, bringing him to his knees, but it couldn't stop him. Nothing would stop him from getting to her. Clawing through snow, he discarded the gun he'd taken from her duffel bag inside the cabin after he'd woken and slipped his uninjured arm around her limp body. Fresh blood dripped from her nose and mouth, her skin too pale. He pressed his index and middle finger to the base of her throat, and a rush of relief flooded through him. Her heartbeat pulsed against his finger, slow, thready, but there. "Come on, Ana, open your eyes. Look at me."

No response.

Hauling her upper body out of the snow, he gritted through the pain in his shoulder and skimmed the pad of his thumb across the bluish tint in her lips. The bastard who'd shot him had run before Benning had gotten another shot off, but it was the bright red stain of blood that had pooled beneath her, such a sharp contrast in the snow, that hiked his blood pressure higher now. Hell, she looked like she'd gone four rounds with a professional boxer and been stabbed in the process. He had to get her inside. Had to get her warm. He brought her into his chest, then scanned the tree line twenty feet to the north. The bullet to his shoulder had taken him down for a few minutes, and when he'd come back around, the shooter and his daughter were gone. Where was Olivia? Every muscle down his spine tightened with battle-ready tension, and Benning shook the woman in his arms. "Ana, wake up. You have to get up. You have to tell me where Olivia is."

He'd searched the cabin after he'd woken alone in the snow. No one—not even the bastard who'd attacked him—had been inside. Which meant his daughter was somewhere out here or…or the killer had taken her, too. If the same man who'd tied him to a tree was responsible for taking his son, the SOB had made a grave mistake. Benning set his hand over Ana's heart, blood crusting to her angled features. The skull was still out there. Benning didn't know where, or who had taken it from the fireplace, but he'd be damn sure the shooter never got his hands on it.

"Benning." His name struggled past her lacerated lips, barely a whisper over the constant whine of the wind through the trees.

He fisted her T-shirt in his hands and pulled her upright. Desperation and hints of anger bled into his voice. "Ana, where is Olivia? I need to know what happened to my daughter."

"I couldn't stop him." Hazel-green eyes struggled to focus on him. Her hands fell limp at her sides, and for the first time he noted her bloodied knuckles and what looked like a knife wound across the top of her arm. "I tried, but I wasn't strong enough. I screamed at her to run. I don't know where she is."

"You told her to run?" He loosened his grip on her shirt, and everything—the darkening bruising around her throat, the busted lip, the torn stitches, and her black-and-blue index finger—rushed into focus. Sweat sheened across her flawless skin, dark circles more prominent than a minute ago. He recovered the gun he'd dropped and shoved the barrel down the back of his jeans. "Hang on to me."

A groan ripped from his throat as he hauled her into his chest and got to his feet, and the hollow space behind his sternum ripped wider. In these temperatures, combined with the loss of blood, her body was bordering on hypothermia and shock. He'd prioritized his daughter's life over hers.

Without Ana, he and Olivia would already be dead. He owed her his life.

His legs burned as they climbed the stairs, maneuvered her through the sliding glass door and swung her down onto the nearest couch in the living room. First-aid kit. He'd left it on the kitchen table after stitching her the first time, but first, he had to get her core temperature back up. Ripping every blanket he could find from the beds, he dashed back into the living room to find her struggling to her feet. "What are you doing? You've lost a lot of blood, but stitches aren't going to do a damn bit of good if you die from hypothermia."

"You know you're bleeding, too, right?" Heavy eyelids drooped lower as she shuffled toward him.

"Bastard shot me after Olivia attacked him. Now I don't know where she is. At least I can say I shot him back." But the man in the mask had slipped away before Benning could get the answers he needed. The echo of Olivia's scream still played in his head, the memory of the suspect advancing on his daughter fresh. The cut on the back of his head throbbed. "Now, get back on that couch so I can keep you alive."

"She's a smart girl, Benning. We're going to find her." Ana fell against the kitchen table, strands of beautiful dark hair sticking to her skin and neck. Her gasp destroyed the lingering effects of their last conversation and pressurized the air in his lungs. "I promised I would keep your daughter safe, and that's exactly what I'm going to do. Right after we take care of that wound of yours."

"Damn it, Ana." He lunged forward before she hit the floor. Taking her weight, he settled her back against his chest as he slowly lowered them both to the hardwood. Her skin was hot, sweat slicking down the side of her temples despite having been discarded in the snow for who knew how long. "How the hell are you going to do that when you can't even stand?"

"I'm not going to lose you again, Benning." Long lashes rested against the tops of her cheeks as she closed her eyes, but when she opened them again, a fire he'd never seen before burned in the depths. "And I'm not going to lose her, too. I can't."

Her voice broke, right along with his heart. Something shifted then. Something he couldn't explain as she rested against him. He'd been wrong before. She'd detached herself from the people she'd been assigned to find, but not because she didn't want to feel the pain and loss of another victim, someone she cared about. How hadn't he seen it before now? It'd been there in the way she'd kept her bullet wound to herself to get them to safety, the way she'd shouldered the blame of Samantha Perry's death, how she'd sacrificed herself to give his daughter a chance to run. Even now, she was determined to put his medical needs above her own, despite the fact she was on the verge of passing out.

She wasn't protecting herself from being hurt again.

She was punishing herself.

For what'd happened to her sister, what'd happened to Samantha Perry seven years ago. All of it. She'd taken the blame and twisted it into her own personal responsibility, leaving her wrung out and nothing more than the empty shell he'd accused her of becoming. She'd cut herself off from the things—the people—she cared about the most, not because they were a distraction, but because she didn't believe she deserved them to be part of her life. That because she'd failed, she didn't deserve to be cared for. Benning swept her hair out of her face. He held her tighter, counted her slowing inhales and exhales. No. She wasn't going to die here. Her lashes dipped to the tops of her cheeks once again, and his eyes burned with the possibility of losing her all over again. "You're not a ghost of the woman I fell in love with. I was wrong. I know now why you left, why you think you need to put your own life on the line for everybody else to make up for the past, but if you keep going like this, you're not going to have anything left to give, Ana, and my kids need you." He took a deep breath as the truth surfaced. "I need you."

"It's my fault." Her voice vibrated against his chest. She struggled to open her eyes, her hands limp by her sides. "I was the one who was supposed to be watching my sister the day she went missing. I'm the one who should've found something we could use on Harold Wood before he killed that girl. No one else. Me."

Warmth spread through him as he set his cheek against the crown of her head.

"You were five years old when your sister was taken, Ana. Five. You couldn't have even saved yourself at that age, let alone someone else. You were a child, and nobody in their right mind blames you for what happened. Just as nobody blames you for what happened to Samantha Perry." Tension built at the thought of how many times she'd internalized that blame, made it a part of herself, carried it on her shoulders day after day, how it affected her life. Her happiness. "The criminals who abducted them, they're the ones who need to answer for their crimes. Not you. Don't you see that?"

She didn't answer.

"You told me the work you do makes it so you have to walk in the dark, and I believe you." He smoothed blood from her bottom lip, and a new level of awareness heightened his senses, chased back the pain in his shoulder. He shouldn't be surprised. She'd always had this effect on him, always been able to shut out the chaos around them, grounded him, kept him in the moment. Gave him confidence. "But nobody said you have to do it alone or that you don't deserve to see the light."

She shook her head. "I should've been able to save her."

"Think of how many others you have saved, Ana. They're alive because of you." He'd been down this road, blamed himself for not being strong enough to protect Owen and Olivia, but in the end, that wasn't what mattered. He could tell her it was because his kids were out there, possibly in the hands of a killer, that he'd laid it all out there, but that wouldn't be the truth. He cared about her. From the moment she'd walked onto that construction site asking him questions about the Samantha Perry case seven years ago, he'd known she was the kind of woman he wanted to spend the rest of his life with. She was intelligent, independent, insightful and caring when she let that part of herself show. And, damn it, she deserved more than this, more than a life filled with unanswered questions, heartache and pain. She deserved to be happy. He and the twins, they could make her happy. The thought should've scared him, but a sense of rightness, conviction, burned behind his sternum. Hadn't he'd always felt that way when it came to her? "This obsession you have with saving everyone but yourself only has one end. Yours." A hint of anger bled into his voice. "Damn it, Ana, you have people that care about you, but you're too consumed by your own mistakes to see it."

She hauled the gun off the floor and struggled to her feet, unstable. Eyes heavy, she limped toward the kitchen table and collapsed into the same chair she'd sat in as he'd stitched the wound in her side. "There are only two people I care about right now, and after you help me stitch up this wound, I'm going to find them."

Chapter Eight

She wiped crusted blood from her face, flashlight to the ground.

The power was still cut from the cabin, but they didn't have time to fix it now. Olivia was out here, in the cold and on the run. Whoever'd pushed Ana through that window would be on the girl's trail. Had maybe even caught up with her already. The thought exposed the very real fear climbing her spine, but she pushed forward, forcing her attacker's parting words to the back of her mind. She might not be strong enough to beat this particular threat, but she'd sure as hell slow him down. As for Benning... Whatever illusions he had about her would have to wait. The kidnapper had given them twenty-four hours to hand over the evidence Benning had pulled from that wall. They had three hours left until the deadline. Not enough time to recover the skull, find Olivia and save Owen, but Ana would fight until the end. "Over here."

Small footprints interrupted the smooth surface of fresh snow between larger divots, heading south, away from the cabin and into the tree line. Olivia had gone out the cabin's front door after Ana had screamed at her to run, but according to Benning, the girl had attacked the shooter just before he'd put a bullet in Benning's shoulder and been gone when he'd woken. From the looks of it, she'd changed direction when she'd run and tried to hide her tracks by dragging something behind her. A smile tugged at one side of Ana's mouth. Good girl.

No fresh tire tracks interrupted the area around the cabin. Their attacker hadn't driven a vehicle straight up to the safe house. Too obvious. They would've heard him coming the moment he'd hit the head of the driveway, which meant he had to have come from the tree line. A snowmobile or an ATV? Either would get him on and off the property relatively quickly. Silence pressed on her from every direction. He had to know the area. Had to know the layout of the land and all the best places to attack from. He'd known exactly how to find them and when they'd been the most vulnerable.

Raising the flashlight to follow the trail, she struggled against the invisible lead in her legs as they headed into the woods. The hand-sewn stitches in her thigh wouldn't last long, but they'd have to do for now. Benning seemed to be handling the bullet in his shoulder. Or maybe desperation had finally caught up with him and the pain didn't matter. "I can't decide if your daughter is a genius or if she's read too many mystery novels."

"Both." Benning kept a safe distance from behind, but she could still feel him on her skin. Could still feel his chest pressed against her back as he'd held on to her, remembered the vibration of his words against her spine, and her body heat hiked a few more degrees. Then again, it could be the shock of losing so much blood finally starting to take a toll. Either way, she had to focus, had to keep moving. Because the longer they were out here, the higher chance Olivia would succumb to the elements. "You should see her room. She's decorated it in crime-scene tape."

Benning helped her as she hauled her injured leg over a fallen tree, still following the trail in the snow. Her toes and fingers had already gone numb from dropping temperatures, and she couldn't imagine Olivia much better off. Had the girl even been wearing a jacket? Or shoes? Ana couldn't remember. Stabbing pain had dulled to an ache around the wound, but there was still a chance the glass had nicked something larger. The possibility of not making it out of these trees alive, of failing Olivia, Owen, Benning, just as she'd failed Samantha Perry, pushed her harder.

There wasn't a doubt in her mind she could've saved that girl if she'd been focused on doing her job and not the man at her side, but she couldn't get his admission out of her head. He needed her, cared about her. Not the emotionally isolated investigator she'd presented to her team and to the world, but the woman hiding behind the mistakes she'd made. The real her, the one he'd claimed he'd fallen in love with before her world had been ripped apart. She leaned into his hard frame for support. Did that woman even exist anymore? She wanted her to, if for nothing else than to shed the guilt that had taken control of her life for so long, to carve her own path. To be the kind of woman Benning would be proud to have in his and his kids' lives. The idea thickened the saliva in her mouth. She wasn't sure that future was a possibility anymore. Not for her. "You were right before."

This close, his body heat tunneled through her coat, and her exhales started crystallizing on the air as they moved as one. He took most of her weight, but even with the bullet in his shoulder, his control never broke. "About what?"

"I've been blinded by my mistakes. My...failures." The word turned bitter on her tongue. "I detached myself from the people who care about me, from everyone, because it was the easy thing to do." Her breath shuddered in her chest as they navigated through the trees. "I blamed myself for what happened to Samantha Perry. I thought since she didn't get to be with the people who loved her, the least I could do is put myself in the same position to try to make up for my mistake, which doesn't make sense, I know. But now I'm not sure redemption is an option. At least, not for me."

He slowed, staring down at her with that unreadable expression. Mountainous shoulders blocked moonlight filtering through the trees, but she didn't need to see him clearly to know what he was thinking. She'd memorized every angle of his features the first day they'd met, and while seven years had gone by, he hadn't changed much. He'd become part of her, and there was nothing—no one—who could change that. Least of all her. "Caring about someone doesn't limit your ability to do your job, Ana. It's because you're emotionally invested in the people you're assigned to protect and recover that makes you such a good agent."

He meant every word, conviction strong in his voice.

She raised her gaze with his. "You really believe that."

"Yeah, I do." His voice dipped into dangerous territory, the scent of pine and soap diving into her lungs as he inched closer. "I know you, and I know despite the effort you go through to prove nothing gets past that guard you've built, you're one of the strongest, most caring and competent women I've had the pleasure of knowing. Of all the agents I could've requested to re-cover my son, I chose you. Because you're all I need."

Her throat swelled. All he needed? "I—"

A scream turned her blood cold.

"Olivia." Benning ran toward the sound, his back slightly hunched as he clamped a hand on his wound in his shoulder.

The darkness seemed thicker then. She raced after him, every cell in her body focused on getting to his daughter. They'd made it about fifty yards—maybe a bit more—into the wilderness, but it sounded as though the scream had come from the cabin. The possibility they were walking straight into a trap crossed her mind, but she struggled through the snow in spite of that. They had to take the risk. Thin twigs and branches caught on her coat sleeve as she tried to keep up. She hit the button on the flashlight and threw them into complete blackness. If the shooter saw them coming, he might do something rash, irreversible. Sweat built along her hairline as she forced one foot in front of the other. The pain was back, stitches stretching with every step. She couldn't stop. She had to find Olivia, had to bring her brother home. Blood soaked through her jeans and T-shirt, but the clock hadn't stopped because she was on the verge of passing out.

They cleared the tree line. Motion-censored lights kicked on, blinding her for a split second. She raised her hand to block the light, and there, positioned near the stairs, Ana made out his outline. The man who'd kicked her through a second-story window waited, his weapon in hand. And beside him, the shape of a six-year-old girl who'd known nothing but fear and loss these past two days.

"Didn't think you had what it took to survive a fall like that, Ramirez." The way he said her name, as though they knew each other, grated on her nerves. A gloved hand rested over Olivia's shoulder, pulling her into his side. "You're going to need to have more than that leg looked at when we're finished here, though."

"You say that like you think I'm going to let you walk away." Not happening. She raised her gun, taking aim with both hands gripped on steel. Benning shifted beside her, but didn't protest the fact with one wrong move, one pull of the trigger, she might accidentally hit his daughter. Tension rolled off him in waves, but she'd promised to protect his girl. That was exactly what she was going to do. "Hand over the girl, give me the location on her brother and I'll consider not pulling the trigger."

The mask covering his face shifted as though he couldn't help but smile despite the brand-new bullet hole in his own shoulder, courtesy of Benning. The shooter fanned his gloved grip over his gun, and a rush of nervous energy shot down her spine. "Tell you what. I'll make you a deal. Seeing as how I don't particularly enjoy hurting kids, I'll make a trade. I'll give you the girl and the location of the son, in exchange for Mr. Reeves."

"And what's to stop me from shooting you right now and putting an end to all of this?" she asked.

"Because I'm the only one who knows where the boy is." Slowly, the shooter reached into his pocket and extracted his phone. Turning the screen toward them, he tossed the device at her feet. "Kill me, and you kill Owen Reeves, Agent Ramirez. Is that what you want?"

Forcing herself to keep her expression blank, Ana braced her feet apart and picked up the phone. Her insides jerked as she recognized the little boy from the file Director Pembrook had handed to her less than twenty-four hours ago. Owen Reeves. The footage looked as though it'd come from a hidden camera tucked into a corner of a small, dark room. And there he was. Alone. Afraid. Tears cutting streaks through the dirt on his cheeks.

Benning in exchange for his children.

No. There had to be another way out of this. She just had to find it. Olivia's sobs broke through her racing thoughts. She shook her head to clear out the chaos, but the answer was there, right on the tip of her tongue. The bastard had been playing games with them this entire time. Bringing the Samantha Perry case into this, leaving the charm at the crime scene on Benning's property, destroying evidence. He was trying to manipulate her. Offering a deal had to be another move in a long line of manipulation he'd put into play from the beginning, and she couldn't let herself fall for it. "No. No deal—"

"I'll do it," Benning said.

Her heart plummeted as she realized he'd seen the footage from the phone. She couldn't take her eyes off the shooter but kept Benning in her peripheral vision. This was not up for discussion. "No. We will figure this out together. The second he gets what he wants from you, he'll come back for your children to cover his tracks, and I'm not going to let that happen. My job is to protect you—"

"Your job is to recover my son." Benning tossed the

gun he'd taken from her duffel bag a few feet away. Hands raised in surrender, he stepped away from her, toward the shooter. Shoulder-length hair hid his features as he increased the distance between them. "I'm counting on you to do it."

ONE STEP AT a time. Benning tensed as the bastard holding his daughter hostage slid his hand off her shoulder. With a nudge, the man who'd shot him forced her forward but kept in line with Olivia's every move. The weight of Ana's attention from behind tunneled through his coat and under his skin. His heart rate throbbed around the site of the new hole in his shoulder, but knowing she'd be the one protecting Olivia and that she'd do whatever it took to find Owen, eased the uncertainty tearing through him. The SOB behind the mask hadn't given him a choice. Not really. This was the only way to ensure his mistake didn't haunt his children forever. The spotlights positioned around the cabin reflected off the tears streaking down Olivia's face as he closed in on her. "It's going to be okay, baby. Ana's going to watch you for a little bit until I can come get you. Okay? Everything's going to be fine."

"Daddy, I want to go home." Her sob broke through her tough personality, and she suddenly became the defenseless, vulnerable little girl he'd held after she'd been born, who'd cried until he'd picked her up.

"You're going home, Liv. You just have to be strong for a little bit longer. This will all be over soon. I promise." The words choked in his throat. He'd never lied to his kids, but this lie had slid from his mouth easily enough. He wasn't coming home. Ana was right. As soon as the shooter got ahold of the skull Benning had taken from that wall, all of this would be over, and his children will have lost both parents before they turned seven. But he couldn't watch them suffer for his sins any longer. Not when he could end this nightmare right now. Curling his hands into fists to keep himself from reaching out for her—to keep himself from doubting his decision—he faced the bastard who'd ripped his family apart. "You can take your hands off my daughter now."

Wrenching free, Olivia ran straight for him and wrapped her arms around his neck as he crouched to catch her weight. "No, Daddy! No. You have to come with me."

"So very touching," the shooter said. "But I'm starting to run out of patience, Mr. Reeves. The more time you waste here, the less time your son has."

His heart threatened to shatter into a thousand pieces right there in the snow between a federal agent and an armed gunman. He turned slightly, and, raising his gaze to meet Ana's, he straightened with his daughter in his arms. This wasn't how it was supposed to be. "You have to go with Ana now, Liv. You have to go. I love you, but you have to go."

"You can do this, Olivia." Ana kept her gun trained on his kids' kidnapper, every bit the federal agent he'd relied on to get him and his twins through this. "Think of all those times the investigators in your favorite books had to make a hard choice, but in the end, the hard choice is what moves the story forward and solves the case, isn't it? Otherwise, the characters wouldn't find out how strong they really are."

Olivia unwrapped her arms from around his neck. She sniffled, her big blue eyes holding on to unshed tears, but he couldn't release her. Not yet. "Yes."

"In the end, the investigator always gets the bad guy, right?" Ana glanced toward him, a single nod all the warning she gave him a split second before understanding hit. She wasn't talking about him or Olivia. She hobbled between the shooter and Benning, weapon raised. "They always get justice."

"You're making a mistake, Agent Ramirez." The shooter took a single step forward. "If I leave empty-handed, Owen isn't the only one who will suffer."

"I've made a lot of mistakes over my career. This isn't going to be one of them." Her shoulders rose and fell on steady inhales. Right before she pulled the trigger.

Benning twisted away from the fight, his hold on his daughter tight. Pumping his legs as hard as he could, he took cover behind one of the trees with Ana close on his trail. Bark exploded to his right as a bullet impacted mere inches from his head, and he slid to his knees, shoving Olivia behind him. Ana pressed her back into the tree beside him. "What the hell are you doing? He's the only one who can tell us where Owen is!"

"He was never going to reveal that information, Benning. He's a killer. Killers only want one thing— to keep from getting caught." She returned fire as the SOB took cover behind the pile of firewood Benning had been chopping that stood between them and their only way out of here. The SUV. "Wherever Owen is, there's too much evidence that could point back to him. The only way to find your son is to identify the owner of the skull you pulled out of that wall, and we can't do that here." She fired another three rounds, then the gun clicked empty. They were out of ammunition. Tossing her weapon, she double-checked the shooter's position.

Pain contorted her features as she placed both hands against her thigh, and his heart jerked in his chest. "We have to get to the SUV."

"How?" Damn it. She wasn't in any condition to go up against this guy again. Neither of them was. He bit back the agony tearing through his shoulder. Olivia huddled into his side as another bullet ripped past them.

"There's nowhere you can run, Mr. Reeves," the man in the mask said. "Nowhere you can hide that I won't find you. One way or another, I will recover what you took from me, and when I do, I'm going to enjoy what comes after."

"This guy is so full of himself, but he is the one with the gun." She shook her head, keeping tabs on their attacker. "Do you trust me?"

Benning slowed his hand's path along Olivia's back. Despite the fact Ana had walked away from him all those years ago, she'd nearly died protecting his daughter from the madman on the other side of that woodpile, stepped between him and a loaded gun and calmed Olivia through this whole thing. Trust her? Hell. He'd take another bullet if that was what she needed of him. "Yes."

"Then I'm going to go for the gun you tossed when you decided to surrender yourself over to this psychopath." She shoved the phone the shooter had handed over into her coat pocket. Her voice remained level despite the lack of color in her face and the fact her hands were shaking as she repositioned herself behind the tree. "When I give you the signal, you and Olivia make a run for the SUV. A spare set of keys are in the glove compartment. The SUV has a tracking device. My team will be able to find you."

Warning screamed through his system. "Ana, wait.

You don't know how many rounds are left in that gun. You'll be exposed for however long it takes you to find where I dropped it."

She crossed the open space between the trees they'd taken cover behind, staying low. Another bullet flew over their heads, but with those mesmerizing hazel-green eyes locked on his, the world around the three of them disappeared. "No matter what happens, I need you to promise me you won't come back for me. Take your daughter and get as far from here as you can. Understand?"

Blood drained from his face and neck as her words registered. She didn't think she was going to make it out of here alive. "Ana, no. You're not—"

"Yes, I am." Fisting her hands in his T-shirt, she crushed her mouth to his. She pierced the seam of his lips with her tongue, and, for a brief moment, they were back in the cabin. Her covered in cookie dough, him desperate to taste her one more time. In those short seconds, everything had felt so…right between them. As though she'd never left. He'd been complete. But sooner than he wanted, Ana pulled away, and the cold crept back in. Releasing her grip from his shirt, she stood as best she could with the wound in her thigh. "You promised Olivia she could tour TCD headquarters when this was over."

He hugged his daughter tighter as he stared up at the woman who'd saved his life, saved his family. "Thank you."

"Don't come back for me." She took a deep breath, almost steeling herself, and charged from the tree line.

Gunfire exploded around them as Benning hauled himself and Olivia to his feet and raced as fast as he could through the trees. His daughter's weight tugged on the bullet wound in his shoulder as snow threatened to trip him every step of the way. He couldn't look back, couldn't slow down as his daughter's tears soaked into his neckline, couldn't stop the hole in his chest from splintering wider. His instincts screamed for him to turn around, but Ana had ordered him to get Olivia as far from here as possible. He had to keep going. He had to leave her behind. He curled his hands tighter in his daughter's pajamas. This was the choice Ana had asked him to make. "We're almost there, baby. Close your eyes. We're almost there."

Olivia beat against his back with her small hands. "Daddy, we have to go back! Ana needs our help! Go back!"

"We can't go back, Liv." His eyes burned at her pleas. His daughter wasn't the only one who'd gotten attached to the federal agent assigned to recover his son, but he'd keep his promise. The SUV came into view, and Benning left the protection of the trees. The back window had been shattered, glass crunching under his boots as he rounded the driver's side of the vehicle. He wrenched open the back door and buckled Olivia inside, then climbed behind the wheel. "Ana's going to be okay. She's a federal agent, remember? She's trained for this."

Whether he'd meant the words for his daughter or for himself, he didn't know.

A final gunshot echoed off the mountains, and he slowed his reach for the glove compartment. Ana. His heart threatened to beat straight out of his chest as the seconds ticked by. Maybe a full minute. No other shots registered. Did that mean—

Movement shifted in the rearview mirror.

"Get down!" He spun in his seat a split second before a bullet cracked the front windshield. Olivia's scream spurred Benning into action. He reached for the keys in the glove box, hit the remote start, and shoved the vehicle into Drive. Snow kicked up behind them, blocking his view of the shooter as they fishtailed onto the main road. Leaving the cabin, the deadline and Ana behind.

FLAKES FELL IN even sheets as Agent Evan Duran followed the fast-vanishing trail of footprints around the back of the property. The TCD safe house had been compromised by a single shooter determined to get his hands on the skull Benning Reeves had recovered from a Britland Construction property. Only now the evidence was missing. Along with Ramirez.

"What the hell happened here?" JC Cantrell straightened from a crouch beneath the shattered window on the north side of the house.

"I have no idea." Snow had been falling for the past few hours—long before he and Cantrell had tracked Ramirez's SUV and recovered Benning Reeves and his daughter on the shoulder of the 441—but failed to hide the stark pool of blood stained into the white backdrop. *Mierda.* Whether it'd come from the attacker or Ramirez, he didn't know, but whoever they were, they didn't have much time after losing that much blood. Whatever'd occurred here, Benning and Olivia Reeves were obviously lucky to be alive, even if that man had walked away with a fresh bullet in his shoulder. "I count three sets of adult footprints, one child. All of them coming from the back of the house."

"Let's move." JC withdrew his service weapon

and raised it shoulder level. "If that blood belongs to Ramirez, we might already be too late."

In the year Agent Ramirez had joined Tactical Crime Division, there wasn't a lot she'd revealed to the team about her past. She'd transferred from missing persons, but other than that, she liked to keep to herself, which he respected. Every agent on their team had secrets. The TCD worked together, trusted each other with their lives when it counted, but that didn't mean they had to give up their entire personal histories. He imagined Ana Sofia Ramirez had one hell of a story to tell. Evan had noted the way she isolated herself from the rest of the team, insisted on them calling her by her last name, how she took on every case with a detachment he usually only saw in veteran agents who'd seen too much over the years. There was a reason behind it, a familiarity.

She'd lost someone close to her—violently—and in that regard, he and Ramirez were probably more alike than she realized. If it hadn't been for Annalise, he never would've seen past all that anger, that pain that came with losing the person he cared about to circumstances he couldn't control. Even worse, the guilt that if he'd only been strong enough, fast enough, he could've stopped it from happening in the first place. No matter how old he'd been at the time when his sister was taken.

Ramirez carried that same guilt now and had been investing it into saving as many lives as she could as though she was searching for some kind of redemption. He didn't know for whom, didn't have to, but it wasn't any way to live. The Tactical Crime Division had been created for rapid response, but even then, it was impossible to save everyone. As long as Ramirez refused to accept that, she'd destroy everything and everyone she cared about in the process. Then again, she had to have survived whatever had happened here to get that chance. Evan tapped JC on the shoulder twice. "On your six."

Unholstering his own weapon, he pressed his shoulders against the exterior of the cabin and put one foot in front of the other until they reached the corner. He waited until JC cleared them to move and followed close on his partner's heels. His heart pounded loud behind his ears as they neared the large pile of wood straight ahead. Countless bullet casings peppered the snow, more blood. Someone had taken cover behind the wall of wood, and another... He traced the path of footsteps near the tree line. And caught sight of a body twenty feet ahead. "JC."

"I see it." They moved as one, ready for anything in case whoever'd ambushed the safe house hadn't gotten far. Wouldn't be the first time a killer had stuck around to soak up the aftermath of what they'd done. Weapons raised, both agents searched the area for signs of movement as they closed the distance between them and the unidentified victim. The remains burned to a crisp in the fireplace on Benning Reeves's property, the charm linking back to one of Ramirez's old cases, now this. The bodies were piling up, too fast to keep up with.

JC crouched beside the body, rolling the victim onto their side. Long, dark hair spilled away from a familiar face, and dread fisted a tight knot in Evan's stomach. Blood drenched the front of her body from what looked like two bullet wounds—one in her side and one above her right breast—and a wound that'd obviously been a rushed patch job in the field in her left thigh. How she'd survived long enough to ensure Benning Reeves and his daughter had escaped, he didn't know, but they sure as hell owed her their lives. "Ramirez. *Hijo de*—"

"She's alive. I've got a pulse, but barely." Pulling his bare hand from her neck, JC holstered his weapon, then ripped her coat down the middle. "We can't move her like this, and it'll take two hours before EMTs can get here by road."

In a single breath Evan had his phone in his hand and pressed to his ear. The line connected directly to Director Jill Pembrook's private cell almost instantly. A gust of frigid air worked under Evan's jacket as JC stared up at him, his partner's expression blank, helpless. They didn't have a lot of time. Not if they were going to save Ramirez's life. The line connected. "I need a chopper to the Sevierville safe house now." He studied the lack of color in Ramirez's face, then let his attention drift lower to her injuries. "We've got an agent down."

Chapter Nine

Numb.

She couldn't feel her fingers, toes, or anything in between, but the soft beeping from nearby said she wasn't dead. If she was, heaven sucked. Ana struggled to open her eyes. Dim fluorescent lighting, scratchy sheets, uncomfortable bed with a remote next to her hand. Hospital. But the weight pressing into her left side didn't fall in line with previous experiences she'd had in places like this. Raising her head, she stiffened as her chin collided with a head of soft, beautiful auburn hair.

"She didn't want you to have to wake up alone." That voice. His voice. The IV in her hand ensured she couldn't physically feel the pain her body was in, but she still felt the tug of her insides when he spoke. Bright blue eyes steadied on her, and everything that'd happened since he'd inserted himself back into her life vanished. Leaving only him, leaving Olivia.

"You weren't…supposed to come back for me." Her mouth tasted dry, bitter. How long had she been here? Hours? Days?

"That credit goes to your team. Agents Cantrell and Duran tracked the SUV's location after I called them from a burner phone you'd left in the glove compartment." He rested his elbow on his knees, one hand intertwined with hers. Shadows darkened under his eyes, his voice choked by something she couldn't put her finger on. "I wasn't going to leave you there to die, Ana. Not after everything you've done for us."

Was that why he was here? Because she'd done her job and he thought he owed her some semblance of repayment? Pain worked through her chest as she tried to sit higher in the bed, but the morphine dripping from the clear bag above her head should've taken care of that. No. This pain was something she hadn't allowed herself to feel for a long time. She'd spent so long trying to control her feelings, trying not to let people get close. While she and Benning had reunited after all these years in grief, held together by blood and fear, facing down the man who could've taken it all away had brought one life-altering realization into focus: moving on to the next case would hurt far more than ever before. In a matter of days, he and the precious soul tucked into Ana's side had carved their way into her heart without her realizing it until it was too late. Leaving would take everything she had left.

"How is she?" Ana set her mouth at the crown of Olivia's head and inhaled the scent of shampoo. Memories flashed like lightning across her mind. She'd provided cover for Benning and Olivia as they'd raced through the trees toward the SUV. Only…she'd taken another bullet before they'd reached the vehicle. She'd tried to stay on her feet, tried to give them a chance, but she'd lost too much blood and her body hadn't been able to take any more. She'd collapsed. The man in the mask had stood over her, weapon aimed directly at her head, but then…she'd blacked out.

"She's fine. Thanks to you. We made it to the SUV and were able to get out of there before he could get to us." Benning rubbed circles into the pressure point between her index finger and thumb, and an immediate sense of calm flooded through her. "You saved our lives, Ana, and I'll never be able to repay you for that, but don't ever do that again. We almost lost you."

Air caught in her throat. The way he'd said those last four words almost made her believe his concern was more than professional courtesy, and her insides warmed. Did that mean... No. He might've been right about the fact her guilt had colored her relationships with the people around her, but she wasn't stupid enough to believe that any feelings built from their stress-induced situation were real. Or would last. She couldn't give in to that hope. Not when she still had so much work to do. Smoothing Olivia's hair out of her face, she rested her cheek on top of the girl's head. "I gave you my word. I'm not going anywhere. Not until I find your son."

The blue of his eyes deepened in color. Sliding his hand from around hers, he leaned back in his chair and ran his uninjured hand through his hair. "They lost the shooter's trail about a quarter mile into the woods. He must've had an ATV or a snowmobile waiting. He'd planned everything before he'd even walked into that cabin. And without him, I don't know if I'll ever see my son again." He picked up the phone she'd taken from the shooter, the one loaded with video of Owen. Alone, in the dark. The hospital staff must've recovered it with her personal effects when she'd been brought in, but seeing Benning with it pooled dread at the base of her skull. "Except with this."

"How many times have you watched that?" she asked.

"I lost count after they brought you out of surgery." He smoothed the pad of his thumb across the screen, and, even though she couldn't see the video clearly, she had the feeling he was imagining smoothing his son's face. "Your team is still processing my house, and they won't let me go inside, so this is all I have of him right now. A video."

"Benning, you have every reason to hate me right now for turning down that bastard's offer, but I promise you, he was never going to give up Owen's location. He would've baited you until you were no longer useful, then killed you both, and I couldn't let that happen." She wanted to reach out for him, take the phone from him, protect him from the pain so obviously pushing him to his breaking point. And protect herself from feeling that same pain.

"I don't hate you." His words barely registered over the beeping of the monitors at her side. "I tried. Those first few weeks after I'd found out you'd requested to be transferred back to Washington, I was angry. At first, I didn't understand what I could've said or if I'd done something wrong." His gaze narrowed on her, head cocked to the side. "But no matter how many times I tried to move on, even after I married Lilly, had the twins, lost her, you were still in the back of my mind. I hated myself more for not being strong enough to realize you weren't coming back than I ever hated you. Now you're the only one standing between my family and the man who wants us dead."

"I'm sorry." She didn't know what else to say but understood those two words couldn't possibly make up for the months—years—of raw pain Benning had endured.

She rolled her lips between her teeth and bit down, but the morphine made it hard for her to know how much pressure was too much, and after a few seconds, she tasted salt in her mouth. A small price to pay for what she'd left behind. "It sounds grim, but the shooter still has the leverage to use your son in order to recover the skull. I know it doesn't seem like it, but we still have a chance to bring Owen home."

"No, we don't." His humorless laugh tugged at something deep inside. He sat fully back in his chair, shadows deepening the exhaustion etched into his expression. He studied the phone in his hand one more time before setting it facedown on the end table beside her bed. "I don't know where the damn thing is."

"What do you mean?" She tried to sit up in the bed, but Olivia's weight pinned her to the mattress, and her strength wasn't what it used to be before taking two bullets and having her leg punctured by a window. "You told me—"

"That I hid it inside that fireplace where your team found Jo's body, and I did," he said. "But they didn't recover it, the killer doesn't have it and I'm not the one who moved it."

The scorched remains belonged to Benning's nanny? Her heart sank as she studied the bandage taped over her broken trigger finger. So much blood, so many innocent lives just…gone. It was her job to protect the innocent and find the guilty, but she couldn't even stomach looking at the damage to the rest of her body. Not without reminding herself of who'd she'd almost lost in the span of a few hours. How much more she would've lost if it hadn't been for him. Raising her gaze to his, she tried to clear her head of him, of his daughter pressed against her side, of all the distractions that could get in the way in finding the scared little boy in that video. But over the course of this investigation, Benning Reeves had made it very hard for her to stay numb.

Owen and Olivia's abductor had returned to the scene to clean up his mess, but he hadn't found what he'd killed an innocent woman over. If Ana had been able to physically feel anything in that moment, she would've had a headache pounding behind her ears. This didn't make sense. Someone else had gotten to the evidence before they could, but that still left the question of how Owen's kidnapping connected to the Samantha Perry case. It wasn't a coincidence that the charm had showed up at the scene of a body dump, and it wasn't a coincidence the shooter had blamed her for that girl's death. There had to be something linking the two investigations. Something she wasn't seeing. "Who else knew about the skull?"

"Nobody." Benning shook his head, that dark, shoulder-length hair stark against his white long-sleeved shirt. He'd showered, changed, but the shadows under his eyes said he hadn't rested during the time she'd been recovering. He'd stayed. Maybe at his daughter's insistence, but still, it meant a lot. More than it probably should have. There weren't a whole lot of people in her life that would've done the same.

"I need to brief my team." The dim lighting was suddenly too bright then, her body aching more with each passing second. The key piece of evidence in this case was missing, Owen Reeves was still out there and the shooter had nearly killed them all in the process. Ana sat up, ripping the IV from her hand, and Benning shot to his feet.

"What are you doing?" He peeled Olivia from her side.

Infierno, her body hurt, but Ana couldn't just sit here. The SOB shouldn't have been able to find them. Not unless he'd hacked into her vehicle's GPS system, which meant her entire team was officially at risk. "The shooter knew where to find us. I want to know how."

SOMETIMES THE AIR stilled before the onset of a hurricane.

Ana hadn't said a word since her discharge from the hospital, but he had no doubt in his mind that her silence wasn't a sign of weakness or pain. She'd survived two bullet wounds and a nick to her femoral artery from being shoved out a second-story window. If anything, the intensity in which she studied what had been left of his house, the way she curled her uninjured hand into a fist, could be seen as the calm before the storm. Because he wasn't sure there was anything that could bring her down.

Olivia barreled past both of them on her way toward the hallway leading to the back bedrooms. "Ana, come see my room!"

The woman at his side let a laugh escape past her lips, and Benning held on to that sound for as long as he could, committed it to memory. He didn't think he'd hear it again after what'd gone down at the safe house, but it was good to know it was still there. Buried, but there. "Thank you. For letting me stay here. I know it's not ideal, having to come back here after everything that's happened, but I'll make sure you get reimbursed for any damage the crime scene techs or my team might've caused."

"I don't care about any of that. What matters is that

you have a place to recover while we figure the rest of this out. I think it'll be good for Olivia, too. Being somewhere familiar." He tried to ignore the fact all his furniture had been moved or that the rug his mother had woven by hand before he'd been born had disappeared from the living room. The property, including the house his father had built with his own two hands, had been left to him by his parents when they'd passed a few years ago. It'd always felt like home, a sanctuary where he and the kids could let go at the end of the day, stay away from the fast-paced, ever-growing city. A place he could build a family. Only now it felt…cold. Empty. Like something was missing.

Benning cleared his throat. Hiking her duffel into his good hand, he nodded down the hall. "You're welcome to take my room. It's not much, but you won't have to sleep on a twin-size bed that may or may not have cookie crumbs in the sheets." Benning shifted his weight between both feet as a smile pulled at the edges of his mouth. "Owen doesn't think I know he gets up in the middle of the night to steal cookies out of the pantry. He's not very quiet, for one, and he usually has a chocolate mustache in the morning."

"Has problems with authority, huh? Good luck with that." Her gaze met his, and the smile relaxed as his own words settled between them. Something *was* missing, and it had been since the night he'd been knocked unconscious on this very floor. Hints of her sultry scent filled the space between them as she faced him, her hand grazing his arm. Bruising darkened the thin skin along the column of her throat as she stared up at him, and he rested his uninjured hand against the markings. Her pulse raced under his touch, and he couldn't help but revel in the knowledge he'd done that to her. He'd affected her, just as she affected him. "Benning, you don't have to do this until you're ready. We can get a couple rooms in town or find another safe house—"

He lowered his mouth to hers.

Hell, she was so damn perfect, so damn strong. She stood there as though everything that'd occurred hadn't fazed her when his entire world had been ripped apart. She was everything he needed right now—his anchor, his confidante, his motivation to keep going—and he'd almost lost her. Again. Only this time had been different. This time he'd truly believed he'd never see her again, and that knowledge, combined with Olivia's pleas to turn the SUV around, nearly had him putting his daughter's life at risk to go back for her. Her hand latched on to his arm as though she'd needed him as much as he'd been craving her, and he brought her fully against his body. Desire burned through him as she rose on her toes best as she could to get that much closer. His uninjured hand gripped her waist as he maneuvered her backward toward the hallway. "End of the hall."

Her exhales mingled with his as she nodded confirmation.

The Tactical Crime Division was still running background checks on Britland Construction employees, trying to find a weakness that would lead them to a suspect in this case. Confirming his nanny had been the victim recovered from the fireplace and the discovery of the charm that might have significance to the Samantha Perry case, solidified his hunger for the woman in his arms. With all the chaos and fear spreading around them, this was what they needed. A chance to block it all out, to escape. To remember. There was nothing left for them to do tonight. Nothing that could keep them apart, and for the first time in seven years, he'd have exactly what he—

"What are you doing?" a familiar voice asked.

Benning jumped as he realized his daughter had been standing less than a foot away, his heart jerking in his chest. He fought to control his breathing as he stepped back from Ana. Running a hand through his hair, he tried to put a lid on the heat exploding from behind his sternum, but it was no use. He'd never been able to control himself when it came to Ana Sofia Ramirez. "What have I told you about sneaking up on people?"

Bright blue eyes that matched his own shifted from him to Ana and back. "How am I supposed to be a private investigator if I don't sneak?"

Ana's laugh raised his awareness of her all the more. She tried to hide the tint of red climbing from her neck into her cheeks with one hand, and he couldn't help but feel a bit of that embarrassment. "She has a good point."

"I thought you were supposed to be in bed." Crouching, he wrapped Olivia in a one-armed hug and tried not to think about the fact he'd nearly undressed the federal agent assigned to protect them without knowing his daughter had been in the room.

"I want to have a sleepover in your room," Olivia said.

"Baby, Ana is going to sleep in my room tonight, and I'm going to be in Owen's room." At least, that was the plan now. Benning raised his gaze to Ana as she gave them some space as though she didn't want any part of the conversation. He hadn't exactly been dedicated to the idea of filling the hole Owen and Olivia's mother had left behind when she'd died, but Ana was as much part of this family as his wife had ever been now. Maybe even more so considering what'd happened over the past three days.

"No, that's okay." Ana reached for her duffel bag, pain filling her expression as she hauled it to her side. "You guys can take the big bed, and I can sleep in Olivia's room. I'll be fine."

"We should all sleep over in Daddy's bed!" An exaggerated gasp filled the living room. Excitement lit Olivia's features as she bounced in his arms. A brightness he hadn't seen in days filled her eyes, and he couldn't help but enjoy the effect. Three days. Her twin brother, the person she'd never lived a single day of her life without, had been missing for three days. Benning would take all the smiles and jumping he could get out of her.

Then he realized what she was asking. "Honey, I'm sure Ana wants her own bed. You remember she got hurt fighting off that bad man? She needs her rest, and you have a lot of energy when you're sleeping."

"But I want to have a sleepover with Ana." In an instant his daughter—the master of manipulation—wiped the excitement from her features. Tears welled in her eyes, and everything inside him surrendered.

Benning relaxed his chin toward his chest, pulling on the bullet wound in his shoulder. "You've got to be kidding me."

"Uh, yeah. We could do that. It'll be fun," Ana said.

He snapped his head up. "What?"

Ana's attention bounced between him and Olivia as she motioned to his daughter's unicorn pajamas. "It's just… I don't have anything to wear."

"I have something! It was my mom's! I'll go get it."

Olivia raced through the kitchen toward the other side of her house to her room, the tears gone in an instant.

"It's a sleepshirt I kept of Lilly's after she died. I thought Olivia might want to wear it when she was big enough. You know, just something she could have of her mom's." Benning straightened. What was happening? He was the one who was supposed to be sleeping over with Ana. Not the three of them in the same bed. "But you don't have to wear it, and you don't have to let her guilt you into a sleepover. She denies it flat out, but she kicks in the middle of the night. Hard."

Hesitation tensed her shoulders.

"Benning, I don't want to insert myself somewhere I shouldn't. I'm not her mom, and we're… We're not together anymore. So if you think this is a bad idea, I can take her twin-size bed or find a hotel room for the night." Ana swiped her tongue between her lips, homing his attention to her mouth, and every nerve ending he owned fired in response. "But I'm not going to lie, that girl is hard to say no to."

"I should've warned you, she's a professional manipulator." He slid his hand into hers. "Lilly and I had an arrangement after we found out she was pregnant with the twins. We would raise our kids together to give them a stable home, love them, provide for them, but that was where our marriage ended. We were open to the possibility that, maybe, down the line there would be more between us, but it didn't work out that way, and Owen and Olivia have never known their mother. I can't say I didn't care for her at all. I did. Without her, I wouldn't have the two best humans I could've asked for, but I need to make one thing clear with you, Ana."

He traced the tendons along her inner wrist, locking his gaze with hers. "I never stopped loving you."

Her mouth parted, her kiss-stung lips begging for his attention again.

Olivia raced into the room. "I found it!"

What was with this girl having the worst timing imaginable? Did she wait around corners for the chance to ambush him and Ana at every turn? Hell. His body wasn't going to be able to take this much longer.

"Great." Pulling her hand from his, Ana took the sleepshirt from his daughter and smiled. Her hand found its way into Olivia's as they all headed down the hallway toward his bedroom. Ana cast a glance over her shoulder toward him. "Looks like we're ready for that sleepover."

Chapter Ten

The sound of utensils scraping against glass plates pulled her back into reality.

Warm blankets had been piled around her, hints of pine and soap tickling her nose, but the rest of Benning's queen-size bed was empty. She'd fallen asleep at the edge, pressed right against the snoring six-year-old who'd worked past her defenses and straight into her heart. And the man on the other side? She could still feel the warmth of his hand sliding across hers against the headboard as Olivia slept between them. Minutes had gone by, maybe hours, as they'd drifted off to sleep, their gazes connected with one another in the dark, and she couldn't remember a time when she'd slept so well.

Her entire body ached, muscles she hadn't even known existed protesting as she slowly eased her legs over the side of the bed. The wound from the pane of glass in her thigh dulled to a low throb as she settled her toes into the plush rug perfectly centered around the bed. The space—Benning's room—was simple. Wooden nightstands on either side of the bed, with lamps that looked like they'd come straight from the pile of firewood she could see out the window now. Framed pictures of the twins had been strategically placed so he had to see them first thing in the morning, no matter which side of the bed he rolled out of.

Ana couldn't help but pick up the one nearest her. Of Owen. He must've been two—maybe three—when the photo had been taken. He'd lifted his arms straight up in the air as though he'd made a touchdown from his position in the middle of the kitchen. Then she noticed the full-size carrots set on top of each of the cabinet drawer pulls, and she couldn't help but laugh. Pain rolled across her chest from the second bullet she'd taken, and she set her hand over the bandage. Blood soaked through the gauze, staining the sleepshirt Olivia had let her borrow. She carefully replaced the frame on the nightstand and used her uninjured leg for balance to stand. *"Maldicion."*

"One of these days you're going to have to translate all the swear words you say when you think nobody is listening." His voice coiled through her, reaching past the aches and pains, deep into the self-doubt and fear that'd plagued her since she'd taken on this case.

"I got blood on Lilly's shirt." She faced him, nearly knocked back by the primal attraction heating her veins as she looked at him. He leaned against the door frame, muscled arms crossed over his chest, and for a split second, she couldn't remember what she'd been so upset about. He'd changed his clothes, kept his hair damp from his most recent shower and brought her a plate of something that smelled so good her stomach lurched. *Infierno*, he was a god among mere mortals. And she'd been stupid enough to walk away from him. "I'm sorry. I'll wash it before Olivia notices."

"Honestly, she'll probably love it even more now." He moved into the room, hints of the scent she'd caught from the sheets intensifying tenfold, and she couldn't get enough. Of him. Of this place. Of the smiling faces in the picture frames set around the room. It was everything she hadn't realized she'd wanted until now as he pinned her with that bright blue gaze. He stepped closer, offering the plate. "Thought you might be hungry."

"Thank you." Awareness of how very little clothing she'd gone to sleep in warmed her straight through. The T-shirt and pair of his oversize sweats were enough to keep her warm when Olivia had stolen the blankets in the middle of the night but felt like nothing when he studied her from head to toe as he did now. She took the plate from him, her body tingling with the unrequited desire that'd shot down her spine last night before Olivia had caught them kissing. She tried focusing on the plate in her hand and not the fact they were seemingly out of range of his daughter. Eggs, waffles and bacon warmed her palm through the plate. Her favorites. Had that been on purpose? "But I should tell you my team hasn't been able to link any of Britland Construction's employees to this case, or the charm they recovered from your property. Whoever has Owen could've just taken advantage of an opportunity to hide the skull on that site. Official access be damned. I have my team looking for the rest of it. Hopefully, we can find something that will give us an ID in case the skull is never recovered."

"They couldn't match ballistics from the bullet casings they recovered at the safe house, either." Her gaze snapped to his. Pressure built behind her sternum the longer he invaded her personal space—that rich, addictive scent of his filling her lungs. He cocked his head to one side, a playful smile tugging at one corner of his mouth. A mouth she'd kissed less than twelve hours ago, a mouth she wanted more of now. Her gaze dropped to his lips in memory. No matter what happened at the end of this investigation, she'd remember that kiss. Remember him. "Agent Cantrell stopped by to fill me in this morning while you were still sleeping. I didn't tell him you'd spent the night in my bed fighting a six-year-old for a corner of the mattress."

A laugh escaped her chest, and she flinched against the ache, sliding her hand over the wound. She set the plate on the end of the bed to avoid dropping it at her feet. "Don't make me laugh. It hurts too much."

"Here." Benning helped her down onto the bed with his uninjured hand, then disappeared into the bathroom for two breaths before reappearing with a bottle of rubbing alcohol, medical tape and fresh gauze in hand. "We should change your bandage."

"Already prepared," she said. "Were you expecting I'd get shot?"

"I live with two sociopaths who don't learn their lessons about running through the house with sharp objects." Setting everything across the end of the bed one-handed, he crouched in front of her, his gaze level with her chest. Callused fingers made quick work of pulling the collar of her shirt lower, removing the bandage over her stitches and cleaning both fresh and crusted blood from the area. Every move he made, every swipe of his fingers against her skin, hiked her heart rate into overdrive. All she had to do was reach out and touch him…and she'd have everything she'd ever wanted. "I can't tell you how many times I had to clean the gash on Owen's head after he ran into the brick fireplace because he wouldn't leave the damn thing alone."

She hissed as the cotton swab he was using pulled at her stitches, and stinging pain slipped past her constant hold on her reactions.

"Sorry," he said. "I've got to clean it all or it might get infected."

"It's fine." She wanted to turn away, to hide the fact she wasn't completely under control at that moment from him, but there was nowhere for her to run. She wanted to be the woman who'd stopped at nothing to protect him and his children from harm for him, who'd stared down a killer without blinking, but the numbness and mental distance had started to fade. He'd gotten beneath her skin, lit the darkest parts of herself she'd kept hidden from everyone around her, and she was starting to lose the battle. Physically. Mentally. Emotionally. Locking her teeth together, she released the breath she'd been holding as the stinging dulled and studied his work. "You're pretty good at this."

"Well, you're pretty good at getting yourself shot." He trailed his hands to the bandage strapped across her upper thigh, igniting a path of heat and goose bumps. "And stabbed. Like I said, I've had a lot of practice."

"Hey, let's get one thing straight, okay? The window stabbed me, and that was not my fault." His smile melted the remaining tension down her spine and fisted tight around her heart. Always the giver, always looking out for someone else. That was the kind of man he was. Caring, considerate. She didn't deserve him. "Would you change any of it? The calls from school, the trips to the emergency room, sweeping cookie crumbs out of sheets on a daily basis."

"Not a thing." Peeling back the tape from the wound in her thigh, he changed out the dressing quickly, but his hand didn't fall away when he was finished. In an instant a rush of sensation fired through her. There was a breath, one moment, where her fear released its hold on her, and she leaned in to finish what they'd started last night.

"Daddy?" Olivia asked from the door.

"Damn it, I really need to put a bell on that girl." Benning ducked his head, his hand sliding from her thigh, and he turned toward his daughter standing in the door frame. "What is it, baby? Are you still hungry?"

"I miss Owen." Sunlight streamed through the windows centered over each nightstand beside the bed, highlighting the well of tears in the girl's eyes, and something inside Ana broke. Something she hadn't let herself feel since realizing her baby sister wasn't going to be coming home. No matter how many times Ana and her brothers had searched, they'd had to accept their sister was gone. "Can he come home now, Daddy? Please?"

In three steps Benning had his daughter wrapped in his big arms, her face buried in his shoulder as he stroked her hair. "Everything is going to be okay, Liv. Owen is going to be home soon. I promise. We're working with Ana's team to find him, and he'll be annoying the heck out of you sooner than you think."

Turning her attention to getting dressed, Ana was aware the moment wasn't meant for her. No matter how easy it'd been to fall back into old habits, familiarities and jokes, she wasn't part of this family. And she never would be. The work she did couldn't be compromised. Not by her past experiences. Not by the six-year-old girl who'd wrapped her arms around Ana as she'd gone to

sleep last night, and definitely not by the man determined to take up too much space in her head.

"Will the skull you put in the fireplace help find him
faster?" Olivia asked.

Ana twisted around, her heart in her throat. "What'd
you say?"

Maneuvering Olivia back at arm's length, Benning
wiped his daughter's tears with the pads of his thumbs,
then gripped both her arms. He lowered his voice. "Olivia Kay Reeves, tell me you aren't the one who took
that skull from the fireplace."

"I wanted to solve the case." Olivia's face fell as another round of tears streaked down her flawless cheeks.
"I brought it to my lab."

"What lab?" Ana took a single step forward.

Benning slid his hands down his daughter's arms as
he turned to face Ana. "She and Owen built a fort in
the backyard where they like to pretend to solve cases.
The skull must be there."

"She really is one hell of an agent," Ana said.

"I wish that made me feel better." All this time the
evidence he'd removed from Britland's construction site
had been right in his own backyard. Well, it'd been in
his backyard before, but his daughter wasn't supposed
to be the one who'd found it. His stomach knotted. This
was the kind of thing nightmares were made of, and Olivia had... Hell, she'd done what any good investigator
would've done and preserved the evidence. "Six-year-
olds aren't supposed to hide bones from their parents
in a fort in their backyard."

The forensic techs pulled the evidence from the
makeshift fort his kids had built out of extra two-by-

fours and subfloor from one of the sites he'd inspected last summer. Owen and Olivia had spent every waking second in their hideout when the weather was good. In fact, he'd had to drag them into the house by their ears for dinner on many occasions. Now it was a crime scene, stained by the very thing he was trying to protect them from.

"We have the skull now. My team will run DNA and dental records, and we'll figure out time and cause of death." Ana slipped her hands into her jacket pockets. "If Olivia hadn't moved it, the killer would've gotten ahold of it first and destroyed the evidence, Benning. Getting an ID on this victim is how we get your son back."

She was right, but at what point would it be okay to say his family had been through enough? How much more blood, fear and near-death experiences did he and his kids have to take before what he'd built cracked beyond repair? Olivia could obsess over becoming an investigator all she wanted, but there was a difference between reading about this kind of stuff in her mystery novels and seeing it firsthand, and he didn't want any part of it. Not for her. Not for the woman at his side. What kind of life was that? What kind of person wasn't affected by this kind of work on a deep, scarring level? Benning knew the answer the second the question had crossed his mind, and right then he understood. Understood the deeper reason why Ana had chosen to cut herself off from her family and friends…from him. Understood why she'd kept her emotions out of relationships, and how she was able to step onto scenes like this over and over again with a kind of numbness and detachment. Because without that boundary in place, she risked the people she cared about the most. No-body—not even she—could handle a lifetime of that kind of guilt if something happened to one of them. "How do you do it? All the pain, the death, the risk of endangering the people you care about. You've made a career out of stuff like this, and I can't even handle it for a few days."

One breath. Two.

"You know as well as I do it doesn't come without a cost, but I realized a long time ago giving people an-other chance to live their life is worth the sacrifice." Ana limped toward the scene, then paused, turning back toward him. Controlled chaos played out behind her, but the world seemed to disappear in the moment her eyes lifted to his. No crime scene techs, no body parts being collected and bagged in his backyard. It was just the two of them. Hints of red colored the tip of her nose and cheeks, the confidence in her eyes overwhelm-ing. "You're stronger than you think you are, Benning. The only reason your kids are still here is because you fought to protect them. Remember that the next time you ask yourself if you're doing enough. You're every-thing to them."

Yet, he'd been the one to put them in danger in the first place.

A car door slammed from the other side of the prop-erty, and he turned his attention to the older, white-haired couple headed for the front of the house. Lilly's parents.

Benning faced the elongated front porch he and his father had built a few years ago, studying Olivia with her notebook and pen in hand as she rocked back and forth in the hanging swing. He used to rock her and

Owen to sleep as babies on it. It'd been the three of them, one of them in each arm, and the crickets on that swing when he'd promised to protect them for the rest of their lives. For the first time he could remember, he'd failed.

The brightness in Olivia's expression gripped his heart in a vise as he climbed the stairs and sat beside her. She was obviously having the time of her life watching real investigators and technicians collect evidence, taking notes on what they did, what they said, how they bagged the evidence. He swiped his uninjured hand down his face. She'd found a human skull in their fireplace and had moved it without hesitation to solve the crime herself. Hell, he had to start watching what kind of stuff she was reading. "Liv, I need you to go spend a couple nights with Grandma and Grandpa while I help the FBI look for your brother. It'll be safer for you there."

He and Lilly hadn't had the greatest relationship. Really, they'd only gotten married to make it easier on the kids as they got older, but he'd always liked and respected her parents, and they loved their grandchildren despite the choices he and Lilly had made. He trusted them to watch over and be there for his daughter in case…he couldn't. Benning bit the inside of his cheek to counter the sinking sensation in his stomach.

The scribbling on her note pad slowed. "I want to stay with you."

He moved a piece of long brown hair out of her face and tucked it behind her ear as his insides tore bit by bit. He should've gone straight to the police after he'd found the skull instead of coming home because Owen had been sick. Should've been strong enough to fight off the bastard who'd taken his kids. Should've gone after Ana seven years ago when he'd had the chance so there wasn't this invisible distance between them now. His life was full of wrong choices, but he'd never forgive himself if something happened to Olivia because of his own selfish need to keep her close. "I know, but think of it this way. Grandma has a whole bunch of mystery novels you haven't read yet."

Curiosity pulled her attention from the crime scene, and those beautiful blue eyes widened. "How many?"

"She told me she ordered a ton of new ones for you last week." He settled one elbow on his knee, leveling his shoulder with hers. Nudging her with his arm, he unbalanced her enough to keep her attention on him. "Thirty. Maybe more."

"And I get to read them all?" she asked.

"I told Grandma you get to read as many of them as you want." Threading his hand in hers, he helped her off the swing and nodded toward Lilly's parents. Within two minutes Olivia, her booster seat and the bag he'd packed for her were loaded into the back of his in-laws' pickup truck. "I'm going to see you in a couple days, okay?"

"Okay." She hugged her bag tighter. "Don't forget to call me tonight when I go to bed."

"I will, baby. See you soon." He kissed the top of her head, memorized the way the scent of her shampoo tickled the back of his throat, then shut her inside and stepped back. Slush kicked up behind the pickup's tires as his daughter centered her face in the rear window and stared back at him with a small wave. He waved back, and something inside him cracked. First, Owen had been taken from him. Now he needed Olivia as far from this case as possible.

"You made the right decision." Ana stepped into his side, her soft, dark hair lifting into his face as wind ripped through the trees, and a shiver raced down his spine. She'd been there nearly every step of the way, protected his daughter from harm, nearly died to ensure he and Olivia had made it to safety at the cabin, and was working tirelessly to locate his son. Where his heart threatened to shred in his chest as his in-laws turned onto the main road back toward Sevierville, Ana was there trying to hold him together. She'd always been there. Because he hadn't been able to let her go all this time.

"There was nothing to think about. Every second she's around me is another chance that bastard can get his hands on her." Warmth spread down his arm as she curled her fingers around his inner elbow. "I should've gotten her out of town when I had the chance, but I couldn't…"

"Stand the thought of losing her, too? I might know a little something about that." She did. More than he ever would. She buried her nose beneath the high collar of her jacket, then tucked her hands into her pockets, taking the heat she'd generated with her. "I could tell you it gets easier over time to help you feel better, but it'd be a lie."

"Has anyone ever told you your bedside manner could use some work?" he asked.

"I don't think anyone but you would have the guts." Her laugh pierced through the unsettling haze closing in on his thoughts as the pickup dipped below the horizon, and hell, he loved that sound. Loved the way her smile reached her eyes, how her smile lines perfectly framed her full lips, loved the way that laugh shot heat straight through his system. She nodded back over her shoulder toward the house. "Come on. It'll be a few hours before forensics has any information on the skull. Until then, we can make up for the sleep your daughter stole from us last night as soon as the tech team is finished. Then we can review the list of Britland Construction employees together. Make sure there's not someone on that list we need to take a closer look at."

The gut-wrenching weight of sending Olivia to his in-laws' farm for a couple days started to lift. How was it possible, in the most terrifying circumstances he'd ever imagined, Ana still kept him grounded, kept him from losing control? If he hadn't requested her to work this case, would he have been able to keep it together this long? Would the killer have gotten exactly what he'd wanted, and taken Benning and his twins down with him? The answer was already there, already cemented in reality. Without Ana, he would've lost everything. "I warned you what would happen if you agreed to a sleepover. You knew the risks going in, Agent Ramirez."

"Like I said, it's hard to say no to her," she said.

Benning slipped his hand into hers as she struggled to retrace her steps through the snow on her injured leg, and in that moment he found himself never wanting to let go. "Wait until she asks you to let her drive your SUV."

Chapter Eleven

This whole investigation would be easier if the evidence spelled out who'd taken Owen Reeves from this very house. Ana studied the official crime scene photos taken of the charm JC had recovered from Jo West's body disposal site. She and Benning had stayed up most of the night reviewing the employee list from Britland Construction, but none of the names—no matter how many times she'd read them—had jumped out at either of them. No criminal charges other than a few speeding tickets, no massive amounts of debt or visible connection to the Samantha Perry case either of them could see. From the outside it looked as though Britland Construction hired the best and most trustworthy assets despite the negligence Benning had uncovered and the skull he'd pulled from one of their project walls.

She'd gone over the interviews she and her partner had conducted seven years ago during the Samantha Perry case, searching the transcripts, rereading the file over and over until the words had started blurring together. Director Pembrook confirmed Samantha's best friend, Claire Winston, was currently serving her country in Afghanistan with her military unit and still wore the bracelet the friends had exchanged in high school while she was off duty. The charm had to belong to the teenage girl Ana hadn't been able to save, the one whose case had changed everything. It had to. It was too much of a coincidence for it to be random.

"There has to be something here." She fought to keep her eyes open, her entire body giving in to the exhaustion she'd been ignoring for the past three days. But she couldn't sleep. The kidnapper's twenty-four-hour deadline had expired. They should've uncovered a lead by now. Should've heard from the *bastardo* who'd taken Benning's son. But there'd been nothing. Tears burned in her eyes as defeat clawed through her. The all-too-familiar sinking sensation she'd worked hard to bury since she'd requested a transfer to Washington broke through her defenses. She had to find Owen, needed to find the boy who'd topped each of these cabinet pulls with carrots in that photo next to his father's bed. Because if she couldn't do this… If she couldn't bring that little boy home, it would destroy the man who'd worked past her defenses and given her a glance at what real happiness could look like. And she'd lose him all over again.

The thought sparked a chain reaction of disbelief and rage. She stilled, but her heart raced out of control. Three days. That was all it'd taken for Benning to put her right back in the same position she'd been in when she'd received the call that Samantha Perry's body had been recovered. She'd become emotionally involved. Attached. Blind to the evidence right in front of her. She'd broken her own rule to keep her distance and fallen in love with the idea she wouldn't have to leave. But if she couldn't find Owen, his small, perfect family would be the ones who paid the price.

She shoved the stack of papers off the kitchen island with every ounce of anger and frustration and disappointment building inside, but spun too fast and stretched the stitches in her side. Pain spread fast, the air rushing out of her, and she had to catch herself before the gray wood-like tile throughout the kitchen rushed up to meet her. Bent over the bar stool, she clamped onto her side as the stinging dulled. She couldn't breathe, let alone think. "What have I done?"

Strong hands slid along her spine, and she twisted around to fight as his arms secured her against his muscled chest. No. She couldn't break. Not in front of him. The bullet wound beneath her collarbones protested as she pushed away from him, but he only held her tighter as the sobs broke past her control. Her knees threatened to give out, but he was there. Lending her his strength, letting her take what she needed from him. She fisted her unbroken fingers into his shirt as tremors racked through her. "What am I missing?"

Benning stared down at her, not an ounce of blame or hatred in his expression, only sympathy. And suddenly the agent she'd been fighting so hard to become shattered into a thousand pieces right in the middle of his kitchen. The hurt, the loss, the grief, the anger she'd had to live with each and every day broke through. She felt it all—everything she'd been trying to hide over the years—in a matter of seconds until her body couldn't take it anymore. He'd been right before. Detaching herself from feeling anything for the people she cared about had been tearing her apart, and she didn't know how to fix it. The tears streaked down her face as the truth she'd been holding on to for so long bubbled to the surface. "I couldn't save them. My sister, Samantha. I...failed."

"But you did everything you could, Ana, and that's

what matters." He bent at the knees, scooping her into his arms, and it was then she'd noticed he wasn't wearing his arm sling. He was at risk of doing more damage to his shoulder, but he kept his attention focused on her. Always on her. The main level of his house passed in a blur as he carried her down the hall and into his bedroom. Laying her in his bed, his hands trailed to her boots, and he unlaced each one before discarding them onto the floor. Slowly, carefully. Treating her as though she were glass. Had anyone taken such care with her before? The mattress dipped as he took position beside her, his gaze centered on her. "You've been so focused on saving everybody else. But who's going to be there for you when you need it?"

She didn't know what to say, what to think. The Tactical Crime Division—JC, Evan, Smitty, Davis, all of them—had become a large part of her life over the past year since Director Pembrook had requested her reassignment from missing persons, but there were still pieces of her she kept hidden from her team. From everyone. Her parents, her three brothers, the friends she'd cut from her life. Any one of them would race to help if she asked, but she didn't deserve their support. Not after what she'd done. He traced her jawline with callused fingers, and right then she couldn't escape the feeling he might know her better than she knew herself. In ways no one else had. "I…"

He leaned into her, pressing his mouth to her forehead as she slid her hand around his wrist, begging him not to leave. Closing her eyes, she reveled in his touch, in the way he always smelled of pine and outdoors, in how he made her feel wanted and strong and beautiful.

Trailing a path of soft kisses to her temple, then lower

toward her ears, he brushed his beard against her over-sensitized skin, and she shuddered. "Let me be that man who can be there for you, Ana. Tell me what you need. Don't think about it. Tell me what you need right now."

The answer sat on the tip of her tongue, but she didn't have the courage to say those words. Instead, she opened her eyes, framed his face between both hands and brought his mouth to hers. She kissed him hard, desperation sliding into every stroke of her tongue against his. She felt as if she'd been starving for air, and he was oxygen. He was her whole world in that moment, the only one who mattered. Her weaknesses, the lack of evidence, the night she'd walked away. None of it existed inside the bubble they'd created. Him. She needed him.

He leveraged his injured arm on the other side of her head, then latched on to her hip before his fingers moved beneath her shirt. Eyes—brighter than the clear blue sky—roamed down the length of her body, and every cell she owned heightened as though he'd physically touched her. "You are the strongest, most dedicated and beautiful woman I've ever known, and you deserve someone who's going to treat you like the queen you are, who will put your needs first and make you happy for the rest of your life."

"You make me happy." Her admission slipped past her lips without her permission, but she couldn't take it back now. She wouldn't. Because it was the truth. The three months they'd been together all those years ago had been the best of her life. Until now. These past few days, seeing him again, seeing him as a father to an amazing little girl and how dedicated he was to protect his children, had shifted something inside her. Opened up a lifetime of possibility she'd never considered before. Given her hope.

A slow smile stretched his lips thin. "You make me happy, too."

Carving a path through his beard with her fingernails, she lifted her mouth to his. What their mutual admission meant for the future, if they even had one, Ana didn't know, but excitement coursed through her as she committed herself to finding out and chased back the fear burning through her. She'd spent her career dedicated to saving as many victims of violence as she could, put her entire life on hold to give them a chance to live the rest of theirs, but maybe she'd finally sacrificed enough to make up for her past. Maybe it was time for her to take that same chance she'd battled so hard to give to the victims who'd been taken. With him. With Owen and Olivia. "We have the house to ourselves now."

"Believe me, that's all I've been thinking about since we finished running through the Britland Construction employee directory." His voice graveled, warming her from the inside. He hauled her off the bed, careful of her injuries, and carried her into the attached bathroom. The same gray wood-like tile directed them toward a large open shower set at the farthest end of the space. Sharp layers of stone and rock made up the back wall of the shower, two square rainshower heads lighting up as Benning twisted on the water. In seconds he'd stripped himself, discarding his clothing outside the reach of the water pooling at their feet, and closed in on her. All predator. All hers. Ridges and valleys of muscle carved shadows across his abdomen, and her mouth watered. "I've been waiting for this moment for seven years."

Slowly pulling her shirt over her head to avoid the pain in her chest and shoulder, Ana gasped as he swept her under the shower spray with most of her clothes still on. A laugh escaped up her throat as she slid her now-wet hair out of her face. "You couldn't wait five more seconds?"

He kissed her again, his body pressed against the length of hers. "Not for you."

HE COULDN'T SLEEP, couldn't take his eyes off her, and after what they'd shared over the past three days, he knew why. He'd fallen in love with her all over again. This intelligent, confident, beautiful creature who'd slipped in and out of his life. But this time he wasn't going to let go. Chasing Olivia down with cookie dough at the safe house, sharing his bed with his daughter sandwiched between them, gasping his name as he'd memorized her body all over again in the privacy of the shower last night. It was as though she was already part of their lives, and, damn it, he didn't want to lose her again. Couldn't.

Long, dark eyelashes rested against her cheeks, but the change in her breathing patterns homed his attention to the light brown flawless skin of her neck and chest visible above the sheets. "I can feel you staring at me."

Pain filtered through his nerve endings and he realized he'd propped himself up on the wrong arm for a mere chance of seeing her clearly. "Does Quantico train all their agents in the art of having a sixth sense, or just you?"

"You don't need to flirt with me." Hazel-green eyes centered on his as her smile pierced straight through him. Leveraging her elbow into her pillow, mirroring him, she rested her head against her palm. And in that moment the woman he'd built in his head was more beautiful and mesmerizing than ever before. Exactly where she belonged. "You've already seduced me with your good looks."

"Is that all it takes?" He couldn't keep his laugh to himself, brushing one hand down his beard. "Damn. Wish I would've known that before now. Could've saved me a lot of time and frustration."

"Don't get me wrong, the free cookie crumbs in the sheets and the rainfall showerheads are a bonus." Skimming her hand across his chest, she shifted closer, her lips barely grazing his as she traced the muscled lines of his abdomen below the sheets. Instant desire seared through him, and he half expected his daughter to interrupt the moment, but the cabin remained silent. "I'm starting to wish we hadn't wasted so much time apart."

He closed his eyes. "Ana, I—"

Her phone vibrated from the nightstand, and she set her forehead against his chest. Reality penetrated through the haze they'd created since he'd witnessed her coming to terms with the past in the middle of his kitchen last night, and guilt ripped through him. He couldn't lie to himself. He'd needed the distraction from the case—from the anxiety he'd never find his son—as much as Ana had, and he wouldn't regret that, but they couldn't ignore their respective duties any longer. He needed to find his son, and she needed to find the SOB responsible for taking him. She reached for the phone before the device dipped off the edge of his nightstand, tapped the screen and brought it to her ear. "Ramirez."

Benning slipped from the bed, reaching for his clothes. He couldn't hear the voice on the other end of the line but imagined if there'd been news on his son's location, she'd get the message across.

"Are you sure?" The color drained from her face. Her attention drifted to him, and everything inside him tensed. Ana pinned her phone between her shoulder and ear as she rushed to get dressed. "I'm on my way. Have the director get in touch with Claire Winston again. I want her found. Now." Ana ended the call, and the hairs on the back of his neck stood on end. Something was happening. "That was Evan—Agent Duran. The forensic lab was working on identifying the owner of the skull, but when they went to compare dental records, they noticed something had been locked between the victim's teeth on the X-rays."

"Locked?" Intentionally or forced? Didn't matter. Whatever it was, it could lead them to the next step in this case, the next step to finding Owen. His throat dried as she bolted from the bed and started getting dressed. "What did they find?"

"A scales of justice charm. Exactly like the one we recovered from your property after Jo West's body was found in the fireplace." She slowed, facing him, her boots pinched in her grip. "So now we have two. One could belong to Samantha Perry and the other—"

"To her best friend. Claire Winston." Hell. Were they about to find another body? Benning sank onto the edge of the mattress, the past few hours evaporating as though they'd never happened. How many more people had to die before they were able to bring this bastard down? How many more had to suffer? "You want Claire found in case she's another victim. I thought your director confirmed she's serving with her unit in Afghanistan."

"As far as I know, that's the truth, but it wouldn't be hard to get someone to cover for her. And the army hasn't always been forthcoming about admitting one of their soldiers might be missing in action," she said.

"Why would she…" That didn't make sense. If Samantha Perry's best friend from high school had been targeted by the killer, how would she know she needed to lie about her whereabouts? Benning stood, his instincts screaming. "They got an ID on the skull, didn't they?"

"Yes." She tightened her broken hand around the phone but didn't even seem to notice the pain. "They were able to match both DNA from the bone marrow and dental records to Harold Wood."

Gravity cemented him in place. Samantha Perry's killer.

His mouth dried. "You think Claire might be involved in Owen's kidnapping?"

"I've seen people kill for much less than getting revenge for a best friend who never saw justice. Shoving a charm Samantha Perry wore up until her death in the mouth of her killer is personal. It's sending a message, and it's possible Claire is the one behind it." Ana's voice dropped, almost monotone, as the agent he'd gotten to know over the past few days surfaced. "But if Claire Winston is involved, she's not working alone. The attacker at the safe house was male. Trained, possibly former military. She'd have an extensive network of possible partners from her unit alone. All she'd have to do is convince one of them to help her get justice for Samantha."

"Claire killed Harold Wood and hid his body—or what was left of it—on the construction site, and I uncovered the evidence. She knew the charm and motive would link back to her if he was ever found." He pushed off the bed. Tension bled back into his shoulders and hands as the puzzle pieces started fitting together. "That's why my son has been kidnapped? So she wouldn't have to answer for the fact she killed her best friend's murderer?"

"We don't know that yet, Benning." She hauled the black duffel bag always within reach onto the bed, and dumped a box of bullets onto the sheets, and reloaded the magazine to her new service weapon. She was far more comfortable around a weapon than he was, and damn, he was thankful for it now. "We have to get to Claire's house. There might be something there we can use to prove she's involved, but we have to go now. The skull you pulled from the wall has been identified. Whoever took your son is going to try to make sure we can't connect his death back to them."

Benning studied how quickly she was able to assemble her weapon and holster it, even with a broken trigger finger wrapped in a brace and tape. The air crushed from his lungs as the realization hit. Hell, he loved her. He loved the strong, badass agent who'd protected him and his daughter from a killer, the vulnerable woman who couldn't forgive herself for her past failures. No matter how hard she tried to bury the side that made her more human, he loved her. Had never stopped loving her. He rounded to her side of the bed. "Ana, wait."

He'd told her the truth before. He'd tried hating her, tried focusing on making his marriage with Lilly work despite the fact neither of them were interested in anything more than being parents to the kids they'd created. But his heart had always had other ideas. Something deep down understood that what he felt in this moment was real, and certainty clicked into place. He wanted Ana Sofia Ramirez. Wanted her in his life, in his kids' lives, wanted her when times got hard, when she dropped her guard and especially when she tried to shut him out. He wanted every piece of her, and he didn't give a damn about how much it might hurt in the long run. Loving her would be easy. The rest of it? They'd just have to figure it out together. As a family. But he had to protect his kids at the same time.

"There's something I need to say to you first." His stomach flipped. Would she even want the responsibility of being with a man who had kids? She'd gotten along well enough with Olivia because his daughter was borderline obsessed with what Ana did for a living, but she'd never met Owen. Would the kids want her around, or would they see her as nothing more than a replacement for what they'd lost the day they were born? Would her job put Owen and Olivia at risk? Would she detach herself from them when a case went sideways as she'd done to him all those years ago? This sure as hell wasn't simple lust, but it was starting to turn more complicated all the same.

"Benning?" Ana maneuvered around the end of the bed, slowly closing the distance between them, and every nerve ending in his body went haywire. For her. Because of her. Handing him her backup weapon grip first, she stared up at him, concern etched into her expression.

"I want you to stay here after we recover Owen. With me," he said. "With us."

Her eyes widened, that legendary control failing her, and his heart jerked behind his rib cage at the pure emotion playing across her features. She dropped the weapon she'd offered him to her side as his request settled between them. Hesitation pulled her shoulders back as she prepared to run, but she couldn't deny the connection between them, what they'd shared since she'd answered his request to work this case. "Benning, I don't know what to say."

"Say you forgive yourself and that you've done enough. Say you've saved enough lives to make up for the past, Ana." His voice grew stronger as he became more sure of himself than he'd ever been before. "You deserve to be with someone who loves you. You deserve a life that doesn't force you to detach yourself from everyone around you or that puts the people you care about at risk." He took her free hand in his. "I love you, and I want to build a life with you. I want you to be around for Owen and Olivia, and answer calls from the school and help them learn and grow, but..."

He dropped his chin to his chest as he realized what he had to ask her to do. She'd already sacrificed so much for him and his kids. How could he possibly ask her for more?

Her thumb smoothed over the side of his hand. "But what?"

"I need to know you won't hurt my kids the way you hurt me." He forced himself to look at her. His insecurity, anxiety, his need for her support, all of it bubbled to the surface as though he was still the same guy who'd just discovered the woman he'd been seeing had requested a transfer back to Washington. "That you won't leave without warning, that you won't cut yourself off from them if another victim turns up dead."

Air caught in his throat. "I need you to quit the Tactical Crime Division."

She sucked in a deep breath, her hand shaking in his. Seconds ticked by, a tension-strained minute, before she finally opened her mouth to respond. She tugged her hand from his, that invisible guard slamming back into place as her shoulders stiffened. "You love me, but you want me to choose between you and your family or my duty to save lives."

"I know what I'm asking, and that this won't be an easy choice for you, but as much as I want you in our lives, I also have to think of Owen and Olivia. I wasn't strong enough to protect them from their abductor, and I won't submit them to another layer of trauma if I can prevent it." Benning read her decision as coldness swept over her expression, and the heat she'd ignited in his veins iced.

"You know why I do this job, why I push so hard. I can't just give that up, Benning." She took a step away from him, and the world threatened to rip out from under his feet. She was... She was choosing her job over him, over the twins. She was leaving. Again. "I'm sorry."

He nodded, not really knowing what he was agreeing to, but it didn't matter. He took the gun she'd offered, the steel heavy in his hands. They had a lead, and any ideas or fantasies about what kind of life he and Ana would have had to wait. "I guess that's it, then. When this is over, you'll go back to Knoxville, and I guess... I'll finally have the chance to move on with my life."

He maneuvered around her toward the bedroom door,

the muscles in his jaw aching. Owen was still out there, and Benning wasn't going to stop looking until he found him. With or without Ana at his side.

Chapter Twelve

Over an acre of uneven green grass stretched between them and the light gray rambler on Maplewood Circle. Sevierville PD's SWAT team took position with a single wave of Ana's fingers toward the east side of the house as she, Agent JC Cantrell and Agent Evan Duran arced wide through a patch of trees at the opposite side of the property. No cars in the long driveway alongside the opposite end, nothing to suggest Claire Winston wasn't in Afghanistan with her military unit as Director Pembrook had reported, but that didn't mean someone wasn't home. Or waiting.

The low crackling of static from the device in her ear kept her focused, her movements steady despite the pain in her leg. She'd left Benning in the SUV for his own protection with an armed officer, but knowing he was on the other side of that signal still didn't settle her nerves. He'd asked her to give up a shot at redemption for the chance of being with him, with Owen and Olivia, a sacrifice he had no right to demand of her. She'd spent the past seven years trying to atone for her sins, and he just wanted her to walk away? To forget the people out there who needed her help?

She forced herself to focus. No matter what happened

out here, he'd be safe. The wound in her chest ached as she pressed the stock of her rifle against her shoulder, but two bullets and a pane of broken glass wasn't going to stop her from finding Benning's son. Gravel crunched beneath her boots as she and her team slowly broke from the trees. "Our suspect has been trained in weapons and combat and has a .45 caliber Beretta M9 registered in her name. Eyes and ears open."

"Copy that, Ramirez," JC said.

Both JC and Evan had been military trained. If there was anyone from Tactical Crime Division she'd want at her side, it was them, but tension still crept across her shoulders as they closed in on the back door of the house. Red wood shudders groaned as a brush of wind barreled down the thin section of patio between the back door and the fence, and Ana raised her hand to signal the team to stop. The fence intersected with the back-east corner of the house, cutting off their access to the SWAT team and vice-versa. Her instincts screamed for her to get the hell out of there, but they hadn't gotten the chance to search the house yet. They had to keep moving. Owen's life depended on it. She motioned toward the back door. "Break it down."

Agent Evan Duran climbed the four stairs to the small back deck and tested the doorknob. With a single shake of his head, he adjusted his rifle, then slammed the heel of his foot near the knob. The crack of wood seemed overly loud as the wind died in an instant, and a shiver chased across Ana's shoulders. The door slammed into the wall behind it. Silence. No alarm. No explosion of gunfire. Nothing but the darkness waiting inside. Maybe Claire Winston really was serving with her unit overseas, but they had to be sure. Someone had stuffed Samantha Perry's killer's skull behind all that drywall, and the only motive that explained why was to hide something the killer hadn't wanted them to see.

Ana nodded to breach, taking up the rear behind her team, and swept into the house. It took a few seconds for her eyes to adjust to the low light, but it was clear nobody had been here in a while. Stale air dove deep into her lungs, a hint of moisture clinging to her face and neck. Dust floated in front of her face. She ran her finger through a thin layer coating the kitchen table to her left.

"Ana? You okay?" Benning's voice from her earpiece pierced through the steady pounding of her heart beating behind her ears. She could still smell him on her, that light hint of pine and man. They'd spent the night memorizing each other's bodies all over again, releasing the stress, fear and frustration of the past few days to the point neither of them could move. There'd been unspoken promises as she'd stared into his eyes and the world exploded around her, and she knew. Knew she'd failed in keeping emotional detachment from this case. Knew she wouldn't be able to walk away this time. Knew she couldn't spend the rest of her life living as a ghost. Knew she'd fallen in love with him and his fearless six-year-old in a matter of days. But then he'd asked her to sacrifice the one thing that'd given her purpose over the years, the one thing that'd kept her going and the guilt at bay. The only thing that could help her redeem herself. "Ana?"

Her throat tightened. She couldn't do it. She couldn't risk more victims for her own shot at happiness. She removed the device, dropped it on the floor and severed the connection between them with the heel of her boot.

JC and Evan took position on either side of the door leading into the basement, each of them waiting for her signal.

Ana raised her rifle. All her life this darkness—a physical hole in her chest—had followed her around after her sister had gone missing. She'd watched what that single event had done to her family, how her brothers vowed to uncover the truth, how her parents hadn't been able to live in the town they loved anymore. All that hurt, that pain, had been reignited the night her former partner had called to tell her he'd found Samantha Perry's body in that alley, and she'd only let that hole become bigger since. Now it didn't seem so deep, so... empty. And the credit had to go to Benning. To the way he cared for everyone else first, how he encouraged his kids to be the best versions of themselves without tearing them down, and how he was so determined to make her understand she deserved better. Deserved to be happy for once in her life. Shaking her head, Ana rested her cheek against the stock of her weapon. "Let's do this, guys. We've got a missing boy that needs to get home to his dad."

"On your signal." JC locked his hand on the doorknob.

She took another deep breath to settle her racing heart rate. "Go."

The door swung outward, and they all closed in. Their boots thudded on the unfinished stairs leading down into the house's basement as they cleared the corner and descended onto cement. Old two-by-fours had been stacked to the wall at their right, giving way to an underground cold storage stocked with cans, bags of flour and shelves of supplies.

Raising her weapon toward the ceiling, she flipped on her rifle's flashlight and skimmed the open cords and piping above. Cobwebs and dust glared back as they maneuvered down what she imagined would be a hallway if the basement had been finished, and into an open space. A single window allowed light to spill across the settling concrete, narrow cracks disappearing under a large piece of carpeting to one side. Only the carpet didn't look as level as it should be against a flat surface. It dipped toward the center. Ana trained her flashlight on the spot and kicked at one edge. "I've got something over here."

Two other flashlight beams centered on the carpet at her feet as JC and Evan closed in. Crouching, she tugged the corner of the rough makeshift rug, then tossed it aside—and froze. Chunks of cement fell into the hollowed-out floor from the edges underneath the carpet. A hole, approximately six feet long, had been dug into the foundation. There, at the bottom, a plastic bag stained red remained. Flies buzzed past her ear, the slight hint of decomposition chasing back the scent of pine in her lungs. The plastic wasn't clear enough to see through, but she had a good idea of what was inside. Ana covered her mouth with the back of her hand, but nausea still churned.

"Lo que en infierno...?" Evan said. "What the hell is that?"

"My guess is the rest of Harold Wood." Ana's gut tightened. But why separate the skull from the body, and why dig it up after all this time? "We need to get forensics in here to confirm, but we have to clear the rest of the property first. Move."

"You don't have to tell me twice." JC slowly headed back the way they'd come.

Something wasn't right. Even if Claire Winston wasn't involved in Owen's kidnapping and serving with her unit overseas as she'd claimed, there was a strong connection between this case and the last case that'd brought Ana to Sevierville. Harold Wood. Pressure built behind her sternum as she caught sight of a small red light in one corner of the room, one she hadn't noticed before. The LED flashed once, then faster until she couldn't tell the difference between fluctuations. Warning launched her into JC's side. "Get down!"

Heat and debris seared across her vest as she took most of the blast to protect her teammate. She hit the ground hard face-first, her weapon pinned between her and concrete. Her ears rang as static crackled from the radio on Evan's chest, her vision darker around the edges. Stabbing pain kept her conscious. She tried to push up but couldn't get her balance. Where was JC? Evan? Were they injured? Alive? Her eyes watered as layers of dust filtered sunlight coming through the window. Someone had rigged an explosive to keep them from leaving with the remains. She coughed, sending more debris into the air. "Guys." No answer from her team. "Evan? JC?"

More static. Pressing one palm into the floor beside the hole, she was able to flip onto her back. Skeletal dust clung to the rafters and cords above. The explosive had to have been set underneath the rug. She must've triggered it when she'd uncovered the remains, and now Harold Wood had become more decoration than evidence.

Heavy footfalls vibrated through the floor as she

gave in to the heaviness pulling her eyes closed. SWAT would've heard the explosion. She, JC and Evan would be okay. They'd be... She closed her eyes as water pounded onto her vest from above. Two steps. Three. Then silence as her ears stopped ringing. She struggled to open her eyes, the blurred outline of a man above her, and she gripped her weapon, only to have it taken from her. "You should've walked away when you had the chance, Agent Ramirez."

BENNING PUSHED OUT of the SUV as what felt like a punch of vibration shook the ground. "What the hell was that?"

"Sir, I need you to stay in the vehicle." The officer assigned to protect him raised his hands. Voices and static battled for dominance from the radio strapped to his chest. "SWAT's reporting an explosion from inside the house, possibly the basement."

An explosion? Blood drained from his face and neck. "Ana."

He shoved past the officer and bolted for the west side of the house toward the back, where Ana and her team had breached. Following the gravel driveway, he ignored the shouts telling him to stop and pumped his legs as hard as he could. The bullet wound in his shoulder screamed for him to slow down, but he pushed the pain to the back of his mind. If Ana had been down there when the explosion happened... His lungs burned with icy dread. He pounded up the four stairs of the back deck and raced inside the house. His heart threatened to beat out of his chest as he pushed deeper into the sparsely furnished home and caught sight of the open door leading down into the basement. White dust particles coated his neck and face as he neared. Cement? "Ana!"

No answer. He wasn't a federal agent, he wasn't SWAT and he didn't have a weapon or backup, but nothing was going to stop him from getting to her. He took each step one at a time. If he'd learned anything working in construction for the past two decades, it was that explosions affected more of a building than the blast radius. One wrong step and he could be added among any casualties. A crack of wood shot his heart into his throat a split second before footsteps reverberated above him on the main floor. SWAT had breached the house from the front. He had to move. The first chance they got, they'd secure him away from the scene, possibly in cuffs. Ana might not have that much time. His boots hit cement, dust clinging to his clothing and face. The cold storage straight ahead didn't look like it'd suffered any damage, and he followed the curve of the hallway around until he found the epicenter of the explosion.

A beam fell from the ceiling, wood on concrete loud in his ears, and he raised his hands to block the blast of dust coming straight at him. The unfinished door frame held strong against the explosion, but what he imagined used to be an open living space had been closed off by twisted ducting, broken plumbing and exposed wiring. Damn it. He had to get in there. Had to get to Ana. Water splattered against the floor, but he couldn't tell from where. It carved rivers around his boots to the drain where a bathroom would sit if the construction had been finished. At least the place wouldn't flood. Dust worked down into his lungs, and he coughed into the crease of his elbow. "Can anyone hear me?"

A groan broke through the rush of water, just on the

other side of the ducting blocking his way into the room, and Benning shoved the metal shaft off to one side. The hole in his shoulder screamed, but after everything the Tactical Crime Division had done for him and his family, getting Ana and her team the help they needed was the only thing that mattered right then. The drain behind him was backing up, making it hard for his boots to get any leverage to move the piece of ducting. The groan he'd heard had been distantly male, which meant Ana hadn't heard him or she was unconscious, and this damn section of ducting was keeping him from getting to her. "Somebody shut that water off!"

Multiple sets of boots echoed off the unfinished stairs as SWAT descended into the basement. "You heard him! You, find the main water valve and shut it down. You two, get over there and help him get that debris out of the way. We've got agents in there."

Two armed SWAT members made quick work of clearing a path into the main room where the explosion had originated, and Benning hefted the last of the debris out of his way. "Holy hell."

Blood. A lot of it. His stomach wrenched as he homed in on the massive hole in the middle of the foundation. A bag had been torn to shreds by the blast, but he didn't have time to figure out what—or who—had been inside. Movement registered off to his left, and he caught sight of a boot pinned beneath more debris. His heart rocketed into his throat. Ana? Hauling more ducting and beams out of his way, he struggled to keep the panic clawing through him at bay. She'd already taken two bullets and a window pane through her femoral artery. If she'd been injured in the blast, how long before her body decided it'd had enough? "Ana. Talk to me. Tell me where you are."

Another groan cut through the patter of water on cement. Lifting a panel of drywall off the agent, Benning froze. Agent Duran. Dropping beside the hostage negotiator, he tried to plug the blood trickling from below Duran's vest with both hands and applied pressure. Pieces of concrete bit into his knees as he searched the rest of the scene. The sound of metal hitting cement caused his ears to ring as the other two members of SWAT cleared a path to another agent a few feet away. Agent Cantrell. No. No, no, no, no. She was here. She had to be. He turned back to Duran. "Where is she? Where's Ana?"

"The body…" Small muscles flexed in the agent's jaw as he tried lifting his head off the floor. "Rigged to blow."

"Body?" His pressure on Duran's wound faltered. The bag in the hole, the one covered in chunks of cement. The pounding at the base of his skull increased. "Who's body? Who was in the bag?"

"Harold… Wood." Sweat built along the hostage negotiator's hairline. "Someone unburied it from under the cement and… Ana shouted for us to get down." Wet coughing arced Agent Duran off the floor. The blast must've punctured a lung. "The bomb was a… distraction."

"What do you mean, a distraction?" Benning fought to catch his breath as a pair of EMTs stepped in to take control of the agent's injuries. He straightened, circling the area, searching every square inch of the space, under every piece of debris. EMTs pulled both Agents Cantrell and Duran from the scene on stretchers, but they still hadn't found Ana. The bomb was a distraction. A distraction from what? Running his hands through his hair, he ignored the thin layer of blood on his hands as the single window at one end of the room came into focus. "She's not here."

Ana wouldn't have left her team to bleed out. Wouldn't have left the scene of a crime without telling anyone. Especially if she'd been injured as badly—if not worse—than Cantrell and Duran. Distraction. He understood how explosives worked. Depending on the setup, whoever had set that charge would've had to have been within proximity to trigger the explosion. They would've needed to watch the house in case the Tactical Crime Division identified the skull he'd pulled from the construction site and needed to tie up loose ends. Ana would've known that, too. He didn't see any evidence the basement was being surveilled. Then again, there wasn't much of a basement left. Claire Winston—or whoever was responsible—could still be close if it had been triggered remotely. Had Ana realized the same and gone after that person? No. Cantrell and Duran barely survived that close-quarters blast. Ana wouldn't have been able to get out on her own, which meant someone had to have dragged her out.

Benning wound his way through the scene, back to the stairs leading to the main floor of the house, and out the way he'd come in. Crisp air picked up, and the hairs on the back of his neck rose on end. Thick trees lined the back of the property on the other side of the fence, leaving miles of open wilderness. Curling his fingers into his palms, he battled against the uncertainty threatening to break him. No new leads on Owen, and now Ana had gone missing. No. He wasn't going to lose them. He couldn't. Branches shifted with the wind and exposed a dark green structure set back about an acre behind the main property. Something he never would've seen if he hadn't still been standing on the back deck. Slats in the wooden fence swung loose with another gust, and he stepped down—and froze. A swipe of blood on one of the slats. Fresh from the looks of it. "She left a trail."

Or whoever'd taken her had.

SWAT and the rest of the Tactical Crime Division were focused on the scene, and Benning couldn't waste time trying to convince someone to follow his hunch. He had to go now. Kicking the bottom of the fence, he wrenched a few more slats loose until he could fit, and slid to the other side. Flakes worked down into his boots, but it'd be easy to avoid if he retraced the large set of footprints interrupting the smooth surface of recent snowfall. Warning exploded behind his sternum as he closed in on the seemingly unused structure ahead. Tractor storage? A door on one side had been left partially open. He pressed his back against the opposite door and twisted around to see inside the other. No movement. Nothing to make him think someone was inside, but the footprints—Ana's or the attacker's—had led straight to the garage.

Old hinges protested as he pried the door wider, and he stepped inside. Darkness bled around the edges of his vision before his senses adjusted. His exhales crystallized in front of his mouth, but something other than low temperatures chased a shiver down his spine. He slid one hand along the cold metal wall until he found a light switch, but flipping it on did nothing. Someone had fled from Claire Winston's house and come here.

Why? As far as he could tell, the shed was empty, and there were no fresh tire tracks to suggest a vehicle had been waiting here.

Except...

Except the small LED light casting a red glow across the metal sheeting on either side of it hadn't been there when he'd come in. Benning hit the light switch again, and the light disappeared. His footsteps echoed off cold cement and thin metal walls as he stretched one hand above his head and ran it over where he'd noticed the light. There. Ripping the device from its position, he turned to face the light coming in through the doors. Severed wiring brushed against the palm of his hand, a small lens reflecting the sunlight. "A camera? Why would you need a camera in—"

The video from the shooter's phone. Owen had been crouched in a dark room like this. Alone, crying, scared. Benning spun around, fixating on the exact position his son would've been sitting for the camera to catch that angle of his face, and something inside him broke. He smoothed one hand over the cold flooring as he nearly crushed the camera with his other. The cement was still warm compared to the area around it. This was where they'd held his son. In a cold, barren tractor shed where no one would find him. Where they'd let him cry for hours with no one to tell him it'd be okay. Rage replaced the gut-wrenching desolation. He pocketed the camera and stood. "I'm coming for you, buddy. Both of you."

Chapter Thirteen

Her ears were still ringing.

She couldn't move her hands or legs, couldn't get enough air. It felt as though an elephant had sat on her chest and was refusing to move. She'd taken the brunt of the blast in Claire Winston's basement. She remembered that, but then…nothing. Her team had been there. JC and Evan. Were they okay? Had they gotten out alive? *Infierno.* It hurt to breathe. She must've cracked a—

"Please don't be dead," a small voice said.

Every cell in her body stilled, only the sound of a low humming audible over her uneven heartbeat. Ana struggled to open her eyes, met with only more darkness. Not a hospital. Tugging at her wrists, she battled gravity and a headache to pull her head off the floor of wherever she'd ended up. The floor underneath her was cold, but she wasn't alone. She could barely make out the shape of a small outline resting across her midsection. Her head fell back to the floor. The weight on her chest wasn't from an elephant. "I'm not dead. Are you?"

"No." The boy's voice shook. "But I'm cold and my tummy hurts. And I want to go home."

"My name is Ana." Relief coursed through her. He was alive. She'd found him. She pulled at the zip ties securing her wrists and ankles. Where the hell were they? Flashes of memory ignited in the front of her mind. The explosion had knocked her face-first onto the floor. There'd been water pounding down on her back, but over that, she'd heard footsteps. Then he'd been standing over her. The man who'd shoved her through the window at the safe house. Her head throbbed. He must've taken her from Claire Winston's basement somehow and brought her here. Wherever *here* was. Barely making out a row of shelving beside her as her vision adjusted, she swallowed the chemical burn at the back of her throat. Industrial cleaner? "Your daddy sent me to find you, Owen."

A combination of excitement and hope bled into his voice. "You know my dad?"

"Yeah." She nodded but wasn't sure he could even see the motion. "We're friends. He's been worried this entire time you've been gone, so he called me and asked me to help find you. I'm here to take you home."

Pain arced through her as the six-year-old tablet enthusiast with a pension for stealing cookies in the middle of the night pressed his hands into her side to sit up. "How are you going to do that with your hands and feet tied?"

"That's a good question." No windows. A slight hint of humidity in the air, like a basement. Bare cement bit into her elbows as she shifted enough to sit up against the metal shelving. There had to be something—anything—she could use to break these ties and figure out where their kidnapper had brought them. In an instant Owen had curled back into her side. If her hands had been restrained in front, she would've captured him inside the circle of her arms. But the best she could do was set her cheek against the top of his head. The odor of gasoline and dirt in his hair chased back the smell. "I don't know yet, but I'm sure we can figure something out. As long as we're together, we'll be okay. I promise."

Short hair bristled against her Kevlar vest, and she imagined he was nodding, but the tremors rolling through him said he didn't have much time. The boy was alive, but she had no idea what kind of circumstances he'd been held, if he'd been given food and water, been able to sleep. Setting her head back against the metal shelves, she stared up at the blackness above them. First things first, she had to get out of these ties, but she needed his help. She thought back to what Benning had told her about his son. "Okay, Owen, I need you to stay awake as long as you can, okay? Because we're going to play a game."

"What game?" he asked.

She had to keep him talking, keep him moving, before the cold set in too deep, and he stopped fighting. "How about a treasure hunt? Do you like those?" He nodded against her vest again. "Great. First piece of treasure we need to find is my flashlight. Do you see where it's attached on my vest?"

In less than two breaths, he detached the flashlight and hit the power button. Bright light punctured through the blackness surrounding them, and for the first time, she was able to see him clearly. Dark smudges across his features highlighted crystal-clear blue eyes. Just like his father's. "I found it."

With one look this sweet boy had reminded her how tightly closed in on herself she'd become over the years—since Samantha Perry's body had been found—and how very exhausting it was to keep going. Cut off

from everyone around her. There, but never committed. She'd been living, surviving by giving her body the
basic needs that would keep it going, ensuring everyone
she'd been assigned to find got their happily-ever-after,
but that wasn't a life. Benning was right. She deserved
more. She wanted more. She wanted…something for
herself. Benning had tapped into the things she'd tried
burying and exposed them for the world to see, and
there'd been a sort of freedom in that. He'd broken her
open and shown her what could be. What they could be.
Together. If she only had the courage to give up her shot
at redemption. But how long—how many lives—would
it take to achieve it? How long did she expect to play
hero without knowing an exact number of victims she
would have to bring home to their families while she
put off the chance of having a life of her own?

Ana studied Benning's son in the castoff from the
flashlight's beam. There was a hole in the sleeve of his
pajama shirt and not much color in his face, but otherwise he seemed unharmed, and that was what mattered.
Tears burned in her eyes as pride transformed his features from hopeless to excitement. "Great work. You're
really good at this game."

"What's next?" The tremors tensing his small muscles hadn't abated, even with him tucked into her side.
Her breath materialized on the air. He'd been taken from
his home—from Benning—in the middle of the night
in his pajamas. No coat. No socks. Nothing to keep his
body from dropping into hypothermia while he'd been
held. They had to get out of here. Now. Before his or-
gans started shutting down.

"Okay. Now we need to find something that can
cut through these ties on my hands and feet. Shine the

light over here." She pressed her heels into the floor to sit higher and twisted her head around to search the shelves. The flashlight beam wavered over the shelves filled with cleaning supplies, rolls of toilet paper, cleaning rags and paper towels for steel bathroom dispensers. No tools. Nothing that could cut through plastic. "I don't see anything, but that doesn't mean we've failed. Here, move over here. I don't want to accidentally hit you."

He did as asked, bringing the light back to her as she rocked forward onto her knees and stood. Increasing the tension between her wrists, she bent forward slightly, then slammed her wrists against her lower back. Plastic cut into her skin, and she bit back a groan and tried again. Taking a deep breath, she kept her gaze on Owen's. If she couldn't get out of here, they were both going to die. Ana closed her eyes and slammed her wrists down one more time. Her arms shot out to the sides as the zip tie fell away.

"Whoa!" Owen's eyes widened in delight. "How did you do that?"

"My three older brothers made sure I knew how to escape any kind of situation when I was younger." Her stomach clenched as she thought back to the countless hours they'd spent in their family basement practicing escape tactics, and the reason why, but all of it had paid off. In this moment. Dropping into a fast squat, she smiled as the ties around her ankles snapped and she handed the plastic to Owen. "After we get you home, I'll teach you."

"Cool." He took the zip ties, then handed her the flashlight. "I'm going to tie up my sister and see how long it takes her to get out. She's always hiding my stuff in our fort."

"Yeah. I've been on the receiving end of that. Here, put these on." She pulled off her windbreaker, followed by the Kevlar vest, and unlaced her shoes to get to her socks. If it hadn't been for Olivia's interception of Harold Wood's skull, they never would've connected Owen's kidnapping to Claire Winston. Although, it would've been nice to have known she'd taken it in the first place. Ana handed over her socks and helped Owen with the oversize windbreaker. Strapping her vest back into place, she ignored the slight chill on the air and tunneling deep into her bones. She'd give him everything she was wearing to ensure his body temperature came back up, but the best thing she could do for both of them right now was get the hell out of here. Ana used the flashlight to search the rest of the room. Shelves stocked with cleaning supplies, a few mops, brooms, a single drain in the center of the floor and a rolling bucket. It was a janitor's closet. But where? She tested the doorknob. Locked. But had she expected any differently? A large vent rained dust down from overhead as the air kicked on. "Here, hold the flashlight and point it toward this vent."

"Why?" he asked.

"Because I'm getting you out of here." Dragging the mop bucket from the corner, she centered it beneath the vent. She balanced on the cheap plastic, the bottom of the bucket threatening to cave in from her weight, and she stretched slowly toward the ceiling. Swiping her fingers along the edges, she found the single screw in each corner but couldn't get any of them to turn. Disbelief pierced through the small amount of hope that'd surfaced. The vent had been welded shut, and unless she found something to carve out the sealed edge, they were trapped. For as long as their kidnapper wanted.

The door swung open.

Ana jumped from the bucket, maneuvering herself in front of Owen as the man in the ski mask centered himself underneath the door frame. Her heart pounded loud behind her ears, every breath still strangled from the pressure of her cracked rib. "You."

"I was getting worried I'd packed too much explosive into the device under Harold Wood's remains." Pulling his gloves from his hands, the man in the mask widened his stance, as though expecting a challenge. "Don't get me wrong, I didn't want anyone to find him in Claire's basement or the skull behind that wall, Agent Ramirez, but I'm coming to realize it's going to take more than a window and a bomb to shake you from this case. But you've always been that way, haven't you? Like a pit bull with a bone. You just couldn't let it go, and well, neither could I. Now, here we are."

She pushed Owen behind her, ready to fight the bastard for however long it took to give the boy a chance to run. "What do you want?"

"The same thing I've wanted from the beginning." Their abductor reached for the mask covering his head and pulled the fabric free, and shock coursed through her as recognition flared. He closed the door behind him, closing off their only chance of escape. "To finish what I started."

THE FOOTPRINTS VANISHED once Benning reached the road. The SOB who'd taken his son could've gone anywhere, could've had a car waiting, or been working with Claire Winston this entire time. One person to recover the skull, one to keep watch on Owen. Hell. He clutched the camera he'd taken from the tractor shed and spun around to search for a sign of where the bastard might've gone. The signal on a device like this couldn't have reached far. It wasn't powerful enough. The kidnapper would've had to remain within a few blocks, maybe a mile, in order to access the surveillance feed. Damn it. That still left a lot of options. Too many. "Come on."

There had to be something he could use, but the spatters of blood had ended at the edge of the pavement. Right along with the trail. Agent Duran had said the body in the hole in Claire Winston's basement had belonged to Samantha Perry's killer. Could she have been involved from the start? In an effort to find Samantha some semblance of justice, had it been Claire's plan to leverage Benning's son, in return for the evidence she'd committed murder? He searched every loose piece of gravel under his boots, every tire tread imprinted in slush along the side of the road. Nothing. Ana and Owen were gone.

Branches swayed behind him on a strong gust of wind. He was a building inspector. Tracking killers and missing persons? This wasn't his world. He hadn't been trained for this, and that inexperience would keep him from finding two of the most important people in his life, but he couldn't give up. Not when Ana had finally come back into his life, when everything had started falling into place and they were so close to finding his son.

His stomach soured. He'd asked her to give up the only chance she had of forgiving herself for the sake of the twins, but faced with the possibility of losing her, of losing Owen, he knew he hadn't been think-ing of anyone but himself. He'd asked her to sacrifice a significant part of her life in order to protect himself from getting hurt again. Damn it. He'd been an idiot. Ana wasn't just an agent. Helping those who couldn't help themselves made her into the woman he'd fallen in love with. Now she was gone. They had a real chance to make this work between them and the twins, but that wasn't going to happen if he couldn't get to her to tell her the truth. Guns, blood, fear… This was her world, but he'd become part of it the second he'd removed Harold Wood's skull from that construction site. He'd fallen in love with a dangerous woman determined to go to the ends of the earth to ensure he and his kids made it out alive, and he couldn't leave her out there alone. Benning curled his fingers around the camera in his palm. He was the one who'd put Owen and Ol-ivia in danger in the first place and brought Ana into the investigation. He'd started this. He was sure as hell going to finish it. "Think, damn it."

All of this tied back to that case from seven years ago, and while he hadn't been involved, there'd been enough in the news and from conversations between him and Ana for him to fill in a timeline. Harold Wood had been a model employee at Sevier County High School where both Samantha Perry and Claire Win-ston attended. Samantha had been well liked, a favorite of her teachers, a fast learner and dedicated to achieving valedictorian during her senior year. The perfect target. According to her best friend, Samantha could become friends with anyone, made sure to smile at the kids who sat alone at lunch, as well as the janitor who kept to him-self most of the time. Harold Wood. Claire's statement after Samantha had gone missing had gone public after the girl's body had been found in that alley in Knoxville. Benning studied the spot where the footprints ended. What had she said? He closed his eyes. The girls had been halfway home in Claire's car when Samantha realized she'd forgotten a textbook she needed in order to study for a test the next day. Claire had driven them back and waited in the parking lot, but after more than thirty minutes, she went in to look for her friend. And never found her.

Goose bumps rose along his arms as another gust shuddered through the trees. He opened his eyes. The school. That was where all of this started that day seven years ago, and that was where it would end. He was sure of it. This entire investigation had linked back to Samantha Perry's disappearance, and the school would be within signal range to stream the footage from the camera in his hand. Whoever was behind this—whoever'd taken his son—would be there.

He jogged east down the long, winding road in the direction of the high school despite the pain arcing through his shoulder. He wouldn't give up on Ana. Not a chance in hell. Because when it came right down to it, she wouldn't give up on him or his family. She hadn't shared her secrets with anyone. Not her team. Not her boss. Only him. She'd punished herself for failing to bring down a killer—had walked out on him because of it—but he would spend the rest of his life trying to help her work through that pain to lighten her burden. As long as it took. She'd dedicated her life to taking care of so many others, always putting everyone else's needs ahead of her own, and it hadn't been fair of him to ask her to give that up. This was his chance to take care of her, to make it right. He didn't know what the future held for them—if they had one at all—but he'd sure as hell give it everything he had. Whether that meant him and the kids driving to Knoxville to see her or her coming to visit between cases, it didn't matter. As long as they were together.

Because he loved her.

The past didn't matter. He wanted her present, her future. Anything she would give him, Owen, Olivia and he would take. She'd been missing from his life for too long, had taken a piece of his soul with her when she'd run, and he had a chance to get it all back. He'd already lost her once. He wasn't going to let it happen again. "I'm coming, baby."

His muscles protested as he pushed himself harder. The large white dome over the main building had been buried beneath several inches of snow, the grounds pure white. There were still a few cars in the main parking lot, and too many footprints for him to isolate the ones he'd followed from that tractor shed. Despite the personal nightmare tearing apart his family's life, students were still living out their lives by trying to survive math class. However, after more than one hundred school shootings across the country in the past year alone, security measures wouldn't allow anyone in the building without checking in with the office first. And police would've already been on location if the bastard had been dragging Owen behind him. So the man in the ski mask had to have gotten inside another way. Jogging along the east side of the structure, Benning kept his back to the light reddish-brown bricks. School had ended a few hours ago, most of the students and teachers off campus, but there was still a chance any one of them could be put in danger. He should've informed the rest of the Tactical Crime Division, only there hadn't been time. He was on his own.

Benning tested the door trying to blend in with the same color paint as the bricks around it at the back of the building. He'd gone to school here over twenty years ago but couldn't exactly remember what was on the other side of the barrier. The knob turned in his hand easily. Unlocked. His stomach clenched. This was it. They had to be here. He threw the heavy metal door out wide and rushed inside. In a single breath, the door slammed closed behind him on automatic hinges and cast him into darkness. His exhales echoed in the small space as he raised his hands out in front of him. No voices. No footsteps. Nothing but stale, humid air slipping through his fingers.

Sweat built along his spine despite the temperatures growing more frigid as he took the stairs one by one. The sound of his boots on cement broke through the groan of piping and electrical humming. The basement. Pushing his hair back behind his ears, he narrowed his gaze ahead as the stairs ended. His blood pumped hard at the base of his head as he pushed one foot in front of the other, slowly working down the long corridor stretched out in front of him. Every cell in his body vibrated with awareness. Every sound, every smell, every blink of the old fluorescent lighting at the other end of the hall. Cracks mapped out dendritic patterns across the cement, up the cinderblock walls and along the edge where the wall met the ceiling. A constant dripping ate away at his senses as he closed in on the end of the corridor.

They had to be here. Because if they weren't... No.

There were no other options. He couldn't spend the rest of his life wondering what'd happened to his son and the love of his life. Couldn't live with the thought that he could've done more. The muscles in his jaw clenched hard. He'd seen what Ana had put herself through. Cutting herself off from her family, from the people who loved her, from feeling anything. He wouldn't do that to Olivia. This ended now.

A shadow darted across the wall ahead.

Benning froze. He hadn't been sleeping well, hadn't been taking as much care of himself as he should have since the twins had been abducted, and he'd been hit not once but twice in the back of the head over the past few days, but he hadn't imagined that. The hairs on the back of his neck stood on end. Warning slithered through him, and he stretched his hand out toward a supply shelf bolted into the wall to his right as he passed. Cold steel warmed in his hand as he gripped a crowbar. The weight of metal tugged on the stitches on his shoulder, but the pain wouldn't slow him down this time. There was too much at stake.

The shadowed outline of a man came into focus at the end of the corridor, but in the next second disappeared. A deep laugh echoed off the cinderblocks around him and settled in his gut, and Benning strengthened his hold on the crowbar. He wasn't alone down here. "I brought your camera back, you bastard."

Chapter Fourteen

Familiar dark eyes locked on hers, and she couldn't move. Couldn't think. All this time, it'd been him from the beginning? "You kidnapped Owen and Olivia. You attacked us at the safe house. You buried Harold Wood's body in Claire's basement. All of it. It was you. Not her."

Her partner when she'd first been assigned the Samantha Perry case.

Agent Ericson York.

It'd been years since they'd worked together, but this didn't make sense. He'd taken an oath to uphold the law and seen firsthand the kinds of monsters that were out there. Monsters like Harold Wood. Her fingers brushed against Owen's arm behind her as she cornered the boy as far from Ericson as she could. The theory Claire Winston had somehow found Harold Wood and gotten the justice for Samantha fizzled right in front of her. Claire had the means and motive to exact revenge, but the FBI hadn't been able to locate Wood for almost a decade. How would she have been so fortunate? The answer stood right in front of her. "Claire didn't kill Harold Wood. You did."

"That bastard deserved everything that came his way, Ramirez." Dark clothing hid mountains of muscles and determination Ana had already gone up against once. And lost. A high widow's peak reflected the light coming from the bare bulb above off Ericson's shorn head. They'd worked side by side, taking down the monsters after witnessing exactly what they were capable of, for years. She'd trusted him to have her back, and she'd had his. But after the Samantha Perry case, he'd gone dark. Left the FBI, wouldn't answer her calls, moved out of his apartment. Now she was the only thing standing between him and his determination to get away with murder. He tossed the mask to the floor near the drain, keeping his hands free for his next move. "You weren't there. You didn't have to see what he'd done to her. You were thirty miles away with that local contractor while I was left to clean up Harold Wood's mess." He took a single step forward, shortening the distance between them and the space she'd have to defend herself and Owen. Ericson's voice dropped into dangerous territory. "So yeah, I did whatever it took to hunt him down. I kept tabs on his sister in case he reached out for help. I sat on his apartment for months at a time. I busted anyone he'd go to for a fake ID because I knew he wasn't finished. You want to know how I finally found him, Ramirez? What he did to get himself caught?"

He took another step toward her, and her breath shuddered in her chest. The closet he'd held them in suddenly seemed so much smaller than it had a few minutes ago.

"The sick SOB had the nerve to go after Claire," he said. "He couldn't stop himself. Didn't matter how many agents and law enforcement organizations were out there looking for him. Harold Wood saw something he wanted, and he tried to take it. Only this time I wasn't going to let him get away with it." The scent of new car smell filled her lungs in the small space, exactly as she remembered from the safe house. He'd shoved her through a window, tried to kill Benning and his family. Had taken Owen and left him for days at a time to freeze and starve to death. This wasn't the agent she'd worked beside. The Ericson York she remembered wouldn't have gone after innocent children to solve a case. "You promised the Perry family we would find their daughter. Do you remember that? You let them down. You let the entire Bureau down. As far as I'm concerned, that makes you as guilty as Harold Wood ever was."

"We would've found him, Ericson. We were closing in, but instead you took the law into your own hands and murdered someone." She shook her head. "If anyone is as guilty as Harold Wood, it's not me. It's you. We swore to protect the innocent, but what you're doing—"

"That oath is nothing!" His exaggerated breath rose and collapsed his shoulders, and she turned to hug Owen closer. A crazed mania bled into the brown of his eyes for a few seconds before he seemed to get control over himself. "I spent over a decade with the FBI hunting the scum who get off on hurting people, only to watch them walk free on technicalities and plea deals." He rolled back his shoulders. "They deserve better than that, Ramirez. Samantha Perry deserved better than that, and I'm finally doing something about it."

The muscles down her spine hardened. She'd seen this side to her former partner before, the caged obsession he hadn't been able to keep locked away during interrogations and investigations, equal to the all-consuming fixation to destroy the criminals they brought to justice. Only, back then, she'd taken advantage of all that intensity, used it to break suspects, to get the confessions they needed, and do their jobs to protect the victims of the cases they took on. She'd never been the target, and now, she and the six-year-old boy behind her would be the ones standing in his way. But there was still a chance they could all get out of here alive.

"You're right. I wasn't there. I wasn't focused on the investigation and an innocent girl paid the price because of it, and I'm going to have to live with that the rest of my life." The hollowness in her chest throbbed. Ana shifted her weight between both feet but nothing could relieve the pressure. Because the truth was she and Ericson weren't so different. That case had changed them both for the worse, taken away any semblance of good in their lives, but she'd found her way back. To Benning. If he hadn't requested her to work this case, would she be the one standing on that side of the room in a few years? Less? Would she be the one hunting down the murderers who hadn't answered for their sins? "I've spent the past seven years punishing myself day in and day out by cutting myself off from the things and the people who made me happy because of that case. I overcommitted myself to the job thinking I could make up for my mistake, but there's nothing that will ever bring Samantha Perry back. No matter how many lives we save, Ericson, it's never going to be enough." Her mouth dried as her own words released the vise she'd carried all this time from around her heart. "Believe me, ignoring the grief and the anger only makes it worse. The only way we're going to get past this is if we take responsibility, find a way to move on and make the most of the life we have left."

"And leave behind all the innocent victims that killers like Harold Wood got their hands on?" he asked.

"What about Owen here? And Olivia? What about Jo West and Benning Reeves? Claire has been falsely suspected in helping you cover up Harold Wood's murder. What about those innocent lives?" she asked. "None of them deserve what you've done. Are you going to be able to live with that for the rest of your life?"

"I never meant for any of them to get tied up in this." He cast his gaze to Owen behind her, his expression stoic, and a hint of the agent she'd known returned. The thick beard growth along his jaw and around his mouth aged him another ten years in an instant, and for a moment hope blossomed behind her sternum. He was telling the truth. He hadn't wanted any of this, but that didn't excuse him from what he'd done. "I knew the moment Benning Reeves called you, we'd be here. With you on one side and me on the other. Even after realizing you played your own part in what happened to Samantha Perry, this isn't what I wanted. I meant what I said before I pushed you through that window. You were always one of the good ones."

That small sense of hope shattered as tension flooded his shoulders and arms, and she leveled her chin with the floor. "So were you, but we both know I can't let you walk away from this, Ericson."

"I know. That's why this is going to hurt me more than it's going to hurt you." He arced his right arm back, and Ana reached for the first thing she could get her hands on along the shelves behind her and Owen.

Threading her fingers through the handle of a heavy gallon jug of bleach, she swung it into Ericson's head as hard as she could. Her former partner stumbled back into the door he'd come through a few minutes ago and it slammed open against the wall behind it. He didn't take long to recover. Rushing toward her, Owen's scream loud in her ears, Ericson swung his fist aimed at her face. She thrust his wrist out of alignment, barely missing the knuckles to her jaw, but the pain from the explosion slowed her down. She wasn't fast enough to block the second swing. Lightning struck behind her eyes as momentum threw her around into the shelves and pinned Owen between her and the metal. A kick to the back of her injured leg brought her down. She clutched onto the shelves for support but couldn't get to her feet in time.

"I'm sorry, Ramirez. I really am, but I can't let you take me in." Ericson closed in again, his massive outline blocking the light from the bulb hanging from the ceiling. "I'm not finished with what needs to be done."

"Leave her alone!" Owen rushed forward, beating his small fists against their kidnapper's leg, but it wouldn't be enough. Ana struggled to regain her balance as the boy did everything he could to protect her. "I'm going to tell my dad on you!"

With a single swipe of his hand, Ericson shoved Owen out of his way and into a collection of brooms and mops in the corner.

She pressed her weight into palms on one of the shelves and cringed as pain flared from the bullet wound in her chest. This was it. Her chance to get him back to Benning. Ana latched on to her former partner to keep his focus on her. "Owen, get out of here! Run!"

The six-year-old ran into the darkness on the other side of the door just as Ericson's right hook slammed her into the floor. She bounced off the cement as his boot landed in her side, knocking the air from her lungs. Searing pain spread across her scalp as he fisted a handful of her hair and dragged her back into his chest. "It's just the two of us now, partner, and only one of us is getting out of here alive."

"You're right." She hauled her elbow back into his solar plexus. "And it's going to be me."

BENNING PUMPED HIS legs as fast as he could. He hadn't mistaken that scream. Ana had yelled for Owen to run. His son was here. He was alive. He turned another corner where he thought the bastard in the mask had disappeared but collided with a pint-size child instead. He hit the ground, the surprised scream coming from the boy barely registering over the crowbar pinging off cement. Owen. Locking his hands on his son before he could dart away, he pulled the boy to his chest. "Owen! Buddy, it's me. Daddy. I've got you. You're safe. I've got you."

He threaded one hand through his son's hair, holding on to him as hard as he could without crushing him.

"Daddy!" The six-year-old seemed so much smaller than he remembered then. More frail. His son shook in his arms. His skin was clammy with a thin sheen of sweat and cold as sobs racked through his tiny frame. The overwhelming relief Benning felt in that moment was all consuming. But in an instant Owen pulled away, latching on to Benning's hand to try to get him to his feet. "Daddy, she's hurt. The man is hurting her. We have to help!"

Ana.

Dread clenched in his stomach. Unfiltered terror at the idea of leading Owen back toward his kidnapper flared hot under his skin. After everything they'd been through, the last thing he wanted right then was to let his son out of his sight, but Ana needed his help. She'd sacrificed herself before, to save him and Olivia at the safe house, and nearly died for it. He couldn't let her go through that again. "Owen, listen to me. I need you to find a spot to hide and stay there until I come get you."

"Don't leave me." Owen's voice slid into a notch above fear, and everything inside Benning urged him to get his son the hell out of there. But he couldn't leave Ana without backup. Not again. "I want to stay with you."

"I know you do, but I can't lose you again." He smoothed his hand over Owen's hair, the sickening scent of neglect heavy in his lungs. He had no idea what his son had gone through the past four days. How horribly he'd been treated, how many times he'd begged to go home without getting an answer from the darkness that'd surrounded him in that tractor shed. This wasn't a choice between his kids or the woman who'd risked her life for them. There was no choice. He'd left Ana behind once and she'd nearly died for it. He wouldn't make the same mistake twice. "I have to help Ana, but I can't do that if I'm worrying about you at the same time. So I need you to hide."

Owen nodded. "Okay."

"Good." Benning led his son back toward the same supply shelf he'd taken the crowbar from and hefted the boy onto the top. "Stay low. Don't make any noises. If you see someone coming, don't move, understand?"

"Yes." Owen slid onto his stomach and laid his head down.

"Good boy." Ruffling his son's hair, he took a step

back to ensure he wouldn't be spotted the moment someone came around the corner into the corridor. "I love you, buddy. I'm coming back for you. I promise."

"Love you, too," Owen said. "Don't die, okay?"

"Okay." He couldn't fight the tug at one corner of his mouth. Collecting the crowbar from the floor where he'd dropped it after slamming into Owen, Benning retraced the boy's steps through a maze of corridors and open spaces containing old desks, a set of lockers and tables. His fingers ached as tension locked his hand around the only weapon he had against a trained professional determined to rip apart his entire life. His shallow breaths cut through the silence, mouth dry. He turned another corner.

And slowed as light spilled into the hallway from a single door up ahead. A body fell back onto the cement in the frame of light, a full head of long brown hair hiding her face, but instant recognition flooded through him. Ana. She wasn't moving, didn't even seem to breathe, and the world stopped. He wasn't too late. Couldn't be. Benning pressed his back into the wall behind him as he heel-toed closer. Blood dripped from the corner of her mouth, sliding along the column of her throat. Get up. She had to get up.

"You're only dragging out the inevitable, Ramirez." The man stepping out of the room and standing above her had the same voice of the one who'd interrogated him against that tree, but the mask was gone. Shorn hair, thick eyebrows arching over narrow eyes. Heavy facial hair had aged the man's face over the years, but Benning still recognized the agent Ana had been partnered with during the Samantha Perry case. Agent Ericson York. Benning had watched the man's press conferences, listened to his pleas for any witnesses to come forward. He'd been the face of the investigation. Now he seemed to be behind two kidnappings, attempted murder of a federal agent and the murder of Jo West.

"As long as you're…stuck here with me, you're not going…after Owen." Her laugh lifted her chest off the cement, followed by a deep, wet cough. Rolling onto her side, she pegged him with those hazel-green eyes, but kept moving to stand. "I'll drag…this out as long… as I have to."

Her attacker pulled a weapon from under his leather jacket at his low back and took aim at Ana. "Let's see how long you last with a bullet between your eyes."

Benning raced to intercept. Gaining the agent's attention, he slid into the bastard's feet as Ericson turned the gun on him. The crowbar hit the floor. In his next breath, he hauled his boot up and kicked the weapon free from Ericson's hand. The gun vanished into the corner of the room, out of sight. The SOB who'd taken his son slammed a fist into the side of his head. Pain exploded through the left side of his face, and he stumbled back. Before the white lights behind his eyes cleared, a feminine growl filled his ears.

Ana launched herself at Ericson from behind, locking her forearm around his throat and pulling the agent away from Benning with a hard thrust. Ericson's hands went to her underarms a split second before he hauled her over his head and slammed her down onto her back. Her gasp of pain tunneled through the haze of both hits to his face, and Benning lunged for the crowbar. He swung as hard as he could, but Ana's former partner shot back on his heels and dodged the swipe and landed another shot to Benning's kidneys. He dropped to one knee as the pain shot through his side and down one leg, but Ana refused to go down.

She caught Ericson's wrist and wound it over her head before twisting around to crush his nose with the base of her other palm. His scream bubbled beneath a fresh wave of blood. Taking advantage as he stumbled back, she kicked him square in the chest. He hit the floor, a groan slipping past the former agent's lips.

She stood over Ericson, every bit the woman Benning had fallen in love with. Strong, protective, determined. His. Blood had already started drying along her face and neck. Swiping the back of her hand across her mouth, she swayed slightly as Benning got to his feet. "You can try to kill me as many times as you want and threaten to hurt the people I love, Ericson, but it's not going to change what happened to Samantha Perry, what you've done, or make up for the people you've hurt." Her voice shook as though her throat had tightened, and she relaxed her fists at her sides. "I'm sorry I wasn't as focused on the case as I should've been and an innocent girl died. I'm sorry I wasn't there for you after you found her body in that alley and that I didn't have the courage to make it to her funeral, and I'm sorry that you think this is the only way to bring Samantha justice." She shook her head. "But I've punished myself long enough. Now it's your turn."

The air rushed from his lungs. He couldn't speak. Couldn't even breathe. She'd done it. She'd finally forgiven herself. The tension in Benning's shoulders drained, and the pressure around his wound ebbed. Damn, he loved this woman. No matter how well he thought he knew her, she'd hit him with another surprise, and he only hoped he and the twins would be able to keep up with her when all of this was over. If she'd forgive him.

"You think you've paid for what you've done because you can admit you made a mistake?" Ericson spit a mouthful of blood off to his right, then recentered his focus on Ana, a cruel smile contorting his mouth. Sweat slipped down the man's temples, his chest rising and falling with shallow breaths. "You haven't even begun to pay, Ramirez."

Dim lighting reflected off a piece of metal in Ericson's hand as the bastard shot to his feet, and Benning lunged.

"Ana!" He collided with her former partner but came up short from tackling Ericson to the floor. The world threatened to drop right out from under his feet as screaming pain slashed through his gut. One second. Two. He stumbled back. Confusion built a wall between rational thought and the fact the blade had embedded deep into his body. Nausea churned in his stomach as Benning fell to both knees, dizziness throwing him off balance. His head felt heavy, but he somehow managed to level his gaze with Ericson's.

"Now you've paid." Ana's partner pulled the blade free, his expression smooth. As though he'd done this a hundred times and was prepared to do it a hundred more.

"No!" Ana shot forward, hiking her shoulder into Ericson's midsection and hefting him off the ground before she slammed him back into the nearest wall. Fists connected with bone, groans and blood cutting through the air as the woman he'd fallen for fought with everything she had left to protect him.

The gun. Benning could make out the grip highlighted beneath a pulsing fluorescent tube above. He clamped a hand over the stab wound in his gut, blood slipping through his fingers. Locking his jaw against the agony, he forced himself to his feet and stumbled forward to grab it. The weight felt solid in his hand as he turned and took aim. "Stay the hell away from my family."

Ericson positioned Ana in front of him as a human shield. The former agent's dark gaze cut to Benning, and dread curdled in his stomach. "I can kill her faster than you can take that shot, Mr. Reeves. Are you willing to take that chance?"

"She would do the same for me." Benning pulled the trigger.

Chapter Fifteen

It was over.

Red and blue patrol lights skimmed across her vision as Ana studied the scene from her position in the ambulance. Officers and emergency personnel almost seemed to move in slow motion, the strong thud of her heart beating at the base of her skull. There, in the middle of it all, Benning sat with his son on the back of another ambulance as snow fell across the parking lot. The man who'd risked everything that mattered to him in order to find her, and nearly died from a stab wound in the process.

Pressure built behind her rib cage, but not from the two broken ribs she'd cracked after the explosion in Claire Winston's basement. No. For the first time she could remember, she hadn't been the only one fighting. He'd fought Ericson York with her, for her. From the internal desolate landscape she'd created by detaching herself from everyone around her, he'd nurtured an ember and turned it into a wildfire. He'd shown her how to hurt, how to bleed, how to heal and how to feel again. None of which she could've done without him.

The Sevier County medical examiner and her assistant led the charge with Ericson York's body sealed into a dark bag on the gurney behind them, and her heart jerked in her chest. Her former partner had been a good agent, one of the best she'd worked with before transferring back to DC, then into the Tactical Crime Division, but neither of them had handled the repercussions of the Samantha Perry case well. The only difference between the paths they'd chosen had been that small piece of her that'd belonged to Benning Reeves the day she'd met him, and she'd never forget that.

Brilliant blue eyes settled on her as Benning recounted his statement to the Sevierville PD officer at his side, chasing back the nightmare of the past few hours. Owen was alive. Dehydrated, bruised, starved, but alive. She hadn't failed this time, and she realized Benning had been right from the beginning. Isolating herself from the people who cared about her—from the victims of her cases—didn't make her a better investigator. The detachment she'd relied on for so long had merely been a crutch to try to ebb the punishing guilt she'd taken on once Samantha's body had been found in that alley. A guilt that still weighed on her chest. Not as heavy, but there. She'd meant what she'd said to Ericson before he'd tried to kill her the second—third?—time. There was no magical number of lives saved or criminals punished to ease the blame they carried. The only way she was going to get past what'd happened on that case was to accept she'd done enough, but seven years of punishment wouldn't disappear overnight. It'd take time, support and help. Benning smiled at her from where EMTs stitched his wound, with Owen squished right alongside him. Luckily, she had all the support she'd need.

"I can see you didn't take my advice to be careful."

Director Jill Pembrook leaned her shoulder against the back door of the ambulance, gray hair tied back in a severe bun that reflected the steel resolve inside. "What was it, two gunshot wounds, a pane of glass through your leg and a broken rib all within the span of four days?"

"Two ribs, and don't forget my broken finger, too." Ana pressed her palms into the gurney mattress in an attempt to sit higher when faced with her boss, but whatever the EMTs had given her to manage the pain hadn't kicked in yet. Pain shot through her midsection, and she pressed the crown of her head against the flat pillow as hard as she could to keep from groaning aloud. The fight with Ericson had been the most brutal battle not only for her life but also Benning's, Olivia's and Owen's, as well. She would've done anything—sustained anything—to make sure they'd made it out of this investigation alive. Because she loved them, all of them, as though they'd always been part of her life. Always been hers. She wanted to keep it that way, to wake up beside Benning every morning and fall asleep beside him every night, to respond to calls from the school when Olivia brought another dead animal to autopsy in the school's science lab, to brush the cookie crumbs out of Owen's bed before he went to sleep at night and compete with him on his newest game obsession. She wanted it all. The good parts and the messy parts, but she wasn't finished saving lives, either, and she wasn't going to let the director bench her because she hadn't followed Pembrook's orders to not let her emotions get in the way of doing her job. Swallowing through the tightness in her throat, she curled her uninjured hand into a fist to distract herself from the pain. "Do you have an update on JC and Evan yet?"

"Agent Cantrell sustained a mild concussion when the explosive went off but is expected to return to the field in a few days. Agent Duran, on the other hand, is currently in surgery to remove a piece of shrapnel from his side. He'll be out for longer, but his prognosis is looking good." Pembrook folded her arms over her pressed blazer and crisp white shirt, her expression controlled. "From what they've been able to tell me, they wouldn't have made it out of that basement alive if it hadn't been for Mr. Reeves disobeying SWAT's orders to stay away from the scene and risking his life so he could get to you." A hint of a smile pulled at one edge of the director's mouth, and Pembrook relaxed her hands to her sides as she straightened. "You're both idiots, but you obviously deserve each other. In any case, I expect you back on your feet and in the field as soon as possible, Agent Ramirez. The people we help still need you."

"Yes, ma'am." Ana rolled her lips between her teeth and bit down to fight back her own smile as Director Pembrook headed toward a beautiful African American woman dressed in military fatigues behind the perimeter of yellow crime scene tape.

Her smile slipped. Claire Winston. It'd been seven years since Ana had been face-to-face with Samantha Perry's best friend, but she would've recognized her at any age. Nausea worked through her. Ericson York had forced that poor woman to relive the nightmare of losing her closest friend so violently when he'd left one Libra charm on Benning's property and the other inside Harold Wood's mouth. *Infierno*, he'd even buried the rest of the killer's body in Claire's basement as some sick token of pride. But…that still didn't answer the question of why Ericson had removed Harold Wood's skull and hidden it separately from the body. Claire stretched her right hand to meet the director's in a handshake, and Ana narrowed her gaze on the woman's wrist.

A hint of a silver bracelet glimmered under the aura of patrol lights.

No charm.

Hadn't Claire told the director over the phone she still had her charm and wore the bracelet off shift while on tour? So then why wouldn't she be wearing it now?

"Tell me you're okay, and I won't have to shoot anyone else tonight." Benning slid into her peripheral vision, Owen petting one of the canine units with another officer a few feet away.

"Help me up," she said.

"What?" Disbelief widened his eyes at the edges.

"Claire Winston isn't wearing her charm, Benning." Ana kept her voice low as she scooted down the length of the gurney toward the end. She slipped from the ambulance, relying on his support to stay on her feet. "Why would she tell the director otherwise unless she didn't want one of the charms we found during the investigation to be connected back to her?"

He searched the scene until his attention landed on Director Pembrook and the woman in fatigues near the perimeter. Turning back to her, he clamped his hand into hers and pulled her into his side. "You think she and Ericson were working together."

"Ericson told me Harold Wood made the mistake of going after Claire." She strengthened her hold around his hand as she studied the exchange between Pembrook and Claire Winston. "It wouldn't be a stretch to believe Claire might've helped get rid of the evidence once she learned she'd become Wood's next target. Why else would Ericson use her basement to hide the body?"

He kept his voice low. "Maybe to frame her in case he was caught."

"Ericson saved her life. He wouldn't have implicated her for a murder he was proud he'd committed, and he wouldn't give her up if she'd been involved in Owen's kidnapping, either." She shook her head. "Despite how far gone he'd become, he cared about her enough to make sure Harold Wood never got his hands on her."

"Then how do you prove she was involved?" he asked.

"I need to see Ericson's gun." Within minutes, Sevierville PD handed her the bagged weapon Benning had used to shoot her former partner and stop a killer, effectively saving her—and so many others. Releasing her grip on Benning, she turned the evidence over in her hand, the plastic sticking to the tips of her fingers. "This is a Glock 22, which shoots .40 caliber rounds, standard issue for FBI agents. Harold Wood was killed with a .45. The same caliber that would fire from the Beretta M9 registered in Claire Winston's name." The air rushed from her lungs as the pieces of the puzzle fell into place. "She did it. She's the one who killed Harold Wood, and Ericson hid the proof on the construction site in case the body was found. He tried to take the fall for her, and when you found the skull, he abducted Owen and Olivia to force you to give it back."

"Why would he take the fall for her?" Benning asked.

Claire Winston's dark, watery gaze followed the ME's movements as she loaded the bag with Ericson's body sealed inside, then rose to meet Ana's.

In an instant she knew the answer. "Ericson blamed himself as much as anyone else for what happened to Samantha Perry. I think he believed protecting Claire was how he was going to finally redeem himself."

The confidence in Claire's expression bled to fear a split second before the woman ran from the scene. Only she didn't make it far. Without hesitation, Director Pembrook ordered officers to close off her escape, and Claire Winston raised her hands in surrender.

"You don't have to do this," she said. "The doctor said I'm fine on my own as long as I take it slow."

"That is in no way what she said. That's what you wanted to hear." But that wasn't the only reason he'd convinced her to recover in Sevierville instead of Knoxville. He'd almost lost her. Twice. Right along with the two most important humans in his life, who, he could see through the front window, were currently jumping up and down with excitement. His in-laws waved from behind Owen and Olivia before giving the twins each a hug and heading for the back door, which would take them to their pickup at the side of the house.

Maybe he hadn't chosen the right location for Ana to recover from her injuries, but he couldn't turn back now. He'd already informed the twins of his plan. Any deviation would only throw him into a world of whining and questions. He brushed his fingers against her low back as she stepped over the threshold to assure her he was there if she fell, but he knew without a doubt she wouldn't let things get that far. "I know exactly how long you'll rest before you try to convince the director you're ready for field work. You're staying here where I can keep an eye on you."

She slowed before reaching the entryway, those mes-merizing hazel-green eyes dark with suspicion. One hand tightened on the single crutch supporting her be-neath her arm. "You don't trust me."

"With my life, yes. With your own, no." Staying close as she navigated slippery terrain on her way into the house—unassisted—Benning swung the front door open to clear her path and immediately held out one hand, palm forward, to stave off the twins from tack-ling her to the floor.

Owen and Olivia bounced in place, their grins bigger than he'd seen them in a long time as Ana stepped into the house. Over the past few days, he'd struggled to get their lives back to normal, but so much had changed. Owen had spent two days in the hospital fighting off dehydration and pneumonia but was acting more him-self a little bit more every day, aside from the apparent break he was taking from his tablet, which Benning wouldn't complain about. Olivia had moved into sleep-ing in her brother's room, to make sure no one would take him from her. His heart had nearly broken all over again when she'd admitted how scared she'd been for her twin. But Owen was home now. They were safe, but Benning wouldn't be pulling any more skulls off con-struction sites anytime soon. As for Benning... Well, the biggest change for him was the woman insisting she could get herself into the house in a timely manner.

Ana's laugh cut through the off-the-charts energy emanating from the kids, but he couldn't blame them for not being able to hold back. He was just as excited—and nervous—for what came next. Only difference was he had more control over his body, and emotions and pretty much everything else. Except when it came to

Ana Sofia Ramirez. "You sure you're up for this? I'm pretty stubborn, but those faces will knock me down with one hit. It's going to be chaos. I'm going to be giving them everything they ask for while I'm here."

"I think I'm up for the challenge." He turned toward the twins to distract himself from the heat climbing up his neck and into his face. "Why don't you guys take Ana to see what you made for her while she was in the hospital."

"It's not another skull, is it? Or a foot or something? I don't think I could take any more body parts right now." She leaned heavier into her crutch as Benning moved to close the front door behind them, then pulled back before the stampede of six-year-olds racing toward their rooms ran her over. Turning her gaze up to meet his, she silently questioned his motives.

"Guess they're excited." He motioned her to lead and followed close on her heels, head down to avoid eye contact. Every cell in his body rose in awareness as she limped along ahead of him down the hall, but he didn't have the capacity to overthink it as they entered Olivia's room.

Ana froze, the muscles down her spine pulling her shoulders tight. "What is this?"

Maneuvering to her side, Benning took in the sight of Owen and Olivia standing at the center of her room. In the middle of the crime scene they'd created together. After convincing one of the agents on Ana's team to hand over a brand-new roll of crime scene tape, his daughter had gone overboard with decorating her room until the pink paint faded into the background. But more horrifyingly cute was the white chalk outline Olivia had traced around her brother on the blue tarp from one of his inspection sites. Along with evidence markers, thinned out ketchup for blood, one of Olivia's favorite books, Owen's tablet, a hammer and a small velvet black box near evidence marker number three. "I know it seems terrifying, but they wanted to plan the whole thing and make sure a little bit of each of us was in there. Hence the book, tablet and hammer."

"I see. Olivia is the book, Owen is the tablet and you're the hammer?" She nodded slowly, taking it all in, but he couldn't read her expression. Cocking her head to one side, she narrowed her gaze. "And am I represented by the dead man in the middle or the blood?"

He pointed to the black velvet box off to one side. "I think that is supposed to be for you."

Owen collected the box from the floor and tipped the lid back on its gold hinges. Stepping near the perimeter of the scene, he stared up at Ana with a whole other level of excitement inching his smile wide. "Will you marry us, Ana?"

"Please?" Olivia asked. "We want you to stay. Forever."

The rush of air escaping from between Ana's lips cut through the hard beat of his heart behind his ears. She wiped the tears streaming down her cheeks with the back of her hand as another laugh escaped her control. Balancing the crutch under her arm, she sank a bit deeper on her uninjured leg to take the box from Owen. She turned toward Benning.

"I know I asked you to give up working for TCD to protect the kids, but it wasn't fair and it wasn't my place." He removed the ring from the box, the round diamond set in the platinum band strong enough to sustain any damage accrued during her future investigations.

"I realized too late I was protecting myself. I wanted a promise you wouldn't disappear when the case was over, but asking you to stop helping people in need is like asking you to stop being the woman I fell in love with. And I love you just the way you are. I always have. Ana Sofia Ramirez—" he dropped to one knee, ignoring whatever sludge he'd just knelt in and slipped the ring onto her finger "—will you marry me?"

She smoothed her thumb across his bottom lip, the diamond sparkling from the low light coming through Olivia's window. "I told you I can't say no to those faces."

"Is that a yes, then?" he asked.

"Yes!" She tilted her head up to kiss him as he stood, and the excited screams from his kids fell into the back of his mind. Right then, there was only Ana. His strong, beautiful, determined FBI agent who hadn't just saved his kids' lives but completed his. "I love you. I've always loved you. You've always owned this part of me, and I know without a doubt you're the reason I didn't follow in Ericson's footsteps, Benning."

"I love you." He framed his hands around her face and kissed her again with everything he had. "And I'm always here for you. No matter what. But given your choice of career and the fact we have two humans to watch out for together, I think it's time I learned how to properly use a gun."

"Ewww." The tandem protest from Owen and Olivia cut through the heat searing across his skin where Ana touched him.

He laughed.

"This is only the beginning. It's going to get worse. Day. Night. In the bathroom. They're everywhere." His heart squeezed as she stared up at him with that gut-wrenching smile. Benning tightened his hold on her, a promise to have each other's backs. Forever. "Are you ready for your next assignment, Agent Ramirez?"

She studied the scene the twins had made in Olivia's bedroom, then faced him again. "I think I'm up for the challenge."

* * * * *

COMING SOON!

We really hope you enjoyed reading this book.
If you're looking for more romance, be sure to
head to the shops when new books are
available on

Thursday 11th June

Sensual love stories featuring smart, sassy heroines you'd want as a best friend, and compelling intense heroes who are worthy of them.

MILLS & BOON

MODERN

Power and Passion

Prepare to be swept off your feet by sophisticated, sexy and seductive heroes, in some of the world's most glamourous and romantic locations, where power and passion collide.

MILLS & BOON
MEDICAL
Pulse-Racing Passion

Set your pulse racing with dedicated, delectable doctors in the high-pressure world of medicine, where emotions run high and passion, comfort and love are the best medicine.

MILLS & BOON

THE HEART OF ROMANCE

A ROMANCE FOR EVERY KIND OF READER

MODERN

Prepare to be swept off your feet by sophisticated, sexy and seductive heroes, in some of the world's most glamourous and romantic locations, where power and passion collide.
8 stories per month.

HISTORICAL

Escape with historical heroes from time gone by. Whether your passion is for wicked Regency Rakes, muscled Vikings or rugged Highlanders, awaken the romance of the past.
6 stories per month.

MEDICAL

Set your pulse racing with dedicated, delectable doctors in the high-pressure world of medicine, where emotions run high and passion, comfort and love are the best medicine.
6 stories per month.

True Love

Celebrate true love with tender stories of heartfelt romance, from the rush of falling in love to the joy a new baby can bring, and a focus on the emotional heart of a relationship.
8 stories per month.

Desire

Indulge in secrets and scandal, intense drama and plenty of sizzling hot action with powerful and passionate heroes who have it all: wealth, status, good looks…everything but the right woman.
6 stories per month.

HEROES

Experience all the excitement of a gripping thriller, with an intense romance at its heart. Resourceful, true-to-life women and strong, fearless men face danger and desire - a killer combination!
8 stories per month.

DARE

Sensual love stories featuring smart, sassy heroines you'd want as a best friend, and compelling intense heroes who are worthy of them.
4 stories per month.

To see which titles are coming soon, please visit

millsandboon.co.uk/nextmonth

JOIN US ON SOCIAL MEDIA!

Stay up to date with our latest releases, author news and gossip, special offers and discounts, and all the behind-the-scenes action from Mills & Boon...

 millsandboon

 millsandboonuk

 millsandboon

It might just be true love...